Peter the Whaler

by

William Henry Giles Kingston

Peter the Whaler

by William Henry Giles Kingston

Copyright © 2024

All Rights reserved.

ISBN: 978-93-64288-41-5

Published by

DOUBLE 9 BOOKS

2/13-B, Ansari Road
Daryaganj, New Delhi – 110002
info@double9books.com
www.double9books.com
Tel. 011-40042856

ABOUT THE AUTHOR

William Henry Giles Kingston (1814-1880) was an influential English writer, best known for his adventure novels targeted at young readers. His works, particularly those with nautical themes, have captivated audiences with tales of heroism, exploration, and moral integrity. Debut: Kingston's literary journey began with the publication of "The Circassian Chief" in 1844. Genre: He specialized in seafaring adventure stories that were highly popular in the Victorian era. Output: Prolific in his writing, Kingston authored over 130 books, many focusing on nautical adventures and aimed at young readers. "Peter the Whaler"(1851): One of Kingston's early successes, detailing the adventures of a young whaler.

"The Three Midshipmen"(1873): Part of a series chronicling the exploits of British naval officers.

"The Three Admirals" (1891): Continuation of the naval adventure series, showcasing themes of bravery and exploration. Impact on Children's Literature: Kingston's adventure stories have had a lasting impact on children's literature, particularly in the adventure genre. Kingston's contributions to literature have made him a celebrated author, particularly known for his ability to inspire and entertain with stories of exploration and heroism. His works remain a testament to the adventurous spirit of the 19th century and continue to be enjoyed by readers around the world. Enduring Popularity: His tales of the high seas and distant lands continue to be appreciated for their timeless appeal and adventurous spirit. Kingston's contributions to literature have made him a celebrated author, particularly known for his ability to inspire and entertain with stories of exploration and heroism. His works remain a testament to the adventurous spirit of the 19th century and continue to be enjoyed by readers around the world.

CONTENTS

Chapter One 7

Chapter Two 13

Chapter Three 19

Chapter Four 24

Chapter Five 32

Chapter Six 38

Chapter Seven 42

Chapter Eight 47

Chapter Nine 53

Chapter Ten 59

Chapter Eleven 62

Chapter Twelve 66

Chapter Thirteen 70

Chapter Fourteen 77

Chapter Fifteen 87

Chapter Sixteen 94

Chapter Seventeen 103

Chapter Eighteen 112

Chapter Nineteen 118

Chapter Twenty 127

Chapter Twenty One 133

Chapter Twenty Two 141

Chapter Twenty Three 149

Chapter Twenty Four 155

Chapter Twenty Five 163

Chapter Twenty Six 172

Chapter Twenty Seven 181

Chapter Twenty Eight 188

Chapter Twenty Nine 195

Chapter Thirty 205

Chapter Thirty One 214

Chapter Thirty Two 223

Chapter Thirty Three 229

Chapter Thirty Four 237

Chapter Thirty Five 247

Chapter Thirty Six 252

Chapter One

"Peter," said my father, with a stern look, though the tone of his voice had more of sorrow in it than anger, "this conduct, if you persist in it, will bring ruin on you, and grief and shame on my head and to your mother's heart. Look there, boy, and answer me: Are not those presumptive evidences of your guilt? Where did they come from?" He pointed, as he spoke, to several head of game, pheasants, partridges, and hares, which lay on the ground, while I stood before him leaning on my gun, my eyes not daring to meet his, which I knew were fixed on me. My two dogs crouched at my feet, looking as if they also were culprits and fully comprehended the tenor of his words.

My father was a clergyman, the vicar of a large parish in the south of Ireland, where the events I am now narrating took place. He was a tall man, with silvery locks and well-formed features. I think his hair was prematurely grey. The expression of his countenance was grave, and betokened firmness and decision, though his general character was mild in the extreme. He was a kind parent, in some respects too kind; and he was very indulgent towards the faults and errors of those not immediately connected with him. He was on good terms with the Roman Catholics of the neighbourhood, of which faith were the large majority of the population, and even with the priests; so that our family had few enemies, and were never in any way molested by the peasantry.

That, however, we had some foes, I shall have occasion presently to show. But I must return to the scene I was describing. I may be pardoned for first giving a slight sketch of myself. I hope that I may escape being accused of vanity, as I shall not dwell on my personal appearance. I believe that I inherited some of my parents' good looks; but the hardships I have endured have eradicated all traces of them. I was well grown for my age (I was barely fifteen), but, dressed in my loose shooting-costume, my countenance ruddy with fresh air and exercise, I looked much older.

"What do you suppose would be the lot of a poor man's son, if he were to be discovered acting as you are constantly doing in spite of my warnings and commands?" continued my father, his voice growing more serious and his look more grave. "I tell you, boy, that the consequences may and will be lamentable; and do not believe, that because you are the son of a gentleman, you can escape the punishment due to the guilty.

"You are a poacher. You deserve the name; and on some occasion, when engaged in that lawless occupation, you will probably encounter the gamekeepers of the persons on whose estates you are trespassing, and whose property you are robbing. Now hear me out. They, as in duty bound, will attempt to capture you. You and your companions may resist; your weapons may be discharged, and life may be sacrificed. If you escape the fate of a murderer, you may be transported to distant lands, away from friends, home, and country, to work for long years; perhaps in chains among the outcasts of our race, fed on the coarsest food, subject to the tyranny of brutalised overseers, often themselves convicts; your ears forced to listen to the foulest language, your eyes to witness the grossest debauchery, till you yourself become as bad as those with whom you are compelled to herd; so that, when the time of your punishment is expired, you will be unfit for freedom; and if you venture to return home, you will find yourself, wherever you appear, branded with dishonour, and pointed at as the convict.

"Think, Peter, of the grief and anguish it would cause your poor mother and me, to see you suffer so dreadful a disgrace—to feel that you merited it. Think of the shame it would bring on the name of our family. People would point at your sisters, and say, 'Their brother is a convict!' they would shake their heads as I appeared in the pulpit, and whisper, 'The vicar whose son was transported!' But more than all (for men's censure matters not if we are guiltless), think how God will judge you, who have had opportunities of knowing better, who have been repeatedly warned that you are doing wrong, who are well aware that you are doing wrong: think how He will judge and condemn you.

"Human laws, of necessity, are framed only to punish all alike, the rich and educated man as well as the poor and ignorant; but God, who sees what is in the heart of man, and his means of knowing right from wrong, will more severely punish those who sin, as you do, with their eyes open. I am unwilling to employ threats; I would rather appeal to your better feelings, my boy; but I must, in the first place, take away your means of following your favourite pursuit; and should you persist in leading your present wild and idle life, I must adopt such measures as will effectually prevent you. Give me your gun."

I listened to all that was said in dogged silence. I could not refuse to give up my dearly-beloved weapon; but I did so with a very bad grace; and I am sorry to say that my father's words had at that time little or no effect on my heart. I say at the time, for afterwards, when it was too late, I thought of them over and over again, and deeply repented of my wilful obstinacy and folly.

Alas! from how much suffering and grief I should have been saved had I attended to the precepts and warnings of my kind parent—how much of bitter self-reproach. And I must warn my young friends, that although the adventures I went through may be found very interesting to read about, they would discover the reality to be very full of pain and wretchedness were they subjected to it; and yet I may tell them that the physical suffering I endured was as nothing when compared to the anguish of mind I felt, when, left for hours and days to my own bitter thoughts, I remembered that through my own perverseness I had brought it all upon myself.

Often have I envied the light hearts of my fellow-sufferers, whose consciences did not blame them. Let me urge you, then, in your course through life, on all occasions to act rightly, and to take counsel and advice from those on whose judgment you should rely; and then not only in the next world will you have your reward, but, in this, through the severest trials and bodily suffering you will enjoy a peace of mind and a happiness of which no man can deprive you.

My parents had four sons and five daughters. My eldest brother was studying for the bar in Dublin; and, as the family fortune was limited, we were somewhat cramped to afford him the requisite means for his education. I was consequently kept at home, picking up, when I felt disposed, any crumbs of knowledge which came in my way, but seldom going out of my way to find them; nor had I, unfortunately, any plan fixed on for my future career.

My mother, was constantly employed with my sisters, and my father with his clerical duties or his literary pursuits; so that I was forgotten, and allowed to look after myself. I am unable to account for the neglect to which I was subjected, but such was the case; and consequently I ran wild, and contrived, to become acquainted with some scampish youths in the neighbourhood, in every way my inferiors except in age; and they gave me lessons which I was, I own, too willing to learn, in all that was bad.

Sporting was my greatest amusement; and, for my age, I was perhaps one of the best shots in all the country round. While I confined myself to my father's glebe, and to the grounds of two or three friends who had given me leave to shoot, he did not object to my indulging my propensity; but, not content with so narrow a sphere of action, I used frequently, in company of some of the youths I speak of, to wander over property where I not only had no right to kill game, but where I had positively been forbidden to trespass, and where I even knew people were on the look-out to detect me.

I had just returned from one of these lawless expeditions, when I was encountered by my father, laden with game, and the scene I have described took place. As I before said (and I repeat it with shame), I felt the loss of my gun more than I cared for the lecture, or the grief my conduct caused my father. I can scarcely now account for the obstinacy and hardness of heart which made me shut my ears to all remonstrances. I have since then grown wiser, and I hope better; and I feel that I ought at once to have asked my father's forgiveness, and to have cheerfully set to work on some occupation of which he approved. With me, as it will be with every one, idleness was the mother of all mischief.

For two days I sulked, and would speak to no one. On the third I set off to take a walk by myself, across the bogs, and over the hills in the far distance. I had got into a better spirit from the fresh air and exercise; and I truly believe that I was beginning to see my error, and was resolving to do my best to make amends for it, and to give up my bad habits, when who should I encounter but Pat Doolan, one of the wildest of my wild acquaintances!

Before a word of salutation had passed, he asked me why I had not got my gun with me; and after a weak and vain endeavour to avoid answering the question, I confessed all that had occurred. He sneered at my fears and my fathers' warnings, and laughed away all my half-formed good resolutions,—telling me that I might just as well go and borrow one of my sister's petticoats at once, for to that I should come at last if I was going to give up all manly pursuits. Unhappy, indeed, it was for me that I listened to the voice of the tempter, instead of keeping my good resolutions safely locked up in my own breast, and instantly hurrying away from him, as I ought to have done. Or perhaps I might have answered him, "No; I must not, and will not, listen to you. I know that what I have resolved to do is right, and that which you want to persuade me to do is wicked—an instigation of the evil one; so go away and leave me." And if he persisted in remaining near me, I should have set off and run from him as hard as I could go. This is the only way to treat temptation in whatever form it appears. Fly from it as you would from the slippery edge of a precipice.

Instead of acting thus, I sat down on the heather by his side, and, looking foolish and humbled, I began plucking off the crisp flowers and leaves, and throwing them to the winds. He asked me if I knew where the gun was locked up. When I told him that it was not locked up at all, but merely placed on the mantelpiece in my father's dressing-room, he laughed at me for fool because I had not before re-possessed myself of it. Fool I was, in truth; but it was to yield to the bad advice my false and false-hearted friend tendered. I own that I at first was rather shocked at what he said;

but still I sat and listened, and made only weak objections, so that he very speedily overcame all my scruples; and I undertook to get back my gun at all cost, and to join him on the following morning on a shooting expedition on the property of a nobleman, some part of which was seen from the hill where we had posted ourselves.

Doolan could make himself very entertaining by narrating a variety of wild adventures in which he or his companions had been engaged, or, I may say, in some of which he pretended to have been engaged; for I since have had reason to believe that he drew considerably more on his imagination than on truth for the subjects of his tales, for the purpose of raising himself in my estimation, thereby hoping to gain a greater influence over me.

I have often since met such characters, who are very boastful and bold in the company of lads younger than themselves, or of persons whom they think will believe them, but cautious and silent in the presence of those whom they have sufficient discernment to perceive at once take them at their true value. Observe one of those fellows the instant an educated gentleman appears in the circle of which he is the attraction,—how his eye will quail and his voice sink, and he will endeavour to sneak away before his true character is exposed. I need scarcely advise my readers not to be misled by such pretenders.

The property on which we had resolved to poach was owned by Lord Fetherston. We knew that he maintained but few keepers, and that those were not very vigilant. He also, we believed, was away from the country, so that we had no fears of being detected.

I said that my father had few enemies. For some reason or other, however, Lord Fetherston was one. I did not know why; and this fact Doolan, who was well aware of it, took care to bring forward in justification of the attack we purposed to make on his property. I should have known that it was no justification whatever; but when people want reasons for committing a bad act, they are obliged to make very bad ones serve their purpose.

Pat Doolan was my senior by three years. He was the son of a man who was nominally a small farmer, but in reality a smuggler, and the owner of an illicit distillery; indeed I do not know what other lawless avocations he carried on.

Very inferior, therefore, as he was in position in life, though Pat Doolan was well supplied with money, he considered it of consequence to be intimate with me, and to gain an ascendency over my mind, which he might turn to account some time or other. He kept me sitting on the heather, and listening to his good stories, and laughing at them, for upwards of two hours, till he felt sure that my good resolutions would not come back. During this time he produced some bread and meat and whisky, of which latter he made me drink no small quantity, and he then accompanied me towards my home, in sight of which he left me, with a promise to meet him on the same spot at daybreak on the following morning.

Even that very evening, as I sat with a book in my hand pretending to read, in the same room the family occupied, and listened to the cheerful voices of my light-hearted innocent sisters, I began to repent of my engagement to Doolan; but the fear of his laughing at me, and talking again about my sisters' petticoats, made me resolve to adhere to it.

Chapter Two

That night was far from a happy one, for I knew all the time that I was doing what was very wrong. I waited till I thought that my father and all the household were asleep; and then, with the sensations I should think a thief experiences when about to commit a robbery, I crept along the dark passage towards his dressing-room. I trembled very much, for I was afraid that something would awake him, and that he would discover what I was about. I was aware that he would learn what I had done, the first thing in the morning; but then I should be far off, enjoying my sport, and I thought not of the consequences. I felt my way along the passage, for it was quite dark. I heard a noise—I trembled more and more—I expected every instant to be discovered, and I should have retreated to my room, but that the thought of Pat Doolan's laughter and sneers urged me on. I held my breath while I stopped to listen. There was again a dead silence, and I once more advanced. Presently something brushed against me. I was almost driven to cry out through terror, though I believe it was only the cat, whom I had disturbed from her slumbers on a rug at the door of the room occupied by my sisters. I was, I may say, constitutionally brave, almost to fool-hardiness, and yet on this occasion I felt the veriest coward in existence. Again I went on—the door of the dressing-room was ajar—I was afraid to push it lest it should creak on its hinges—I slowly moved it a little, and crept in. The moonlight was streaming through an opening in the upper part of the shutter on the coveted weapon. I grasped it eagerly, and slinging the shot-belt and powder-horn, which was by it, over my shoulder, I silently beat my retreat.

Now that I had won my prize, I felt much bolder, and without accident I reached my room. Sleep I could not; so, carefully closing the door, I spent the remainder of the night in cleaning my gun and getting ready for my excursion. I got out of the house without being perceived, and, closing the door behind me, even before the time agreed on I reached the spot where I was to meet Doolan. A hoar frost lay on the grass, the air was pure and bracing, my gun was in my hand, and plenty of powder and shot in my belt; and this, with the exercise and excitement, enabled me to cast away all regrets for my conduct, and all fear for the result.

I anxiously watched for my companion as I walked up and down the road to keep myself warm, till at last I began to fancy that some accident must have happened to prevent his coming. It never occurred to me that he could play me false. I had not learned to be suspicious of any one. At last I saw him trudging across a field towards me, and whistling as he came.

I could not have whistled if I had tried; but then, bad as he was, he was not, like me, disobeying a kind parent. When I remember the sort of person Doolan was (for his appearance was coarse and vulgar in the extreme), I wonder he could have gained such an influence over me. I believe that it was the boastful way in which he talked made me fancy him so important. I was very innocent and confiding, in spite of the bad company into which I had fallen; and I used to believe all the accounts he gave me of his own adventures, and those of his own particular friends. I have, fortunately, seldom met a man who could tell a falsehood with such a bold, unblushing front. I had a great horror of a falsehood, notwithstanding my numerous faults; I despised it as a mean, cowardly way of getting out of a difficulty, or of gaining some supposed advantage. I did not believe that a person older than myself could possibly be guilty of telling one. I fancied that only very little miserable children, or mean contemptible people, told stories; and I therefore could not fancy that such a person as Doolan would even condescend to say what was not true. I honestly say that I always adhered to the truth myself; and to this circumstance I ascribe my not having irretrievably sunk into the grade of society to which my too frequent companions belonged. I have mentioned Doolan, whose faults I would rather have forgotten; but I naturally wish to excuse myself as much as I can, and to account for the influence he had gained over me—an influence he never would have obtained had I known him to be what I now know he was.

It would indeed be happy for the young if they always could learn the true characters of their companions; and it is in this point that the advice of their older friends is so valuable. They, by their experience of others, are generally able to judge pretty correctly of persons, and often discern very dangerous qualities which young people cannot perceive. Therefore I say to my young friends, Avoid the acquaintance of those against whom your relations, or those who take an interest in your welfare, warn you, although you may think them, in your blindness, very fine fellows, or even perfect heroes. I wish that I, Peter—your friend, if you will so let me call myself— had thus followed the oft-repeated warnings of my kind father, and kept clear of Pat Doolan.

Doolan's loud cheer, as we met, raised my spirits still more, and away we trudged gaily enough towards the scene of our intended sport. He laughed and talked incessantly without giving me a moment for thought, so that when we reached the ground I was ready for anything. A hare crossed my path. It belonged, I knew, to Lord Fetherston. I fired, knocked it over, and bagged it; and while Doolan was applauding me, a pheasant was put up, and in like manner transferred to my game-bag. Never before had we enjoyed such capital sport, till, weary with our exercise, we sat down to partake of the provisions, not forgetting a whisky bottle which my companion had brought with him. While we were eating, he amused me with an account of an intended run of smuggled goods which was to be made on the coast two nights thence; and without much difficulty I agreed to join the party who were to assist in landing the things, and in carrying them up the country to the places where they were to be concealed.

On these occasions, conflicts between the coastguard officers and the smugglers often take place, and lives are frequently lost. This I well knew, though perhaps I did not think about it. I was pleased with the idea of the danger, and flattered by having so much confidence placed in me. I thought it was a very manly thing to assist the smugglers, while Doolan all the time wished to implicate me, to be able, should we be discovered, to shield himself by means of me. After breakfast we resumed our sport. Our game-bags were full and very heavy, and even we were content. My companion at last proposed to return home. "Home," I remarked unconsciously. "How can I return home? How can I face my father after having thus disobeyed him?" I thought. This feeling had not before occurred to me. I already repented what I had done. "I can't go home now," said I to Doolan aloud.

"Why not?" said he; "you've a mighty fine faste to place before your dad; and, faith, if he's a sinsible man, he'll ax no questions how you came by it." Such were my companion's notions of morality; and in this instance he spoke what he thought was the truth, for he had been taught no better, and he knew that thus his own father would have acted.

"It won't do; I cannot look my father in the face, and must go to your house now; and I will creep home at night, when there's no one to see me."

"Well, Pater, you must do as you like," he said, laughing; "you're mighty welcome to come to our house and to stay there as long as you plase; at the same time that I see no reason at all, at all, why your dad shouldn't be glad to see such an illigant stock of game for his dinner."

"I know my father better than you do, Pat," said I, for the first time in my life asserting a little determination with him. "Home I will not go this day."

So it was settled; and we were bending our steps in the direction of Doolan's house, through Lord Fetherston's property, when another pheasant got up before me. My gun was loaded, and I could not resist the temptation to fire. The bird fell, and I was running forward to pick it up, when three persons appeared suddenly from a path through a copse close to me. Doolan, who was a little in advance, ran off as fast as his legs could carry him, throwing away his game-bag in his fright, and leaving me to take care of myself as I best could. Two of the strangers, whom I guessed to be keepers by their dress—indeed one I knew by sight—rushed forward and seized me roughly by the collar.

"What are you doing here, you young scamp?" exclaimed one of them. "Killing our lord's game, and caught in the act," he added, picking up the still fluttering bird. "Come along, and we'll see what he has to say to you."

The other immediately made chase after my companion; but Doolan ran very fast, and was in good wind, which the keeper was not, so that the former soon distanced him. The keeper gave up the chase, calculating that, having caught one of us, he should be able to lay hands on the other whenever he chose.

On his return, with many a cuff he dragged me along towards the third person I spoke of, and whom I at once recognised as Lord Fetherston himself. He did not remember me; but the keepers did, I suspect, from the first.

"What is your name, youngster?" said his lordship in a severe tone.

I told him, with the shame I felt strongly depicted on my countenance.

"I am sorry to hear it," he replied. "And that of your companion?"

"Pat Doolan, my lord." I said this with no vindictive feeling, or with any idea of excusing myself; but I was asked a question, and without considering what might be the result I answered it.

"A pretty companion for the son of the vicar of —. Take away his gun, O'Rourke," he said to the keeper, "and the game: to that he has no right. And now, young gentleman, I shall see your father on this matter shortly. If he chooses to let his son commit depredations on my property, he must take the consequences."

"I came out without my father's knowledge, and he is in no way to blame," I answered quickly; for I could not bear to have any reflection cast on my father through my fault.

Lord Fetherston looked at me attentively, and I think I heard him muttering something like, "He is a brave lad, and must be rescued from such companionship;" but I am not quite certain.

"Well, sir, you at all events must not escape punishment," he replied aloud. "For the present, I leave you in the custody of my keepers. You see the condition to which you have reduced yourself."

He then gave some orders to one of the keepers, which I did not hear; and without further noticing me he walked on, while they led me away towards Fetherston Abbey, his lordship's residence. I need scarcely say that my feelings were very wretched, and full of shame; and yet perhaps I would rather it should thus have happened, than that I should have been compelled to go back to my father. It was perhaps somewhat of a consolation to feel that I was being justly punished, and yet not by my father's hand. I don't know that I thought this at the time, but I know that I did afterwards. And then, when days had passed, and many other events had occurred, I felt very grateful that Providence had thus disposed of me, and had preserved me from a fate which in all human probability would have been mine had I this time escaped with impunity.

Lord Fetherston was a magistrate, and consequently in the Abbey there was a strong room, in which, on occasion, prisoners were locked up before they were carried off to jail. Into this room I was led, and with a heavy heart I heard the key turned in the lock, and found myself alone. If I had wished to escape I could not; and there were no books, or other means of amusement, so that I was left to my own reflections. A servant, who would not answer any questions, brought me in some dinner, which I could scarcely taste; and at night a small bed, ready-made, was brought in, and I was again left to myself. Two days thus passed away: my obstinate spirit was completely broken, and I must say that I truly had repented of all my folly and idleness. On the third day the door opened, and my father appeared. He looked very sad, but not angry. He took a chair and sat down, while I stood before him. For more than a minute he could not speak.

"Peter," he at length said, "I do not come to reproach you: the grief I and your mother feel, and what you will have to endure henceforth, will be, I trust, sufficient punishment. We must part with you, my son; we have no choice. You must go to foreign lands, and there retrieve your name, and, I trust, improve and strengthen your character. You have placed yourself and me in Lord Fetherston's power. He insists on it, that you shall forthwith be sent to sea; and on that condition he promises to overlook all that has occurred. He did not even speak harshly of you; and I am fain to believe that what he has decided is for the best. At my earnest solicitation, he consented that you should take only a short voyage first to North America, provided that you sail without delay. Accordingly, I have agreed to set off to-morrow with you for Liverpool, whence many ships sail for that part of the world, and I dare say that I shall find some captain to take charge of you. Do you consent to abide by this arrangement?"

"I think Lord Fetherston is right," I replied. "The life of a sailor, if what I know of it is correct (little in truth did I know of it), will just suit me; and though I regret to go as I am going, and grieve to wound my mother's heart, yet I consider that I am very leniently dealt with, and will gladly accept the conditions." So it was settled, and my father led me out of my prison. Lord Fetherston met us as we left the mansion.

"My son gratefully accepts your conditions, my lord," said my father, colouring. His pride, I fear, was humbled to the dust (alas! through me) when he said so. "I shall fulfil to the letter your lordship's commands."

"I am glad to hear it, Mr Lefroy; depend on it, you act wisely," said Lord Fetherston. "And I trust that we part without malice, young man," addressing me. "You have my well-wishes, I can assure you." He held out his hand, and I shook it, I believe gratefully, though I said nothing; and without another word I jumped into the car which had brought my father, and we drove home.

There was much grief and sorrow when we got there, and many a tear in the eyes of my mother and my sweet, ever kind, sisters as they packed up my little kit; but not a word of reproach. Thus passed the last day for many a long year that I spent at home.

Let me tell those who wish to quit their homes to go roaming round the world in search of what they know not, that though they chance to bring back shiploads of riches, they will find no jewels comparable in price to a another's fond love, a father's protecting affection, the sweet forbearing regard of tender sisters, a brother's hearty interest, or the calm tranquillity of the family roof.

I write for the large and happy majority of my readers: some few are less fortunate, and they in truth deserve the sympathy of the rest. Cherish, I say, while you can, the affections of your home; and depend on it, when far away, the recollection alone will be like a refreshing spot in the weary desert through which your path in life may lead you; for be assured that there is no place like home.

Chapter Three

I remember very little of my journey to Dublin, except that it was performed on the top of the mail. My father went outside also, which was not his usual custom; but he did not like to expose me to the inclemency of the weather while he was comfortably ensconced within (another proof of his love), and he could not spare money to pay for my fare inside.

We saw my eldest brother for an instant, just for me to wish him good-bye, and the same afternoon we went on board a steamer bound for Liverpool.

She was very different to the superb vessels which now run twice a day from one place to the other, making the two capitals, for all intents and purposes, not so far off as London and Winchester were not a hundred years ago. She was in every respect inferior; but I thought her, as she was indeed, a very wonderful vessel. I was never tired of examining her machinery, and in wandering through every part of her.

I had never before been on board a steamer; and as I was naturally of an inquiring disposition, I had numberless questions to ask to learn how it was the steam made the engines work, and the engine made the large paddle-wheels go round. This occupation prevented me from thinking of what had occurred, and kept me in good spirits.

Arrived at Liverpool, we went to an inn, and my father immediately set out with me to inquire among the ship-brokers what ships were sailing for British North America.

"You shall go to an English colony, Peter," said my father. "Wherever you wander, my son, remember you are a Briton, and cease not to love your native land."

Liverpool was then, I thought, a very fine city. I was particularly struck by the fine public buildings; the broad streets, full of richly-stocked shops; and more than all, by the docks, crowded with shipping. Since then, several of the streets have been widened, the docks have been increased, and many fine buildings have been added; and as the wealth of Liverpool continues to increase, many more will be added, till it vies with some of the proudest cities in the world. Such is the result of commerce, when guided by a wise and liberal policy.

Had my father known more of the world, I am inclined to think that he would have waited till he could procure an introduction to some respectable ship-owner, who would have selected a good honest captain with whom to place me. Instead of so doing, he walked into several offices by chance, over which he saw written "Shipping Agent and Broker." Some had no ships going to the British North American ports, others did not know of any captains who would take charge of a raw youngster like me. One said if I liked to go to the coast of Africa he could accommodate me, but that he could not say that I might not have to spend two or three months up some of the rivers, waiting for a return cargo of ivory and gold dust. Another said he could secure me a trip to China if I would pay a premium; and three others offered me cruises to the West Indies and North America. The fact was, that the navigation of the mighty river Saint Lawrence was scarcely open, and consequently few ships were ready to sail for Quebec. At last a broker into whose office we entered, informed us that he was agent for one of the first emigrant ships which would sail that year; that her captain was a very superior man, a great friend of his; and that he doubted not for a small premium he would take charge of me. Mr John Cruden, our new friend, insurance broker and general shipping agent, was a very polite man, and extremely soft-spoken; but he was of an extremely inquisitive disposition, I thought, for he asked my father numberless questions about himself and me, to all of which he returned the short monosyllable "H'm," which did not inform us whether he was satisfied or not. I found all the time that he was merely trying to discover what amount of premium my father was likely to be able to pay, that he might ask accordingly.

The office, in which we stood, was very small for the large amount of business Mr Cruden informed us he transacted in it, and very dark; and so dirty, that I thought it could never have been cleaned out since he commenced his avocations there. There were sea-chests, and cases, and small casks of all sorts piled up in all the odd corners. There were also coils of rope, and bottles, and rusty iron implements, the form of which I could not discern, and bundles of old clothes and canvas bags, and compass-boxes in and about the cases, and hanging from the ceiling; while a tarry, fishy, strong shippy odour pervaded the room. I was particularly struck with the model of a ship fully rigged on a shelf over the mantelpiece; but she also was as much covered with dust as the ship in which the ancient mariner went to sea would have been, after he had shot the albatross, could any dust have reached her. I observed all these things while our new friend was talking to my father.

"You will doubtless like to make the acquaintance of Captain Elihu Swales, Mr Lefroy," said Mr Cruden. "I expect him here every instant, and I shall then have the pleasure of introducing him to you, and we can arrange matters forthwith. You will find him, sir, a very amiable, excellent man—indeed you will, sir—a very proper guardian for a young man."

Whether this description was correct or not I had then no means of judging. The subject of this eulogium appeared while it was being uttered; indeed I suspect he heard a portion of it, for, suddenly turning my head after growing weary of looking at the dusty ship, I saw a man, whom I instinctively suspected to be the captain, standing outside the little paddock in which we were enclosed, called by Mr Cruden his counting-house, with a very peculiar smile on his countenance. Had I not turned, I think he would have burst forth outright into laughter. I must remark that my father's back was towards him, and that Mr Cruden, unless he was very near-sighted, could scarcely have helped seeing when he came in.

"Ah, there is at last my excellent friend," observed the agent when he perceived that I had discovered the captain. "Mr Lefroy, allow me to introduce Captain Swales to you. Captain Swales, this gentleman has a son whom he wishes to send to sea. You will take charge of the lad. You will be a second father to him. I can depend on you. Say the word, and all parties will come to terms."

"Day, sir," said Captain Swales, making as if he would take off his hat, which he did not. He was a very respectable man, as far as dress went; that is to say, he was clothed in a suit of black cloth, with a black silk handkerchief—nothing very remarkable, certainly: most masters and mates of merchantmen wear such on shore. His figure was short and square, there was nothing rounded about him; his features were all angular; and though there was a good deal of him, it was all bone and sinew. His countenance was brown, with a deep tinge of red superadded; and as for his features, they were so battered and seamed with winds and weather, that it was difficult to discern their expression. I remember, however, that the first glance I caught of his eye, as it looked inquiringly towards Mr Cruden, I did not like, even though at the time he was smiling.

"You wish to send your son to sea, sir," he continued to my father. "As Mr Cruden says, I'll look after him as if he was my own boy, sir. I'll keep him from mischief, sir. Lads always gets into mischief if they can; but with me, sir, they can't—I don't let 'em. I look after them, sir; and when they knows my eye is on them, they behaves themselves. That's my principle, sir; and now you know me."

He said this in an off-hand, bluff, hearty way, which made my father fully believe that he had fallen in with a prize—indeed, that he was supremely fortunate in having secured so kind a protector for me. It was finally arranged that he was to pay Captain Elihu Swales the sum of fifteen pounds; in consideration of which, in addition to any service I could be of, I was to mess at his table, and to learn what I could of a seaman's duty, till the ship returned to Liverpool.

The *Black Swan*, the name of Captain Elihu Swales' ship, would not be ready for sea for some days, he informed my father; and till she was so, as he was compelled to return home immediately, Mr Cruden kindly undertook to board and lodge me at the rate of twelve shillings a week. I was to go on board the *Black Swan* every day, to see if I was wanted; and I was to return to Mr Cruden's in the afternoon, or when I was not wanted. My father considered this a very admirable arrangement, and was perfectly confident that he had done the best circumstances would allow, and that he had left me in safe and honourable hands.

On our way to our inn, we met one of the brokers to whom we had spoken in the morning. He asked if we had found what we wanted. "Oh yes," replied my father, "an excellent man, Captain Swales, a friend of Mr Cruden's—very superior—very superior indeed." The broker, I thought, looked odd at this, and was at first apparently going to speak; but on second thoughts he seemed to consider that it was no business of his, and he passed on with a cold "Oh, really—good-day, sir." It was afterwards only, perhaps, that his manner struck me; at the time I supposed that it was usual to him.

We spent most of the afternoon in purchasing a sea-chest and an outfit for me, according to a list furnished by Mr Cruden, to whose office my traps were transferred forthwith. We did not go down to see the *Black Swan*, because Captain Swales said she was a long way off, and was not fit to receive visitors, but that she would be in a few days. He then remarked that she was one of the finest and fastest craft out of Liverpool. "Nothing could beat the *Black Swan* when she had a mind to put her best foot foremost." I was wondering whether ships really had feet. I afterwards found that this was a figurative way of expressing that she sailed fast. These observations were made when we returned with my chest to Mr Cruden's, where we again met my future captain; and when the sum agreed on for my voyage was paid into the hands of the first-named person, my father's heart was softened towards me; and after he had exhausted all the good advice he could think of, and had given me several useful books, and many little articles of his own property, he made me a present of six pounds as pocket-money, and to purchase anything I might wish to bring back from America. He took his watch out of his fob, and would have given me that also, but

I persuaded him to keep it, assuring him that I did not require it, and that I should certainly break it, or lose it overboard, as would have been the case probably the first time I went aloft. The next morning my poor father returned by the steamer to Dublin. He felt very much, I am sure, at parting from me, more than he would have done under other circumstances, though by a considerable effort he mastered himself so as not publicly to betray his emotions. He was gone; and I was left alone in the big world to look after myself, with little more experience of its ways than a child.

Chapter Four

When my father was gone, I went back to Mr Cruden's office and asked him to tell me where I could find his house, at which I understood I was to lodge.

He looked up from the book in which he was writing, with an air of surprise, and replied, "You are mistaken, my lad, if you suppose that I am about to introduce into the bosom of my family one of whom I know nothing. Your father is a very respectable man, I dare say, and you may be a very estimable youth, for what I know; but it is generally a different sort who are sent to sea as you are being sent; and therefore it is just possible you may be a wild young scamp, whose face his friends may never wish to behold again—hark you."

I blushed as he said this, and looked confused; for my conscience told me that he spoke the truth.

"Ah! I guessed I was right," he continued. "Now, to answer your question. While you remain on shore, which won't be for long, you may swing your hammock in the loft over this office; and for cooking, you won't require much of that. This will break you in by degrees for the life you've to lead, and will do you good, my lad. So I hope you will be grateful."

From the determined manner he had about him, I supposed that all was right; and had it been otherwise, my spirits at that time were too low to allow me to remonstrate. I asked him next if I could not go on board the *Black Swan*, to make myself useful.

He gave a peculiar smile, the meaning of which I did not comprehend at the time, as he replied, "By all means. You will probably find Captain Swales on board—at all events his first mate; and you may offer your valuable services to them. When they have done with you, you may come back here. By keeping along the quays to the right, you cannot miss the ship if you ask for her."

I had scarcely fancied that there were so many ships in the world as I saw crowded together in the Liverpool docks, as I passed through them for the first time in my life. It gave me a great notion of the wealth and commerce of the place. "And these will all be gone in a few weeks," I thought, "scattered far and wide to all parts of the world, and their places will be filled by others now on their homeward voyage, which will have again to make way for a totally fresh set." I inquired for the *Black Swan* of the seamen and porters loitering about the quays, but I did not get very satisfactory answers. Some told me that she was drunk last night, and had not got up yet. Others said she had sailed yesterday, for they had seen her dropping down with the tide. The boatmen invariably wanted me to take a boat to look for her, as the only chance I had of finding her; but I saw that they were trying to impose on me, and passed on. At last, when I had got very near to the west end of the docks, I asked a man whom I saw standing in a meditative mood, with his hands in his pockets, if he would tell me where the *Black Swan* was to be found.

"Why, I calculate, if you look right before your nose, young one, you'll see her as big as life," he answered, pointing to a large ship lying along the quay, on board which a number of men were employed about the rigging; while others, with a peculiar song, were hoisting in the cargo. I found that the first were riggers, and that the others were dock porters, and that neither belonged to the ship; the regular crew, with the exception of two mates and the cook, not being engaged till just before the ship was ready for sea.

I must notice here the very bad system which has long prevailed with regard to British merchant seamen. The moment a ship arrives in harbour, the crew are paid their wages and discharged. On this they are immediately set upon by Jews and harpies of every description. I do them no wrong when I say that they are the very worst of the human race: the fiercest savages have some virtues—these wretches have none.

The poor seamen are cajoled by them with every artful device; nor do the miscreants cease till they have plundered them of all their hard-earned gold. Not content with this, these crimps—for such is the name by which these persons are known—encourage the seamen to get into their debt, chiefly for liquor; and they then go to the masters of merchantmen looking out for crews, and make any arrangements they please. Part of the seamen's wages are paid in advance, and this goes into the pockets of the crimps. I have known men put on board in a state of brutal intoxication, without knowing who were their officers, or where they were going to. Thus the men were kept in a state of absolute slavery, without self-respect or a chance of improvement.

I speak of the system as it was till lately. I trust that a better state of affairs is now being introduced; at the same time, as there is a tendency in most things to let abuses creep in, I must entreat you, my young friends, in your several capacities when you grow up, not to forget the interests of our brave seamen. On those seamen depend greatly the prosperity, the glory, the very existence of England; and, whether as legislators or as private gentlemen, I tell you it is your duty to inquire into their condition, and to endeavour to improve it by every means in your power.

But to return to the *Black Swan*, and the man who had pointed her out to me. There was something I remarked very peculiar about the said man, so I will speak of him first. He wore a straw hat with a very broad brim, a nankeen jacket, though the weather was still cold, Flushing trousers, which did not near reach to his ankles, and a waistcoat of fur—of beaver, I believe, or of wild cat. He had a very long face, and lantern jaws. His nose was in proportion, and it curled down in a way which gave it a most facetious expression; while a very bright small pair of eyes had also a sort of constant laugh in them, though the rest of his features looked as if they could never smile. His complexion had a very leathery look, and his figure was tall and lanky in the extreme. I could not have said whether he was an old or a young man by his appearance.

"Well, there's the ship," he observed, seeing that I was looking at him instead of going on board. "*Do* you know me now?" with an emphasis on the *do*. "That's kind now to acknowledge an old friend. We was raised together, I guess; only you wasn't weaned till last summer, when the grass was dried up."

I saw that he was laughing at me; but as I felt that I had been rude in staring at him, I said I begged his pardon, but that he made a mistake in supposing we were acquainted, unless he had visited the south of Ireland, seeing that I had never been out of that part of the country before. This seemed to amuse him mightily, for he gave way to a quiet and very peculiar laugh, which I heard as I passed on towards the ship.

There was a plank placed from the quay to the deck of the ship, and by means of it I stepped on board the *Black Swan*. No one took any notice of me, so that I had time to look about me. She was a ship of some eight hundred tons burthen, though she was advertised as of twelve hundred. She had a raised poop aft, which I may describe as an additional house above the deck, the doors of which opened on the deck. There was a similar raised place forward, called the topgallant forecastle. Under the latter the seamen and mate lived, while the captain and passengers inhabited the poop. The space between decks was open fore and aft, and fitted up with standing bed-places. This was for the abode of the poorer class of emigrants. The hold, the remaining portion of the ship below the main deck, was filled with cargo and provisions.

All this I discovered afterwards, for at first everything appeared to my sight an inextricable mass of confusion and disorder. After watching for some time, I observed a man whom I concluded was the first mate, by the way he ordered the other people about and the air of authority which he assumed; so at last I mustered courage to go up to him.

"Please, sir," said I in an unusually humble tone, "are you the first mate of the ship?"

"Well, if I am, and what then?" was his not very courteous answer.

"Why, it's settled that I'm to go in this ship to learn to be a sailor, so I've come on board at once to make myself useful," I replied.

He eyed me curiously from head to foot as if I was some strange animal, and then burst into a loud laugh. "You learn to be a sailor?—you make yourself useful?—you chaw-bacon. Why, the hay-seed is still sticking in your hair, and the dust ain't off your shoes yet. What can you do now?" he asked.

I confessed that I knew nothing about a ship, except the machinery of a steamer, which I had examined in my passage across from Dublin; but that I would learn as fast as I could.

"And so you are a young gentleman, are you?" he continued, without attending to my observations. "Sent to sea to learn manners! Well, we'll soon knock your gentility out of you, let me tell you. Howsomdever, we don't want no help here, so be off on shore again; and when you meet John Smith, just ask him to take you a walk through the town, and not to bring you back to make yourself useful till the ship's ready for sea, d'ye hear, or you'll wish you'd stayed away, that's all."

I must say that even at that time I thought such a man was not fit to be placed in command of others, and yet I am sorry to say that I met many others no better fitted to act as officers. I did not answer him; and though I did not understand what he meant about John Smith, I comprehended enough of his observations to judge that it would be more advantageous for me to keep out of his way; so I walked along the plank again to the quay. There was the man I have described, standing as complacently as ever. As smoking is not allowed in the docks, for fear of fire, he was chewing.

"And so, young 'un, you've done your business on board; and what are you going to do next?" he asked, as he saw me sauntering along. I felt that there was a kind tone in his voice, so I told him that I had nothing to do, as the mate of the *Black Swan* did not require my services.

One question led on to another, and he very soon wormed my whole history out of me. "And your name is Peter Lefroy, is it? Then mine's Silas Flint, at your service. And now, as neither of us has anything to do, we'll go and help each other; so come along." Saying this, he led the way out of the dock.

I wondered who Mr Silas Flint could be, and yet I had no mistrust in him. From his manner, and the tone of his voice, I thought he was honest, and meant me no harm; and my heart, I must own, yearned for companionship. He did not leave me long in doubt; for after I had told him everything I had to tell about my previous life, he began to be equally communicative about himself. "You see, Peter, I've secured my passage in the *Black Swan*, so we shall be fellow-voyagers; and as I've taken a sort of liking to you, I hope we shall be friends. I come from 'Merica, over there, though I don't belong to the parts she's going to; but you see I've got some business at Quebec, and so I'm going there first." I cannot pretend to give his peculiar and quaint phraseology.

I soon learned that he was raised, as he called it, in the Western States of America; that he had spent much of his life as a hunter and trapper, though he was a man of some little substance; that having accidentally seen an advertisement in the paper, stating that if the heirs of the late Josiah Flint, of Barnet, in the county of Hertfordshire, England, would apply to Messrs Grub and Gull, Fleece Court, Chancery Lane, London, they would hear of something to their advantage, he, believing himself to be a descendant of the said Josiah, had come over to hear the welcome news. He remarked, with his peculiar smile, that he had *heard* a great deal which might be very advantageous to him, and which might or might not be true, but that he had got nothing—that he had established his undoubted claim to be one of the heirs of the said Josiah, but that he had fifty cousins, who had turned up in all directions, and whom he would never otherwise have had the happiness of knowing. The gain in this case did not seem great, as they none of them showed any cousinly affection, but did their best to prove that he was an impostor. Thus all the share of his grandfather's property went in law expenses; and he was going back to the land of his father's adoption considerably poorer than he came, and in no loving humour with England and his English cousins.

Such is the brief outline Silas Flint gave me of his history, as we strolled together through the streets of Liverpool. If, however, I continue describing all the characters I met, and all the strange things I saw, I shall never get on with my history. Silas made a confession which much pleased me: it was, that although he had lived many years in the world, he still felt that he had much to learn, and was constantly doing things he wished to undo: the last was paying his money for his passage, before he had made any inquiries about the ship. He hinted that Mr Cruden was not as honest as he might be; that he suspected Captain Swales was no better; and that the way the poor emigrants who had come to Liverpool from all parts to go by the ship were treated, was most shameful.

He told me that, in the first place, they were attracted there by advertisements long before the ship was ready for sea, partly that the ship-brokers might make certain of having the ship filled, and not a little for the benefit of the inns and lodging-house keepers. As soon as they arrived—most of them absurdly ignorant of what was to be done, and of the necessaries required for the voyage—they were pounced upon by a set of harpies, who misled them in every possible way, and fleeced them without mercy. There existed—and, I am sorry to say, exist to the present day—a regular gang of these wretches, by profession lodging-house keepers, ship-chandlers, outfitters, and provision merchants. So notorious have they become, that they now go by the name of the Forty Thieves, for to that number amount the worthy fraternity.

Silas Flint took me round to a number of our intended fellow-voyagers; and we found them loud in their complaints of the treatment they had received, though, when he had discovered them, he had been able to preserve them from much further expense by describing the character of the country to which they were going, and the things they would most require. Among them were a great many of my countrymen. They were generally the most forlorn and heartbroken, though they had indeed little to leave behind; but then the slightest incident would make them forget their grief, and clap their hands with shouts of laughter.

The sorrow of the English was less loud; but it took much more, I observed, to make them smile. They were better dressed, and seemed to have made more provision for the voyage. They had also been proportionably more fleeced by the Forty Thieves. When so many of our poor countrymen are leaving our shores annually to lands where they can procure work and food, we should have a far better supervision and a more organised system of emigration than now exists. And again I say to my young countrymen, when you grow up, make it your business to inquire into the subject; inquire with your own eyes, remember; do not trust to what is told you; and if you do not find such a system established, strive with heart and hand, and weary not till you have established it; at all events, correct the abuses which too probably by that time will have sprung up. You will all have the power of aiding that or any other good work. If you are not in influential positions, if you have not wealth at command, you at least have tongues to speak with, pens to write with; so talk about it in private, speak in public, write on the subject, and, depend on it, you will ultimately gain your object.

It was very late in the day when I returned to the office. Mr Cruden was about to go away. He told me, that as I had chosen to be absent at the dinner hour, I must be content with what I could get; and he pointed to some musty bread and cheese, and a glass of sour, turbid-looking ale which stood on the desk. I was, however, too hungry to refuse it; so I ate it as soon as he was gone. An old porter had charge of the premises, and he now beckoned me to follow him to a sort of loft or lumber-room over the office, where he had slung a hammock, which he told me I might sleep in, or I might, if I liked, sleep on the bare boards outside. "The hammock's more comfortable than it looks, young 'un, so I'd advise you to try it," he remarked; and I found his remark true. As I was very tired, I was glad to turn in early and forget my sorrows in sleep. The next day I fared no better than the first, and all the time I boarded with Mr Cruden the only variation in my food from bread and cheese was hard biscuits and very doubtful-looking pork and beef. When I told Silas Flint of the treatment I had received, he shrugged his shoulders.

"Can you mend it?" he asked.

I told him that I could complain.

"To whom?" he said. "You have no one to complain to—no friend in the place. Now let me advise you to do as I do. When you can't cure a thing, grin and bear it; but if you see your way out of a fix, then go tooth and nail at it, and don't let anything stop you till you're clear. That's my maxim, youngster; but there's no use kicking against the pricks—it wears out one's shoes, and hurts the feet into the bargain. Now, soon after I took my passage in this here *Black Swan*, I guessed I had made a mistake; but what would have been the use of my going to law about it? I knowed better. I should only have sent my last dollar to look after the many which have gone to prove I was first cousin to a set of people, who would all rather have heard my father was drowned years ago than have set eyes on me. I tell you, Peter, you must grin and bear it, as you'll have to do many things as you get through life."

I found that my friend practised what he preached; for so completely were his finances exhausted by his law expenses, that he had to husband all his resources to enable him to return home. In board and lodging he was worse off than I was; and, as he said, he was accustomed to camp out at night, to save the expense of a bed. He used to amuse himself in the day by walking about to look out for a snug place to sleep in at night, either in the city or its neighbourhood, and he seldom occupied the same spot two nights running. He assured me, and I believed him, that it was far pleasanter than sleeping in the close atmosphere of a crowded room; and it reminded him faintly of his beloved prairies, on which he had spent the greater part of his life. The chief portion of every day, for a week before the ship was reported ready for sailing, I passed with my new-found friend; and, as may be supposed, I did not again offer my valuable services to the mate of the *Black Swan*, nor was any inquiry made after me by her worthy captain.

Chapter Five

At last I was informed by Mr Cruden that I might transfer my chest and myself on board the *Black Swan*. Accordingly, the old porter wheeled the former down to the docks, while I walked by its side. I gave the old porter a shilling for his trouble: his eye brightened, and he blessed me, and muttered something about wishing that I had fallen into better hands; but he was afraid, apparently, of saying more, and casting another glance at me, I suspect of commiseration, he tottered off to his daily avocations. My chest, which was a very small one, was stowed away by one of the seamen under a bunk in the forecastle. I thought that I was to have a cabin under the poop, and to mess with the captain; but when I made inquiries, no one could give any information, and the captain was nowhere to be seen. Everything on board appeared in the wildest confusion; and I must own that I got most unaccountably in everybody's way, and accordingly got kicked out of it without the slightest ceremony.

Silas had not arrived, so I could not go to him for information. I therefore climbed up out of the way, to the boat, placed amidships, on the top of the booms. Soon afterwards the emigrants' bag and baggage began to arrive. I was amused by observing the odd and mixed collection of things the poor people brought with them, some of the more bulky articles of which were not admitted on board. The Jew harpies were on the quays ready to snap them up, giving little or nothing in return. I thought that it was a great pity that there were no means to enable these poor people to obtain better information before they left home, to have saved them the expense of dragging so much useless lumber about with them. I pitied them, not because they were going to another land where they could get food and employment, but for their helpless ignorance, and the want of any one fit to lead or direct them, as also for the treatment they were receiving at the hands of the countrymen they were leaving for ever.

Many of them resented bitterly the impositions practised on them; and I saw some of them, with significant gestures, take off their shoes and shake the dust over the ship's side as they stepped on board, while they gave vent to their feelings in oaths not lowly muttered. Henceforth, instead of friends and supporters, they were to be foes to England and the English—aliens of the country which should have cherished and protected them, but did not. Such things were—such things are: when will they cease to be? What a strange mixture of people there were, from all parts of the United Kingdom—aged men and women; young brides and their husbands; mothers with tribes of children, some with their infants still unweaned—talking many different dialects, weeping, laughing, shrieking, and shouting! At last they got their berths allotted to them, and they began to stow away their provisions and baggage between decks. Some kept going backwards and forwards from the ship to the shore, and no notice being given, many of them were left behind when the ship hauled out of dock, and had to come on board in boats, at a considerable expense, after being well frightened at the thoughts that we had sailed without them.

We lay out in the stream for another whole day, with the Blue Peter flying, to show that we were ready for sea, and to summon any passengers who might yet remain on shore. Silas Flint was one of the last to come on board, before we left the dock. He appeared following a porter, who wheeled down his chest, containing all his property. He did not even give me a look of recognition as he passed me; but he at once plunged below with his chest, and he studiously avoided coming near me. This I thought odd and unkind, nor could I comprehend the cause of this behaviour.

I was sitting very disconsolate by myself among the emigrants, and wondering when the captain would come on board, and when I should begin to learn to be a seaman, when I felt the no pleasing sensation of a rope's end laid smartly across my shoulders. I turned quickly round to resent the indignity, when I encountered the stern glance of the first mate, Mr Stovin, fixed on me, while the "colt" in his hand showed that he was the aggressor. "And so you are the youngster who wanted to make himself useful, are you?" he exclaimed in a sneering voice.

"I am," I replied; "and I'll thank you in future not to take such liberties with my back."

He burst into a loud laugh. "O my young cock-a-hoop, you show fight, do you?" he exclaimed. "Well, we'll see what you are made of before long."

"I'm ready to do my duty when you show me the way," I answered in as calm a voice as I could command; and I believe this reply, and the having kept my temper, gave him a more favourable opinion of me than he was before inclined to form, and somewhat softened his savage nature.

"A willing hand will have no want of masters," he observed. "And mind, what I tell you to do you'll do as well as you can, and we shan't fall foul of each other."

I will now describe the *Black Swan*. She measured nearly eight hundred tons, was ship-rigged, and had been built many years. She carried eighteen hands forward, with two cooks and a steward, besides the captain, four mates, and a doctor.

There were about four hundred and forty steerage passengers, who, I may explain, are the poorer classes; and I think there were ten cabin passengers, who berthed in the cabin and messed with the captain. The steerage passengers brought their own provisions, but the captain was obliged to provide them with water and biscuit, just to keep life in them; indeed, without it many of them would have died. It was, I felt, like severing the last link which bound us to our native shores, when the pilot left us at the mouth of the Mersey, and with a fair wind we stood down the Irish Channel.

I cannot say that before I quitted home I had any very definite idea of the life of a sailor; but I had some notion that his chief occupation was sitting with his messmates round a can of grog, and singing songs about his sweetheart: the reality I found was very different.

The first time I had any practical experience of this was when, the pilot having left us, and the wind having veered round to the north-east, the captain ordered the ship to be kept away before it. His eye happened to fall upon me for the first time, dressed in my sea toggery, and seated, with my hands in my pockets, on the booms.

"Hillo, Jim—what's-your-name—we'll have none of your idling ways here if you belong to this ship, as I've a notion you do," he exclaimed. "Aloft there with you, then, and help furl the mizzen topsail. Be smart about it, or I'll freshen your way with a rope's end, and we'll see if you give me an answer."

By this last observation, I guessed that the mate had told him of the answer I had given him, and I felt that the wisest thing I could do was to obey him without making any reply. What, however, he meant by "furling the mizzen topsail" I had not the slightest notion; but as I saw that he pointed to the mizzen-mast, and that several lads and men were ascending the mizzen rigging, I followed them. I was a good climber, so I had no fear of going aloft; and while I was in the top, luckily one of my new messmates, who was already lying out on the yard, exclaimed, "Hillo, Peter, lend us a hand here, my lad." On hearing this, I immediately threw myself on the yard, and following his directions I made a very fair furl of it. I got no praise certainly for this, but I escaped blame; and I saw by the way the other mizzen-top men treated me, that they considered me a smart lad, and no flincher.

From that moment I was never idle. I followed a piece of advice honest Dick Derrick gave me on this occasion: "Never let go with one hand till you've got a good gripe with the other; and if you cannot hold on with your hands, make use of your teeth and legs; and mind, clutch fast till you've picked out a soft spot to fall on." Dick Derrick taught me to hand, furl, and steer, to knot and splice, to make sinnet and spun-yarn, and the various other parts of a seaman's business. I was ambitious to learn; and I found the work, when taught by him, both easy and pleasant.

I was placed in the second mate's watch, and had to keep my watch regularly. In this I was fortunate. William Bell was his name. He was a quiet, gentlemanly young man, who always kept his temper, however roughly spoken to by the captain. It was through no want of spirit that he did not reply to the abuse thrown at him, as I afterwards discovered, but because it was the wisest and most dignified course to pursue. As I said before, I expected to mess in the cabin, and to be a sort of midshipman; but when I went up to the captain and told him so, he laughed at me, and asked me if I would show him any written agreement on the subject, for that he knew nothing at all about it. All he could say was, that I was entered as a ship's boy; that as such I must be berthed and messed, and do duty. If I did not like it, he would see what Mr Stovin had to say to me. I saw that there was no help for me; so, following Silas Flint's advice, I determined to grin and bear it.

We sighted Cape Clear, the south-westernmost point of Ireland. I longed to be able to swim on shore and return home. I did not the less wish to see the world, but I did not much like the company with whom I was likely to see it; Mr Stovin and his rope's-ending were not agreeable companions. From Cape Clear we took a fresh departure. A ship is said to take her departure from a point, the distance and the bearing of the point being ascertained when her course is marked off from the spot where she then is. At four p.m. Cape Clear bore five miles north-east of us, or rather we were five miles south-west of the Cape. This spot was marked on the chart; and the distance run, and the course by compass, were each day afterwards pricked off in like manner on the charts. The distance run is measured by the log, which is hove every two hours.

The log is a small triangular piece of wood, secured to the end of a long line, on which divisions are marked, bearing the same proportion to a mile which a half-minute bears to an hour. One man holds a half-minute glass in his hand—another a reel on which the line is rolled—a third, the mate, takes the log and heaves it overboard, drawing off the line with his left hand. Thus, as the log remains stationary in the water, according to the number of divisions or knots run off while the sand in the glass is running, will be shown the number of miles the ship is going in the hour. Instead of miles, the word knots is used, evidently from the knots marked on the line.

The mode I have thus briefly described of finding the ship's course is called "dead reckoning." This, of course, is liable to errors, as careless steering, the compasses being out of order, or a current, may carry her far from her supposed position; at the same time, when the sky is obscured, it is the only mode of finding the way across the ocean. It can be correctly ascertained by observation of the sun, moon, and stars, taken with a sextant and a chronometer; but I shall be led to give an epitome of the science of navigation if I attempt to explain the mode of using them.

In shallow waters, where the bottom has been accurately surveyed, a clever pilot will find his way with the lead. At the end of the lead a cavity is made, which is filled with grease; and according to the sort of mud, sand, or shells which adhere to it, he tells his position. This, and many other parts of navigation, Mr Bell, during our night watches, took great pains to explain to me; but it was not till I had been some time at sea that I comprehended them clearly.

Mr Bell never spoke to me in the day-time; for if the captain saw him, he was certain to send me to perform some kind of drudgery or other. I was set to do all the dirty work in the ship, to black down the rigging, to grease the masts, etcetera, etcetera; indeed, my hands were always in the tar-bucket; but it served the useful purpose of teaching me a seaman's duty, and of accustoming me to work. The captain and first mate's abusive language, however, I could not stand; and my feelings resented it even more than the blows they were continually dealing me.

I have said little about the emigrants. If my lot was bad, theirs was much worse. They were looked upon by the officers as so many sheep or pigs, and treated with no more consideration. Crowded together below, allowed to accumulate filth and dirt of every description, their diet bad and scanty, and never encouraged to take the air on deck, disease soon broke out and spread among them. Old and young, married and single of both sexes, were mingled indiscriminately together; and the scenes I witnessed when I was obliged to go below turned me sick with disgust, as they made my heart bleed with sorrow.

The surgeon had little more knowledge of his profession than I had, and had not the slightest notion of what ought to be done to stop the ravages of disease. He physicked indiscriminately, or bled or starved his patients, without paying the slightest regard to their ailments. When they died they were thrown overboard, with scant ceremony; but the men had the greatest difficulty in tearing the bodies of the Irish from their friends, or of children from their wretched parents; and it was heart-rending to listen to the shrieks and howls of grief as this was attempted to be done.

However, I do not wish to dwell on these scenes, or to discourage emigration. I fully believe that by thoroughly cleansing the ship, and by serving out good provisions, disease might then have been arrested. The object is to prevent the occurrence of such disorders for the future, by the introduction of a well-organised system. In spite of all obstacles, emigration will go forward; but it depends on every one of us, whether it will prove a curse or a blessing to those who go forth, whether the emigrants are to be in future friends or deadly foes to the country they quit.

Chapter Six

For ten days we had fine weather and light winds; but a southerly gale sprang up, and drove us to the northward, and I then found out what it was to be at sea. Of course I had to do duty, as before, aloft; and following Derrick's advice was of service, or one night, while furling top-sails, and when the ship was pitching tremendously, I should certainly have been killed. On a sudden I found myself jerked right off the yard; but I fortunately had hold of the gasket, which I was passing through the mizzen top-sail, and by it hauled myself up again and finished the work. After the gale had lasted a week, the wind came round from the northward, and bitter cold it was. We then stood on rather farther to the north than the usual track, I believe.

It was night, and blowing fresh. The sky was overcast, and there was no moon, so that darkness was on the face of the deep—not total darkness, it must be understood, for that is seldom known at sea. I was in the middle watch, from midnight to four o'clock, and had been on deck about half-an-hour when the look-out forward sang out, "Ship ahead—starboard—hard a star-board!"

These words made the second mate, who had the watch, jump into the weather rigging. "A ship!" he exclaimed. "An iceberg it is rather, and—All hands wear ship," he shouted in a tone which showed there was not a moment to lose.

The watch sprang to the braces and bowlines, while the rest of the crew tumbled up from below, and the captain and other officers rushed out of their cabins: the helm was kept up, and the yards swung round, and the ships head turned towards the direction whence we had come. The captain glanced his eye round, and then ordered the courses to be brailed up, and the main top-sail to be backed, so as to lay the ship to. I soon discovered the cause of these manoeuvres; for before the ship had quite wore round, I perceived close to us a towering mass with a refulgent appearance, which the look-out man had taken for the white sails of a ship, but which proved in reality to be a vast iceberg; and attached to it and extending a considerable distance to leeward, was a field or very extensive floe of ice, against which the ship would have run had it not been discovered in time, and would in all probability instantly have gone down with every one on board.

In consequence of the extreme darkness it was dangerous to sail either way, for it was impossible to say what other floes or smaller cakes of ice might be in the neighbourhood, and we might probably be on them before they could be seen. We therefore remained hove to. As it was, I could not see the floe till it was pointed out to me by Derrick.

I was on deck, with my eyes trying to pierce the darkness to leeward, and fancying that I saw another iceberg rising close to the ship, and that I heard strange shrieks and cries, when I felt a hand placed on my shoulder: "Well, lad, what do you think of it?" said a voice which I recognised as that of Silas Flint.

"I would rather be in a latitude where icebergs do not exist," I replied. "But how is it, old friend, you seemed to have forgotten me altogether since we sailed?" I added.

"It is because I am your friend, lad, that I do not pretend to be one," he answered in a low tone. "I guessed from the first the sort of chap you've got for a skipper, and that you'd very likely want my aid; so I kept aloof; the better to be able to afford it without being suspected, d'ye see? You lead but a dog's life on board here, Peter, I am afraid."

"It is bad enough, I own," I answered; "but I don't forget your advice to 'grin and bear what can't be cured'; and Mr Bell and some of my messmates seem inclined to be good-natured."

"Maybe; but you, the son of a gentleman, and, for what I see, a gentleman yourself, should be better treated," he observed. "If I was you, I wouldn't stand it a day longer than I could help."

"I would not if I could help it; but I cannot quit the ship," I answered.

"But you may when you get to Quebec," he remarked. "I wouldn't go back in her on any account, for many a reason. There's ill luck attends her, trust to that." What the ill luck was, my friend did not say, nor how he had discovered it.

Flint spent the night on deck, and during it he talked a good deal about America, and the independent wild life he led in the backwoods and prairies. The conversation made a considerable impression on my mind, and I afterwards was constantly asking myself why I should go back in the *Black Swan*.

When daylight broke the next morning, the dangerous position in which the ship was placed was seen. On every side of us appeared large floes of ice, with several icebergs floating like mountains on a plain among them; while the only opening through which we could escape was a narrow passage to the north-east, through which we must have come. What made our position the more perilous was, that the vast masses of ice were approaching nearer and nearer to each other, so that we had not a moment to lose if we would effect our escape.

As the light increased, we saw, at the distance of three miles to the westward, another ship in a far worse predicament than we were, inasmuch as she was completely surrounded by ice, though she still floated in a sort of basin. The wind held to the northward, so that we could stand clear out of the passage should it remain open long enough. She by this time had discovered her own perilous condition, as we perceived that she had hoisted a signal of distress, and we heard the guns she was firing to call our attention to her; but regard to our own safety compelled us to disregard them till we had ourselves got clear of the ice.

It was very dreadful to watch the stranger, and to feel that we could render her no assistance. All hands were at the braces, ready to trim the sails should the wind head us; for in that case we should have to beat out of the channel, which was every instant growing narrower and narrower. The captain stood at the weather gangway, conning the ship. When he saw the ice closing in on us, he ordered every stitch of canvas the ship could carry to be set on her, in hopes of carrying her out before this could occur. It was a chance whether or not we should be nipped. However, I was not so much occupied with our own danger as not to keep an eye on the stranger, and to feel a deep interest in her fate.

I was in the mizzen-top, and as I possessed a spy-glass, I could see clearly all that occurred. The water on which she floated was nearly smooth, though covered with foam, caused by the masses of ice as they approached each other. I looked; she had but a few fathoms of water on either side of her. As yet she floated unharmed. The peril was great; but the direction of the ice might change, and she might yet be free. Still on it came with terrific force; and I fancied that I could hear the edges grinding and crushing together.

The ice closed on the ill-fated ship. She was probably as totally unprepared to resist its pressure as we were. At first I thought that it lifted her bodily up; but it was not so, I suspect. She was too deep in the water for that. Her sides were crushed in—her stout timbers were rent into a thousand fragments—her tall masts tottered and fell, though still attached to the hull. For an instant I concluded that the ice must have separated, or perhaps the edges broke with the force of the concussion; for, as I gazed, the wrecked mass of hull and spars and canvas seemed drawn suddenly downwards with irresistible force, and a few fragments, which had been hurled by the force of the concussion to a distance, were all that remained of the hapless vessel. Not a soul of her crew could have had time to escape to the ice.

I looked anxiously: not a speck could be seen stirring near the spot. Such, thought I, may be the fate of the four hundred and forty human beings on board this ship ere many minutes are over.

I believe that I was the only person on board who witnessed the catastrophe. Most of the emigrants were below, and the few who were on deck were with the crew watching our own progress.

Still narrower grew the passage. Some of the parts we had passed through were already closed. The wind, fortunately, held fair; and though it contributed to drive the ice faster in on us, it yet favoured our escape. The ship flew through the water at a great rate, heeling over to her ports; but though at times it seemed as if the masts would go over the sides, still the captain held on. A minute's delay might prove our destruction.

Every one held his breath as the width of the passage decreased, though we had but a short distance more to make good before we should be free.

I must confess that all the time I did not myself feel any sense of fear. I thought it was a danger more to be apprehended for others than for myself. At length a shout from the deck reached my ears, and looking round, I saw that we were on the outside of the floe. We were just in time, for, the instant after, the ice met, and the passage through which we had come was completely closed up. The order was now given to keep the helm up and to square away the yards; and with a flowing sheet we ran down the edge of the ice for upwards of three miles before we were clear of it.

Only then did people begin to inquire what had become of the ship we had lately seen. I gave my account, but few expressed any great commiseration for the fate of those who were lost. Our captain had had enough of ice, so he steered a course to get as fast as possible into more southern latitudes. This I may consider the first adventure I met with in my nautical career.

Chapter Seven

I was every day improving my knowledge of seamanship, though my schooling was, it may be supposed, of the roughest kind.

The feelings Captain Elihu Swales exhibited towards me did not grow more tender; but hitherto I had kept my temper, and had flown to obey his orders without answering his abuse. At last, however, one day when the ship was caught in a heavy squall, we were somewhat slow in reefing the mizzen topsail; and as we descended on deck he laid a rope's end across the shoulders of several of us. I could not stand this; for I and another of the topmen, generally the smartest, had hurt our hands, and ought not properly to have gone aloft at all. "How dare you strike me, Captain Swales?" I exclaimed. "I paid you a sum for my passage, as also to learn seamanship, and not to be treated as a slave."

It was the first time I had replied to him. Perhaps speaking increased the anger I felt, perhaps it was that I saw his eye quail before mine; but, be that as it may, a handspike lay near, and almost unconsciously I grasped it, and made as if I would strike him in return.

"A mutiny!" he exclaimed, with an oath.

"A mutiny!—knock down the rascally mutineer."

"A mutiny!" repeated Mr Stovin, the first mate; and suiting the action to the word, he dealt me a blow on the head with his fist, which sent me sprawling on the deck.

Several of the crew, as well as the emigrants, who had seen what had occurred, cried out "Shame, shame!" but they were afraid of interfering, so that my enemies had it all their own way.

I was forthwith dragged forward by Stovin and two or three of the men, who made up to him, and lashed down to the foot of the bowsprit, where I was most exposed to the spray which flew over the ship, and could be watched from every part. "You'll cool your temper and your heels there, my lad, till I let you go," whispered my old enemy in a tone of voice which showed the vindictive triumph he felt.

For the whole of that day I was kept there, watched by one of the mate's creatures, so that no one with friendly feelings could come near me. Some mouldy biscuits and a piece of hard junk were brought to me long after the dinner hour, and when I was almost too sick with hunger to eat. When night drew on, I asked my guard if I was to be released. "Maybe not till the end of the voyage," was the satisfactory answer. "They hangs mutineers."

Though I did not for a moment suppose such would be my fate, I yet bitterly repented having, by giving way to my temper, allowed my enemies to get an advantage over me. The wind fell, and there was less sea; but still the night was a very dreary one to me, and, besides other physical discomforts, I was half-starved. There has been seldom, however, a time when some ray of comfort has not shone from above, or some human sympathy has not been shown for my sufferings. It had just gone two bells in the first watch, when I saw a figure creeping cautiously upon the forecastle to where I was sitting. "Hush!" he whispered; and I knew by the voice it was Silas Flint. "You've friends who'll help you when the time comes. I've been watching an opportunity to bring you something more fit to eat than the horseflesh and beans I hear you've had. Eat it while you can." Saying this, he put into my hand some potted meat and fine biscuits, which I found very refreshing. I must observe that my hands were only so far at liberty that I could get them to my mouth, but I could not move them to cast off my lashings.

The brutality to which I was subject is only a specimen of what seamen are exposed to from ignorant and rude shipmasters. In my time I have seen much of such conduct; and though I have known many very excellent and superior men commanding merchantmen, I have met as many totally unfit for the post. This state of things will continue till higher qualifications are required from them—till they are better educated—till their social position is raised—till they have more power placed in their hands; also till the condition of the seamen under them is improved, and till both parties may feel that their interests are cared for and protected. I do not mean to say that I thought thus at the time. I felt only very angry, and a strong desire to be in my berth.

After I had eaten the food I became very drowsy, and should have gone to sleep had I not continually been roused up by the showers of spray which came flying over me, as the ship, close hauled, ploughed her way through the waves. The nights were long in reality, and I thought daylight would never come. It was just at the end of the middle watch, and, in spite of the wet and my uncomfortable position, I had dropped off asleep, when I was aroused by loud shrieks and cries, and a rush of people on deck. The awful words, "Fire! fire! fire!" resounded through the ship. Several, in the first paroxysm of alarm, leaped overboard; and, no one regarding them or attempting to rescue them, they were drowned. I was a witness of their fate, but could make no one attend to me. The watch below and the officers were instantly on deck; but for some time nothing was done, and the ship continued her course in darkness over the deep.

"Silence, fore and aft!" shouted the captain, who believed that it was a false alarm. "Those who spread this report deserve to be hove overboard. I'll take care to make inquiries about it—in the morning. What frightens you all so?"

"Fire! fire! fire!" was the answer of others rushing up from below.

For some minutes the shrieks and cries and confusion prevented me from hearing anything more; nor could the exertions of the officers serve to maintain order. At last the captain, who had been incredulous, or pretended to be so, became convinced that there was some cause for the alarm, and on going round the lower deck a strong smell of fire was perceived, and smoke was found to be issuing from the fore-hatchway over the hold. No flames were seen, so it was evident that the fire was among the cargo in the lower hold. The hatchway was accordingly opened, and immediately dense volumes of smoke arose, and almost stifled me where I remained lashed.

When it was discovered that the fire was forward, the ship was hove to, thus, under the idea that as fire works to windward, to prevent its being driven so rapidly aft as it would otherwise have been. Buckets were now cried for; and the crew, and all the emigrants whose fears had not mastered their senses, were engaged in filling them with water and in heaving it down below. A pump was also rigged and manned, which, with a hose attached to it, played down the hatchway.

After some time this appeared to have effect; and Mr Bell, who, quiet as he generally seemed, was now the soul of everything, volunteered to go down in order to discover the exact position of the fire. Securing a rope round his body, while some of the crew on whom he could depend held on, he boldly threw himself into the midst of the smoke. Not a quarter of a minute had passed before he sang out to be hauled up again. When he reappeared he was insensible, and it was some time before he recovered. They brought him up to the forecastle close to me, and the first words I heard which he uttered were: "She's all on fire below, and I doubt if water will put it out."

This was very dreadful; and I began to consider whether I was fated to be roasted and then drowned, when I saw my friend Silas Flint creeping cautiously up to me. "Hillo, Peter, my lad, you seem to take it coolly enough; but you shan't, if I can help it, be roasted like a lark on a spit, so I've come to give you a chance for your life. I did not come before, not because I had forgotten you, but because I knew that wicked captain of ours was watching me, and would have prevented me from setting you at liberty if he could: however, he's enough else, I guess, to think of just now."

"Thank you, Flint—thank you for your kindness," I answered as he was cutting the lanyards which confined me. "Do you think there is any danger, though?"

"The ship may burn till she's too hot to hold us," he replied laconically; "and then it is not easy to say where five hundred people are to find standing-room. There is danger, Peter; but a stout heart may face and overcome it."

"What do you propose to do?" I asked.

"Get into a boat if I can, or else build a raft and float on that. I'll not go down as long as I can find something to keep me up."

Flint's calmness gave me courage; and after that, notwithstanding the dreadful scenes I witnessed, I did not feel any fear. As soon as I was at liberty, I set to work with Flint to make myself useful; and though I was close to Captain Swales while we were working the pump, he did not observe me. An event of the sort I am describing shows people in their true colours. While some of the passengers threw off their jackets and set to with a will, several had cast themselves on the deck, weeping and groaning among the women; and Flint and one of the mates had actually to go and kick them up before they would attempt to perform their duty.

It is difficult to describe the horrors of that night, or rather morning, before the day broke—the ship rolling and pitching on before a heavy sea (whither she went no one considered, provided she was kept before the wind)—the suffocating smoke which rose from the depths of the hold—the cries of despair heard on every side—the scenes of cowardly fear and intense selfishness which were exhibited. Still we floated; but I expected every instant to see the ship plunge head-foremost down into the depths of the ocean; for I thought the fire must soon burn a hole through her planks. I was not aware how long fire takes to burn downwards. One of the greatest cowards of the crew, and a big bully he was, happened to be at the helm when the fire was first reported; and as soon as the captain and mates went forward to attend to rigging the pumps, his fears overcame him, and he dastardly deserted his post.

Fortunately, one of the crew was aft, and went to the helm and kept it up, or the ship would have broached to, and, before she could have been put on her course, the sea would have swept over our decks, and the destruction of all would have been expedited. At the same time a number of the passengers made a rush at the larboard-quarter boat, and, while some got into her, others lowered her down, intending to follow. Going fast, as the ship was, through the water, of course she was immediately swamped, and every soul in her perished. Three or four of those who were about to follow, so great was their eagerness, before they understood what had occurred, leaped where they expected to find her, and met the fate of the rest.

This was reported to the captain, who at once set a guard over the other boats. Indeed, as yet, there was no necessity for any one to quit the ship. The boatswain, however, who had charge of the boats, followed by the fellow who had quitted the wheel, the cook, and one or two others, soon afterwards collecting some provisions, sails, compasses, tools, and other things they thought necessary, deliberately lowered her, and getting into her, veered her astern, where they remained, careless of what became of the rest of us. Such was the state of things when the sun shone forth on the ocean world.

The decks, covered with women and children, and even many men lying prostrate, looked as if just swept by the shots of an enemy. Such countenances, too, of terror, agony, and despair as were exhibited, it is difficult to describe. Many had fainted, and some had actually died through fear, and lay quiet enough. Others rushed about the decks like madmen, impeding the exertions of the officers and crew, and crying out that the ship should be steered to the nearest land, and insisting on being set on shore immediately. Had the captain been a man of firmness and moral courage, to whom his officers and crew had been accustomed to look up, much of the disorder would have been prevented, and perhaps the lives of all might have been saved; but they knew him to be a bully and a coward, and the first impulse of each was to think of his own individual safety, as they knew he would do of his. Thus not one quarter of the necessary exertions were made to save the ship; indeed Mr Bell and his watch were the only part of the crew who really did any good.

Most of the cabin passengers, and some of the second and steerage passengers of the English, at once came forward and offered their services to work the pumps and to hand down the water-buckets. The poorer Irish, on the other hand, would do nothing to help themselves, but sat shrieking and bewailing their cruel fate till they could shriek and cry no longer.

Chapter Eight

It is my belief that, if proper measures had been taken the moment the fire was discovered, it might have been extinguished, and if not, its progress might have been retarded. The ship had a large quantity of coals among her cargo, and there is no doubt it originated in it by spontaneous combustion. Some said it had been smouldering away ever since we left Liverpool. What would have been our sensations had we known that we had a volcano on board? When some of the passengers saw that the object of our exertions was to fill the hold with water, they began to cry out that the quickest way would be to start the water-tanks on deck. The captain, on hearing this, immediately exclaimed that if they did so they would repent it, for without water they could not live, and that this was the only fresh water at which they would shortly be able to get. On learning their mad design, he should instantly have placed some of the crew on whom he could depend, with arms in their hands, to guard the tanks, and with orders to cut down any one who should attempt to touch the bungs. Instead, he contented himself with pointing out the folly of the proceeding.

His words were not heeded; and without any attempt to prevent them, several of the madmen started the water from the tanks. "Hurrah!" they shouted as they performed this feat. "The fire will now be put out, and we shall be saved." The hidden fire laughed at their puny efforts, and the wreaths of smoke came forth as dense as ever.

A consultation among the officers was now held; and it was their opinion that we were in as good a position as could be for being fallen in with by ships crossing the Atlantic, and that therefore we should continue as we were—hove to. We all watched with deep anxiety the progressive increase of the smouldering furnace below us. Fortunately the flames did not begin to burst forth.

Dreadful as the day was, it passed more rapidly than I could have expected. There was nothing to mark the time; there were no regular meals, no bells struck, no watches set. The captain, on seeing the want of effect produced by the water thrown on the cargo, abandoned all hopes of saving the ship, and thought only how he might best secure his own safety. The stern-boat was, as I have said, towing astern. I now saw him go aft, and with the aid of some of the people, to whom he had spoken privately, he lowered down the starboard-quarter boat, having first put into her compasses, provisions, and water. The first mate meantime baled out the other quarter boat, and in like manner provisioned and stored her. Three hands being placed in each, they were veered astern. The captain and mate knew that these men would not desert them, because without their assistance they would be unable to find their way to any port.

I took my spell at the pumps, and on several occasions the captain passed me and gave me a scowl, by which I knew that he recognised me, and probably contemplated leaving me behind in the burning ship; at least so I thought at the time, and resolved to frustrate his kind intentions. The captain next gave orders to the crew to hoist out the long-boat, as the sea had gone down sufficiently to enable this to be done without risk. The long-boat is stowed on the booms amidships, and it requires tackles to the yard-arms, and considerable exertion, to launch her. It was the first time I had ever observed Captain Swales and Mr Stovin really energetic in their exertions when they were getting this done; and I very soon found that they had a reason for it, as they intended to take possession of her for themselves, and those they most favoured. She at length was launched and dropped astern; and, being hauled up under the cabin windows, the ladies and other cabin passengers were lowered into her. She was likewise provisioned; and compasses, charts, sails, and oars were placed in her.

I thought that the captain, as a precautionary measure, wished to place the passengers in comparative safety; but what was my surprise, to see him lower himself into the boat, and drop her astern, virtually abandoning all command of the ship! This vile example was followed by Mr Stovin, who took possession of one of the quarter boats. The greater part of the crew, and all the steerage and second-class passengers, still remained in the burning ship, of which Mr Bell now took the command. When the people saw the captain deserting them, they rushed aft, some with piteous cries, exclaiming, "O captain dear, save us! save us!" Others cursed him as a traitor for leaving them to their fate; and I believe, had they known what he was about to do, they would have torn him in pieces before they would have let him go. (See Note 1.) He shouted to them in return, that he was not going to desert them, but that his presence was required in the boat. I have always held that the captain should be the last man to quit the deck of his ship; and every true seaman thinks the same, and would scorn to do otherwise.

"A pretty job, this is," observed Dick Derrick, who was working away at the pumps close to me. "We were nearly squeezed to death by the ice a few days ago, and now it seems we are to be roasted with fire. Are you prepared for death, Peter?"

I replied that I would rather live.

"Then the sooner we begin to knock some sort of rafts together, to float a few of these poor people, the better," he observed. "I'll just hint the same to Mr Bell."

I saw him go up to Mr Bell, and, touching his hat, speak earnestly to him.

"You are right, Derrick," remarked the second mate as he passed me. "We must keep the passengers working at the pumps though, to the last, while the crew build the rafts."

As soon as the plan was conceived, all hands set to work to collect spars, and to knock away the fittings of the lower deck, the bulkheads, and the bulwarks. We thus very soon formed three small rafts, each capable of supporting thirty or forty people in calm weather—a very small portion of the poor wretches on board.

Mr Bell urged the crew to continue their exertions, and not to launch the rafts till the last moment. "We do not know where the rafts may drive to; and as we are now in the usual track of ships bound to America, our signal of distress may be seen, and we may be saved without more risk," he observed, addressing several who seemed about to launch one of the rafts. His words, however, had not much effect; for a few minutes afterwards their fears overpowered their better judgment, and one of the rafts was launched overboard. It was with some difficulty that it could be kept alongside. They fitted it with a mast and sail, and a few casks of provisions, but no water was to be found, except in a small keg.

While some of the people who intended to embark on it were looking for more, a fresh puff of smoke forced its way up near the mainmast; and this so frightened the emigrants, that a general rush was made to get on the raft. About thirty were already on it, and so alarmed were they lest the number crowding on it might capsize it, that, ill provisioned as they were, they cut it adrift. What became of them I know not; for the night coming on, they were soon lost sight of, and we never saw them again. That night was far more dreadful than the first; for, though the terror of the people was not so loud, their despair was more pitiable. The remainder of the crew still worked, spell and spell, at the pumps, but the fire gained upon us. At length some of the steerage passengers broke into the cabins, which they rifled of everything on which they could lay their hands, and unfortunately discovered several cases of brandy and wine.

Now began the most horrible orgies imaginable. Men, women, and even children, became speedily intoxicated, and entirely forgetful of their fears and awful position. They were, in fact, like the fiercest savages, and, like them, danced and shouted and sang, till some of them fell down in fits on the deck. In the cabins they found several muskets, and, taking it into their heads that the crew had been the cause of the disaster, they set upon Mr Bell and those of us who remained, and, had we not struggled desperately, would have thrown us overboard. They could, fortunately, find no powder and shot, or they would certainly have killed some of the people in the boats. We retreated before them forward and then, aided by Flint, and some of the more reputable English who had kept sober, we made a rush at them and wrenched their arms from their grasp. So infuriated had they become, that while some of us worked at the pumps and rafts, the rest had to stand guard and keep them at bay. Fortunately the wind fell, and the sea went down with the sun, or it would have been still worse for us.

In one respect the calm was bad, as no ship was likely to come to our rescue. One might have passed within a very short distance of us, and would not have discovered us, as we had no guns on board, nor any blue-lights or rockets, to make signals. We had four old rusty muskets, it is true, but there was scarcely powder enough found to fire them a dozen times. For the best part of the night we were employed in defending our lives from the attacks of the drunken emigrants. After being defeated they would return to the cabin to search for more liquor; and, not finding any, they would again make a rush upon us, declaring that we knew where it was hid, and that they would have it. I must do the crew justice to say, that, with few exceptions, they all kept sober,—and those under Mr Bell behaved very well. The second mate's conduct was above all praise; for, though repeatedly invited by those in the larboard-quarter boat to come off and to take command of her, he refused to quit the ship.

At length, when the maddening effects of the spirits had worn off, the emigrants sank down exhausted on the deck, and, had the fire then reached where they lay, they would have been burnt, unconscious of their fate. We were now left to consider what was next to be done. Gradually the fire continued creeping aft, as we could tell by the increasing heat of the lower deck; and I can scarcely describe the feelings I experienced as, putting my hand down on the planks, I found them growing hotter and hotter. The hatches over the hold were, however, wisely kept closed, to prevent the flames from bursting forth. The ship was already so full of water, that it would have exposed us to the danger of drowning if we had pumped more into her. A second day dawned on the same scene.

We anxiously scanned the horizon in the hopes that a ship might appear to rescue us, but not a sail was in sight to relieve our anxiety. As the people woke up from their slumbers, the general cry was for water; but no water was to be procured. They had uselessly squandered what might have preserved them. "Water! water!" was repeated by parched mouths, which were fated never to taste that fluid again. Some stood aft, and shouted to the captain, who sat comfortably in the boat astern, and made gestures at him for water. Some, in their madness, broke open the surgeon's dispensary, and rifled it of its contents, swallowing the drugs indiscriminately. The effects on them were various, according to the nature of the drugs. Some, overcome with opium, fell down speedily in a state of stupor; others were paralysed, and others died in dreadful agonies.

Burning thirst drove some mad, and several leaped overboard in their delirium. Many died where they lay, on the deck; women and several poor children quickly sunk for want of water. No sooner had the breath departed from the body, than we were obliged to throw them overboard, as the corpses lay in our way as we hurried about the decks. I forgot to mention that there was a Romish priest on board, Father Slattery by name. He was a coarse, uneducated man, but the influence he exercised over the poor people was very great; and I must do him the justice to say, that in this instance he exercised it for a good purpose, in endeavouring to calm the fears of his followers, and in affording them the offices of their religion. From the moment the danger became apparent, he went among them confessing them and absolving them from their sins, and giving them such other consolation as he had to offer; but this did not seem to have any great effect, for the moment he left them, they began to howl and shriek as loud as ever. As to attempting to help themselves, that seemed far from their thoughts. Few of them could be induced to work at the pumps, or to assist in building the rafts. Yet, miserable as was their condition, the love of life appeared stronger in them than in the English.

When the captain dropped astern in the long-boat, there was a general rush to follow him; and I remember seeing two girls lower themselves down by ropes over the taffrail, where they hung, their feet in the water, entreating to be taken in. "Oh, captain, dear, sure you won't let us be drowned now!" they exclaimed in piteous accents. For some time those in the long-boat were deaf to their entreaties, and I thought the girls would have lost their hold and have been drowned, for they had no strength left to haul themselves on board again. Feeling that their destruction was inevitable if they were not rescued, I slipped a running bowline knot over the rope to which one of them was hanging, and then gliding down, I passed it over her shoulders. I was up on deck again in a moment, and hauled her up, though I must own she did not like my interference. The other girl let go her hold, and would have been drowned, had she not been caught as she floated past the boat, when she was taken in.

But I could scarcely have believed that human nature could become so depraved, as an instance I witnessed with my own eyes convinced me it might be. I saw two Irishmen, who had their wives and families on board, slip over the ship's side, and drop down towards the boat, with ropes in their hands. Little as they deserved it, they were not prevented from climbing on board; and there they remained, in spite of the bitter cries of those they had so basely deserted.

> Note 1. I regret to say that the whole account of the burning ship is perfectly true. Incredible as it may seem, the fire continued smouldering for nearly a week before the flames burst forth.

Chapter Nine

The unhappy people were more quiet the second day than during the first; for they were worn out with fatigue, terror, and hunger. Our ensign, reversed, was flying, as a signal of distress, but to little purpose; for there was no one who could see it to help us. Two more rafts were constructed; and the carpenters set to work to raise the gunwales of the boats, and they also nailed canvas round their sides, so as to be able to cover them completely in.

Those in the boats appeared very uncomfortable; and certainly they were much worse off than we were, if it had not been for the uncertainty when the fire might break forth from beneath our feet. Every instant I expected that to take place; and I certainly felt it difficult to say by what means I should make my escape.

A few jars of fresh water were found in the cabin; and, among other provisions, a cask of flour, with which the cook instantly set to work to make bread, and the whole of the day he was engaged in making and in baking it in the caboose. This very seasonable supply of wholesome food kept many on board from dying.

Mr Bell took off, in the dingy, a fair proportion to the boats. The people in them begged him to remain, telling him that the ship might suddenly go down, and that he would be lost; but he replied that he would not desert her and the people, and he instantly returned.

The day passed away without a sail appearing in sight; and darkness, with its attendant horrors, again drew on. Dreadful, indeed, was that night; but it was very different to the last. There was then excitement and activity. Now there was a calmness—at times almost a total silence; but it would speedily be broken by the groans of the dying, and the wails of those who mourned for them.

All attempts to stop the progress of the fire were abandoned as useless. The officers and crew who remained faithful to their trust, took such rest watch and watch, as the state of the case would allow; but we were wet through, and our bed was the hard deck.

Somewhere towards the morning, as I was still asleep, I felt my shoulder touched, and the voice of Flint whispered in my ear, "Peter, my lad, rouse up, and come with us. The ship won't much longer give us any footing; and it's as well to leave her when we can."

"What do you mean, Flint?" I asked, in the same low tone. "You would not have me quit my shipmates?"

"What I mean is, that some thirty of us—some of the crew and some emigrants—have resolved to trust ourselves to a raft, rather than to these burning planks; and that, if we wait till daylight, so many will be attempting to get on it, that we shall be all lost together. I don't ask you to desert your shipmates, Peter; but self-preservation, you know, is the first law of nature."

I considered a moment before I spoke. "I am grateful to you, Flint, for your kindness; but I cannot desert Mr Bell," I replied. "I don't blame you, remember, for going; but I am differently situated. I am in the second mate's watch—under his command, as it were; and while he sticks to the ship, so must I."

While I was speaking, I saw a party of people cautiously engaged in launching the raft. After no slight exertions, they succeeded in getting into the water, though the noise they made disturbed a number of the emigrants.

"I understand your motive, my lad, and I suppose you are right," replied Flint. "I wish you could come with us; and I am half inclined to stay by you—that I am."

"I should be very unhappy if you were the sufferer in consequence of so doing," I answered; "so pray go, if you think the raft affords the greatest safety."

"No, lad, I care little for my own safety; but I promised these people to go with them, and to act as their captain. I did so, thinking you would be certain to go too."

I again assured him that nothing would induce me to desert Mr Bell. So, expressing his sorrow, he shook me warmly by the hand, and slid down the side of the ship on to the raft. I assisted in casting it off, before the rest of the emigrants, who were awake, discovered what they were about, or else they would senselessly, as before, have attempted to get on it, to the almost certain destruction of them all. Flint and his companions hurriedly shoved off, and then hoisted their sail. I watched the raft as long as it could be seen, standing directly before the wind to the northward; and I remember at the time my heart misgave me, and I feared that I should never again see my kind but eccentric friend. If a sea should get up, I thought they in all probability would be drowned. I felt very grateful, also, that I had decided to remain. However, I was too weary to think much about any subject, and I was very shortly again fast asleep on the deck.

As suffering and misery will, after a time, come to an end, and it would be well if we could always remember this when we ourselves are in that condition, so did this night of dark horror, and another morning dawned on the burning wreck. Clouds, streaked with bright red edges, were gathering on the eastern horizon, as I went aloft to look out for a sail, though with little expectation of seeing one. I had just reached the main-topgallant-mast head, and was sweeping my eyes round the horizon, when I saw, just under the brightest part of the glow caused by the rising sun, a dark spot, which I thought must be the topsail of some square-rigged craft. I looked again; I felt that I could not be mistaken. I shouted out the joyful intelligence—

"Sail ho!—ho!—over the larboard quarter."

Instantly the second mate, followed by several others, who had strength remaining, ran aloft to ascertain the fact. They also all clearly saw the ship. The people in the boats understood what we were pointing at, and a feeble shout, indicative of their joy, rose from all hands. The question now was, which way she was steering. If to the westward, we had a good chance of being seen by her; but if not, she might pass us by unheeded. This uncertainty was, perhaps, still more painful to endure than our previous hopelessness.

While we were watching the stranger, the clouds gathered thicker in the sky, and the sea began perceptibly to get up, though as yet there was no increase of wind. "I don't altogether like the look of things," observed Derrick to me. "The sea getting up before the wind comes is a pretty sure sign of a heavy gale; and if it does come on to blow, Lord help us, my boy!"

"Amen," said a deep voice near us, which startled me. It seemed not like that of a mortal; it was, however, that of Father Slattery, who was at that instant passing us. "And so, my son, you think there is more danger than before?" he asked.

"If it comes on to blow, and keeps blowing with a heavy sea, I say it will be no easy matter to carry women and children from one ship to another, even if that sail yonder should come any way nigh us; that's what I say, your honour," answered Derrick.

"I understand you, my son," said the priest; "we'll be in a worse position with regard to affairs temporal than we are at present."

"Yes, your honour; it looks brewing up for a regular tempest, as you say, and no mistake," observed Derrick.

Even while they were talking, we heard the wind whistle in the rigging, and the ship began to surge heavily through the rising waves.

The people in the boats at this were evidently alarmed, and one of the gigs hauled alongside, several persons in her preferring to trust themselves to the burning ship rather than to her. I must remark that a feeling almost of security had come over many of us, and that for my part I could not help fancying that it was nothing unusual to live on board a ship full of fire. Of course I knew that some time or other the flames must burst forth; but I looked upon this event as likely to happen only in some remote period, with which I had little to do. Our sufferings were greatest from want of water, and on that account we were most anxious for the coming of the stranger. Mr Bell, Derrick, and I were again aloft looking out for the ship. The captain hauled up under the stern, and hailed to know which way we made her out to be still standing. "Right down for us, sir," answered the mate. "She's a barque, and seems to be coming up with a strong breeze."

It is difficult to describe how anxiously we watched for her. On she came for perhaps half-an-hour, though to us it seemed much longer, when suddenly we saw her, to our dismay, haul her wind and stand away to the north-east. I felt almost as if I should fall from aloft, as our hopes of being rescued were thus cruelly blasted. Few of the emigrants understood the change, but the seamen did, and gave way to their feelings in abuse of the stranger, who could not probably have seen our signal of distress. With heavy hearts we descended to the smoking deck.

The wretched emigrants, on discovering the state of the case, gave fresh vent to their despair; some, who had hitherto held up more manfully than the rest, lay down without hope, and others actually yielded up their spirits to the hands of death. Meantime the sea increased, clouds covered the sky, and it came on to blow harder and harder. I had returned aloft, when, to my delight, I saw the stranger again bear away and stand for us. I shouted out the joyful information, and once more the drooping spirits of my companions in misfortune were aroused. The sound of a gun was heard booming along the waters. It was a sign from her that she saw our signal of distress. Now she crowded all the sail she could venture to carry in the increasing breeze. Her captain was evidently a humane man anxious to relieve his fellow-creatures, though he could scarcely have guessed at our frightful condition. There was no mistake now, and on she came, and proved to be a large barque, as Mr Bell had supposed.

"We have a good chance of escaping a roasting this time," I observed to Derrick, as we watched the stranger.

"But not quite of drowning, lad," he answered. "Before one quarter of the people about us can placed on her deck, the gale will be upon us, and then as I said before, how are we the better for her being near us? Howsomdever, we'll do our best, lad; and if the old ship goes down, mind you look out for a plank to stick to, and don't let any one gripe hold of your legs."

I promised to do my best; but I confess I did not like the prospect he held out.

The barque approached and hove to. A shout of joy escaped from the lips of most of those on board, who had still strength to utter it. On this, immediately Captain Swales cast off his boat, his example being followed by the others; and without attempting to take any of the people out of the ship, he pulled on board the stranger. There was little time to lose; for scarcely had they got alongside than down came the gale upon us.

In the condition our ship was, the only course was to run before the wind; so we once again kept away. The stranger soon followed; and as she carried more sail than we could, we saw she would soon pass us. Hope once more deserted us; for it was possible that the master, finding that there were so many of us on board, might think himself justified, for the safety of his own people, to leave us to our fate. I confess that on this I regretted that I had not gone off with Silas Flint on the raft; but then I remembered that I had done my duty in sticking to my ship to the last. It seemed dreadful, indeed, to be thus left to perish. However, just as the stranger was about to pass us, a man in the rigging held up a board on which was written the cheering words, "We will keep near you, and take you off when the weather moderates."

Suppose, I thought, the weather does not moderate till the flames burst forth, at any moment they may break through the deck!

I am afraid of wearying my readers with an account of our sufferings.

Our greatest want was water. We fancied that, if we could have had a few drops to cool our lips, we could have borne anything else. Some drank salt water, against the warning of the mate, and in consequence increased their sufferings.

Worn out with fatigue, the crew every hour grew weaker, so that there was scarcely a man left with strength to steer, much more to go aloft. Night came on to increase our difficulties. The stranger proved to be the *Mary*, bound from Bristol also to Quebec. She at first kept a short distance ahead, showing a light over her stern by which we might steer.

I ought to have said that the captain had taken the sextant, chronometer, and charts with him, and that in their mad outbreak the emigrants had destroyed the binnacle and the compasses in it, so that we had the *Mary's* light alone to depend on. Mr Bell had divided those who remained of the crew, and some of the emigrants willing to exert themselves, into two watches.

I was to keep the middle watch. I lay down on the deck aft to sleep on one of the only few dry or clean spots I could find. I was roused up at midnight, and just as I had got on my feet, I heard a voice sing out, "Where's the *Mary's* light?" I ran forward. It was nowhere to be seen.

Chapter Ten

Fortunately a star had appeared in a break of the clouds, and by that we continued steering the same course as before. Once more we were alone on the world of waters, and in a worse condition than ever; for we had now no boats, and the sea was too high to permit us to hope for safety on a raft. Weary and sad were the hours till dawn returned. Often did I wish that I had followed my father's counsels, and could have remained at home. With aching eyes, as the pale light of the dull grey morning appeared, we looked out ahead for the *Mary*. Not a sail was to be seen from the deck. The lead-coloured ocean, heaving with foam-topped waves, was around us bounded by the horizon. On flew our burning ship before the gale, and we would have set more sail to try and overtake the *Mary*, but we had not strength for it. We steered as near as we could the same course as before.

The ship plunged heavily; and as she tore her way through the waves, she rolled her yardarms almost into the water, so that it was difficult to keep the deck without holding on. Nearly at every roll the sea came washing over the deck, and sweeping everything away into the scuppers. One might have supposed that the water would have put out the fire, but it had no effect on it; and it was evident that the coals in the hold were ignited, and that they would go on burning till the ship was under the waves. I had sunk into a sort of stupor, when I heard Mr Bell from aloft hail the deck. I looked up and tried to comprehend what he was saying. It was the joyful intelligence that the *Mary* was ahead, lying to for us; but I was too much worn out to care much about the matter. We again came up with her; but though the wind had somewhat fallen, the sea was too high to allow a boat to carry us off the wreck.

We acquitted the kind master of the *Mary* of any intention of deserting us. The officer of the watch had fancied that he saw us following, and had not, consequently, shortened sail. Oh that day of horrors, and the still more dreadful night which followed! The fire was gaining on us: every part of the deck was hot, and thick choking smoke issued from numberless crevices. With dismay, too, we saw the boats on which our safety so much depended dragged to pieces, as they towed astern of the *Mary*, as they could not be hoisted on board, and their wrecks were cut adrift. Even the crew, who, more inured to hardships, kept up their spirits the best, could but arouse themselves to take a short trick at the helm. What would we have given, I repeat, for a drop of water! A thousand guineas would willingly have been exchanged for it. The value of riches, and all else for which men toil and toil on while health and strength remain, were becoming as nothing in our sight. One thing alone called any of us to exertion. It was when some wretch, happier, perhaps, than we were, breathed his last, and the shrieks and wails of his relations or friends summoned us to commit his body to the ocean-grave, yawning to receive us all, the living as well as the dead. I must pass over that night. It was far more full of horrors than the last, except that the *Mary*, our only ark of safety, was still in sight.

Another dawn came. The gale began to lull. I was near Derrick. I asked him if he thought we had a chance of escape. He lifted his weary head above the bulwarks. "I scarce know, lad," he replied. "The wind may be falling, or it may be gathering strength for a harder blow. It matters little, I guess, to most of us." And he again sunk down wearily on the deck. How anxiously we listened to the wind in the rigging! Again it breezed up. A loud clap was heard. I thought one of the masts had gone by the board; but it was the fore-topsail blown to ribbons. What next might follow we could not tell. The very masts began to shake; and it was evident that the fire had begun to burn their heels. Their working loosened the deck, and allowed more vent for the escape of smoke. There was again a lull. The foam no longer flew from the white-crested waves; gradually they subsided in height. The motion of the ship was less violent, though she still rolled heavily, as if unable to steady herself.

We at length began to hope that the final effort of the gale was made. The day wore on—more persons died—the smoke grew thicker, and was seen streaming forth from the cabin windows. Towards evening there was a decided change for the better in the weather, and we saw the people in the *Mary* making preparations to lower a boat, and to heave the ship to. Another difficulty arose: to enable the boat to come on board, we must likewise stop the way of our ship, but we had not strength to heave her to.

We were too far gone to feel even satisfaction as we saw a boat pulling from the *Mary* towards us. We put down the helm as she came near us, and the ship rounded to. The fresh crew scrambled on board, and, backing our main-topsail, our ship remained steady, a short distance to leeward of the *Mary*. A few of the emigrants were lowered into the boat; some of the crew remained to take care of us, and the remainder returned on board in safety. This experiment having been successful, another boat was lowered, and more of our people taken off. They brought us also a keg of water; and so eager were we for it, that we could scarcely refrain from snatching it from each other, and spilling the contents. It occupied a long time to transfer the emigrants from one ship to the other. They were so utterly unable to help themselves, that they had to be lowered like bales of goods into the boats, and even the seamen were scarcely more active.

It was thus dark before all the emigrants were rescued; and, what was worse, the wind again got up, as did the sea, and prevented any communication between the ships. In one respect during that night the condition of those who remained was improved; for we had water to quench our burning thirst, and food to quell our hunger; besides which, a boat's crew of seamen belonging to the *Mary* gallantly remained by us and navigated the ship, so that we were able to take a sounder rest than we had enjoyed for many days past. Still the flames did not burst forth, and another night and day we continued in that floating furnace. Towards the evening the wind suddenly dropped; and, while the remaining emigrants were being taken off the wreck, it fell a dead calm.

The last man to leave the deck of the *Black Swan* was Mr Bell. He made me and Derrick go down the ship's side just before him. I trust that we felt grateful to Heaven for our deliverance. Scarcely had we left the deck of the *Black Swan* than the flames burst forth from her hold. They first appeared streaming out of the cabin windows, curling upwards round the taffrail. By this time it was quite dark; and the bright light from the burning wreck cast a ruddy glow on the sails and hull of the *Mary*, and topped the far surrounding waves with a bright tinge of the same hue. Soon the whole poop was on fire, and the triumphant flames began to climb up the mizzen-mast. As the ship lay head to wind, their progress was slow forward, nor did they ascend very rapidly; consequently the mizzen-mast fell before the main-mast was on fire. That shortly, however, followed with a loud crash before they even reached the main-topgallant-yard. Next down came the fore-mast, and the whole hull was a mass of flame. I felt sick at heart as I saw the noble ship thus for ever lost to the use of man. The fire was still raging when, overcome with fatigue and sickness, I sunk on the deck. As the *Mary* sailed away from her, she was seen like a beacon blazing fiercely in mid-ocean. Long those on deck gazed till the speck of bright light was on a sudden lost to view, and the glow in the sky overhead disappeared. It was when her charred fragments sunk beneath the wave.

Chapter Eleven

We were kindly welcomed and cared for on board the *Mary*, though we subjected her passengers and crew to much inconvenience, and to no little risk of starving, should her voyage be prolonged.

There were ladies who attended with gentle care to the women and children, and aided also in nursing the men. Many of the passengers and crew gave up their berths to the sick; but the greater number of our people were compelled to remain on deck, sheltered, however, by every means the kindness of our hosts could devise. There was one fair, blue-eyed girl—can I ever forget her? What a pure, light-hearted young creature she was! I felt at once that I could place the same confidence in her that I could in my own sisters, and that she was a being superior both to me and to any of those by whom I had been lately surrounded. Her name was Mary Dean. She was the daughter of the master of the *Mary*, and the ship was named after her. Mr Bell told the master of my behaviour, which he was pleased to praise, and of my refusing to quit the ship till he did; and Mary heard the tale. The mate also told him that I was the son of a gentleman, and how I had been treated by Captain Swales.

Captain Dean was a very different character to Captain Swales, with whose conduct he was so thoroughly disgusted, that he refused to hold any further communication with him than business actually required. I had held out till I was in safety, and a severe attack of illness then came on. Captain Dean had me removed to a berth in his own cabin, and Mary became my nurse. Where there is sickness and misery, there will the ministering hand of gentle woman be found. Mary Dean watched over me as the ship which bore us steered her course for the mouth of the Saint Lawrence. To her gentle care, under Providence, I owed my life. Several of the emigrants died after they came on board the *Mary*, and such would probably have been my fate under less watchful treatment.

I was in a low fever and unconscious. How long I remained so, I scarcely know. I awoke one afternoon, and found Mary Dean sitting by my side working with her needle. I fancied that I was dead, and that she was an angel watching over me. Although I discovered that the first part of the notion was a hallucination, I was every day more convinced of the truth of the second. When I got rather better, she used to read to me interesting and instructive works; and every morning she read some portion of the Bible, and explained it to me in a manner which made me comprehend it better than I had ever done before.

Ten days thus passed rapidly away before I was able to go on deck. Captain Dean was very kind to me, and often came and spoke to me, and gave me much useful instruction in seamanship, and also in navigation. I then thought Mary Dean very beautiful, and I now know that she was so. She was a child, it must be remembered, or little more than one; but though very small, she was very graceful. She was beautifully fair, with blue, truthful eyes, in which it was impossible guile could ever find a dwelling-place. I have no doubt that my readers will picture her to themselves as she sat in the cabin with a book on her lap, gravely conning its contents, or skipped along the deck, a being of light and life, the fair spirit of the summer sea. Such was Mary Dean as I first saw her. Every one loved her. Her father's heart was wrapped up in her. His crew would, to a man, have died rather than that harm should have happened to her. On sailed the ship. There was much sickness, for all hands were put on the smallest allowance of water and provisions it was possible to subsist on; and we, unfortunately, fell in with no other ship able to furnish us with a supply.

At length the welcome sound was heard of "Land ahead!" It was Cape Breton, at the entrance of the Gulf of Saint Lawrence. Rounding the cape, we stood towards the mouth of the river Saint Lawrence, that vast stream, fed by those inland seas the lakes of Upper Canada, and innumerable rivers and streams. On the north side of the gulf is the large island of Newfoundland, celebrated for its cod fisheries. A glance at the map will show our course far better than any description of mine. I could scarcely believe that we were actually in the river when we had already proceeded a hundred miles up it, so distant were the opposite shores, and, till told of it, I fancied that we were still in the open sea. I was much struck with the grand spectacle which Quebec and its environs presented, as, the ship emerging from the narrow channel of the river formed by the island of Orleans, the city first met my view. It is at this point that the Saint Lawrence, taking a sudden turn, expands, so as to assume the appearance of a broad lake.

The sun had just risen, and all nature looked fresh and green, rejoicing in the genial warmth of a Canadian spring. On the left was the town, the bright tin steeples and housetops of which, crowning the summit of Cape Diamond, glittered in the rays of the glorious luminary. Ships of all rigs and sizes lay close under the cliffs, and from their diminutive appearance I calculated the great height of the promontory. About eight miles off, on the right, I could see the falls of Montmorency, descending in a sheet of milk-white foam over a lofty precipitous bank into the stream, which, winding through a plain interspersed with villages and studded with vegetation, finds its way into the Saint Lawrence. Quebec is divided into two distinct parts.

The lower town, occupies a narrow strip of land between the precipitous heights of Cape Diamond and the river. It is connected with the upper town by means of a steep street, built in a ravine, which is commanded by the guns of a strongly fortified gateway.

The lower town is principally inhabited by merchants; and so much straitened are they for room, that many of their houses are built upon wharfs, and other artificial ground. The streets of Quebec are very narrow, and there is a general appearance of antiquity, not often to be met with in an American town. The suburbs are situated on the shores of the Saint Charles, without the fortifications. But I afterwards found that the most magnificent prospect was from the summit of the Citadel on Cape Diamond, whence one may look over the celebrated Plains of Abraham, on which the gallant Wolfe gained the victory which gave Canada to England, and where, fighting nobly, he fell in the hour of triumph. But my object is rather to describe a few of the events of my early days than the scenes I visited. It was a happy moment when we at length dropped our anchor, and water was brought off to quench the thirst from which all had more or less suffered. As soon as the necessary forms were gone through, the emigrants went on shore, and, with few exceptions, I saw them no more.

I was the only person on board who regretted that the voyage was over. I wished to see the country, and the Indians, and the vast lakes and boundless prairies; but far rather would I have remained with Mary and her father—at least I thought so, as the time for quitting them, probably for ever, arrived. I regretted much leaving Captain Dean, for he had been very kind to me; indeed, he had treated me almost like a son, and I felt grateful to him. It was evening. The ship was to haul in the next morning alongside the quay to discharge her cargo. The captain was on shore and all the emigrants. Except the anchor-watch on deck, the crew were below. Mary and I were the only persons on the quarter-deck.

"Mary," I said, as I took her hand—the words almost choked me while I spoke—"to-morrow I must leave you to look out for a berth on board some homeward-bound ship. You have been very, very kind to me, Mary; and I am grateful, I am indeed, to you and to your father."

"But I do not see why you should leave us, Peter," answered Mary, looking gravely up with a somewhat surprised air. "Has not my father told you that he thinks of asking you to remain with him? And then, some day, when you know more of seamanship, you will become his mate. Think of that, Peter, how pleasant it will be! So you must not think of leaving us."

"I have no wish to go, I can assure you, except that I am expected at home," I replied. "But if I stay, what office are you to hold on board, Mary?" I could not help asking.

"Oh, I suppose that I shall be another of the mates," she replied, laughing. "Do you know, Peter, that if I have you to study with, I think that I shall make a very good sailor in a short time. I can put the ship about now in a very good style, let me tell you."

"That's more than I can do, I am afraid," I observed. "But then I can go aloft, and hand and reef; so there I beat you."

"I should not be a bit afraid of going aloft, if I was dressed like you, and papa would let me," she answered naïvely. "I often envy the men as I see them lying out on the yards or at the mast-head when the ship is rolling and pitching; and I fancy that next to the sensations of a bird on the wing, theirs must be the most enjoyable."

"You are a true sailor's daughter, Mary," I answered, with more enthusiasm than I had ever before felt. "But I don't think your father would quite like to see you aloft; and, let me tell you, when there's much sea on, and it's blowing hard, it's much more difficult to keep there than it looks."

Thus we talked on, and touched on other topics; but they chiefly had references to ourselves. Nearly the last words Mary uttered were, "Then you will sail with father, if he asks you, Peter?"

I promised, and afterwards added, "For the sake of sailing with him, Mary, my dear young sister, if you are on board, I would give up kindred, home, and country. I would sail with you round and round the world, and never wish again to see the shore, except you were there." She was satisfied at having gained her point. We were very young, and little knew the dangerous sea on which we were proposing to sail. I called her sister, for I felt as if she were indeed my sister.

Chapter Twelve

The next morning the *Mary* commenced discharging her cargo. Captain Dean then told me that he hoped I would sail with him, but that, as the ship required a thorough repair, it would be some weeks before she could be at sea again, and that in the meantime he would advise me to employ myself usefully; and he recommended me to take a trip in a trader to Halifax or Saint John's, for the sake of gaining information regarding the navigation of those seas.

"A person who wishes to be a thorough sailor (and if a man is not a thorough sailor he has no business to be an officer)," he observed, "will seek every opportunity of making himself well acquainted with the navigation of every sea he visits, the appearance of the coasts, the set of the currents, the rise and fall of the tides, the prevailing winds, and the weather to be expected at different seasons. He will go afloat in every sort of craft, and be constantly considering how he would act under all possible circumstances. He should never weary of making inquiries of other seamen how they have acted, and the result of what they have done. As navigation was not brought to the perfection it has now attained under many centuries, so no man will become a perfect seaman unless he diligently gathers together the information possessed by all whom he meets, at the same time weighing well their opinions, and adopting them after duly comparing them with others."

I have always remembered Captain Dean's advice, and I advise all young sailors to follow it; indeed, it strikes me that it is applicable to most relations in life.

I looked about for a vessel, but could not find one. Meantime, by the captain's kindness, I remained on board, though he and Mary went to live in lodgings on shore, as, of course, in the state the ship was in, she could have no comfort even in her own cabin. About three or four days after our arrival, I saw a ship ascend the river and come to an anchor not far from where we were lying. Prompted by curiosity, I was looking at her through a telescope, when I observed a group of people on the deck who were gazing apparently with the curiosity of strangers at the shore. A little apart from them stood a form I thought I recognised. I pointed my glass steadily at him.

I felt certain that I could not be mistaken. It was Silas Flint. Then all on the raft, instead of perishing, as it was supposed they would, might have been saved, as he had escaped. I was truly glad, and, borrowing the dinghy from the mate, I pulled on board the newly-arrived ship.

Silas—for I was right in my conjectures—was looking over the side as I climbed up it. He almost wrung my hand off as he took it in his grasp. "I am glad to see ye, I am, Peter!" he exclaimed. "Why, lad, I thought you had gone to the bottom with all who remained on board."

I told him that we had in like manner fancied that all on the raft had perished; and I was glad to find that, with the exception of two, all had been picked up by the ship on board of which they then were. He then asked me what my plans were, and I told him what Captain Dean advised. He next inquired if I had seen Captain Swales. I replied that I had met him twice in the streets of Quebec, and that he had eyed me with no very friendly glance.

"Then depend on it, Peter, he means you some mischief," he observed. "If he gets another ship here, which is likely enough he will, he will want hands; and if he can lay hold of you, he will claim you as put under his charge by your father; and I don't know how you are to get off."

"By keeping out of his way, I should think," I replied.

"That's just what I was going to advise you to do, Peter," observed Silas. "And I'll tell you what, lad, instead of your kicking your heels doing nothing in this place, you and I will start off up the country with our guns as soon as I have done my business here, which won't take long, and we'll see if we can't pick up a few skins which will be worth something."

This proposition, as may be supposed, was much to my taste; but I did not much like the thoughts of leaving Captain Dean and Mary, though I did not tell him so. He, however, very soon discovered what was running in my mind, and set himself to work to overcome the wish I had to remain with them. I had found so few friends of late, that I had learned to value them properly. But Silas Flint wanted a companion, and, liking me, was resolved that I should accompany him. We went on shore together; and before the day was over, he had so worked up my imagination by his descriptions of the sport and scenery of the backwoods, that I became most eager to set off.

I next day told Captain Dean; and as I assured him that it was my father's wish that I should see something of the country, he did not oppose the plan, provided I should return in time to sail with him. This I promised to do; and I then went below to tell Mary, who was in the cabin packing up some things to take on shore. To my surprise, she burst into tears when I gave her the information; and this very nearly made me abandon my project.

When, however, I told her of my promise to return, she was comforted; and I added, that I would bring her back plenty of skins to make her tippets and muffs for the winter, to last her for years.

Three days after his arrival at Quebec, Flint was ready to set out. I had preserved intact the money my kind father had given me, and with it I purchased, at Flint's suggestion, a rifle, and powder, and a shot-belt, a tinder-box, a pipe, some tobacco, a tin cup, and a few other small articles. "Now you've laid in your stock in trade, my lad," he observed, as he announced my outfit to be complete. "With a quick eye and a steady hand you've the means, by my help, of making your fortune; so the sooner we camp out and begin the better."

I told him I was ready, and asked him where we were to go.

"Oh, never you mind that, lad," he replied. "It's a long way from here; but a man, with his eyes open, can always find his way there and back. All you've to do is to follow the setting sun going, and to look out for him rising when coming back."

"Then I suppose you mean to go to the westward?" I observed.

"Ay, lad, to the far west," he answered; but I confess that at the time I had no idea how far off that "far west" was.

We set off the next morning by a steamer to Montreal, and on from thence, past Kingston, to Toronto on Lake Ontario, in Upper Canada. Flint lent me money to pay my way. He said that I should soon be able to reimburse him. I need not say how delighted I was with the fine scenery and the superb inland seas on which I floated. I could scarcely persuade myself that I was not on the ocean, till I tasted the water alongside. Flint told me with a chuckle, that once upon a time the English Government sent some ships of war in frame out to the lakes, and also a supply of water-tanks, forgetting that they would have a very ample one outside. A little forethought would have saved the ridicule they gained for this mistake, and the expense to which they put the country. As my intention is to describe my adventures afloat rather than those on shore, I shall be very brief with my account of the life we led in the backwoods.

From Toronto we crossed the country to Goodrich, a town on the shores of Lake Huron. Here we took a passage in a sailing vessel, trading to the factories on the northern shore of the lake, and at the nearest we landed and prepared for our expedition. Flint observed, that as we were short of funds, we must proceed on an economical principle. He therefore purchased only a small though strong pony, to carry our provisions and the skins of the animals we might kill, while we were to proceed humbly on foot.

We were now in a land teeming with every description of game; and I was able to prove to Flint that I was not a worse shot than I had sometimes boasted to him of being. The weather was generally fine, so that a bark hut afforded us ample shelter at night, and our rifles gave us as much food as we could require. Our greatest enemies were mosquitoes and other flies, and it was only by smearing our faces over with fat that we could free ourselves from their attacks.

We constantly encountered the Indian inhabitants of that territory; but they were invariably friendly, and willing to trade with us. Silas understood their language a little, so that with the aid of signs we could carry on sufficient conversation for our purpose. Six weeks thus passed rapidly away, and I calculated that it would be time for me to return to Quebec; so I told Silas I must wish him good-bye. He seemed very much vexed at this; for I believe that he both liked my society, and found me very useful to him. He had, indeed, formed the intention of keeping me by him, and converting me into a regular trapper and hunter; but, fond as I was of sport, for this I had no fancy, and I therefore persisted in my purpose of returning. Seeing that he could not prevail on me to remain, he accompanied me back to the fort, where he made over to me my fair share of the skins.

After the delay of a week, I found a vessel returning to the lower lakes, and in her I set sail for Quebec. My readers must excuse me for being thus brief in my description of my doings on shore; but it must be remembered that I am writing an account of my sea adventures, and I must defer the former to another opportunity.

Chapter Thirteen

At length I reached Quebec, and hurried to the quay, where I had left the *Mary*. She was not there. I hastened to the dockyard where she was to be repaired; I made inquiries for her of everybody I met. "What, the *Mary*, Captain Dean?" replied a shipwright to whom I spoke; "why, she sailed three weeks ago and better, for the West Indies, or some of them ports to the southward—she's pretty well there by this time."

I felt that he was speaking the truth, and my heart sunk within me; but to make sure, I ran on to the house at which Captain Dean and Mary had lodged. The woman, who was a French Canadian, received me very kindly, and seemed to enter into my feelings when she corroborated the account I had heard. She did not know exactly where the ship had gone; but she said that my friends were very sorry when I did not come back at the time appointed. At last Monsieur the captain grew angry, and said he was afraid I was an idle fellow, and preferred the vagabond life of a hunter to the hardier though nobler work of a seaman; but "*ma pauvre petite,*" as she called Mary, took my part, and said she was certain some accident had happened to me, or I should have been back when I promised. "Sweet Mary, I knew that she would defend me," I muttered; "and yet how little do I deserve her confidence!"

"Ah, she is indeed a sweet child," observed Madame Durand, divining my thoughts; "she cried very much indeed when the ship had to sail away without you, and nothing would comfort the poor dear."

This information, though very flattering to me, added to my regret. I was now obliged to consider what I should next do. After the free wild life I had been leading, the idea of returning to Ireland was odious to me. I can scarcely now account for my conduct in this respect, but I had but once written home on my arrival at Quebec; and during my long excursions to the backwoods, I never had time. I was now ashamed to write—I seldom ever thought of those at home. I had sunk, I felt, from their grade, whenever I recollected them. My whole attention had been for so long occupied with the present, that the past was, as it were, a blank, or as a story which I had read in some book, and had almost forgotten. I therefore hardly for a moment thought of going back, if I did so at all; but I was anxious to fall in again with Captain Dean. I fancied the pleasures of a sea life more than those of a hunter, but I was not yet altogether tired of the backwoods. I had still a hankering to trap a few more beavers, and to shoot some more raccoons and deer.

On making further inquiries of the ship-broker, I discovered that there was a possibility of Captain Dean's going to New Orleans, and I at once formed the idea of finding my way, by land and river, to that city. I knew a little more of the geography of the country than I did on my arrival, but the immense distance no way daunted me. I wanted to visit the States, and I was certain that my gun would always afford me the means of proceeding by any public conveyance, when I required it. I had a good sum remaining from the sale of the peltries I had saved; and with this in my pockets I once more started for the lakes of Upper Canada, purposing from thence to work my way through the western States down the Mississippi to New Orleans.

An American vessel, which I found at Goodrich, conveyed me, through Lake Huron, to a fort at the southern extremity of Lake Michigan, called, if I recollect rightly, Fort Dearborn. The voyage was long and tiresome. The feeling that one is in a fresh-water lake, and at the same time being out of sight of land for days together, is very curious. It gives one a more perfect notion than anything else can of the vastness of the country in which such inland seas exist. I must be excused from giving any minute account of my adventures at this period, as I made no notes, and I do not recur to them with much satisfaction. In fact, I was weary of the solitary life of a hunter and trapper, and longed once more to be among people with whom I could have some thoughts and feelings in common.

Till I got into the settled districts, I shot and trapped as before. My rifle always supplied me with abundance of food; and, whenever I reached a trading-post, I was able to exchange my peltries for a fresh store of powder and shot. When passing through the more inhabited districts, I was invariably hospitably received by the settlers, whatever was the nation to which they before belonged. Travelling through a large portion of the State of Indiana, I entered that of Illinois, and at length I embarked with a party of hunters in a canoe on the river of the same name, which runs through its centre. With these people I proceeded to Saint Louis, a city situated on the spot where the mighty streams of the Mississippi and Missouri join their waters.

Saint Louis was founded by the French, and is still very French in its general aspect. I here easily disposed of my remaining skins for a good sum of money, which I secured in a band round my waist. I remained here only two days, for I was anxious to proceed to the south; and, finding a steamer starting down the Mississippi, I went on board, and for about eight dollars engaged a passage on deck to New Orleans. The passage occupied ten days. By my usual way of proceeding, on foot, I should have been as many months, with a constant probability of dying of fever on the way.

I must make a remark for the benefit of Englishmen who may contemplate settling in the United States. They expect to find land cheap, no taxes, and few laws to hamper their will. In this they will not be disappointed; but there will be a considerable expense incurred in reaching those settlements where land is cheap. They will probably be a very great distance from a market for their produce; and, though they have no taxes and few laws, neither will they have the advantages which taxes and laws afford. They will be far removed from the ordinances of their Church, and the opportunities of education; there will neither be the where to buy nor to sell. In fact, they must be deprived of many of the advantages of civilisation; added to which, many parts of the western States are unhealthy in the greatest degree, of which the wretched, sallow, ague-stricken beings inhabiting them afforded melancholy proof; and these people, I found, were once stout, healthy peasants in England, and would have continued healthy, and gained what they hoped for besides, had they emigrated to Canada or to any other British colony, or even had they possessed more knowledge of the territory of the United States. I do not say that many British emigrants who give up their country, and become aliens in the States, do not succeed, and thus the accounts they send home encourage others to go out; but I do say that thousands of others die miserably of sickness and disappointment, without a friendly hand to help or cheer them, or any one to afford them the consolations of religion, and of their fate we never hear a word.

People talk a great deal of the advantages of liberty and equality, and the freedom of a wild life; but let me assure them that the liberty of having one's eye gouged out, the equality which every ruffian claims, and the freedom which allows a man to die without any one to assist him, are practically far from desirable; and yet such are the false phantoms by which many are allured to a land of strangers, away from the home of their countrymen and friends. However, I am not writing a lecture on colonisation. I will finish the subject, by urging my readers to study it, and to become the advocates of British colonisation.

New Orleans is justly called the wet grave of the white man, for yearly pestilence sweeps off thousands of its inhabitants; and as water is found but two feet below the surface, it fills each last receptacle of the dead as soon as dug. Yet pestilential as is the clime, the scenery is very beautiful. The stream, which is here a mile broad, rolls its immense volume of water with calm dignity, in a bed above two hundred feet deep, past this great commercial mart of the south. The banks on either side are covered with sugar plantations, from the midst of which rise numberless airy mansions of the wealthy owners, surrounded with orange, banana, lime, and fig trees, with numberless other productions of the tropics; while behind them can be seen the sugar-houses and the cabins of the negroes, to remind one of the curse which hangs over the land.

The city itself stands in the form of a half-moon on the banks of this mighty stream, and before it are moored craft of every description—backwood boats, keel boats, steamers and ships, brigs and schooners, from every part of the world. I may remark that directly behind the city is an impenetrable swamp, into which all the filth from the houses is led, for the ground is lower than the surface of the Mississippi; and then we cannot be surprised that plague and fever prevail to a terrific extent.

As soon as I landed I set to work to try and discover the *Mary*, if she was there, or to gain tidings of her should she have sailed, as, from the length of time I had occupied in my journey, I was afraid might be the case. I walked along the quays, examining every ship in the river, and, after a long search, I was convinced that the *Mary* was not there. I next had recourse to the ship-brokers and ship-chandlers, but from none of them could I gain any information. I then began to make inquiries of the people I found lounging about the quays smoking, and otherwise killing the time. At last I saw a man who stood lounging against a post, with a cigar in his mouth and his arms folded, and who, by the glance he cast at me, seemed to court inquiry.

He was, I remember well, a sallow-faced, gaunt fellow, with large expressive eyes and black hair, which hung down from under his Panama hat in ringlets, while a pair of gold rings adorned his ears. He had on a nankeen jacket and large white trousers, with a rich silk sash round his waist, in which was ostentatiously stuck a dagger, or rather a Spanish knife, with a handsome silver hilt. I took him for a Spaniard by his appearance; but when I accosted him in English, he replied in the same language, with scarcely a foreign accent, "And so you are looking for the *Mary*, Captain Dean, are you? Very curious," he observed: "I left her three weeks ago at the Havanah waiting for a cargo; and she won't be off again for another three weeks or more."

"Then I may reach her in time!" I ejaculated.

"Do you belong to her?" he continued. "You have not much the look of a seaman."

He was right; for I was still dressed in my mocassins and hunting costume, with my rifle in my hand, and my other worldly property slung about me, so I must have cut rather a curious figure.

I replied that I was to have belonged to her, and explained how it had happened that she had sailed without me. By degrees I told him more of my history; and finally, without my intending it, he drew the whole of it from me.

"You are a likely lad," he observed, with an approving nod. "The fact is, I sail to-morrow for the Havanah, in the schooner you see out yonder; and if you like to ship on board, you may, that's all." He pointed, as he spoke, to a large square-topsail schooner which lay out in the stream, at a single anchor.

She will not take long to get under weigh, I thought, as I looked at her. Eager as I was to reach the Havannah, I jumped at his offer. "I have not been accustomed to a craft like yours," I replied, "but I will do my duty on board her, to the best of my power."

"That's all we require; and perhaps, if you find your friend gone, you will like us well enough to remain with us," he observed, with a laugh. "We are constantly on the wing, so you will have no time to get weary of any place where we touch, as is the case in those big ships, which lie in harbour for months together. If you want to become a seaman, go to sea in a small craft, say I."

I told him that I did wish to become a seaman; but I did not say that it was for the sake of sailing with Captain Dean, nor did I mention his daughter. Indeed, I had kept her name altogether out of my narrative.

The arrangement being concluded, he advised me to go and get a sea-rig, remarking that my present costume was not exactly suited for going aloft in. There were several outfitting shops, such as are to be found in all seaports, and towards one of them of the most inviting appearance I bent my steps. Before going, however, I inquired of my new friend his name, and that of the schooner.

"The English and Americans call me John Hawk, and my craft the *Foam*," he answered. "Captain John Hawk, remember. The name is not amiss; so you may use it, for want of a better."

"Are you neither an Englishman nor an American?" I asked.

"No, youngster, I belong to no nation," he replied; and I observed a deep frown on his brow as he spoke. "Neither Spain, France, Portugal, England, nor even this free and enlightened country, owns me. Are you afraid of sailing with me, in consequence of my telling you this? If you are, you may be off your bargain."

"No," I answered, "no; I merely asked for curiosity, and I hope you won't consider me impertinent."

"Not if you don't insist on an answer," he replied. "And now go and get your outfit."

As I walked along, I meditated on his odd expressions; but I had no misgivings on the subject. I did not like the first shop I reached, so I went on to another, with the master of which I was more pleased. I there, at a fair price, very soon got the things I wanted, and, going into a back room, rigged myself out in them; while my hunting costume I did up in a bundle, to carry with me, for I was unwilling to part from so old and tried a friend.

As I was paying for the things, the whole of which cost somewhere about fifteen dollars, a stout, good-looking, elderly man came into the shop. I at once recognised him as the master of an American brig on board of which I had been in the Liverpool docks. I felt as if he was an old friend, and could not help speaking to him. He was very good-natured, though he did not remember me, which was not surprising. I asked him if he had met the *Mary*.

"I left her at the Havanah, for which place I sail to-morrow," he answered.

"So does Captain Hawk, of the *Foam*," I observed. "I have just shipped on board her."

"Youngster," he said, looking grave, "you do not know the character of that vessel, I am sure, or you would not willingly set foot on her deck. She is a noted slaver, if not something worse; and as you put confidence in me, I will return the compliment, and would strongly advise you to have nothing to do with her."

"But I have engaged to sail with Captain Hawk, and he seems a fair-spoken man," I urged.

"If you choose to trust to his fair speeches more than to my blunt warnings, I cannot help it," he answered. "I have done my best to open your eyes for you to his true character. If you persist in following your own counsel, you will soon have to open them yourself very wide, when it is too late."

I liked the tone of the master's voice, as well as the expression of his countenance; and I therefore felt inclined to believe him. At the same time I did not like to be moved, as it were, from my purpose by every breath of wind.

"I promised to sail with Captain Hawk, or whatever may be his name; and though I cannot doubt but that you have good reason for what you say, sir, yet I don't like to desert him, without some proof that he is the character you describe him," I replied.

"Did he tell you what trade he was in?" asked the captain.

"No, sir," I replied; "he said nothing about it."

"Then be guided by me, youngster, and don't ship with him," he said, speaking most earnestly. "You may make every inquiry about my brig—the *Susannah*, Captain Samuel Searle. You will find all is clear and above-board with me. I want hands, I own, and I should be glad to have you, but that does not influence me in what I say."

The shopkeeper corroborated all Captain Searle had told me, and added so many other stories of the character of Captain Hawk and his schooner, that I felt truly glad there was yet time to escape from him. Bad as he might be, there was something in his manner which made me wish not to desert him altogether, without offering him some excuse for my conduct. I accordingly, leaving my bundle in the shop, went back to the quay, where I found him lounging as before. He at first did not know me in my change of dress when I accosted him.

"You are a likely lad for a sailor," he remarked, as he ran his eye over me approvingly.

"I am glad you think so," I answered; and I then told him I had met the master of a vessel whom I had known in Liverpool, and that I wished to sail with him.

"And he has been telling you that I am a slaver, I suppose, or something worse, eh?" he exclaimed in a sneering tone, and with an angry flash of the eye I did not like. I looked conscious, I suppose; for he continued, "And you believed him, and were afraid to sail with so desperate a character, eh? Well, lad, go your own ways, I don't want to lead you. But I know of whom you speak, for I saw him go into the shop where you have been, and tell him *to look out for himself that's all.*" Saying this, he turned on his heel, and I went back to the shop.

I told Captain Searle what Captain Hawk had said.

"That does not matter," he answered. "He cannot do me more harm than he already seeks to do; so I do not fear him."

I was now pretty well convinced of the honesty of Captain Searle; but to assure myself still further, I called on two or three ship-brokers, who all assured me that his ship was a regular trader, and gave a favourable report of him. When I inquired about Captain Hawk, they screwed up their mouths, or made some other sign expressive of disapprobation, but were evidently unwilling to say anything about him. In the evening I went on board the *Susannah*; and I must say that I was very glad to find myself once more afloat.

Chapter Fourteen

The *Susannah* was a fine brig, of about three hundred tons burden. She had a raised poop, but no topgallant forecastle; so the crew were berthed in the fore-peak, in the very nose, as it were, of the vessel. I had engaged to serve as a boy before the mast. Indeed, perfectly unknown as I was, with slight pretensions to a knowledge of seamanship, I could not hope to obtain any other berth.

The crew were composed of about equal numbers of Americans—that is, subjects of the United States—and of Englishmen, with two blacks and a mulatto, a Spaniard, and a Portuguese. The first officer, Mr Dobree, was a great dandy, and evidently considered himself much too good for his post; while the second mate, Mr Jones, was a rough-and-ready seaman, thoroughly up to his work.

I was welcomed by my new shipmates in the fore-peak with many rough but no unkind jokes; and as I had many stories to tell of my adventures in the backwoods, before we turned in for the night I had made myself quite at home with them.

At daybreak on the next morning all hands were roused out to weigh anchor. The second mate's rough voice had scarcely done sounding in my ear before I was on deck, and with the rest was running round between the capstan-bars. "Loose the topsails," next sung out the captain. I sprung aloft to aid in executing the order. Though a young seaman may not have knowledge, he may at all events exhibit activity in obeying orders, and thus gain his superior's approbation. The anchor was quickly run up to the bows, the topsails were sheeted home, and, with a light breeze from the northward, we stood towards the mouth of the Mississippi.

As we passed close to the spot where, on the previous day, the *Foam* lay at anchor, I looked for her. She was nowhere to be seen. She must have got under weigh and put to sea at night. "She's gone, Peter, you observe," remarked Captain Searle, as some piece of duty called me near him. "I'm glad you are not on board her; and I hope neither you nor I may ever fall in with her again."

From New Orleans to Belize, at the mouth of the Mississippi, is about one hundred miles; and this distance, with the aid of the current and a favourable breeze, we accomplished by dusk, when we prepared once more to breast old ocean's waves. These last hundred miles of the father of rivers were very uninteresting, the banks being low, swampy, and dismal in the extreme, pregnant with ague and fevers. Although I rejoiced to be on the free ocean, I yet could scarcely help feeling regret at leaving, probably for ever, the noble stream on whose bosom I had so long floated; on whose swelling and forest-shaded banks I had travelled so far; whom I had seen in its infancy—if an infant it may ever be considered—in its proud manhood, and now at the termination of its mighty course.

These thoughts quickly vanished, however, as I felt the lively vessel lift to the swelling wave, and smelt the salt pure breeze from off the sea. Though the sea-breeze was very reviving after the hot pestilential air of New Orleans, yet as it came directly in our teeth, our captain wished it from some other quarter. We were enabled, however, to work off the shore; and as during the night the land-breeze came pretty strong, by day-break the next morning we were fairly at sea.

Before the sun had got up, the wind had gone down, and it soon became what seamen call a flat calm. The sea, as the hot rays of the sun shone on it, was, as it were, like molten lead; the sails flapped lazily against the mast; the brig's sides, as she every now and then gave an unwilling roll, threw off with a loud splash the bright drops of water which they lapped up from the imperceptibly heaving bosom of the deep. The hot sun struck down on our heads with terrific force, while the pitch bubbled up out of the seams of the deck; and Bill Tasker, the wit of the crew, declared he could hear it squeak into the bargain. An awning was spread over the deck in some way to shelter us, or we should have been roasted alive. Bill, to prove the excess of the heat, fried a slice of salt junk on a piece of tin, and, peppering it well, declared it was delicious. The only person who seemed not only not to suffer from the heat, but to enjoy it, was the black cook; and he, while not employed in his culinary operations, spent the best part of the day basking on the bowsprit-end.

The crew were engaged in their usual occupations of knotting yarns, making sinnet, etcetera, while the aforesaid Bill Tasker was instructing me—for whom he had taken an especial fancy—in the mysteries of knotting and splicing; but we all of us, in spite of ourselves, went about our work in a listless, careless way, nor had the officers even sufficient energy to make us more lively. Certainly it was hot. There had been no sail in sight that I know of all the day, when, as I by chance happened to cast my eyes over the bulwarks, they fell on the topsails of a schooner, just rising above the line of the horizon.

"A sail on the starboard bow!" I sung out to the man who was nominally keeping a look-out forward. He reported the same to the first mate.

"Where away is she?" I heard the captain inquire, as he came directly afterwards on deck.

"To the southward, sir; she seems to be creeping up towards us with a breeze of some sort or other," answered Mr Dobree. "Here, lad," he continued, beckoning to me, "go aloft, and see what you can make of her. Your eyes are as sharp as any on board, if I mistake not, and a little running will do you no harm."

I was soon at the mast-head, and in two minutes returned, and reported her to be a large topsail schooner, heading north-north-east with the wind about south-east.

"I can't help thinking, sir, from her look, that this is the same craft that was lying off New Orleans two days ago," I added, touching my hat to the captain. I don't remember exactly what made me suppose this, but such I know was my idea at the time.

"What, your friend Captain Hawk's craft, the *Foam*, you mean, I suppose?" he observed. "But how can that be? She was bound to the Havanah, and this vessel is standing away from it."

"I can't say positively, sir; but if you would take the glass and have a look at her, I don't think you would say she is very unlike her, at all events," I replied.

"It's very extraordinary if such is the case," said the captain, looking rather more as if he thought I might be right than before.

"Give me the glass, and I'll judge for myself, though it's impossible to say for a certainty what she may be at this distance." Saying this he took the telescope, and in spite of the heat went aloft.

When he came down again, I observed that he looked graver than usual. He instantly gave orders to furl the awning, and to be ready to make sail as soon as the breeze should reach us. "The youngster is right, Mr Dobree," he said, turning to the mate, and probably not aware that I overheard him.

"It's that piccarooning craft the *Foam*; and Mr Hawk, as he calls himself, is after some of his old tricks. I had my suspicions of him when I saw him off New Orleans; but I did not think he would venture to attack us."

Peter the Whaler | 79

"He's bold enough to attack any one, sir," said the mate; "but we flatter ourselves that we shall be able to give a very good account of him, if he begins to play off any of his tricks on us."

"We'll do our best, Mr Dobree," said the captain; "for if we do not, we shall have but a Flemish account to render of our cargo, let alone our lives."

I do not know if I before stated that the *Susannah* carried four guns— two long and two carronades; and as we had a supply of small arms and cutlasses, we were tolerably able to defend ourselves.

The captain walked the deck for some time in silence, during which period the stranger had perceptibly approached to us. He then again went aloft, and scrutinised her attentively. On coming down he stopped at the break of the poop, and, waving his hand, let us know that he wished to address us. "My lads," he began, "I don't altogether like the look of that fellow out yonder, who has been taking so much pains to get up to us. He may be honest, but I tell you I don't think so; and if he attempts to molest us, I'm sure you'll one and all do your duty in defending the brig and the property on board her entrusted to you. I need not tell you that pirates generally trust to the saying, that dead men tell no tales; and that, if that fellow is one, and gets the better of us, our lives won't be worth much to any of us."

"Don't fear for us, sir; we're ready for him whatever he may be," sung out the whole crew with one voice.

The stranger brought along the breeze with him, but as yet our sails had not felt a particle of its influence. At length, when he was little more than a mile off, a few cat's-paws were seen playing on the water; they came, and vanished again as rapidly, and the sea was as smooth as before. In time they came oftener and with more power; and at length our topsails and topgallant-sails were seen slowly to bulge out as the steadier breeze filled them.

The wind came, as I have said, from the south-east, which was directly in our teeth in our proper course to the Havanah. The stranger had thus the weather-gauge of us; and a glance at the map will show that we were completely embayed, as, had we stood to the eastward, we should have run on the Florida coast, while on the other tack we must have run right down to meet him. We might possibly reach some port; but the probabilities were that he would overtake us before we could do so, and the appearance of fear would encourage him to follow us. We had therefore only the choice of running back to Belize, or fighting our way onward. Captain Searle decided on the latter alternative; and, bracing the yards sharply up on the starboard tack, we stood to the eastward, intending, whatever course the stranger pursued, to go about again at the proper time.

The schooner, on seeing this, also closely hugged the wind and stood after us. There could now be no longer any doubt about his intentions. We, however, showed the stars and stripes of the United States, but he hoisted no ensign in return. It was soon very evident that he sailed faster than we did, and he was then rapidly coming within range of our guns. Our captain ordered us, however, on no account to fire unless we were struck, as he was unwilling to sacrifice the lives of any one unnecessarily, even of our enemies.

Every stitch of canvas the brig could carry was cracked on her: all would not do. The stranger walked up to us hand over hand. Seeing that there was not the slightest chance of escaping by flight, Captain Searle ordered the foresail and topgallant-sails to be clewed up, and, under our topsails and fore-and-aft sails, resolved to wait the coming up of the enemy, if such the stranger might prove.

On came the schooner, without firing or showing any unfriendly disposition. As she drew near, I felt more and more convinced that she must be the *Foam*. She had a peculiarly long cutwater and a very straight sheer, which, as she came up to the windward of us, and presented nearly her broadside, was discernible. As she heeled over to the now freshening breeze, I fancied that I could even discern, through the glass, Captain Hawk walking the quarter-deck. When she got about a quarter of a mile to windward of us, she hove to and lowered a boat, into which several people jumped and pulled towards us. At the same time up went the Spanish ensign at her peak.

Captain Searle looked puzzled. "I cannot make it out, Dobree," he observed. "I still doubt if that fellow is honest, and am half inclined to make sail again, and while he bears down to pick up his boat, we may get to windward of him."

"If he isn't honest he'll not trouble himself about his boat, but will try to run alongside us, and let her come up when she can," answered the mate. "There is no trusting to what such craft as that fellow may do."

"Oh, we'll take care he does not play off any tricks upon us," said the captain; and we waited the approach of the boat.

As she drew near, she was seen to contain eight men. Four were pulling, one sat in the bows, and the other three in the stern-sheets. If they were armed, it could not be discovered. When they got within hail, the captain asked them what they wanted.

They pointed to their mouths, and one answered in Spanish, "Aqua, aqua, por amor de Dios."

"They want water, sir, they say," observed the first mate, who prided himself on his knowledge of Spanish.

"That's the reason, then, that they were in such a hurry to speak to us," said the captain. "But still, does it not strike you as odd that a vessel should be in want of water in these seas?"

"Her water-butts might have leaked out; and some of these Spanish gentry, sir, are very careless about taking enough water to sea," replied the mate, who was biassed by the pleasure he anticipated of being able to sport his Spanish.

"Get a water-cask up on deck, and we'll have it ready to give these fellows, whatever they may be," said our humane captain. "Have some pannikins ready to serve it out to them. Thirst is a dreadful thing, and one would not keep a fellow-creature in that state a moment longer than one could help."

I do not know what the second mate thought of the strangers, but I remember several of the crew saying that they did not like their looks; and I saw him place a cutlass close to the gun nearest the starboard gangway, while he kept eyeing them in no very affectionate manner. Notwithstanding the heat of the weather, the men in the stern-sheets wore cloaks. On observing this, Bill Tasker said he supposed it was to hide the shabby jackets they wore under them. The other men were dressed in blue shirts, and their sleeves rolled up to the shoulder, with the red sash usually worn by Spaniards round their waist, in which was stuck the deadly *cuchillo*, or cut-and-thrust knife, in a sheath, carried by most Lusitanian and Iberian seamen and their descendants of the New World.

They pulled up at once alongside, and before any one attempted to stop them they had hooked on, the man in the bows climbing up on deck, followed by his companions in cloaks, and two of the seamen. The other two remained in the boat, pointing at their mouths, as a sign that they wanted water.

Seamen, from the sufferings and dangers to which they are exposed, are proverbially kind to those in distress. Our men, therefore, seemed to vie with each other who should first hold the pannikins of water to the mouths of the strangers, while a tub, with the fluid, was also lowered into the boat alongside. They eagerly rushed at the water, and drank up all that was offered them; but I could not help remarking that they did not look like men suffering from thirst. However, a most extraordinary effect was produced on two of them, for they fell down on the deck, and rolled about as if in intense agony. This drew the attention of all hands on them; and as we had no surgeon on board, the captain began to ransack his medical knowledge to find remedies for them.

While he was turning over the pages of his medical guide to find some similar case of illness and its remedy described, the schooner was edging down towards us. As she approached, I observed only a few men on board; and they, as the people in the boat had done, were pointing at their mouths, as if they were suffering from want of water. The boat was on the lee side.

I think I said that there were some sails, and two or three cloaks, apparently thrown by chance at the bottom of the boat. While all hands were engaged in attending to the strangers, and for some minutes no one had looked towards the schooner, on a sudden I heard a loud grating sound—there was the wild triumphant cry of a hundred fierce voices. The seemingly exhausted men leaped to their feet; the helmsman and our captain lay prostrate by blows dealt by our treacherous foes; the second mate and several of the men were knocked down; and before any of us had time to attempt even any defence of the brig, a set of desperadoes, of all colours and nations, were swarming down on her decks from the rigging of the schooner, while others, who had been concealed in the boat, sprang on board on the lee side. Never was a surprise more complete, or treachery more vile. In an instant we were helplessly in the power of as lawless a band of pirates as ever infested those seas. The captain and mates were first pinioned; the men were sharing the same treatment. I was at the time forward, when, on looking aft, who should I see but Captain Hawk himself walking the deck of the brig as if he were her rightful commander! He took off his hat with mock courtesy to poor Captain Searle, as he passed him. "Ah, my dear sir, the fortune of war makes you my prisoner to-day," he said, in a sneering tone. "Another day, if my people do not insist on your walking the plank, you may hope, perhaps, to have the satisfaction of beholding me dangling at a yardarm. By the bye, I owe you this turn, for you shipped on board your craft a lad who had engaged to sail with me; and I must have him forthwith back again, with a few other articles of your cargo which I happen to require." As he said this, his eye fell on me, and he beckoned me towards him. I saw that there was no use hanging back, so I boldly advanced. "You are a pretty fellow, to desert your colours," he continued, laughing. "You deserve to be treated as a deserter. However, I will have compassion on your youth, if you will swear to be faithful to me in future."

"I never joined your vessel, so I am not a deserter. I cannot swear to serve a man of whose character I know nothing, except that he has taken forcible possession of a peaceable trader." I said this without hesitation or the least sign of fear. The truth is, I felt too desperate to allow myself to consider what I said or did.

"You are a brave young bantam," he answered laughingly. "And though all the rest may hang or walk the plank, we will save you to afford us sport; so set your mind at rest on that point."

"Thank you for my life, for I have no wish to lose it, I can assure you," I replied; "but don't suppose I am going to spend it in your service. I shall do my best to get away from you as soon as possible."

"Then we must tie you by a lanyard to the leg," he answered, without at all appearing angry. "Here, Mark Anthony,"—he beckoned to a tall, ill-looking black who had been busy in securing the rest of the crew,—"take charge of this youngster, and render an account of him to me by and by, without a hair of his head injured, mind you."

"Yes, sare," said the Roman general, who I afterwards found was a runaway slave from Kentucky. "I'll not singe his whiskers even. Come here, massa;" and seizing me by the shoulder, he dragged me forward away from the rest of the people. "What's your name?" asked my black keeper, as he made me sit down on the bits of the bowsprit.

"Peter, at your service, Mr Mark Anthony," said I in as fearless a voice as I could command; for having once taken a line of conduct which seemed to answer well, I determined to persevere in it.

"Den, Massa Peter, you sit dere quiet," he said with a grin. "I no break your skull, because Captain Hawk break mine if I do. I no let anybody else hurt you for same reason."

From his look and voice I certainly did not flatter myself that he refrained from throwing me overboard from any love he bore me; but, on the contrary, that he would have been much more gratefully employed in making me walk the plank, or in tricing me up to the foreyard.

Meantime the pirates were busily employed in ransacking the vessel, and in transferring everything of value to them which they could find from her to their own schooner. The captain and mates were threatened with instant death if they did not deliver up all the money they had on board; and even the crew were compelled to hand over to our captors the small sums they possessed. To make them do this, they were knocked about and beaten unmercifully. And even those who possessed watches and rings were deprived of them, as well as of any clothes which appeared worth taking.

I had often read the history of pirates and of their bold exploits, till I almost fancied that I should like to become one, or, at all events, that I should like to encounter them. But I can assure my friends that the reality was very different to the fiction; and as the hideous black was standing over me, ready every moment to knock out my brains, and my companions were suffering all sorts of ill-treatment, I most heartily wished that such gentry as pirates had not been allowed to exist.

Though I tried to look as indifferent as possible, the black would have observed me trembling, had he not been watching to see what his friends were about, no doubt eager to obtain his share of the plunder. The work the pirates were engaged in went on for some time, till even they had tolerably satiated their eagerness for booty; and then I fully expected to see them either heave my shipmates overboard as food for the sharks alongside, or hang them at the yardarms, and then set the ship on fire, as Mark Anthony insinuated, for my satisfaction, that they would do. Instead of this, to my surprise Captain Hawk went up to Captain Searle, and said, "I sent a message by that youngster there to you to look out for yourself, and I never threaten in vain. He goes with me. I want a good navigator; and as your second mate seems a likely sort of person, I shall take him also. The rest of you may go free; but remember, that if any of you attempt to betray me, or to appear as witnesses against me, you will dearly pay for it."

Our poor captain, who was almost ruined and heart-broken by the pillage of his ship, said nothing, but bowed his head on his breast, looking as if he would as soon have been killed outright. The unfortunate mate, Abraham Jones, seemed horrified at hearing what his fate was to be; but he knew enough about the pirates to be aware that it would have been worse than useless to attempt to escape accompanying them. He, however, took the precaution of calling on the crew of the *Susannah* to bear witness that he was compelled through bodily fear and by force to join the pirates; and he made the best show of resistance that under the circumstances he could venture to do.

From what I saw of him, I do not think that he had so great an objection to joining them as some men might have had. Indeed, I confess that I was very wrong in doing so; and I feel that a person ought rather to sacrifice his life than consent to commit a crime, even though driven to it with a dagger at his throat. However, both Jones and I fancied that the only chance of saving our own lives, and those of our shipmates, was by our going on board the schooner.

"Remember, Captain Searle, if we get into any misfortune through you, these two will be the first to suffer, and then again I say, look out for yourself," exclaimed the chief pirate, as he quitted the deck of the *Susannah*.

His people then hove her guns overboard, and removed the small arms on board their own craft, to which the mate and I were also transferred. They also cut the standing and running rigging, which would effectually prevent her from making sail for a long time to come.

The first mate was next released, and was ordered to stand on the poop, on pain of being shot down if he attempted to move while the schooner was near. Her boat was then hoisted in, she was cast off from the brig, and with a cheer of triumph from her crew, she stood away from the *Susannah*.

The first mate wisely did as he was ordered; and it was not till we had got to such a distance that there was little fear of his being hit, that I saw him jump down to release his companions. It was with a sense of misery and degradation I have never before experienced, that I watched till we lost sight of the unfortunate *Susannah*.

Chapter Fifteen

A week passed away on board the *Foam*. Whereabouts we were I had no means of telling; for the captain kept me in his cabin, and would not allow me to go on deck without first asking his leave, nor would he permit me to communicate with Mr Jones. He treated me very kindly, and even gave me books with which to amuse myself; but I was very far from happy. I felt that the schooner might some day be captured by a ship of war, and that I might probably be hung as a pirate before I had an opportunity of establishing my innocence. I also did not like to be a prisoner, even though I was kindly treated; and I thought that most probably, when Hawk found I would not join in any piratical acts, and I had resolved that nothing should compel me to do so, his behaviour would change, and that if I escaped with my life, I should no longer be treated as before.

Abraham Jones had, I am sorry to say, as far as I was able to judge from appearances, taken readily enough to the office imposed on him, and on two occasions when I went on deck, I saw him doing duty as the officer of the watch. My opinion of him was, that he would not have sought to become a pirate, but that, having no nice sense of right and wrong—finding himself thrust, as it were, into the life—he did not think it worth making any exertion to escape from it.

Whether we went to the Havanah or not I did not know. We certainly were once at anchor, and three times we either chased vessels or were chased by a superior force, from the eager tone in which the captain ordered sail to be made. Once we fired several shots, and were fired at in return; and I suspect it must have been at some vessel on our beam chasing us, and that some of her rigging or her masts must have been cut away, from the loud cheers the pirates gave, perhaps they sunk the enemy.

An hour afterwards, Hawk came down into the cabin, looking as cool and unconcerned as if nothing had happened. I tried to gain some information from him, but he would answer none of my questions. He only gave a ghastly smile when I asked if the vessel at which he had fired had sunk; and he then took up a book, in which he soon seemed to be deeply absorbed. After some time the book dropped from his hand, and he sat for half-an-hour in a state of abstraction, unconscious of where he was, or who was present.

He was roused by the black, Mark Anthony, putting his head in at the door and saying, "A sail on the lee bow."

He sprang on deck in a moment, all life and activity. Instantly all sail the schooner could carry was packed on her, and we were bowling along with a fine breeze in chase of the stranger. This I could only surmise, however, by the way the vessel heeled over to the breeze, for I was still kept in the cabin.

Presently Hawk came down again. "Peter," he observed, "you have disappointed me. I thought you would not be content to lead the idle life you do; I fancied you would like the excitement of the chase and the fight better than sitting alone in the cabin all day, like a young girl."

"I am not content, Captain Hawk," I replied; "but a prisoner has no choice."

"No one is allowed freedom on board here, unless he has taken the oaths of allegiance to the captain and our laws," he answered, looking steadfastly at me.

"Nothing could induce me to take one or the other," I exclaimed; "so I suppose I shall remain a prisoner till you release me, or I die."

He seemed to take my answer very calmly; and this encouraged me to proceed and to make an effort to obtain my freedom.

"Captain Hawk," I said, "you have been very kind to me; and though I should have been willing to sail with you before I knew the character of your vessel, I am now most anxious to be put on shore; and if you will liberate me, I will swear most solemnly not to betray you, or any of those who sail with you."

"We do not trust to the oaths of those who do not join us," he answered. "For your own sake, I must make you take part in the next capture we attempt, or else my people will begin to suspect that you are a mere coward, and even I shall be unable to protect you."

"I am no coward, Captain Hawk, and that I will prove any time that I have an opportunity; but I do not choose to commit murder or robbery," I answered, in the same bold tone in which I usually spoke.

"You use harsh terms, youngster, to one who could any moment order you to be hove to the sharks," exclaimed the pirate. "However, I do not quarrel with you for speaking your mind. I once thought as you do, but custom has altered my ideas."

"Then why do you wish me to do what you know I must consider wrong?" I asked.

"Because I have a liking for you, and want a lad of spirit and education to be my companion," he replied. "The old hands I cannot trust—they are as likely to turn against me as to serve me—while you, I know, will be faithful for awhile, till you get hardened like the rest, and then—"

"And then," interrupting him, I said, "what would you do with me? Give me as food for the sharks, I suppose?"

"No, lad; I should let you live to fight your own way in the world, with a charge to keep out of my path," he replied. "But that is not what I wanted to talk to you about. You must come on deck and join in capturing the vessel we are in chase of, for we think she is likely to prove a prize of value."

I am sorry to say that so heartily tired was I of remaining shut up in the cabin, that I was glad of being allowed, on any terms, to see what was going forward on deck.

On this, I suspect, the pirate had calculated. He well knew the force of the French proverb, "It is but the first step to crime which is difficult." He wished me to take that first step, being assured that I should then be his.

I thought when I went on deck that nothing would tempt me to take any part in the acts of the pirates, even as far as in assisting to navigate the vessel; but there is something so exciting in the chase of a vessel, that it is difficult not to wish to come up with her. At first I stood merely looking on; but the breeze freshened and rather headed us, and Hawk issued an order to flatten in the fore-and-aft sails, and to brace up the yards. I flew instinctively to the sheets, and found myself pulling and hauling with the rest.

The captain made no remark, nor did he appear even to notice what I had done. The wind was about south, and the chase was to the eastward of us, standing on a bowline she was a brig of some size, and at the first glance I thought she was a man-of-war; but Hawk pronounced her to be a Spaniard, and homeward bound from Cuba. On hearing this, of course I knew that we must be somewhere to the eastward of that place, and this was the first intimation I had had of our whereabouts.

The chase had not observed us, or if he had, seemed not to be at all suspicious of our character; for he was standing on under easy sail, as if in no way in a hurry to escape from us.

Hawk, who was usually so calm and almost apathetic, walked the deck full of energy and excitement. Every order he gave was uttered in a sharp, quick tone, which demanded instant obedience. Every one partook of the same spirit; and there appeared to be as much discipline and regularity as on board a man-of-war. Even the most lawless vagabonds find this necessary for the attainment of their ends and their own preservation.

We rapidly came up with the chase, and were within about three miles of her, when she began, it seemed, to suspect that all was not right, for sail after sail was set on her till she could carry no more, while she edged away a little from her course, so as to allow every one of them to draw properly. This threw us soon completely to windward, for we held on the same course as before, and she appeared at first to be recovering her lost ground. In a short time we also kept away with the wind almost abeam, a point on which the *Foam* sailed her best.

"Huzza, my lads!" exclaimed Hawk; "in a short time the chase will be ours, and, if I mistake not, plenty of gold doubloons into the bargain, if you can but make our craft walk along faster."

"Huzza!" shouted the English and American part of the crew, in which the people of other nations joined in their peculiar cries.

The brig once more hauled her wind, and this brought us soon nearer again to her.

Hawk thought it was because the captain saw indications of a shift of wind, and hoped to be placed well to windward. He was scrutinising her narrowly through a telescope. "She does not show any guns," he remarked; "but it is no reason that she has not got them. Get all ready for action, in case she should prove a Tartar."

I scarcely knew what I was about; but I confess that I not only assisted to hand up the powder and shot, but to load and run out the guns.

Neither of us made any further variation in our course; but the chase was, it appeared, a very slow sailer, for we so rapidly came up with her, that five hours after she was seen she was within range of our guns. She did not fire, nor did we; for supposing her to be unarmed, Hawk was anxious to capture her without in any way injuring her hull or cargo. We sailed on, therefore, as if we were engaged in a friendly race; and no one, by looking at us, could have supposed that we were deadly enemies.

We were getting very near to the chase, and with our telescopes could almost distinguish the faces of those on board, when I observed Abraham Jones, the new second mate of the *Foam*, hurry aft to the captain with a face pale as a ghost. Hawk laughed and shook his head incredulously. Jones seemed from his manner to be insisting that he was right, for I did not hear what he said. Still we stood on till the chase was within the distance of half the range of our guns. I was again aft. "Hoist our bunting to make him show his colours," I heard Hawk say; "and give him a shot from our bow-chaser to hurry him."

Directly afterwards a broad red flag, without any device, was run up at our peak, and with a spout of smoke a shot went flying over the water, and with a crash which made the splinters fly it struck the dark sides of the brig. The effect was instantaneous, and such as was little expected by the pirates.

A flag was run up to the gaff of the brig; but instead of the Spanish ensign, the stars and stripes of the United States were displayed; and the ports being opened as if by magic, eight guns were run out, and luffing up, she let fly her broadside right into our bows. The shot tore up our decks, and knocked away part of our starboard bulwarks, killing two of the people, and wounding three more, but without injuring our rigging. Then I saw what sort of men I was mingling with. I cannot describe the fierce rage which took possession of them, the oaths and execrations to which they gave vent. The bodies of the two men who were killed, while yet warm, were thrown overboard directly they were found to be dead, and the wounded were dragged below, and left without a surgeon or anyone to attend on them. Instead of the timid Spanish merchantman we expected to get alongside, we found that this vessel was no other than a United States man-of-war sent to look out for the *Foam*—in fact, that we had caught a Tartar. Hawk, to do him justice, stood undaunted, his energies rising with the occasion, keeping away a little, so as to get our broadside to bear, we fired in return, and the guns being planted high, some of the running rigging was cut away, and her fore-topmast was struck, and must have been badly wounded, for some hands instantly were seen going aloft to fish it.

"About ship, my lads—down with the helm; and while she's in stays, give Uncle Sam our larboard broadside."

The sails of the schooner were well full; she quickly came round, and before the brig could follow our example, we sent the shot from our whole broadside flying among her rigging. A loud shout of exultation from our pirate crew showed their satisfaction at the damage they had done; for several spars and sails, with blocks and ropes, were seen coming down by the run on deck.

"Now, my lads, let's up stick and away," cried Hawk. "They thought, doubtless, that they were sure of us; but we'll show them that the *Foam* is not to be caught so easily."

All hands who could be spared from the guns, and I among the rest, flew to their stations to trim sails; the yards were braced sharp up, and with her head to the south-west, the *Foam* stood away on a bowline from her powerful antagonist. We were not to escape, however, with impunity; for as soon as the brig's crew had somewhat recovered from the confusion into which the damage done by our shot had thrown them, such guns as could be brought to bear were fired at us with no bad aim. One struck our taffrail, and another killed a man on the forecastle; but our rigging escaped. Twice the brig missed stays in attempting to come about, from so much of her head-sail having been cut away; and this, as she all the time was sailing one way and we the other, contributed much to increase our distance. The breeze also favoured us further by freshening, making it more difficult to the enemy to repair damages, while, as we were unhurt, it sent us along all the more rapidly. The Americans are not the people to take the treatment we had given them with calmness, especially as we were so much the smaller, and had less force. At last, at a third trial, the brig came about, while she continued without cessation firing at us. Not much damage was done, though our sails had daylight made through them several times by her shot, and another man was killed; but this casualty the pirates seemed to make light of—it was the fortune of war, and might happen every instant to any of us. The bodies, with scant examination, except to discover whether there was money in their pockets, or rings in their ears or on their fingers, were thrown overboard without a prayer or a sigh. As the shot came whistling over us, they laughed when they saw me bobbing down my head in the hope of avoiding them. I had no fancy, I own, to be shot by people with whom I had not the slightest enmity, nor whom I in any way wished to injure.

We soon found that the brig-of-war, instead of being a slow sailer, was remarkably fast, and that, while we were in chase of her, she must, by towing a sail overboard, or by some other manoeuvre, have deadened her way, on purpose to allow us to come up with her. We had now, therefore, to put the schooner's best leg foremost to get away from her, even before she had got all her gear aloft again. To try and do her further damage, a gun was got over the taffrail, and a constant fire was kept up from it as fast as it could be loaded.

I was standing in the waist with the black, Mark Anthony, near me. "Well, Massa Peter, if de brig catch we, we all be hung; how you like dat?" he asked, with a broad grin, which made him look far from pleasing.

"I should be sorry to see any of those who have treated me with kindness hung, or otherwise injured," I replied.

"See! Ha, ha! but how you like feel being hung, Massa Peter?" he said, again grinning more horribly than before.

"Why, I have no fear of that sort, Mr Mark, I can assure you," I replied; though I confess the disagreeable idea did come across me, that I might possibly not be able to prove that I was not a pirate should we be captured. "I have had nothing to do with any of the acts committed by the crew of this vessel."

"Ho, ho, ho!" he exclaimed, "den you no pull and haul, and help work de guns which fire at de sip of war? me swear me saw you myself. Ho, ho, ho!"

The black's laughter sounded almost demoniacal in my ears. He spoke the truth, too: I had indeed helped to work the guns; and on the strength of it, like a tempter to evil, he was endeavouring to persuade me, in his rough way, to join the pirates. I did not think it prudent to show him that I clearly saw his aim; but I resolved still to remain firm.

The evening was now drawing on, and fortunately the breeze did not drop. I confess that I was just as anxious to escape from our pursuer as any pirate on board; scarcely more so, perhaps, than the new mate, who had guessed the character of the brig, and had no fancy for having his career cut short so soon.

The brig did not fire at us, as to do so she would have had to yaw and thus lose ground, while we continued to ply her with our long gun. Her fore-topsail could not be set while the mast was being fished. An attempt was now made to hoist it; but the breeze at that instant strengthening, away went the mast, rigging and sail together. A loud cheer arose from our decks: a parting shot was given her from our gun, and in two hours darkness hid her from our sight.

Chapter Sixteen

I dreamed all night that I was in the hands of the Americans, with a rope round my neck and about to be run up at the yardarm. I felt the practical inconvenience of associating with bad company. As soon as I awoke I went on deck, for Hawk no longer placed any restriction on my movements. I fully expected to see the brig-of-war in chase of us. I own I felt somewhat relieved when, on looking round, not a sail of any description was to be seen, and the schooner was still bowling along with a brisk breeze on a westerly course.

Towards evening we sighted land, towards which our course was altered. We ran on, and by marks, which I could not distinguish, steered between coral banks, till on a sudden I found that we were entering a lagoon, with trees towering on either side high above our top mast heads. The wind dropped completely as we got within the passage, and the boats were sent ahead to tow. Hawk ordered me into one of them, and I saw no reason to disobey; indeed, I felt that it would be very foolish not to do my best to please him in matters unconnected with piracy.

The sky was clear overhead, and the stars shone down and were reflected, as in a mirror, on the otherwise ink-black water of the lagoon. As we pulled ahead, we appeared to be passing through a narrow canal, with lofty impenetrable walls on either side, while in the centre rose before our eyes the phantom-like outline of the schooner, her topmast heads and rigging alone being seen against the sky above the dark shadows of the trees. The splash of our oars was the only sound which broke the dead silence which reigned in this sequestered spot; while the only light, except from the glittering stars above us, was from the phosphorescent flashes as the blades entered the water, and the golden drops again fell into their parent element. On looking on that gloomy surface, it seemed as improbable that anything so bright should come from it as that sparks of real fire should be emitted from the hard flint-stone. Mat Hagan, an Irishman, who pulled the bow oar in my boat, declared that our oars were throwing up to the sky again the reflection of the stars, which had no business to be there at all.

We pulled on for about half-an-hour, and then a sort of bay or bight appearing on one side, we brought the vessel into it, and moored her stem and stern fast to the trees. There she lay so completely concealed, that any one passing up the canal could not by any possibility have seen her, even in broad daylight.

Here we lay for several days, repairing damages and refitting the ship. Where we were I could not learn from any one on board; but I suspected that we were in one of the numberless keys among the Bahama or Lucaya Islands; and I had afterward reason to know that I was right.

Some of the booty taken by the pirates was landed, as, on account of the marks on the bales and other signs, it was likely to lead to their detection should they attempt to dispose of it in its present form. Some of the things were hid away; the others, after undergoing various operations, were re-shipped with such perfectly different marks, that it would have been impossible to detect them. Cunning and trickery seemed to be now the means taken by the pirates to carry on their operations, instead of the bold, daring way in which, as I had read, their predecessors formerly plundered the honest trader.

Hawk ordered me to lend a hand in refitting the schooner, so I made myself as useful as my knowledge would allow. I had begun, to entertain a hope of escaping when the pirates were off their guard and fancied that I had become reconciled to my lot. It was against my nature to be in any way treacherous, and I most certainly would not have injured Hawk, on account of the kindness with which he had treated me; but, at the same time, I did not feel that I was acting wrongly in concealing from him my wish to regain the liberty of which he had deprived me.

One morning, while the yards were still on deck and the sails unbent, notice was given from our look-out at the mouth of the lagoon that a sail was in sight, about two miles in the offing.

"What is she?" asked Hawk of the messenger.

"A barque, deeply laden, captain," replied the man, who was an old pirate. "To my mind she looks as if she would not make a bad prize, if we could get hold of her; and, as the wind is dropping, and it will be some time before the sea-breeze sets in, I think there will not be much difficulty in doing that."

The captain was pleased at his follower's suggestion; indeed, he would have risked the loss of his authority had he refused to attend to it. The men were ordered to knock off work, and to get the boats ready, while, those who were away in the interior of the little island were recalled to lend their assistance. Every one was instantly all life and animation: with the prospect of making a prize, even the most sluggish were aroused.

There were three boats, which were soon launched, and oars, arms, and provisions were placed in them. To my surprise, Hawk gave the command of them to Abraham Jones, he himself remaining to take charge of the schooner. From what I heard, I found that the pirates expected no difficulty or danger in making the capture.

I, of course, hoped that I should have nothing to do in the matter. What was my horror, then, when Hawk ordered me into the boats, and my old enemy—for I cannot call him my friend—Mark Anthony, was told to keep me company! I do not know whether this was Hawk's wish, or the desire of the men, who did not like to trust me till I had been guilty of some piratical act. At first I hesitated about obeying; but I soon saw, by the angry looks which were cast at me, that I was doing so at the peril of my life; and at the same instant it struck me, that if I went, I might by some means or other obtain my liberty.

The boats were one long-boat, which pulled eight oars, and carried in all sixteen men, and two large swift-rowing gigs. Jones took command of the long-boat, and I was in one of the gigs. In silence we left the vessel on our nefarious errand—in silence we pulled down the canal with steady and slow strokes, for while the wind held there was no hurry. When we got close to the mouth of the harbour, the boat I was in was sent out to reconnoitre.

The stranger was apparently beating up along shore, towards which her head was now pointed, those who directed her movements little aware of the danger which threatened them. After waiting a short time, during which she had drawn nearer to us, her sails began to flap against the masts, and the ripple which had been playing on the water disappeared altogether. With the last breath of wind she was put about, and attempted to stand off shore; but she was very soon left in what is called the "doldrums," namely, without steerage-way.

I had been watching her attentively. I thought from the first I knew her; and I now felt certain that she was no other than the ship of which I was in search, the *Mary*. With bitter grief I came to this conclusion; for I could not but fear that my friends were on board her, and that Captain Dean and his sweet child would be thrown into the hands of the pirates. What, too, would they think of me? Would they believe me innocent when they saw me in such company? A thought came cross my mind at that instant; I would pretend not to recognise them. At all risks, I would make the pirates suppose that I joined willingly in this expedition, and perhaps I might be the means of preserving their lives, at all events, if not their property. Perhaps, I thought, my steps might have been led providentially through the various adventures in which I had engaged for this very purpose. The very idea made my heart beat quick with a sensation almost of joy. I did not see how it was to be accomplished; but I felt assured that the Power which had hitherto guided me would point out the way.

When the officer of the boat I was in saw the barque becalmed, he gave the signal to our consort, and without further delay we three pulled out together towards her.

For some time no one on board appeared to have observed us. At last some one saw us, and two or three glasses were directed towards us; but we did not seem to have created any alarm or even suspicion among them. Thus we were enabled to approach without any preparation having been made to prevent our getting on board. When it was too late, probably from the eagerness with which they saw us dash alongside, they suspected that all was not right, and a few of the hands ran to the arm-chest, while others attempted to slue round one of the two guns the barque carried, and to point it down at the boats. Before they could do so, we were scrambling up her sides.

"Oh, oh, Massa Peter, you hurry enough now to turn pirate, when you tink someting to be got!" shouted Mark Anthony, as he saw my eagerness to be one of the first on deck.

The cutter boarded on one side, the two gigs on the other—one at the fore-rigging, the other at the mizzen-chains; so that the crew had to separate into three divisions to oppose us. The crew thus weakened, the people from the long-boat gained easily a footing on deck. They drove the crew aft, who were now attacked in the rear by the party from one of the gigs. I was in the foremost gig, and we had no one to oppose us. The only defence made was by the master, his mates, and two of the crew, who had secured cutlasses. They stood together on the larboard side of the poop, and boldly refused to yield up the ship, till they knew the authority of those attacking her.

I saw at a glance that my fears were well founded. There stood my kind friend, Captain Dean, and, in the centre of the group, his sweet little daughter, Mary. Oh, how I wished to have the strength of a hundred men, to drive all the pirates into their boats, and to release my friends!

No sooner had I appeared above the bulwarks than Mary saw me. She uttered a cry of surprise, for she recognised me at once. It attracted her father's attention. His cutlass was struck from his grasp by Jones, the two mates were knocked down, and all further resistance was at an end.

This easy victory prevented the pirates from being as bloodthirsty as they might otherwise have proved; but, as a precautionary measure, Jones ordered both the officers and crew to be bound to the masts and rigging while the ship was being searched.

I had rushed aft, in the hopes of being of some assistance to Captain Dean should he have required it—how, I scarcely knew. I thought I would have interposed my body, should a sword have been raised to strike him: When I saw him no longer making any defence and uninjured, I stopped, and was endeavouring to turn away to consider what I should do; but Mary's eye had followed me, and, as she saw me approaching, she uttered my name in his ear. On losing his sword, he had thrown himself on one of the hen-coops placed against the bulwarks, where he lay, clasping his child in his arms; and even the pirates seemed to respect him, for no one molested him.

Most of the pirates were engaged in dragging the prisoners to the masts to bind them. Jones had gone into the cabin. I saw that no one was observing me. I hurried past my old friends. "Hush," I whispered, in a voice they could just hear; "I am honest still. Do not recognise me—I will save you if I can!"

"I knew he was true and good," said Mary, kissing her father, and trying to turn her eyes from me.

What courage did her words give me! That sweet child's trusting friendship was a reward for all I had suffered. I resolved to abstain still from the evil courses to which my companions were endeavouring to lead me. I gave a glance over the stern, as if I had been looking to see what had become of the gig which had boarded at that end of the ship, and I again passed my friends without noticing them. I guessed that Mark Anthony would have been watching me, and I was right.

"What, you like pirating, Massa Peter! You run about like little dog, quite frisky—not know what to do," he remarked, with a grin. He was fond of giving things their proper names. Jones would have been horrified at being called a pirate; and even Hawk did not like the term, though in his bitter moments he used it.

"I have no help for it," I answered, with, I hope, excusable duplicity. "The fact is, Mark, I had formed a wrong opinion of you gentlemen; and in future I hope to make as bold a robber as the best of you."

"Berry good, berry good, my boy!" said the black, grasping my fist with his huge rough hand. "Me tell Captain Hawk, Massa Peter now take oath." I had not thought of that dreadful ceremony when I boasted of being ready to turn pirate; and, as I had a true idea of the sacredness of an oath, I knew that I must be betrayed if I was asked to take it, by refusing, as I must, to do so.

Jones now came out of the cabin, and went up to the captain. "Captain Dean," he said, "for such, I find, is your name, you must order your people the pirates returned to the schooner for the night, leaving the [with] the third mate and a small guard, including me, in charge of [ ] before he left the vessel, Hawk called me aside.

[ ]ave you on board of the prize, Peter," he said, "because, though [ ] young and untried, yet you have more of humanity about you than [ ] of my followers, and I can place more confidence in you. I must, [ ]er, have you take the oath of our band, to the effect that you will not [ ] the ship, betray a comrade, or separate from the rest till our compact [ ]solved by mutual agreement."

I thought, as seriously and as rapidly as I could, whether such an oath [w]ould not only preclude my own escape, but prevent me from assisting my [fr]iends. "It must effectually bind me to the pirates, and probably cause my [d]eath; but if I refuse to take it, I shall lose all chance of aiding Captain Dean and Mary, so for their sakes I will do as I am asked." I told Hawk I would no longer refuse to take the oath he proposed.

"Then swear," he said, repeating it, while a number of the pirates gathered round.

"I swear," I said, in a voice which must, I thought, betray my emotion. The pirates cheered and welcomed me as a brother among them. At that instant a peal of thunder echoed along the rocks of the shore, and vivid lightning darted from the sky.

I presumptuously thought at the time that the anger of Heaven was thus shown for the crime I had committed. I trembled violently; and had it not been dark, my confusion would have been discovered. The pirates were, however, in a hurry to depart, and, stepping into their boats, which were again deeply laden, they pulled up the harbour, leaving me and my companions in charge of the ship and twice as many prisoners as we ourselves numbered.

into the boats, to tow this vessel close in shore, where you must anchor, to discharge some of your cargo."

"I have no longer command of this vessel," replied the captain; "if the people choose to obey you, I have no power to prevent them."

"We have the means of making them do what we please, though," exclaimed Abraham Jones. "Here, you, get your boats into the water, and tow us ahead." He pointed to several of the Mary's crew, who were released, and compelled by the pirates to do as he ordered. The pirates' long-boat also went ahead, to assist in towing; while four men were stationed at the bows with muskets in their hands, to fire on the boats should they attempt to escape. The rest who remained, I zealously assisting them, cleaved and brailed up the sails. When ordered by Jones, I, without hesitation, seized a musket and pointed it at the boats.

Captain Dean, still holding Mary in his arms, sat aft, without moving. He seemed completely stunned with the blow which had fallen on him, for the cruel robbery would prove his ruin.

It was an arduous operation, towing the vessel in; for a current set along shore, it seemed, and drifted her to the southward of the entrance to the lagoon. I have before described the heat of a tropical sun; and very hot work indeed was this towing. But more particularly disagreeable was it for the crew of the barque, who could not tell but, at the end of it, their lives might be sacrificed by their captors; while the pirates, on the contrary, had the satisfaction of having a rich booty in store. At last, after five hours' incessant labour, we got, as near as the depth of water would allow, to the mouth of the harbour, and the anchor was dropped to the bottom.

Overcome by the heat, the pirates now came out of the boats, and, rushing below, brought a spirit cask on deck, which they forthwith broached. I trembled for the consequences. Jones did all he could to prevent their becoming intoxicated; but they only laughed and jeered at him, and asked who made him an officer over them.

I ought to have said that, as soon as the barque had anchored, those of her crew who were in their boats were turned adrift without oars or masts or sails, or anything to guide them, and allowed to float wherever the current might carry them. As it happened, there was but little current there, and consequently they remained but a short distance off, afraid to attempt either to regain the ship or to reach the shore.

Louder and louder grew the mirth of the pirates, and wilder their looks and gestures, as the powerful liquor they were swallowing took effect on their brains. I saw Mary cling closer to her father in fear and trembling, all the time watching me with furtive glances, lest she should be observed by her captors. I kept my musket in my hand, pretending to be watching the boats; and as they were now astern, I came aft for that purpose. What might have been the result of the prolonged orgies of the pirates it is impossible to say; but just as two or three had begun to stagger on their feet, and, with their knives in their hands, to cast their bloodshot eyes round as if looking for some victim for their insane fury, a small boat shot out of the harbour and rapidly approached the ship.

In a few minutes Captain Hawk stood on the deck of the prize, just in time to prevent one of his men from killing the first mate of the vessel, who remained all the time bound to the mast. He then turned fiercely on Jones, and reprimanded him for not having restrained the people more effectually. With a blow of his fist he knocked down the three most drunken of his followers, and the rest appeared instantly sobered. Without a murmur they threw the remainder of the spirits over-board, and under his directions commenced hoisting out such part of the cargo as he considered most valuable.

Captain Dean was not molested; nor was any notice taken of the boats which were drifting in shore, and would, I hoped, reach it, and thus enable the crews to find means by which to return to the ship, and perhaps to escape. On a sudden it seemed to strike some of the pirates that there was no use working while there were people they could compel to work for them; and to my sorrow two armed boats were instantly sent off to tow back the two which were drifting away. Resistance was vain, so the poor fellows were compelled to work in hoisting the cargo out of their own ship, and afterwards in pulling up the lagoon to the schooner. When I saw that the pirates allowed the strangers to see their place of concealment, I trembled for the fate of the latter, and feared greatly that the result would be their destruction, to prevent their discovering it to others.

The boats were all away, and six of the pirates, with Captain Hawk and myself, were the only persons besides the prisoners who remained on board. Hawk had observed my apparent zeal, I suspect, for he said to me, "I am glad to see that you are overcoming your foolish scruples, Peter; and to show the confidence I place in you, I will give you charge of the old master and his daughter. Take care they do not communicate with any of the other prisoners or assist, to release them."

My heart leaped within me at the chance thus offered of assisting my friends; at the same time I considered whether I ought to betray the confidence placed in me.

"I'll keep an eye on them, sir," I answ[...]
same time I took my post opposite to then[...]
I observed that Mary turned her head away[...]
observe the satisfaction she felt at this arrangen[...]
all his followers, went below to make a more n[...]
nature of the cargo.

As soon as they had disappeared, I ran up to M[...]
knelt down; I kissed their hands, and with tears in my[...]
that I had been long looking for them, and was guiltless of[...]
the pirates. "I will risk my life to liberate you," I added. "B[...]
the watch for whatever may occur. Perhaps to-night something[...]
our projects; perhaps it may be weeks before I find the mean[...]
you."

"I knew you would, I knew you would," exclaimed Mary. "Father,[...]
will help us to escape." Captain Dean, by a strong effort, roused hin[...]
from the state of stupor into which he was near falling. He took my han[...]
and grasped it tightly.

"Peter," he said, "I will trust you, though appearances are solely against you. For the sake of humanity—for this sweet child's sake—I pray that you will not deceive us."

I again assured him that I was true, and that, when I had time, I would explain how it all had happened; and then, fearful of being seen, I retired to my post to act sentinel as before.

On Hawk's returning on deck, he ordered Captain Dean and Mary into the cabin below, and told them that they must remain there till he had determined what should be done with the ship. My poor friend obeyed without a murmur, and, taking Mary by the hand, conducted her to his state-room, into which he entered and closed the door. I heard him say, while I was still close to it, "Kneel, my child, kneel, and pray to God to protect us."

The boats had made only two trips to the shore before it was dark, and still very much of the property the pirates wished to appropriate remained on board. When they returned for the last time, there were various discussions as to what should be done with the vessel. Some were for landing everything of value, and then burning her; others proposed scuttling her, with her people on board; a few suggested that they might be allowed to escape in their boats, as there was little probability of their ever reaching land; while the most humane voted for allowing the ship to depart when they had taken all they required out of her.

Chapter Seventeen

I did not go to sleep, it may be supposed, but walked the deck, considering what I should do. I had never spoken much with the third mate, who was now commanding officer; and I felt less inclination than ever to enter into conversation with him, so I only went near him when I was obliged to do so, to report that all was right.

He was a surly ruffian, in no way superior to the rest of the people, except that, from having been at sea all his life, he was a tolerable seaman. It was with some difficulty that I gained permission from him to carry some food and water to the prisoners, or I believe he would have allowed them to starve. I dared not tell them that I was a friend, lest some might incautiously betray me. Wherever I went, also, Mark Anthony followed, and narrowly watched my proceedings. I observed him, though I pretended not to do so, and was trying to devise some means of lulling the suspicions he evidently still entertained of me.

The mate's name was John Pinto, a Portuguese by birth, though he said he was an American, and he spoke English well. I knew that he was addicted to liquor, when he could indulge in it without fear of the consequences. I had found several bottles of fine old Jamaica rum in the cabin, so I brought one up on deck, with a monkey full of cool water, and saying that I was very thirsty after the day's work, and must have a glass, asked him if he would have one also. He consented, and I poured him out a stiff tumblerful, the strength of which was concealed by the coolness of the water.

"Very good indeed," he growled out. "Peter, you understand these things; give me another." I did so, and made it even stronger than the first. He liked it accordingly even better, and took several others in quick succession. I was not afraid of his growing furious, for, from the nature of the man, I knew that he would only become stupid, and finally would fall asleep. With much satisfaction I saw this effect take place.

"Now I am commanding officer," I thought, "and I will see what is next to be done." Just as I had thought this, and had stood up to look around me, I felt the hot breeze coming off the land. An idea struck me, if I could but liberate the prisoners, they might run the vessel far away to sea before the morning, and out of the reach of the pirates.

How to accomplish this was the next thought. Go with them I could not, on account of my oath, and I was also bound to the rest. There was a sentry placed before Captain Dean's cabin. I determined to make him tipsy also, I had recourse to the old rum, and with the same effect it had on the mate. Two men walked the deck near the main hatchway, the other four were forward. The prisoners were in the hold, and my great difficulty was to get to them.

I went on deck to watch the two men. They were sitting down, and I had hopes were asleep. Mark Anthony, whom I most feared, was forward. The night had become very dark, so I went close to them without being perceived, and I could distinguish by the tones of their voices that all four were talking together. On this I crept back to the cabin. The sentry was snoring in complete insensibility, so I dragged him on one side, and tapped softly at the door of the state-cabin.

"It is Peter," I whispered. "Open the door, I have something to say." Mary knew my voice, and opened it before I had done speaking, for I had unlocked it from the outside.

"Captain Dean," I said, in a hurried tone, "the wind is off the shore; two of your guards are unconscious from drink; and if I can but make the rest so, or you can manage to overpower them, you may regain possession of your vessel. I can neither assist you further, nor can I accompany you, for at all risks I must return to the schooner."

"Oh no, no," exclaimed Mary, "you must go with us; we cannot leave you behind with those dreadful men."

"I have taken an oath, Mary, and I must remain," I replied. "But have no fears for me. I shall, I trust, finally escape from the toils which surround me, and we may meet again." For some time I continued in the same strain, and finally succeeded in winning her over to my view of the case. I had less difficulty in persuading her father that there was no other chance of escape; and I urged on him the duty he owed to his owners as well as to his child, if not to himself.

With several bottles of old rum I returned on deck, and with one in my hand I sat myself down near the two men guarding the hatchway.

"The mate finds this stuff very good," said I; "will you take a glass?" They did not say no, but pronounced it excellent.

"The rest should not be kept out of their share," I remarked; "I'll take them some." To this they would not agree; and wishing to keep it all to themselves, drank it down much faster than they would otherwise have done. I took the empty bottle away, and put a full one in its place, much to their surprise, for they did not suspect my trick. Favouring my design, the others heard them praising the rum, and asked them what they were about. I instantly ran forward with two bottles.

"They have got some spirits which they think very good, and I have brought you some bottles. There are several more stowed away somewhere on deck, and if I can find them I will bring them to you."

"Bear a hand and bring them to us, but do not let Pinto see you, or he will be laying an embargo on them," said one of the men in a low voice, thinking the mate might hear him.

In a short time all the pirates, including even Mark Anthony, were lying about the decks in a state of helpless intoxication.

With my knees trembling with agitation, I hurried aft, and told Captain Dean what had occurred. Leaving Mary in the cabin, he accompanied me on deck, and we instantly set to work to get the hatches off. We succeeded, and, going below, found the mates and crew, most of them overcome with fatigue, fast asleep. It was the work of a minute to rouse them up, to explain what had happened, and to cut loose the lanyards with which they were secured.

I told them that they must make a simultaneous rush on deck; that they must bind me with the rest of the pirates; that they must put us into a boat with a couple of small sculls, just to enable us to reach the shore; and that they must then cut their cable, and get to sea as fast as possible.

"I do not see what should prevent us from carrying all hands off prisoners," said the first mate. The idea that they might do so had not occurred to me. I wished most cordially that they would, but my oath made it incumbent on me to return if I had the power.

"We must do as this young man requires," said Captain Dean. "We will abide by his decision."

"Then I must beg that you will without delay put me and my companions into a boat, and be off yourselves," I answered, with a sinking heart.

I crept first on deck, and lay down among the men forward. Presently the crew rushed on deck, and in a few minutes the previous order of things was completely reversed, and the pirates were bound and floating helplessly in a boat by themselves. The black, who was near me, was the only one who was aroused, and he saw me being bound like himself. He would have cried out, but a gag thrust into his mouth effectually prevented him.

With mingled feelings of pain and joy I saw, through the gloom, the sails of the *Mary* drop from their yards, and her cable being cut, she glided away into the obscurity of the distance. I uttered a prayer for the safety of those on board. I had no fears for myself; but I confess I wished that, notwithstanding my protestations, Captain Dean had forcibly detained me, though I, of course, was compelled to insist on being treated like the rest of the pirates, and he, not knowing my real wish, thought he was bound to do as I desired. Mary was all the time below, or her keen perception would have saved me, as she would have insisted on keeping me, in spite of myself. I repeated the oath I had taken over and over again, and I did not find that it in any way prevented me from liberating the prize. That any one would dream of doing such a thing had, I suppose, never occurred to its framers.

It was broad daylight before any of the people came to their senses. The black had been all the time, in a degree, awake, though his intellects were not very bright; he, however, had been too tightly bound hand and foot to move, while his mouth was too securely gagged to allow him to cry out. I arose with pretended difficulty; I saw his keen eye glaring on me. I looked over the gunwale: the *Mary* was nowhere to be seen. She had then escaped, and I returned thanks to Heaven for her safety.

The boat had been driven by the wind some way out to sea, and it occurred to me that there was a great probability of our being starved before we could regain the shore, should we not be seen by the schooner's crew. This idea gave way to the picture which presented itself of the rage and disappointment of the pirates when they found that their prize had escaped.

"They will wreak their vengeance on us all, perhaps—on my head especially, if it is suspected that I had a hand in liberating the prisoners. How can I avoid being suspected? The mate will recollect that I brought the rum to him; so will the others. They will compare notes, and I shall be accused of having plotted with the crew of the *Mary*. It will be asserted that I intended to accompany them, and to claim a reward—perhaps to bring a ship of war to the spot—and that they had played me false in placing me in the boat. It will not be supposed that I might have escaped, but would not break my oath. My condition is indeed perilous."

I was right in that respect. Never, perhaps, had I been in such imminent danger; but I forgot at the time that there is a higher Power ever watchful over men, and that it will assuredly protect those who act rightly.

Oh, let me urge my young friends, in their course through life, always to do what they know is right, fearless of consequences: let no consideration whatever induce them to act otherwise. They may not—probably do not—see the way by which they are to be preserved, but God, in His good time, will show it to them; or if they are exposed in consequence to suffering, will not fail, beyond all measure, to reward them.

I must explain that I do not feel quite certain that I was right in taking the oath. Even now that years have passed since that time, I am undecided as to that point; and therefore I trust that I may be pardoned if I was wrong in doing so, when I had no time for reflection.

When the black saw me move, he made various strange noises, to call my attention to his condition. I showed him that my hands were bound, but I contrived to crawl towards him; and though his hands were behind his back, he contrived so far to loosen the cords which bound mine (they were, in truth, but slightly secured, and I could have released them without aid), that I got them perfectly free. The first thing I did was to take the gag from his mouth; and oh, what a torrent of abuse flowed instantly out of it! He did not, however, suspect me, as I thought he would. We next released the rest, but they were still too overcome with the liquor to comprehend what had happened.

The wind was still off the shore, and the boat continued drifting out to sea, her speed increased by a current which set to the southward. The black recognised the mouth of the lagoon, which he knew well, but I could not make it out. The two sculls were found, and, bestowing many maledictions on his companions for not being able to drink with impunity, he made me take one of them, and attempt to pull towards the shore.

With the prospects I had in view, I had no particular wish to exert myself, and I saw that, even if I did so to the utmost, we could make no way against the breeze and the current setting in an opposite direction.

The sun rose, and struck down with burning fury on our heads; and I knew, when the wind fell, it would be hotter still. At length I began to feel the pangs of hunger, and, to my satisfaction, I found that some considerate friend had put a few biscuits and a keg of water into the boat. With this I refreshed myself, and so did the black; and I began to hope that he was grateful to me for releasing him from the gag, and that he would bear witness to having seen me bound like the rest.

When we found that we could make no way with the paddles, we gave it up, and set to work to try and revive our companions. We unlashed their arms and legs, and by degrees they came to themselves. They were very much surprised at what had happened, and could not account for it.

"Well, no use talking here," observed Mark Anthony, whose wits being brighter than theirs, was for active measures. "If we no get on shore, we all die togeder."

I suggested that we might manufacture some more paddles out of the bottom-boards; and that by bending our handkerchiefs and jackets together we might form a sail, which, when the sea-breeze set in, might enable us to reach some part of the coast. No one having any better advice to offer, mine was adopted: two more pairs of paddles were formed; but though they enabled us to make some little headway, it was very slowly.

My companions now grew weary; and the looked-for breeze not arriving, they began to lose their tempers, as people are apt to do, even without so much reason, after a debauch.

"It was all your fault, youngster," suddenly exclaimed the mate, turning to me; "you brought me the stuff which capsized me."

"And he brought it to us," said one of the men who had been guarding the main-hatchway.

"And to us also," cried those who had been forward.

"Den," exclaimed the black, giving a most diabolical grin from ear to ear, which made my blood run cold, "he done it on purpose: dere was someting in it, no doubt."

Oh, now my heart sunk within me; for their suspicions once being set on the right scent, I feared they would discover the truth. However, I put a bold face on the matter, and answered, "I found the spirit—I tasted it, and thought it very good, so I brought it to you. I am in as bad a condition as any of you; so I gained nothing by treachery, if I was guilty of it."

"Ah, but you hoped to do so!" exclaimed the mate. "It wasn't your wish to remain with us, but you could not help yourself." Thus the discussion went on, till they arrived very nearly at the truth. I said nothing, but listened, expecting every moment to be my last. Some proposed throwing me overboard at once; but the black suggested that the captain would be angry at such a proceeding, and that it would be far better to carry me in alive, and to torment me before they put me to death.

I told them that they had no proof of my guilt, and that I denied the accusation of having put anything into the liquor, and that I was certain that Captain Hawk would acquit me.

They were still threatening me, when the black, who was standing up, on looking towards the mouth of the harbour, espied two boats pulling out towards us. Our comrades must have seen us with their glasses from the shore, and were coming to our assistance. They could not possibly be more than four miles off. Scarcely had the rest time to discover the specks they seemed on the water, when I observed a sail just rounding the west side of the island, and standing, with a fresh breeze, directly for us. It was not long before she was discovered by the rest.

She was a large brig, and, from the squareness of her yards, she looked like a man-of-war. Down she came rapidly on us, as yet unperceived by the people in the boats, as a point of high land, covered with trees, hid her completely from them. The black jumped up, and watched her, with lips apart and staring eyeballs, for some time.

"De brig we fought de oder day!" he exclaimed. "If he see we, den we all hang." And he sunk down at the bottom of the boat, intimating to the rest to follow his example.

I scarcely knew whether to wish that the American brig-of-war—for such I felt convinced she was—should discover us, or whether we might get into the harbour unperceived.

In the latter case, the probabilities were that the pirates would put me to death. In the former, I ran a great risk of being hung because I was a pirate; or the boat might drift out to sea, and a lingering death would be our portion. Neither alternative afforded a pleasant subject of contemplation.

The boats from the shore were all this time approaching us. At last they saw the topgallant-mast's heads of the brig over the point; but I suppose they fancied they were those of the *Mary*, for they continued their course. In a short time, however, they perceived their mistake; but the brig had got clear of the land, and they were full in view of any sharp eyes stationed on her tops. They directly pulled back, and we lost sight of them almost immediately.

The brig came on, and at first, after rounding the point, stood on a course which would have carried her inside of us, but, on discovering the boat, she again stood towards us. The fright of all hands in the boat was excessive, and the bold blustering pirates proved themselves cowards indeed. The African was the bravest, for the death he expected had few terrors for him. He even had presence of mind sufficient to suggest that we should invent a plausible tale of having been cast adrift by the rest of the crew of a ship who had run off with her: All eagerly grasped at the idea; but before the tale was thoroughly concocted, the brig was alongside of us, and we were very unceremoniously hauled on board.

We were immediately taken before the captain and his officers in full uniform, who stood round him on the quarter-deck.

"What brought you out here?" he demanded of the mate, who from his dress seemed to be the officer. Pinto told the tale which had just been invented.

"And what are those boats doing inshore of us?" was the next question.

"I know nothing of the boats," was Pinto's answer; but the appearance and dogged manner of my companions had raised suspicions in the minds of the American officers which were not easily allayed.

Meantime the brig had hauled her wind, and was standing inshore with the lead going, in the direction the boats had taken. Officers with sharp eyes were also stationed at each fore-yardarm to look out for coral reefs. The *Foam's* boats reached the entrance to the lagoon just as the brig dropped her anchor, it being considered dangerous to approach nearer the shore.

The brig, I found, was the *Neptune*, Captain Faith. She was a remarkably fine vessel, carrying nineteen guns, and had been sent out expressly to look for the *Foam*. Captain Faith and his officers were burning to revenge the insult offered them shortly before by the schooner. It appeared that they had, by some means, notice of her whereabouts, and when they saw the retreating boats, they had little doubt of the true state of the case.

We were all kept separate from each other, and were questioned one by one. What the others said I do not exactly know, but I have reason to believe that not one of them told the same story, I was the last interrogated. "And what have you got to say for yourself?" asked the lieutenant.

"That I was last night put into this boat with the rest, with my hands bound behind my back," I replied.

"And you believe that the people who so treated you have run off with the ship to turn pirates?"

"I do not believe it," I answered. "I knew the captain, who was a kind friend of mine, and the ship was his own. If you ever meet Captain Dean of the *Mary*, he will corroborate what I say."

"This is a new version of the story," replied the lieutenant.

"It is the true one; of that you may be assured," I replied. "I would willingly tell you more, but I cannot, so there is no use questioning me."

"We shall soon see that," he observed. "Those who will not speak when they can, must be made to speak."

I was silent; for if I said more, I was afraid of running the risk of breaking my oath, by betraying Hawk and his followers.

The attention of all on board was now taken up by the manning of the boats, which were, I found, to be sent up forthwith, on an expedition in search of the pirates. Oh, how I longed to warn the brave men I saw with such joyful alacrity getting ready, of the great risk they were about to run!

The schooner, I knew, had ten guns on board, and the pirates would be able so to place her as to offer a stout resistance, if not to defeat the man-of-war's boats completely.

Four of the brig's boats were sent away, to which was added the one in which I had been taken; so that there was a pretty strong flotilla engaged in the expedition. Remembering, however, the extreme narrowness of the passage, I felt that if the pirates landed, and simply fired down upon their assailants, they might pick every one of them off, without the slightest risk to themselves. I was very much afraid of being compelled to accompany the boats—not that I feared the danger, but I thought that Hawk would fancy that I did so willingly; and though he might be defeated and killed, I did not like the idea of his dying with the impression on his mind that I had betrayed him; or, on the contrary, if the boats were destroyed, of course I could expect no mercy at his hands. With aching eyes I saw them enter the mouth of the lagoon; and perhaps no one on board felt a greater interest in their proceedings than I did.

Chapter Eighteen

I was allowed to remain on deck, under charge of a sentry, but was in no other way treated as a prisoner. Half-an-hour elapsed, during which the boats were probably looking for the pirate vessel, without a shot being heard. It was a time of the most intense anxiety. At length, as if to make amends for the previous silence, the roar of big guns and musketry was heard reverberating in quick succession among the rocks. One fancied that one could distinguish as each boat came up to the contest, and the schooner fired at her in return. The wreaths of smoke could be perceived in the atmosphere, rising above the trees. Once there was a cessation; and it appeared that the boats were driven back. One thing was certain, the pirates had not attempted to stop them at the narrow passage, as they might have done; or, if they had, they had successfully passed it.

Five minutes elapsed—they seemed an hour. Then again the hubbub recommenced, with greater fury than before. So excited did many of the men, and even the officers, become, that I almost thought they would leap into the water, and try to swim to shore, to join in the combat. I fancied that I could even hear the cries and shrieks of the combatants—that I could see the whole scene before me, through the trees; the boats at the mouth of the bight, firing away at the schooner, their officers cheering the men on; the pirates, stripped to the waist, working the guns of the schooner, some on board, and others on either point on shore, with small-armed men scattered in every direction around. The prolonged fight made me feel very doubtful of the result of the contest. There was a pause, and then a loud, fearful explosion, and the masts and spars and fragments of the pirate schooner could be seen rising in the air. She had blown up; but still it might be questioned who were the victors.

There was another interval of the most intense anxiety. In vain we waited for the reappearance of the boats, till the *Neptune's* people began to fear that their brave shipmates had been all destroyed. There was only one small boat, the dinghy, remaining on board. The master, the only gun-room officer left besides the surgeon and purser, volunteered to go in and look for them. I was on the very point of offering to accompany him as pilot, when I remembered that I was supposed to know nothing of the place. The commander gave an unwilling consent, for he did not like to risk more of his people. He was just shoving off, when first one boat was seen to emerge from among the trees, then another, and lastly four appeared—thus one only was missing. They pulled slowly on board, and were seen to be heavily laden.

With a shout of joy and hearty congratulation, they were received alongside; but the entire satisfaction at the success of the expedition was somewhat mitigated when it was found that several of their numbers were missing. They had brought off ten prisoners, most of whom were wounded. Some of the packages which had been taken from the *Mary* were also brought on board. Neither Hawk nor Abraham Jones were among the prisoners: I therefore concluded that they were killed or had escaped. The prisoners, to my horror, at once recognised me and the rest of their comrades, addressing us familiarly by our names, and thus completely identified us with themselves. I suppose they did this from a feeling of revenge, from fancying that we had been the cause of their disaster. The captain, on this, ordered us all to be secured and treated as prisoners alike, till he had time to investigate the matter fully.

I heard an account of the expedition from one of the seamen who had been engaged in it, as he described it to a messmate. It appeared that the pirates had at once gone on board the schooner, which they had placed, just as I supposed they would, directly across the entrance of the bight. Here Hawk fought her most bravely, once compelling the boats to retreat.

On a second attempt to board, she was discovered to be on fire, notwithstanding which Hawk had remained in the vessel till the last moment, when, leaping into the boats, he and some of his crew escaped to the shore. Many of them, who could not, were blown up. Fortunately, one boat's crew only of the Americans had got on board by the stern. Several of these poor fellows were lost; but, wonderful to relate, others, by leaping over the taffrail at the moment they felt it lifting under their feet, were saved and picked up by their friends. It was considered useless to pursue the fugitives. The prisoners taken were those picked up in the water, and a few found wounded on shore. Securing them, and attending to the wounded of both parties, as well as collecting some of the booty, had caused the delay. The guns, also, planted by the pirates at the two points of land on either side of the bight, were spiked and thrown into the water, and all arms found about were carried off.

Such was the end of the *Foam*; and such will, in every ease, probably be the concluding scene of piratical craft and their crews now-a-days. They certainly deserve no better; and although their captains, to rise to that unenviable post, must possess some of those fiercer qualities which people are apt to admire, I have no fancy for making them interesting characters, or heroes of romance.

On hearing that there was a considerable amount of booty on shore, the captain despatched fresh hands to bring it off. I longed to caution them that Hawk, if he was alive, was a man very likely to play them a trick, but I had no opportunity of doing so till they had gone. The boats were sent away, and I was afterwards had up for examination. I then, as the schooner was destroyed, no longer felt myself bound by my oath to keep silence; I therefore gave a rapid sketch of my adventures as the best way of accounting for being found in such bad company. The captain laughed at my statements, which, he said, were altogether incredible, and assured me that he fully believed that I deserved hanging as much as the rest.

I assured him that I had not deceived him, and requested him to confront the negro, Mark Anthony, with me, and that he would corroborate all my assertions. Had I known more of the worst part of human nature, I might not have made this request. When the black was brought up, he gave a malicious grin at me, and, putting his hand on his heart, assured the captain and officers that, as he spoke the truth, I was the most wicked, vicious youngster on board the schooner, to which he knew that it was useless to deny that he belonged—that he was perfectly innocent of any piratical act, having been carried off to act as cook—that he had at first taken an interest in me, and had done his best to reform me, but in vain, and that lately he had given my case up as hopeless.

"What do you mean by lately?" I asked.

"Just de last six months or so," he answered, with the greatest effrontery.

"I beg, gentlemen, that his answer may be noted; for I hope to be able to prove that I have not been on board the schooner as many weeks," I said, with a calm voice, which had, I think, some effect on my hearers.

There was such a mass of false swearing and contradictory evidence taken during the examination, that the naval officers were compelled to reserve any judgment on the case till they should arrive in port, when it might be handed over to the lawyers to sift to the bottom. Greatly to my satisfaction, the boats returned laden with further goods taken from the *Mary*; but it required two more trips before they could all be brought off. The task was at last accomplished, without any of the pirates having made their appearance, and sail was then made to the northward.

I found that our destination was Charleston, to which port the brig belonged, and where my trial and that of the other prisoners would take place. Had it been New Orleans, I thought I might have been able to prove that I had gone to sea in the *Susannah*, and Captain Searle might be found, who would give a favourable account of me. While I was thinking of this, I suddenly began to reflect that perhaps Captain Searle might turn upon me as the African had done, though for a different reason. He would be able to prove that I was at New Orleans, certainly, but then the *Foam* was there at the same time. She had watched, attacked, and robbed him, and taken out of his vessel me and another person, who, without any unwillingness, had turned pirate, so that I had perhaps all along been in league with the freebooters, and my pretended ignorance of Hawk and his craft might have been all sham. I might indeed be considered, as the negro declared I was, worse than all the rest.

As I reflected on these things, I remembered that my destiny was in the hands of a higher Power; that I had acted rightly according to the best of my belief; and that He would direct all things for my future good. This feeling gave me strength to endure the present and confidence in the future. I have thus invariably found it in all the affairs of life. When I have conscientiously done my duty, though inconveniences and annoyances may have apparently happened in consequence, the end has always been fortunate when I have been able to arrive at the result. The consequence of many of our acts, we must remember, is yet in the eternal future, unfathomed by mortal ken. To that time we must look forward for the reward of any of our acts which may be considered by our beneficent Father worthy of reward; and also to that time (we must not conceal from ourselves) for punishment for our misdeeds, unless our Saviour mercifully intercede for us.

Our voyage to Charleston was very rapid. I certainly was in no hurry to have it over, when I had so disagreeable a prospect before me as a trial, and not impossibly an execution. I was treated with less harshness than the rest of the prisoners—perhaps on account of my youth—perhaps because some believed me innocent. I fain hoped on the latter account.

At length we arrived. I will not stop to describe Charleston. It is a fine, flourishing city, with a dock-yard, where many of the ships of the American navy are built. I saw little of it, for soon after the *Neptune* had dropped her anchor I was conveyed with the other prisoners on shore to jail.

The Americans are as fond, fortunately, of the go-ahead system in law as they are in everything else. In the settlements founded by Spain and Portugal, we might have been kept six months without being brought into court; here, before as many days were over, our trial commenced. The fate of those taken in the schooner was easily settled. Several robberies were proved against them; and she was sworn to as the same vessel which had fired into the brig off the coast of Cuba, and had there carried the pirate flag, besides having also killed and wounded several officers and men in the United States navy.

The trial of the people in the boat next came on. The others swore that we belonged to the schooner and the negro, in the bitterness of his feelings against me, had acknowledged the same. I told my history as my best defence.

"Ask him if he can swear he no fire de big guns—he no pull and haul—when we fight de brig," exclaimed the malignant black, perfectly indifferent to his own fate. I held my peace.

"Prisoner at the bar, can you swear that you did not aid and abet those engaged in making unlawful war against the United States brig *Neptune*?"

"I cannot swear to that, because, in a fatal fit of forgetfulness, seeing every one excited around me, I might have pulled and hauled at the ropes of the schooner."

"An acknowledgment of his guilt?" exclaimed the counsel for the Government; and I, with all the rest, was adjudged to be hung at the end of the week at the yardarm of the brig which had captured us. Never was a nest of more atrocious pirates broken up, said the public papers, commenting on the trial, and never were men adjudged to meet a more deserved doom.

Now the reader will almost be prepared to know how I was saved. I must own that I never expected to be hung. I felt that I was innocent, and I trusted that some means would be offered for my escape.

Just as I was being led out of court, there was a cry of "Witnesses! witnesses for the trial of the pirates!" Looking up, I saw several seafaring men entering the court, and among them two persons whose appearance at that juncture made my heart leap into my mouth with joy and gratitude, and proved that the finger of God had directed their coming. Need I say that they were Captain Dean and Mary, and that the other people were the crew of the barque, released from the power of the pirates by my means?

Their story created a great sensation in court; and Captain Dean was ready to swear, from his knowledge of me, that I had no willing participation in any of the acts of the pirates. My story was now believed; but I had acknowledged having worked the guns in the action with the brig, and I had, by the evidence of all present, willingly, and of my own accord, rejoined the pirates, though every opportunity had been offered me of escaping.

I urged my oath in extenuation of my conduct, and that I was bound to return. This was not held in law to be any excuse. I had no business to take an oath of that nature, it was asserted by the counsel for the Government. The sentence of death against me was, however, rescinded, on account of the many extenuating circumstances brought forward in my favour; but still I could not be set at liberty.

The sentence of the people who had been found with me in the boat was afterwards commuted to imprisonment for fourteen years; and I was offered a conditional pardon, provided I would volunteer to serve for two years on board a ship of war just then about to sail, and short of hands.

I was sorry to be again thus separated from Captain Dean and Mary; but as I had no dread of the service, I, without much hesitation, accepted the offer. "I will do my duty and retrieve my character," I thought; "and as, I trust, there is no chance of a war with England, I see no reason to prevent me."

Chapter Nineteen

The next day I found myself transferred on board the United States corvette *Pocahuntas*, of twenty guns, and one hundred and fifty men, including officers, marines, and petty officers. I found that she was bound to the North Seas; to look after the interests of the United States fisheries. She was strongly built and strengthened, so as to contend with the bad weather she might expect to meet, and the loose ice she was also likely to encounter. I shall describe her more particularly by and by.

The day after I had become one of the crew, while I was below, I was informed that a person was alongside inquiring for me. I looked over the side, and there I saw, as I expected, Captain Dean and Mary. They came on deck, and Mary was very nearly throwing her arms about my neck and kissing me, while her father took both my hands and held them in his.

"I owe everything to you, Peter," he said, and the tears stood in his eyes—"my life and property, and more, the safety of this dear child; and I do feel most cruelly not being able to make you any return. In England the sovereign would have given you a free pardon to a certainty; here, in such a case as yours, we have no one to appeal to. I have introduced myself to your captain, and, as he seems a kind man, I trust he will interest himself in you. I beg to offer you an outfit, which I have brought on board; and I fear that there is little else I can do for you. When you come back I shall be on the look-out for you, and then you must fulfil your promise of sailing with me. Make yourself a thorough seaman in the meantime, and I think I can promise you very soon the command of a ship."

Mary joined in, and entreated me first to take care of myself, and then to come back to Charleston to rejoin them.

"You know, Peter, I shall be nearly grown up by that time," she said, in her sweet, innocent, and lively manner, though she was half crying at the time. "Then, you know, if you become first mate, I shall be able to act as father's second mate; so we shall have quite a family party on board the dear old ship."

Thus we talked on, joking often through our sorrows, till it was time for my friends to go on shore. With heavy hearts we parted. Had we been able to see the future, haw much heavier would they have been! I found in the chest which they had brought me numberless little things, which all told of sweet Mary's care and forethought. I had just time to write a few hasty lines to my family, but the letter never reached home. While I was in prison, and my fate uncertain, I dared not write.

The next morning, at break of day, the boatswain's whistle roused me from my slumbers, and his gruff voice was heard bawling out, "All hands up anchor," followed with another pipe of "Man the capstan."

To a person accustomed to the merchant service, where, from the few hands which can be employed, the duty must be carried on slowly and cautiously, the work on board a man-of-war appears as if done almost by magic. The rapidity and certainty of action is gained only by great arrangement, method, and practice. Every man on board has his proper post and particular duties; and all are accustomed to listen for and obey the signal of command, be it the human voice, the boatswain's pipe, a peculiar flag, or the report of a great gun or musket. The crew are separated into two divisions, with their respective officers: these divisions are called watches—the starboard and larboard—because one does duty, or watches, while the other rests below.

On important occasions, when greater strength is required, or it is necessary to shorten sail in a hurry, or danger is apprehended, both watches, or all hands, are called. Thus, getting under weigh, or going into harbour, or at divisions and quarters, all hands are at their proper posts at the same time. Each top has its proper crew, who are known as fore-top men, main-top men, and mizzen-top men, whose duty is to tend the sails above them. On deck there are the sheet-anchor men stationed on the forecastle, whose duty is to tend the head-sails, anchors, etcetera, and consequently the most trustworthy veterans are selected for the office. In what is called the waist, or the centre of the ship, the landsmen and least skilful of the crew are placed. They have to pull and haul with the marines, and to clean the decks, and to do various ignoble duties below. From the part of the ship where they are stationed, they are called waisters. The after-guards are stationed on the quarter-deck, and have to tend the spanker and other after-sails, and to haul the main brace.

The officers are divided into commissioned officers, namely, the captain and the lieutenants, the master, surgeon, and purser; the warrant officers, who are boatswain, gunner, and carpenter, and the midshipmen; and, lastly, the petty officers, who have their rating given them on board ship by the captain or first lieutenant, and may be equally disrated by them.

There are slight variations in the British and United States navies; but the latter has adhered very closely to the customs of the former; and however republican our well-beloved cousins may be on shore, afloat they wisely carry out the principles of an absolute monarchy in the most perfect manner.

There are certain general duties in which all hands are engaged, and in which each has a number. Thus a man has one number at mess, another at quarters, and another at divisions. Discipline is everything on board a man-of-war. Without it such a mass of people could not possibly be moved together, and all would be confusion and constant disaster. There must be a head to command, either worn by the captain or first lieutenant. If the latter is a good seaman, all may go well in spite of the incapacity of his superior; but a clever captain will never submit to have a stupid first, so that it is seldom that the office of first lieutenant is held by other than a good seaman. It would take up too much space were I to attempt to describe all the grades and offices on board a man-of-war. It will suffice when I state that every man has his proper place, and that one follows the other in rank, down to the lowest rated officer. I was rated as an able seaman, which I considered a high honour, considering the little knowledge I felt myself to possess, and was placed in the after-guard. I had to take my trick at the helm, which I was also glad of, as it enabled me to perfect myself in steering.

The commander, Captain Gierstien, was a man who had seen much of the world, and was, I have reason to believe, a very good seaman; so was Mr Stunt, the first lieutenant, who was a disciplinarian of the most rigid school; and certainly the ship was in very good order as a man-of-war. But there was a sad want of any of the milder influences which govern human beings. Kind words and considerate treatment were not to be found. This I soon discovered; and it seemed as if a leaden weight were attached to my heart. Strict regulations, the cat, and fear did everything. How the second lieutenant, Mr Dunning, contrived to gain his rank I do not know, for he was nothing at all of a practical seaman but then he spouted poetry, and wrote verses in praise of freedom; and this talent, I conclude, had gained him his appointment, though, by the bye, the verses appeared to be very bad.

There were several of my own messmates with whom I became intimate. Though rough in manner, they were kind of heart; and I will say of two or three of them, that all their sentiments were such as no gentleman need have been ashamed of possessing. I found them both agreeable and instructive companions; and I was glad to enjoy their friendship, the more from the very want of kindly feelings which prevailed generally throughout the ship. Andrew Thompson was my greatest chum. He was a true-hearted seaman, every inch of him. He had been all his life at sea, and had had his eyes open, as the saying is, all the time. He used to take great delight in describing the countries he had visited, and the ports and harbours in which he had brought up, as also in giving me instruction in all branches of seamanship.

My other friend was called Terence O'Connor, an Irishman, as his name betokens, with all the good qualities generally ascribed to the natives of that country. He liked me, as being a countryman, in the first place; and secondly, because I liked him. He was still young, and had nothing of the Mentor about him, like Thompson. He was brave, and true as steel. I should not say that he was a first-rate seaman; but he was active and energetic, and he knew how to obey—indeed, he was a capital hand to have as a mate.

There was also an English lad I liked much, Tom Stokes by name. He was not very bright, and he used to be sadly bullied by the crew; but as I was strong, could and did protect him, and his gratitude won my regard. He had been tolerably well educated; and being fond of reading, with a retentive memory, he possessed a good deal of information. Left an orphan, without a friend in the world, he had come to sea; and quitting his ship at Charleston, he had entered on board the Pocahuntas. I mention these three of my shipmates for reasons which will hereafter be seen. I had several other friends, whom I liked more perhaps than Tom Stokes, and as much as O'Connor, but I need not describe them.

We had fine weather on first putting to sea, and had thus time to let everything shake into its place before a gale came on. It was early in the year, but for some reason or other we were ordered to get northward as fast as we could. For the first week we had calms, and then the wind came ahead, so that our progress was very slow. Instead of running through the Gulf of Saint Lawrence, we were to keep on the eastern coast of Newfoundland, and to approach the northern shore of Labrador.

"You'll want your Flushing jacket and trousers, not forgetting worsted socks and gloves, my boy, when you get there," said Thompson, who gave me this information. "You've never felt anything like the cold, nor seen anything like the fogs, to be found in those parts."

He told me that few Europeans had settled on the coast of Labrador; but that some Moravian missionaries were stationed at four or five spots, for the purpose of converting the Esquimaux to Christianity. "Those must be Christians, indeed, to my mind, who will go and live in such a climate, for the sake of teaching their religion to the ignorant heathen, who would not otherwise have a chance of having the truths of the gospel preached to them," he observed; and I agreed with him. "I've been told," he continued, "that during the winter the thermometer often falls 30 degrees below the freezing point; and though the houses of the missionaries are heated by stoves, the windows and walls are covered all the time with ice, and the bed-clothes freeze to the walls. Rum is frozen in the air as rapidly as water, and rectified spirits soon become thick like oil. From December to June the sea is so completely frozen over that no open water is to be seen. Once some of the missionaries ventured, in February, to visit some Esquimaux forty miles distant, and although wrapped in furs, they were nearly destroyed. Their eyelids froze together, so that they were continually obliged to pull them asunder, and, by constantly rubbing, prevent their closing; while one of them had his hands frozen and swollen up like bladders. During their short summer, however, the heat is excessive; and mosquitoes, in swarms, infest the air."

"I hope we shall not have long to remain in those regions," I remarked.

"I hope not," said Thompson; "but who can tell? Ships, when they get into the ice, cannot always get out again, and some have been frozen up for several years together; yet, by proper precautions, few of the people on board have died, and at length have returned to their friends and country."

"It must be very dreary work, Andrew, having nothing but the ice and snow to look at for such a length of time together," I remarked.

"I'll tell you what, Peter, when you have lived as long as I have, you will discover, I hope, that it is not what one sees on the outside, so much as what is in the inside of a man, which makes him happy and contented, or the contrary," said Andrew. "Now I have met several men, who have passed two winters running in those regions, when the sun was not to be seen for months together, and ice and snow was all around them; but the captain and officers being kind, and doing everything to amuse them and to take care of their health, they assured me they never enjoyed themselves more in their lives."

"I would rather not try it in our present ship."

"Nor would I, Peter," said Andrew; and the subject dropped.

"What an odd name they have given to our ship!" I remarked one day, when Tom Stokes was near; "I cannot think where it comes from."

"Oh, I can tell you, Peter," said Tom, sitting down close to me. "I read some time ago a history of North America, and I remember meeting with the name of Pocahuntas. You must know that she was an Indian princess, that is to say, she was the daughter of a powerful chief inhabiting that part of the country which is now the State of Virginia. A small body of English, had settled there, with a governor, a handsome young man, placed over them. They were cultivating the ground and building houses in fancied security, when the Indians attacked them, killed some, and carried off others, among whom was the governor, as prisoners. It was the custom of the Indians to torture their prisoners in the most dreadful way before killing them. Such was to be the lot of the governor; but, fortunately for him, he was seen by Pocahuntas, who instantly fell in love with him, and interceded for his life with her father. The prayer was granted, on condition that he would become her husband. He was too glad to accept his life on such terms; for the young lady was very beautiful, and he would thereby form an alliance with a very powerful tribe, and secure his countrymen from further molestation. He became much attached to his beautiful and faithful bride; and, having succeeded in converting her to Christianity, he married her according to the rites of the Church. From this union sprung some of the most respectable and wealthy families of the State."

I thanked Tom for his story, and agreed that the Princess Pocahuntas ought to be held in reverence by all true Virginians. Our conversation was interrupted by the cry of "All hands, shorten sail!" We sprung on deck. A heavy gale had come on, and the ship was heeling over to her scuppers under it. I was aloft in an instant, helping to reef the mizzen-topsail; the topgallant-sails and courses had been clewed up.

The wind was about north-west, and blew very cold. The leaden waves rose sullenly on every side, topped with hissing foam, and every instant they leaped higher and higher, as if lashing themselves into fury. The twilight of evening was just giving way to the gloom of night. I never remember a more dismal-looking close to a day.

We had managed to close-reef the mizzen-topsail; but the main-topsail, which was more difficult to manage, was still bulging out above the yard, the hands on which it threatened every instant to strike off, as the ship, with desperate force, kept plunging her bows into the opposing seas.

"Come, bear a hand with that main-topsail there," exclaimed Mr Stunt through his speaking-trumpet, "or—"

What he was going to say I know not, for at that instant there arose the fearful cry of "A man overboard!—a man overboard!"

It sounded like the knell of a fellow-being. Captain Gierstien was on deck. I was near him.

"If I lower a boat I shall lose some other brave fellows," he exclaimed aloud, though he was speaking to himself.

"We'll gladly risk our lives to save him, sir," cried two or three who were near him; "it's O'Connor—it's Terry O'Connor!"

"So would I," escaped from my lips. I had at all events intended to have volunteered to go in the boat.

"Down with the helm! Back the main-topsail!" exclaimed the captain in the same breath. "Stand by to lower a boat; but hold fast. Can any of you see or hear him?" The ship was hove to, and all hands stood peering into the loom and trying to catch a sound of a voice. O'Connor was a first-rate swimmer, and he was not a man to yield to death without a struggle—that we knew.

It must be understood that, though several sentences were spoken, not thirty seconds had elapsed after he had struck the water before the order to heave the ship to was given. She was also going but slowly through the water, though, from the way she was tumbling about, a landsman might have supposed she was moving at a great rate.

"Does any one see him?" asked the captain. Alas in that dark night even the sharpest eyes on board could not discern so small an object as a man's head floating amid those troubled waters.

"Does any one see him?" There was a dead silence. The hopelessness of the case struck a chill through all our hearts. Two minutes—three—passed away. We continued from all parts of the ship peering into the darkness—some to windward, others to leeward, and others a stern. Now I thought I saw something, but it was the dark top of a wave under the glistening foam. Five minutes had elapsed since the accident. Long before this the ship must have left him far astern, and he must have sunk beneath those heavy waves. Such was the feeling gaining possession of many.

Again the captain made the final inquiry, "Does any one yet see him?" An ominous silence gave the sad response. "Then it is hopeless waiting longer. Fill the main-topsail. Up with the helm."

Scarcely had the captain uttered these words in a loud voice, than a hand in the main-top hailed the deck with the words, "I hear a voice from down to leeward, sir."

I had heard it also, I was certain. It was O'Connor's manly voice. It was not a shriek, the death-wail of a struggling wretch, but a bold, nervous hail.

"Hold fast then with the main-topsail braces," cried the captain. There was no need of that order, by the bye. "Keep the helm down. Stand by to lower the starboard quarter boat." It was the lee one.

"Volunteers, away!" Several sprung to the falls. I was among the first; so was Tom Derrick, an active young topman. He leaped into the bow as the boat was being lowered; I into the stern to unhook the after falls; the rest of the volunteer crew followed. The boat was lifting and pitching with fearful violence alongside, to the great risk of being swamped. Poor Derrick stood up to clear the falls, I believe, or to fend off the bow of the boat from the ship's side. I saw his figure in an erect position for an instant—the boat's bow pitched into the sea—the next instant he was gone. In vain the man close to him tried to grasp him—he went down like a shot; not a cry was heard, not a sign of him was again seen.

There was no time to be lost, if we would save O'Connor. Every moment the fury of the gale was increasing. Our oars were out, and over the foaming sea we pulled in the direction whence the voice had come. The ship rose towering astern of us, her dark masts lifting and falling against the leaden sky. By her we guided our course. We thought we must have reached the spot where O'Connor should have been.

"Be alive, shipmates," said a voice close to us. "In bow oar, and lend us a hand." It was O'Connor's voice. He was swimming with perfect composure close to us on the top of a wave, and striking out toward the bows, so as to avoid the stern. He was with some little difficulty hauled on board, for he had not a stitch of clothing on with which we could catch hold of him.

"Thank ye, shipmates all," he exclaimed, as he sprung into the stern-sheets. "But lend us a jacket, some one, will ye? for it's bitter cold out of the water, and I've left all mine, do ye see, for Daddy Neptune, when he wants a new rig-out."

A seaman will joke in the midst of a furious engagement, or at other moments of the greatest peril; and I believe Terence was truly grateful to the merciful Providence who had so wonderfully preserved him. We threw our jackets over him, to shelter him as well as we could, and pulled back as fast as we were able to the ship. There was a short time for talking and hearing how it had happened, as may be supposed. We had great difficulty in getting on board again, and it required extreme caution to prevent the boat being swamped alongside. At last we reached the deck, and the boat was hoisted in.

"Why, you haven't got him," said the captain, seeing the same number come back as had gone away in the boat.

"Yes, sir," we answered; "but poor Derrick has gone;" and we explained how our other shipmate had been lost. So there was a sigh and a tear for poor Derrick; and a cheer and congratulations for O'Connor's preservation.

Our captain ordered O'Connor at once to his hammock, observing that his nervous system must have received a great shock, and that he need not do duty for some days, while the surgeon was directed to see to him. O'Connor very gladly turned in; and the surgeon feeling his pulse, prescribed a stiff glass of grog, a style of medicine of which sailors most approve. After he was made comfortable, I went and sat by him, and congratulated him heartily on his preservation.

"Why, you see, Peter, there's an old saying about a man not being able to drown who is born to finish his career in another way, in which a rope plays a prominent part; but I hope that's not true in my case. You must know, indeed, that when I first struck the water, as I was hove off the yard, I thought I should escape. When I came to the top again, after I had sunk some way down, thinks I to myself, there's no use trying to swim with all this hamper of clothing about me; so the first thing I did was to cast it all adrift, and to kick off my shoes. I had some difficulty in getting out of my jacket, but I succeeded by treading the water with my feet the while. Remember, Peter, always have your sea-going clothes made loose, so as to be able to throw them off in a moment. You never know when you may require to be rid of them. When I was free of my clothes, I thought there would be no use striking out and wearying myself, to try and regain the ship, because I saw that all I could do would not bring me up alongside her again; so I threw myself on my back, with my arms folded on my breast, and lay as quiet as a turtle basking in the sun of Ascension. You know singing out in the water tires a man almost as much as struggling with his arms and legs, so I kept my voice also for when it was wanted. There was no use, you see, singing out at that time, because I knew that there would be a noise on board, and people asking who had gone, and where was. I heard a cry of 'A man overboard!' just as I came to the surface. I could see the ship all the time, and I was glad to find she did not leave me. I don't mean to say, Peter, but what my feelings were very awful, for I knew the difficulty and danger of lowering a boat; but I did not think my shipmates would ever desert me, without trying to pick me up. There I lay, then, tossing on the seas, and looking at the ship. I hoped I should be observed, for I heard the captain ask, 'Does any one see him?' I being to leeward of the ship, his voice reached me; but I did not expect to make any one hear on board. How long the time appeared! At last I heard the order given to fill the main-topsail. 'Now or never,' I thought; and just as I rose on the summit of a wave, I leaped as high as I could, and sung out at the very top of my voice. Never did I shout louder, for it mattered nothing if I burst my lungs, if I was not heard. How thankful I felt when I heard the order given to lower a boat! My advice to you, Peter, is, 'Always keep your presence of mind, and, while life remains, never despair.'"

Chapter Twenty

The *Pocahuntas* continued on her course to the northward, with variable weather. I believe we had got a considerable way to the eastward of where we should have been; but of that I have no certain knowledge, as a foremast man has no means of ascertaining the ship's position, except when she makes the land, unless the officers choose to tell him. At last a fine westerly breeze sprung up, and we went gaily along.

Now, however incredible what I am going to relate may appear especially as happening to O'Connor, yet it is, I can assure my readers, perfectly true. Terence had been sent on the fore-topgallant-yard—what to do I do not recollect, for I was aft at the time—when by some means or other he lost his hold and fell over the yard. Another man, who was on the yard and saw him fall, ejaculated, "Poor Terence, this time it's all over with him!"

Falling from that height on the deck, his brains would inevitably have been dashed out of his head; but, as he fell, the hitherto sluggish wind filled the foresail, on the bulge of which, at the very instant his body striking, it was thrown with considerable force forward right into the sea. As before, Terence preserved his consciousness, or, at all events, recovered it as he struck the water. He struck out bravely alongside the ship.

"Heave us a rope, shipmates," he sung out. I ran to the side, and was just in time to throw him a rope as he dropped past. He caught hold of it, and hand over hand he hauled himself on board into the mizzen-chains. From thence jumping into the waist, he shook himself dry, like a Newfoundland dog, and went forward again to his duty, as if nothing had happened.

"Peter," he observed afterwards to me, when we were together, "if I never had any religion before, I think I should have some now. You see, when I felt myself going, I thought it was all up with me, and never was so surprised in my life as when I found myself in the water. Tell me, Peter, do you think it was God who made the foresail belly out at the moment it did?"

"I think it was by His will it so happened," I answered. "I don't think chance did it."

"But do you think He would take the trouble to look after such a poor fellow as I am?" he asked.

"A sparrow, we are told by the Bible, falls not to the ground that He knows not of," observed Andrew Thompson, who had sat himself down near us. "Then don't you think, messmate, He would look after a human being, with a soul to be saved?"

"I feel that He preserved my life; but I don't understand it," replied Terence.

"No, messmate, none of us can understand His mysteries. We see the earth and the sky and sea—the sun and moon rise and set—we feel the wind blow, and the snow and the rain fall. But we cannot comprehend how all this is ordered, though we must acknowledge that it is for our good; and we feel that the power of the Ruler of all is so much greater than we can understand, that it is hope less to attempt it. But I say, messmate, that is no reason why we should not believe that all these things are; but, on the contrary, that God, who creates and cares for the smallest birds, watches over us also."

We both acknowledged the truth of Andrew's creed; and let me assure my young friends that a blessed comfort it was to us afterwards, when dangers, such as few have surmounted, surrounded us.

We continued standing to the northward; and, as far as we could learn, we were considerably to the eastward of Newfoundland. The change of temperature made us glad of warm clothing; but as yet there was no cold to be complained of. We might have guessed that we were approaching the arctic regions, by the character of the numberless sea-fowl which at times surrounded us. We were now, I believe, in latitude 54 degrees or 55 degrees; but I am uncertain, from the reasons I before stated.

Our officers had their guns on deck, and amused themselves by shooting as many of the birds which came in their way as they could; but my messmates called them by the various names of shearwaters, boatswains, kittiwakes, dovekies, Mollymokes or Mollies, gulls, buntings, and many others, whose names I forget. Those the officers did not want were given to the crew, who were in no ways particular as to the nature of the fresh meat they could procure. The shearwaters especially we found very good, particularly when made into pies. For the purpose of enabling us to make crust, a greater quantity of flour than usual was served out. At first our pies had a very oily and fishy taste; but Andrew showed us that this fishy flavour is confined to the fat, the whole of which is under the skin, and chiefly near the thighs. By carefully skinning the birds, they tasted like ordinary land-fowl; and before the officers found out the secret, we had a capital pie every day for dinner.

Our most constant companions were the Mollies; for which bird the North Sea men have as great an affection and veneration as sailors round the Cape of Good Hope have for Mother Carey's chickens or the superb albatross: They have an idea that the spirits of the brave old Greenland skippers, the successors of the fierce sea-kings, have, when quitting their mortal frames, entered these fleet denizens of the air, still desirous to wander over the scenes of their former exploits. They are very strong and graceful on the wing and though they scarcely seem to move their gracefully-rounded pinions, they can fly in the teeth almost of the fiercest gale—now swooping into the dark troughs of the sea—now skimming over the white foaming crests. They seldom, except during calm and moderate weather, alight on the water, being ever constant on the wing; and they will fly so close to the ship, that I have fancied I could catch them with my hand.

One calm evening, as I was stationed on the poop, one of these birds, with noiseless wing, came flying so close to me that he almost brushed my nose; but before I could lift my hand to catch him, he was gone. Several times some of the pretty little snow-buntings attempted to alight on our rigging; but, like thistle-downs, before they could reach it, they were blown to leeward, and, exhausted and weary, were soon overwhelmed by the waves.

We had fishing-lines on board; and one day, the wind being light, we were told we might try them, when, to our no small satisfaction, we caught some excellent cod and halibut. We were, in fact, passing over a fishing-bank.

The weather now altered for the worse. Sleet, fog, and rain succeeded each other with unvarying rapidity, with an addition generally of a strong gale, coming from the north round to the north-west. For two days it was impossible to lay our course, so we remained hove to, hoping for an abatement of the storm.

I am now coming to one of the most perilous incidents of my life. I think I said that Thompson, O'Connor, Stokes, and I were in the same watch, though we were stationed in different parts of the ship. It had been blowing very hard from the northward during the day; but towards the evening it moderated a little, and the ship was carrying her three whole topsails close-hauled, and looking up to the north-east. No moon or stars were visible, for heavy masses of clouds covered the sky, and seemed to descend till they filled, as it were, the whole space between sky and ocean.

There were look-outs stationed forward, though, as we were supposed to be in the open sea, no danger of any sort was apprehended. Other ships might, by possibility, be crossing our course, but that was not likely; and if, by any wonderful chance, we came near each other, we should probably see and be seen in time to prevent a collision. The larboard watch, to which I belonged, and of which Mr Dunning, the second lieutenant, was officer, had the first watch, namely, from eight o'clock till midnight. At four bells, or ten o'clock, it came to my turn to take my trick at the helm. The weather had become bitterly cold; so I, with the rest, had donned all the warm clothing we could command. I had on a flannel shirt and drawers, with worsted hose and comforter, and over all a thick Flushing jacket and trousers; a Welsh wig, under a south-wester, covered my head, and a thick pair of lined boots my feet, while my hands were encased in woollen mittens—so that I little cared for the inclemency of the weather, provided I had not to face it. This I had to do while at the helm; and I remembered Andrew's account of the Moravian missionaries having their eyelids frozen together, and thought mine would suffer in the same manner.

To say that the night was very dark would not give an idea of the inky obscurity in which we appeared to be sailing. One could scarcely see one's hand with one's arm held out at full length; and as for discerning anything ahead, that appeared impossible. I say appeared, because there is much difference having something to look at and nothing. In the latter case you fancy, because you see nothing, that nothing could be seen if it were there. I heard Mr Dunning, as he passed me, apostrophising the night as dark as Erebus.

The quarter-master, who was conning the ship, was continually exclaiming, "No higher," as I kept her luffing up into the wind, unable to see the shaking of her canvas, which rose dark and towering above me, till it seemed to be lost in the clouds. Indeed, as we sailed on, we seemed literally to be sweeping the sky with our mast-heads. Thus we ploughed our way, ignorant of what was ahead, through the boiling seas during the whole time I had the wheel.

I had just been relieved, and was finding my way forward, knocking my hands against my sides to warm them, when there was a loud cry from the look-out men of "A ship ahead, standing right for us under all sail."

"Under all sail—impossible, in a night like this!" exclaimed the officer of the watch, rousing himself from a reverie.

"Luff all you can luff, and we may weather her," cried the voice from forward, in a tone which showed the emergency of the case; but the lieutenant had seen what he thought was a sail, and exclaimed, "Keep her away—hard up with the helm—hard up." The commands of the officer were obeyed; the spokes of the wheel were turned a-weather; the ship, falling off, felt the full force of the gale, and flew with redoubled speed through the water.

Andrew Thompson, who was standing next to me, had been peering into the gloom ahead. "A sail!" he exclaimed: "that's no sail, but an iceberg—I see its light. We might have weathered it; but now we are on it—and Heaven have mercy on our souls!"

As he spoke, a loud, fearful crash was heard—the stout ship shook and trembled in every timber. I was thrown, as were all near me, to the deck with stunning force. Shrieks and cries arose from every part of the ship; and the watch below, in their consternation, came hurrying up on deck, many without their clothes, others with them in their hands. All was dismay and confusion; while the terrific noise of the wind, and the sea dashing over the ship, and the ship striking against the iceberg (for an iceberg it was in truth against which we had struck), added to the cries of the people, the groans of the ship, and the creaking and crashing of the masts, almost drowned the voices of the officers, who were rushing here and there as they came from their cabins, in a vain endeavour to restore order. Many of the people in their fright sprung overboard, and were instantly swallowed up by the waves. The ship rose and fell with tremendous force as the sea lifted her, and the loud crashing forward showed that her strong bows had been stove in. The fore-mast went by the board, the heel probably lifted right out of its step. Then a terrific cry arose that the ship was sinking, and that all was lost.

The sergeant of marines, a rigid disciplinarian, had at the first alarm collected his men, and by the command of the captain brought them, with their arms in their hands, on the quarter-deck, ready to enforce his orders. No sooner was the cry raised that all was lost, than many rushed forward, with the intention of getting on the iceberg.

"Let no man quit the ship," shouted the captain through his speaking-trumpet. "Beat to quarters, marines; fire on any who attempt to leave the deck."

Andrew Thompson, O'Connor, and Stokes were close to me, just abreast of the fore-mast. Andrew looked round when he heard the bows of the ship being stove in. "My lads," he exclaimed to us three, "the ship won't be many minutes more above water; so if you'd have a chance for your lives, follow me."

This he said just as the captain had ordered the marines to fire on any who should quit the ship. We did not stop to see whether they would obey or not, but, jumping on the forecastle, ran along the bowsprit and down by the dolphin-striker—a spar which hangs perpendicularly under the bowsprit—from whence we dropped down one by one on to a part of the iceberg which the waves did not reach. The ice was very rough, and we were thus enabled to scramble up perfectly clear of the sea.

Several others attempted to follow our example; and the marines, even at that awful moment, obedient to their orders, commenced firing on them. By the flashes of their muskets, as well as from three or four guns, which the gunner and his crew had time to discharge, the whole dreadful scene was disclosed for an instant, never to be erased from my memory: The ship, with her bow run high upon the berg; her tall masts, with their yards and sails going by the board; the dark ocean and the white-crested seas dashing over her stern, amid which stood a mass of human beings, in all the attitudes of agonised despair and dismay, except those few drilled to obedience, who knew not the danger. Then, again, above our heads, rising to the clouds, the white shining iceberg, which at every flash seemed to glow with flames of fire—the bright light reflected from pinnacle to pinnacle, and far into the caverned recesses of its stupendous sides.

Can I ever forget the dreadful despairing shriek which rent the skies, as the bow lifting high in the air, it seemed, the stern sank down, even at the instant the marines fired their last volley: it was a volley over their own graves! Slowly the proud ship glided from the icy rock, on which she had been wrecked, down into the far depths of the ocean. Soon all were engulfed beneath the greedy waves. No helping hand could we offer to any of our shipmates. The taller masts and spars followed, dragged down by the sinking hull; and in another instant, as we gazed where our ship had just been, a black obscurity was alone before us. I say we, for I saw that others were near me; but who they were I could not at the time tell. I called out, and Andrew's voice answered, "Is that you, Peter? I am glad you've escaped, lad. Who is there besides?"

"I'm here, Andrew, thanks to Providence and your advice," cried Terence.

"And so am I; but I don't think I can hold on much longer," exclaimed poor Tom Stokes, who had fallen on his side and hurt himself. Terence and I, who were near him, on this grasped hold of him, and dragged him up to the broad ledge on which we were seated, from the rough points of ice—to which he had been clinging. We then all huddled together as close as we could, to keep ourselves warm.

"Perhaps there may be some one else saved," observed Andrew; so we shouted at the top of our voices, "Shipmates, ahoy! are any of you there?" We listened. The only answering sound was the lashing of the waves against the base of the iceberg; and we were convinced that, out of that gallant crew, who lately trod the deck of the beautiful ship which was now, fathoms down beneath our feet, we four were the only beings left alive.

Chapter Twenty One

I can scarcely picture the horrors of that night. I would fain, indeed, forget them, but that is impossible. We had preserved our lives for the present moment; but what could we expect beyond, but starvation in its worst form? We had also read and heard enough of icebergs to know that, as they are driven to the southern latitudes, their bases, immersed in water much above the freezing-point, rapidly melt, and huge fragments being dislodged, they are suddenly reversed, creating a tumult as if a huge mountain were plunged into the ocean.

"If we have to stay here long, we shall be frozen to death," said poor Stokes, his teeth chattering with cold and fear. He was the only one of us who had got wet. "Trust in Providence, lad," said Andrew solemnly. "He has wonderfully preserved us thus far. He will not desert us, unless it be His good pleasure that we should die; and then we must: meet our fate like reasoning men, thanking Him for His especial mercy that He has given us time to repent of our sins, and has not hurried us, as He has our shipmates, into eternity without a moment's warning."

"Should I never have another opportunity, I thank you now, Andrew, for making me think of such things in the way you have done," exclaimed Terence, from the fulness of his heart. "Had it not been for you, shipmate, I should not have seen the finger of God in the various ways in which He has been pleased to preserve me, and I should have died the ungrateful, unthinking wretch I had hitherto lived."

"I have been but an humble instrument in His hand, Terence," answered Andrew, in his usual calm, humble tone. "You see, I should be very wrong, and very wicked indeed, if, knowing what is right, I did not take every opportunity, when there was no fear of discrediting religion, to teach my shipmates."

"You spoke to me at a proper time, Andrew; and your words had, I hope, a right effect," I observed.

"And to me also," said Tom; "and I thank you."

"Well, shipmates, bad as we are off, and worse as we may be, I don't feel unhappy when I hear you say those words; that I can tell you," exclaimed

Andrew. "It's a joyful thing for a man, when he has seen the sun rise for the last time, to feel that there is a chance of some few things being scored in his favour in the world to which he's bound. But mind you, I don't say it's what I would pride myself on, for I know that the most one can do may count as nothing; but still it's pleasant, and nothing can make it otherwise."

Strange as it may seem, thus we talked on. Indeed, what other subject could we talk on but religion? for every moment we felt that we might be in the presence of our Maker. As Andrew warned us, the shock the iceberg had received by the ship striking against it might have detached what are called calves, great lumps from the bottom, and, should the gale increase, it might capsize in an instant.

We had many hours to wait for daylight. We were so well clothed, from its having been our watch on deck, that we did not feel the cold particularly; but poor Tom continued to suffer. Fortunately Andrew discovered in his pocket his pipe with some tobacco, and a flint and steel. He lighted the pipe, and let Tom have a smoke, which revived and warmed him, and we then all took a few whiffs round. This little luxury seemed to do us much good. We sheltered Tom as much as we could from the wind with our bodies; and we wrung out his wet jacket, and chafed his hands and feet till the circulation was restored. The night, however, seemed interminable. To favour us still further, the wind fell, and shifted further to the south, which made it much warmer. The sea also went down, for it did not seem to lash with such fury as before our floating resting-place.

"What chance have we of escaping?" I asked of Andrew, after a lengthened silence.

"There may be some of the wreck cast up on the berg, and with it we may make a raft, and reach the coast of Newfoundland or Labrador; or the berg itself may be driven ashore, but that I do not think at all likely; or we may be seen by some ship and taken off. I know of no other possible chance of escape."

"Then I trust we may be seen by some ship," I ejaculated. "There must be many whalers in these parts."

"They keep farther to the eastward, generally," replied Andrew. "They are also not fond of icebergs, and try to avoid them."

I own that, seeing him so calm and collected, I fancied he must have some hopes of deliverance, by means of which we were ignorant; so I asked him whether he thought we should find any food to support us.

"I have often heard of people finding means of subsistence when in as bad a condition as we are," he replied. "Providence has decreed that man should require food to support life; and therefore the air and the sea, as well as the earth, afford him food. Even in the cold regions of the north there is an abundance; and the very food which we could scarcely manage to digest in the south is there wholesome and palatable. In the plains of Asia, for instance, where the earth affords the greatest produce, the people care to eat little besides fruit and corn; while in the land of the Esquimaux, where neither fruit nor corn can grow, they thrive on whale's blubber, the flesh of bears and wild-fowl."

"Perhaps we may catch some wild-fowl in the morning," I observed.

"Perhaps we may; but I think we should hear them if there were any perched about the berg, and I have been listening for some time for them without hearing a sound."

By this remark of Andrew's I knew that he had been considering how we should support life, though he was prepared for the worst; and also, probably, how we had best act under all the circumstances which might occur. I might have sailed with Andrew for a long time, in calm weather, without discovering the real heroic qualities which, under his rough exterior, he possessed.

Morning at last dawned; and what a change from the previous day! Then, all had been storm and gloom; now, all around was calm, beautiful, and bright. Before the sun rose, the whole eastern sky was glowing with an orange tinge; while every fleecy cloud around was tinted with gold and red, orange, or pink, and every conceivable intermediate hue; while the clear portions of the sky itself were of the purest and most ethereal blue—the whole sea glowing with the same varied and beautiful colours. But still more beautiful and wonderful seemed the vast mountain of ice on which we floated, as in every fantastic form it appeared, towering above us. The pinnacles and turrets of the summit were tinted with the glowing hues of the east; while, lower down, the columns and arches which supported them seemed formed of the purest alabaster of almost a cerulean tint; and a round us, on either side, appeared vast caverns and grottoes, carved, one might almost suppose, by the hands of fairies, for their summer abode, out of Parian marble, their entrances fringed with dropping icicles, glittering brilliantly.

It is not to be wondered at, if we did not admire the enchanting spectacle as much as it deserved, for we could not forget that we were floating on an iceberg, in the middle of the North Sea; but still the scene made an impression on my mind which I shall not forget. We had struck on the lowest and least precipitous side of the iceberg, there being a wide flat space some distance above the water, with one ledge rising above the other, for some way up,—so that we had ample room to walk about; nor was the ice so slippery as to cause us much fear of tumbling into the water. I had heard a rippling noise during the night, and could not conceive whence it came; but now, on looking around, I perceived that it was caused by a small cascade, which, from the ice at the top continually melting, came trickling down the side.

"We shall have fresh water, at all events, in abundance," I observed to Andrew, who had awoke from a sleep into which he, with our other companions, had fallen.

"Yes, Peter; and from what I see not far off, if I mistake not, we shall have food also," he added, pointing to a dark object which lay on a ledge below us, a little way to the left.

"If looks like an animal of some sort," I exclaimed. "But I am afraid it will be off before we can catch it. Shall we run down and secure it?"

"I have no fear on that score," he replied; "it is a seal, and from the way it is lying, it is, I suspect, dead. Indeed, a live animal would not have got on the ice so early in the morning. They are now feeding, and love to come out of the water to bask at noon in the sun. We will wake up Terence and Tom, and get them to help to drag it up out of the reach of the sea. It will probably not be very palatable, though it will doubtless serve to keep us alive. But before we commence the work of the day, let us return thanks to Heaven for having preserved us through the great perils of the past night."

We roused up our companions; and I believe did most sincerely offer up our thanksgiving for the mercy which had been shown us in saving us out of so many from destruction. We then, with care to avoid falling into the sea, descended to where the body of the seal had been thrown. The animal was dead, but it was quite fresh, and had probably been cast up that very night; at all events, it could not have been there long.

"I doubted not that God would send us food. This did not happen by chance," said Andrew. We found that we could not drag the entire body of the seal up to the higher ledge, so we cut thin slices out of it, hoping by drying them in the sun to preserve them longer. We first skinned it carefully, as Andrew showed us that by stretching out the skin it would afford us some little shelter at night. Having collected a supply of food to last us for many days, we dragged the remainder of the carcase out of the reach of the waves, and carried the meat to the upper ledge.

"Now, my lads," said Andrew, who took the lead in everything, we willingly obeying him, "it is very right to secure some food for ourselves in the first place; but as we shall none of us have a fancy for spending the rest of our days here, we'll look out to see if there's a ship in the offing, and if so, to make some signal to attract her notice."

We all agreed; and before attempting to eat some of the seal, for which, indeed, we had little fancy, we set to work to climb to one of the highest pinnacles of the berg. We found it impossible to reach the highest, but we got some way up; and not a sail was to be seen as far as the eye could reach on the part of the horizon visible to us. Our climb had shown us, however, a considerable portion of the lower part of the berg, and we observed several things lying about, evidently cast there by the waves. We immediately descended to secure them.

There was a hen-coop with some chickens in it, and though they were drowned, they were very acceptable; there were two boarding-pikes, a boat-sail, and several spars and bits of rope, which had been lying in the boats or on the booms. These were all treasures, and, collecting them, we carried them up to our ledge. There were also fragments of wood and chips washed from the cook's galley, and bits of quarter-boat which had gone to pieces with the first sea. These latter we dried in the sun, and afterwards kindled with them a small fire, over which we cooked two of our fowls, and dried the seal's flesh for future use. We without difficulty ate the fowls, but had not yet got up an appetite for seal-flesh.

"We might be worse off, there's no doubt about it," observed Terence; "and it strikes me, Andrew, that what with the hen-coop and the spars, we might build a sort of a raft which would keep us afloat a short time, should the berg take to making a somerset?"

"I was thinking of the same thing," was Andrew's reply. "They will form but a small raft; but if the berg drives anywhere near shore, it will, at least, enable us to reach it. The sooner we set about making it the better. It will keep us off the cold ice in the meantime, and by rigging the boat's sails on the pikes, we shall be sheltered from the wind; and, my lads, let me tell you, we might be much worse off, so let us be thankful."

This conversation took place while we were making our breakfast. Instead of tea, we knocked off, with the boarding-pikes, lumps of ice, which we ate, and found perfectly fresh. This, Andrew explained, arose either from the iceberg having been formed of the accumulation of the snow of many winters on the coast of Greenland, and thus having been always fresh; or if formed out of salt water, from the ice, when freezing, having ejected the saline particles. He told us that water, when freezing, has the property of purifying itself, and of squeezing out, as it were, all extraneous or coarse matter.

Our not over-luxurious repast being finished, Andrew proposed our attempting again to ascend the berg to plant a signal-post and flag to attract the notice of any passing ship. Terence was for spreading out the boat's sail; but Andrew reminded him that on the white iceberg that would not be readily seen, and advised our fastening our coloured handkerchiefs together instead.

"We must first, however, get to the top of the berg," said Terence; "and, to my mind, these boarding-pikes will serve us a good turn."

No sooner thought of than tried. With the boarding-pikes we chopped steps out of the side, where it was too precipitous to surmount without such aid; and by fixing the pikes below us, we shoved ourselves up with them. In this manner, after considerable labour, we reached a high pinnacle of the berg. It was not broad enough for us to stand on without fear of falling off, so we sat astride on it while we chopped a hole deep enough to fix one of the spars in, which we had hauled up for the purpose. At the top we secured four red cotton handkerchiefs, which, as they blew out, might be seen at a considerable distance. We beat the ice tightly round the heel of the spar, and it appeared to stand firmly and well.

"Now, on whatever side of the berg a ship approaches, it will be seen that some human beings are on it," observed Andrew, as we prepared to descend, having first carefully surveyed the horizon on every side.

At this juncture we had a loss, which caused us great dismay, and, we thought, would prove a very serious inconvenience. After lighting the fire, Andrew had put the flint and steel into his jacket pocket, along with his handkerchief, on drawing out which they were jerked out also, and before we could catch them, they had fallen over the steep side of the berg. Away they bounded, from ledge to ledge, till they fell into the sea. Had they lodged in any crevice, one of us might probably have attempted to recover them, and should very likely have fallen into the sea in so doing; so, as Andrew observed, all was for the best. It was fortunate, we observed, that we had dried some of our seal's flesh, or we should have had to eat it quite raw.

We now descended, and commenced at once to form our raft. We had few materials, and our only tools were the knives and the heads of the boarding-pikes. We first made a framework of the spars; and then, knocking the hen-coop to pieces, we nailed the planks on to the top, securing the whole fabric more firmly with ropes. When completed, as we looked at it, we agreed that it was a very small ark to support four people on the stormy ocean.

"I don't think it will have to float me, shipmates," said poor Tom, who had not recovered his hurt. "I feel as if I could not weather out another night like the last."

"On you'll do well enough, lad," answered Andrew, in a kind voice. "Your clothes will be dry, you'll have a dry plank to lie on, and a roof over your head. You'll do yet, trust to me." These encouraging words had an immediate effect on Tom's spirits, and we heard no more of his complaints.

We had observed, as we sat on the top of the berg, several articles floating round the base, and some lodged in crevices which we had not before discovered. Our raft being completed as far as our materials would go, I volunteered to try and get hold of some of the things. To do this with safety, I begged my shipmates to hold one end of a line, which we had formed out of the various pieces collected, while the other I secured round my body. By keeping the line always tight, I was able to lean over the edge and pick up several things in the water. The first was a bucket, in sound condition. This was valuable, as it would contain fresh water, and prevent the necessity of our chewing the cold ice, which chilled us extremely. Then I found some more spars, and the fragments of one of the boats, which must have been stove in and got adrift before the ship went down. These enabled us to increase our raft to a size which afforded us hope that it might support us in our necessity.

When I was tired, Terence followed my example, and also added to our store of valuables. As he was hunting about, almost out of sight, among the rougher parts of the berg, we heard him sing out, "A prize! a prize!" and, standing up, he held aloft an iron pot with the cover on. The cover had been jammed tightly down, so that it had floated like a buoy.

"There is something in it, though," he observed, shaking it; and, on getting off the cover, we discovered a piece of beef ready for cooking. It had evidently floated out of the cook's galley.

"I quite forgot, though, that we had no means of lighting a fire; so, after all, it won't be of any use," sighed Terence, after we had all four collected again on our raft.

"Don't be so sure of that," said Andrew. "I have seen a fire kindled by means which few people would think of, but I am not quite certain that I can manage it; however, I'll try. It's worth the experiment; for if we can light a fire, we may make some soup, which will do us all good."

Saying this, he climbed some way up the berg, where he knocked off a pure piece of ice from one of its sparkling pinnacles. We all sat round, wondering what he was going to do. With the boarding-pike he carefully chopped the lump, till he had made it into a thick circular cake; then he pared away the edges, and afterwards commenced operations with his knife, scraping away, till he had formed both sides into a perfect convex shape. Lastly, he took it between his mittens, and rubbed it round and round till he turned it out with a fine polish.

"There," he said, "there is a fine burning-glass for you."

"A burning-glass!" I answered, laughing. "A piece of ice shaped like a burning-glass; but you will never get anything like fire out of that, I should think!"

"I should think not," said Terence, but not in the same positive way that I had spoken; for he had, justly, a great respect for everything Andrew did.

"Give me your hand here, then," said Andrew to me. I took off my mitten and gave it him willingly. He looked at the sun, which was shining brightly, and held the ice between it and my hand. I saw a little bright spot appear on my hand; but I thought nothing of that, till, feeling an acute sensation of burning, I snatched my hand away in a hurry, to the amusement of my companions.

"I thought it would answer," exclaimed Andrew triumphantly. "I saw the master of a whaler I was once on board make several like this, and play the same trick to his people I played you; and he afterwards explained that any perfectly transparent substance in a convex shape—that is, bulging out like this—will collect the rays of the sun, and form a burning-glass. But now, while the sun is out, and before our burning-glass melts, let us light a fire and boil our soup."

The chips we had collected very rapidly dried; so we soon had a fire kindled by this unexpected means. The soup refreshed us wonderfully; but we were very sparing of it, by Andrew's advice; for we could not tell how long we might have to remain without means of obtaining more food.

Thus passed away our first day on the iceberg, without a sail appearing in the horizon to afford us a hope of rescue.

Chapter Twenty Two

That night, overcome by fatigue, strange as it may seem, we all slept soundly. The sun again rose, and discovered us still floating in safety on our unstable resting-place. The day passed much as the former one had done.

We had been actively employed during the greater part of it, and therefore, in spite of our extraordinary position and the deep anxiety we felt for our future fate, we were all able to sleep, if not very soundly, at least for some hours, when the third night closed in upon us. I need not say that Andrew offered up our prayers aloud for deliverance to the Great Being who had hitherto so mercifully preserved us.

I dreamed, it seemed to me, all night long. Sometimes I was at home with my father and mother and sweet sisters, and they were all laughing and talking, while we stood at the window of the dining-hall and looked out at the beautiful and familiar prospect before it. Someone was describing to them some adventures very similar to mine; but I felt that I could have nothing to do with them, for I was still, I knew, on an iceberg in the Northern Ocean, likely any moment to be overwhelmed beneath it. Then I thought a ship appeared, and Captain Dean was at the helm, and that sweet Mary, dressed in white, and looking like a seraph, stood on the forecastle waving to me to come off to them. I, of course, could not move, for my feet were jammed into a hole in the ice, and I struggled in vain to drag them out. On a sudden a storm arose, and Mary shrieked; and even her father turned pale, as the ship rose on the tops of the angry billows, and rolled over and over, bow foremost, till she was lost to my sight in the distance. I cried out with terror, and my own voice awoke me, when I found that my feet were projecting beyond the shelter of the sail, and were bitterly cold.

I got up to warm them by stamping them up and down, and the noise awoke my companions. They naturally told me to lie down and be quiet; but the night was so fine and calm, that I said I would go a little way from them not to disturb them, and would walk up and down for an hour or so. I had no fancy for any more of those dreadful dreams, and I felt that the exercise would do me good. As I looked out on the tranquil, dark-shining sea, in which the glittering stars floating, so it seemed, in the blue ether above me were reflected as in a mirror, all sorts of strange fancies came into my head. I remembered all I had read or heard of mermen and mermaids, of ocean monsters and sea-spirits, and I could scarcely persuade myself that I did not see some gliding before me. Certainly I could hear them: now there was a distant roar, now a loud snorting noise near me; there were voices wandering through the air, and strains of sweet music seemed to come up from the deep. I was almost positive I could hear music: sweet and faint and soft as a seraph's sigh, it came down to my ear on the gentle wind. I would on no account have missed listening to that enchanting melody.

For a long time I continued gazing on the sea without feeling any inclination to sleep, when I fancied that I saw the dark sails of a ship about a mile off, and directly to windward of us. I peered into the darkness to assure myself, for I did not like causelessly to arouse my companions. How eagerly I looked may be supposed. If there was a ship where I supposed, the music I had heard must have come from her. At last I was almost confident that there was a ship; but as I had my doubts, I went back to Andrew and touched his arm.

"Andrew," I said, trembling all over in my eagerness, "I do not wish to raise false hopes, but look out there and tell me what you see."

"See, lad!—why, a sail; there's no doubt of it," he exclaimed hurriedly. "A barque-rigged vessel standing on a bowline to the north-west. She's a whaler, I suspect; but how to make the keenest ears on board hear us, is a puzzle."

We called Terence and Tom, who instantly sprung to their feet and joined us in looking out for the stranger.

"Could not we make a fire as a signal?" I asked, "that would attract her."

"You forget that our flint and steel went overboard, and the ice without the sun won't light a fire," he answered; "but we will see what our voices can do. Now, my lads, let's hail together."

On that, standing up, throwing out our chests, and putting our hands to our mouths, we gave a shout which none but strong lungs could have uttered. It must have been carried a good mile to windward over the calm sea, but no responding cry came down to our anxious ears.

"There is no use wearing out our lungs with hallooing," said Terence. "They wouldn't hear us, up to windward there, even if they were much nearer. We must have patience, shipmates!—it's no use."

"God's will be done," ejaculated Andrew. "He may yet think fit to send us help."

The tone Andrew gave to our minds prevented us from despairing or sinking into despondency. I do not mean to say that we did not, at first, feel the most bitter disappointment as the ship receded into the darkness which surrounded us, but this feeling did not endure. We, as our wise companion advised us, "trusted in God that He would save us;" and we all along felt that He would do so.

We earnestly watched the ship as long as she was visible, and long after, though we scarcely expected her to tack, or to repass near. At length we returned to our raft, and endeavoured to forget our disappointment in sleep. We lay down, under our sealskin and sail, and after an hour's trial, I once more closed my eyes. How long I had slept I do not know, when I was again awoke by a loud noise and a violent movement of the iceberg.

Andrew suddenly started up, exclaiming, "The time has come! Hold on to the raft, my lads; hold on."

He meantime seized a boarding-pike, ready to steady the raft. His impression was that the iceberg was in the act of rolling over, and that now was the time our raft would be of service, if it could survive the waves caused by the submersion of the snow-formed mountain on which we rested.

We waited in awful suspense, believing that our last moment had indeed arrived. It is difficult to calculate time on such occasions. Gradually the rocking movement of the berg ceased, and we found that the ledge on which we were posted had sloped rather more towards the water than before, so that it was necessary to continue holding on by the boarding-pike to prevent its gliding off.

"What has happened?" I exclaimed, as I first again drew breath freely. "I thought it was all over with us."

"So did I, lad, at first, before I had time to think. I now suspect the cause of the commotion; and it is a mercy that the consequences have not been more terrible. When the circumstance which has just taken place happens, the whalers say that an iceberg has calved—that is, a huge lump of ice has broken away from the base of the berg, and has floated up to the top of the water. The noise we heard was when it struck against other parts, and first came to the surface. The loss of a large mass, of course, makes the berg lop-sided; and should another lump break away, it may go right over. Should we survive till the morning, we shall probably see the calf floating near us. I have known large ships overwhelmed by bergs falling on them. You know that it is the custom to moor ships to the lee side of a berg, to prevent their drifting to leeward with a contrary wind. A friend of mine, who gave me the account, belonged to a whaler, the *Thomas*, of Hull, Captain Taylor, fishing in Davis's Straits. Well, one day they lay moored to an iceberg, with a long scope of warp out, and thought themselves quite secure. On a sudden, without any notice, as they were sitting at dinner, a tremendous noise was heard and a blow was felt, just as if the ship had struck on a rock. Up went the bow in the air, till the keel showed above water, and the taffrail was almost under it. All thought the ship must go down; but still she floated, not much the worse for the blow. It was found, what all the old whalemen knew well enough, that a calf had broken away from the bottom of the berg, but fortunately had struck the keel fairly, without injuring the ship's bottom. Sometimes a calf falls from the top of a berg; but I hope one will not come down on our heads, for if it does, it will settle us outright."

Andrew said this quite calmly, though he felt that what he was describing might any moment happen. He afterwards reminded us that pieces were more likely to fall from the summit in the day-time, when the sun was shining on it, than at night, and that therefore we should not let the thought oppress us.

It may be supposed that we did not sleep, nor attempt to sleep, any more that night. As there was no moon, we had not any means of ascertaining how the time passed; but we calculated that it was about two o'clock in the morning when the last occurrence I have described took place. The air had been very light when I first looked out; now it was a perfect calm, so that not even a ripple was heard against the side of the berg. We were therefore not uncomfortable, as far as our feelings went, could we have divested ourselves of the recollection of the peril to which we were momentarily exposed.

Oh how long that night seemed! I fancied, that it would never have an end: each minute seemed prolonged to an hour—each hour to a winter's night. Sometimes we talked, and listened to Andrew's description of the events which had occurred to him when he before visited the Polar Sea. At other times we were all silent together; but Andrew took care this should not last long; and never did man so exert himself to keep up the spirits of his companions. He was actuated by a true Christian spirit; and nothing else would have enabled him, I am confident, to forget himself and watch over us in the way he did.

There had been a spell of silence, when Terence exclaimed, "What say you, Andrew, if we were to launch our raft, and try to reach the coast of Newfoundland while the calm lasts? It might be done, might it not?"

"I think not," was Andrew's reply. "While we remain on the iceberg, we have a chance of being seen; but, on a raft, a ship may pass close to us and not heed us, while, if a gale should come on, the raft would not live an instant. Even should we near the coast, which I do not think likely, we should probably be knocked to pieces on the rocks; so I say stay to the last extremity. If the iceberg won't hold us, then take to the raft."

Of course we determined to follow Andrew's advice; indeed, we all looked up to him as our guide and captain. With no little thankfulness did we welcome the first streaks of dawn on the eastern horizon. Again we knelt down and offered our prayers to Heaven. We had scarcely risen to our feet when a shout of joy escaped from our lips; for there, in the grey misty dawn, with her canvas hanging against her masts, lay motionless on the calm water a ship—the same, doubtless, which we fancied had passed far away from us in the night. Was that calm sent by Providence to effect, our salvation? The result will prove it, or when His now inscrutable ways are made manifest. How our hearts beat with hope and fear! My first impulse was to scream out to her. I checked myself, and asked Andrew what he would advise. He did not answer for some time.

Eagerly we watched the stranger. She was a barque—a whaler, no doubt. "Will she see us?" we asked one another. "Will she near the iceberg again, or will she sail off in an opposite direction?"

Those who have been placed in a similar position to the one in which we were, can alone truly comprehend to the full the intensity of our feelings. We could scarcely breathe—we could scarcely speak. All our thoughts were concentrated in that one point; our very being seemed wrapped up, as it were, in it. The night had passed slowly away; but still more slow did the light of day seem to creep over the world.

I said we were for some time silent. At last Andrew answered my question by saying, "The first thing we must do, shipmates, is to climb up to the top of the berg, and spread out our red handkerchiefs; so as to show a broad face to those on board yonder vessel. As soon as the sun is high enough, we'll try and light a fire, and the smoke may be seen by them; but if not, then we must trust ourselves to the raft, and try to paddle up to her. Perhaps we may reach her before a breeze springs up; but perhaps not. Yet I don't think it will get up till noon."

"But why not get on the raft at once?" I urged; for I had more confidence in it than he had.

"Because if we do, we may not be able to return to the iceberg, which we should wish to do if we miss the ship," he answered. "But on that point I will agree to what you all wish. What do you say, Tom?—you are the youngest, and should speak first."

"I say, then, let us try the raft," said Tom, who fancied even that he could swim to the ship.

"And so do I," I added.

"And I," exclaimed Terence, eagerly. "We'll drive her up to the ship in no time."

"Then, shipmates, the sooner we are off the better," we all cried out together.

Terence and I climbed up to the top of the berg, and spread out our handkerchiefs between two upright spars, and we thought they could not fail of being seen. Andrew and Tom, meantime, were filling the iron pot with water, collecting some of our seal flesh, and otherwise getting our raft ready. Securing one end of our rope to a point of ice, we eased the raft carefully down into the sea. To our satisfaction it floated well alongside, but it required great caution not to upset it as we stepped upon it. We at once saw that Andrew had good reason for not wishing to trust to it; for no sooner were we on it, than, calm as the sea was, the water washed completely over it, and, had we not placed two planks across it to sit on, we should have been wet through directly. We each of us held a small piece of the boat's planking in our hands to serve as paddles.

"Away we go, my lads," exclaimed Terence, as he gave a strong shove against the iceberg with a boarding-pike; and with a cheer, which, perilous as was our adventure, we could not repress, we began vigorously to ply our paddles. It was a matter of life and death, we saw. If we missed the ship, our chance of returning to the iceberg was small indeed. Our progress was very slow. We might have made a mile an hour—perhaps not so much—and we had three miles to go at least. Still we did not flag in our exertions. We each of us chewed a piece of seal's flesh to stay our hunger, though we had no inclination or power to swallow anything. We scarcely spoke a word all the time, but every now and then we turned a glance back, to judge how far we had got from our late abode.

One mile was passed, and we were not seen. Indeed, so small a speck as we were on the ocean, we could not expect to be observed till the sun had risen. Our great anxiety was respecting the wind—still the sea continued calm as a mirror. On we went—our eyes were on the ship's sails. Alas! a light cat's-paw skimmed across the ocean—the topgallant-sails of the barque blew out; but before they had any influence in impelling her through the water, they again drooped as before. Another cat's-paw came stronger than the first, and rippled the whole surrounding surface.

Oh with what agony we saw the topsails bulge out, and the barque's head turn from us! We simultaneously shouted, or rather shrieked out in our eagerness. It was of no avail. We strove to drive the raft on faster than before. What could our utmost efforts accomplish in overtaking a ship, her sails filled even with the light air then blowing? No longer were cat's-paws playing on the surface of the sea, but a well-defined ripple, almost small waves, were covering every part of it; and, as we worked our way among them, they washed around our feet. Every sail on board the barque began to draw; she had got steerage way, and was standing from us. We were not seen; and hope, which had hitherto sustained us, fled. Our hearts sunk, and scarcely could we longer ply our useless paddles.

"Andrew, what say you to this?" asked Terence at length.

"Persevere to the last, like men," replied Andrew. "We may have to return to the iceberg; but even then we must not lose courage, or our trust in Providence."

Just then the sun rose from his watery bed with glorious refulgence in an unclouded sky. I looked back, to judge how far we had got from the iceberg. Truly if it had appeared beautiful when we were on it, doubly so it did appear now, glittering in the beams of the sun; some parts of alabaster whiteness, and the rest tinged with hues of gold and pink and most transparent blue. It was an object well calculated to attract the eyes of a stranger.

A cry from my companions made me turn my head. The barque's sails were shivering, as she luffed up to the wind. Directly after a boat was seen to be lowered, and quickly being manned, it pulled towards us. Then indeed our hearts rose to our bosoms, and we shouted with joy. Poor Tom, from the great revulsion of feeling, was nearly fainting and falling off the raft, had we not supported him. Still we paddled on, and the boat seemed to fly towards us. She was quite close to us, when, in our joy we waved our paddles above our heads, and gave way to another shout.

"Hillo, who have we here?" exclaimed a voice from the boat. "What, mates, we didn't see you!"

Such was the case; they had seen our signal, but had overlooked us. The surgeon of the ship, never having before seen an iceberg, was gazing at it with his glass, and was the first to remark our handkerchiefs; and not being able to make out what they were, he had directed to them the captain's attention. He was in the boat, and assisted to help us off our raft.

Once on board and safe, the strength which had hitherto supported us, gave way, and we sunk down to the bottom of the boat, overpowered with various emotions. I trust and believe that we were all of us grateful to Heaven for our wonderful preservation.

The boat towed our raft alongside, as it was too valuable for firewood to be lost. We were hoisted on board, unable to help ourselves, and were received by the master, officers, and crew with the greatest kindness and attention. The surgeon ordered us at once to be put into warm hammocks, while some warm liquid was poured down our throats, which soon restored us. However, no one questioned us about our adventures till we were more completely recovered.

Two events occurred which ought to have increased, if they did not, our sense of gratitude for our preservation. Scarcely had our feet touched the deck of the barque than a strong breeze sprang up, which sent her at the rate of some seven knots an hour through the water, far away from the iceberg. Before, however, she had run out of sight of that floating island, its glittering summits were seen to lean forward, and, with a sound which could be heard at that distance, to fall prostrate in the water, while the waves created by its submersion reached so far as perceptibly to lift the ship as they passed. Thus was I, with my companions, preserved from the most awful and perilous position in which I was ever placed.

Chapter Twenty Three

The vessel on board which we so happily found ourselves was called *The Shetland Maid*,—her master, Captain John Rendall. She measured three hundred and fifty tons, was barque-rigged, and perfectly fitted as a whaler, being also strengthened by every means which science could devise, to enable her to resist the pressure of the ice to which such vessels must inevitably be exposed in their progress through the arctic seas. She had forty-two souls on board, including officers, being some few short of her complement, as two fell sick in Orkney before leaving, and two were unhappily lost overboard in a furious gale she encountered soon after sailing.

Andrew, Terence, and I remained two days below under the doctor's care, and by the third had completely recovered our usual strength. Tom Stokes, who had suffered most, and was not naturally so strong, took a week before he came round.

As soon as we appeared on deck, the captain called us aft, and desired to know our adventures. Andrew was the spokesman, and the captain expressed himself much pleased with our messmate's mode of narrating them.

"Well, my men," he said, "I have lost some of my crew, and I suppose you'll have no objection to entering regularly for the voyage in their place. You'll share with the other able seamen eighteenpence for each tun of oil, you know, besides monthly wages."

We told him that we should be glad to enter, and would sign articles when he pleased; and that we would answer for Tom Stokes, that he would do the same.

Behold me at last, then, as I have styled myself, *Peter The Whaler* . We were now standing to the northward, and rapidly approaching the ice. Before, however, I proceed with an account of my adventures, I will describe the ship, her officers and crew, and the peculiar arrangements made to fit her for the service in which she was employed.

Captain Rendall was a well-educated, intelligent, brave, and, I feel sure, a truly religious man. I may say, without more than justice, that he was the father of his crew. His father had been in the same service before him for many years; and he had the advantage of his experience, to which he added the knowledge he himself had gained. I do not give him as a specimen of the masters of all whalers, for I fear there are few like him, though they must of necessity be intelligent and superior men. There were three mates. The chief mate, Mr Todd, was also chief harpooner or specksioneer. Then there were the other harpooners, boat-steerers, line-managers, and coopers, beside foremast-men, landsmen, and apprentices.

It is not the custom to pay simply monthly wages; but, as an inducement to all hands to exert themselves in their several capacities in capturing fish, they receive a gratuity for every size fish caught during the voyage, or a certain sum for every tun of oil which the cargo produces. The master gets scarcely any pay if he has no success in his voyage; but for every whale killed he gets three guineas, from ten to twenty shillings for each tun of oil, and a thirtieth to a twentieth on the value of the cargo; so that he may make as much as five hundred pounds by a single voyage. The chief mate may get nearly a hundred, and the seamen twenty-five pounds each. Many of the ships belong to Hull and other northern ports of England and Scotland; but it is usual to touch at the Orkneys or Shetland, to complete the complement of the crew with the hardy islanders who inhabit them.

A whaler, in order to withstand the shock of the ice, is strengthened inside, both at the stem and stern, by stout timbers placed in various directions, and fastened securely together; while on the outside she is in parts covered with a double, and even a treble planking, besides other thick pieces, which serve to ward off the blows from the parts most likely to receive them. How little all the strengthening which the art and ingenuity of man can devise is of avail against the mighty power of the ice, I shall have hereafter to describe. The masts of a whaler are lower than in a common merchantman, and her sails are smaller, and cut in a different shape, the courses or lower sails decreasing towards the foot, so as to be worked with slight strength. Sometimes this is of importance, as, when all the boats are away together in chase of whales, three or four men alone remain on board to take care of the ship.

A whale-ship, therefore, though she has great care and expense bestowed on her, has not, in port, the graceful and elegant appearance possessed by some other ships, bound to more genial climes. The crew do not sleep in hammocks, as on board men-of-war, but in berths or standing bed-places, erected on the half-deck forward. It is a dark retreat, and not scented with sweet odours, especially after a ship has begun to take in her cargo; but the weary seaman cares little where he lays his head, provided it is in a dry and warm place.

We next come to the boats—a very important part of the outfit. The bow and stern of a whale-boat are both sharp, rise considerably, and are nearly alike. It has great beam, or breadth, to prevent its being dragged, when towed by a whale, completely under the water. The keel is convex in the centre, to enable it to be turned more easily; and for the same reason it is steered by an oar instead of a rudder. The oar can also turn a boat when she is at rest, and can scull her in calm weather up to a whale without noise. A large-size boat is pulled by five oars, and one to steer, and a small one by four oars; the first being from twenty-six to twenty-eight feet long, and the last from twenty-three to twenty-four. A large one is five feet five inches in breadth; and a small one five feet three inches.

The rowers include the harpooner and the line-manager. They are carvel-built—that is, the planks are placed as in a ship. Boats in general are clinker-built—that is, the planks overlap each other; but as they are difficult to repair, the other simpler method is employed. A ship generally carries seven boats—two or more large, and the rest small. They are suspended by cranes, or davits, in a row outside the rigging, on either side of the ship, and another astern, so that they can be directly lowered into the water. A smart crew will man and lower a boat in the space of a minute, and be away in chase of a whale.

When we got on board, the boats' crews were busily employed in getting their respective boats and gear ready for action. Each boat had a harpooner, who pulled the bow oar, a steersman, next to him in rank, who steered, and a line-manager, who pulled the after or stroke oar; and besides them were two or three seamen who pulled the other oars.

The first operation, after cleansing the boats, was to get the lines spliced and coiled away; and when it is remembered that each whale may be worth from five hundred to eight hundred pounds, and that, if the lines are in any way damaged, the fish may be lost, it will be acknowledged that they have good reason to be careful. Each line is about one hundred and twenty fathoms long; so that when the six lines, with which each boat is supplied, are spliced together, the united length is seven hundred and twenty fathoms, or four thousand three hundred and twenty feet.

A few fathoms of the line is left uncovered, with an eye at the end, in order to connect the lines of another boat to it; for sometimes, when a whale swims far, or dives deep, the lines of several boats are joined together. The rest of the line is neatly and carefully coiled away in the stern of the boat.

To the upper end of the line is spliced the "fore-ganger" of a "spanned harpoon," thus connecting the harpoon with all the lines in the boat. A "fore-ganger" is a piece of rope a few fathoms long, made of white or untanned hemp, so as to be more flexible and easily extended when the harpoon is projected from the hand.

As the crew of each boat accomplished the work of coiling away their lines, they gave three hearty cheers, to which we all responded; so we had as much cheering as at a sailing match.

I must try to describe a harpoon, for the benefit of those who have never seen one. It is the whaler's especial weapon—the important instrument of his success. It consists of a "socket," "shank," and "mouth." The shank, which is made of the most pliable iron, is about two feet long; the socket is about six inches long, and swells from the shank to nearly two inches in diameter; and the mouth is of a barbed shape, each barb or wither being eight inches long and six broad, with a smaller barb reversed in the inside. The object of the barb, of course, is to prevent the harpoon being drawn out of the whale after it has been fixed.

The hand harpoon is projected by aid of a stock or handle of wood, seven feet in length, fixed in the socket. After the whale is struck, this handle falls out; but it is not lost, as it is secured to the line by a loop. The line, it must be remembered, is fastened to the iron part of the harpoon.

Harpoon-guns are now frequently used for projecting harpoons. The harpoon for this purpose is made with two shanks, side by side, one of which goes into the bore of the gun; to the other on the outside the line is attached.

On every harpoon is stamped the name of the ship, so that it is at once easy to ascertain, from the weapon in the whale, by whom it was struck. Lances are also used, with long handles and sharp heads, to assist in killing the whale.

Each boat is furnished with two harpoons, eight lances, and some spare oars; a flag, with its staff, to serve as a signal; a "mik," as a rest for the harpoon, when ready for instant service; an axe, ready for cutting the line when necessary; a "pigging," a small bucket for baling out the boat; two boat-hooks, and many other things which I need scarcely name.

A most important contrivance belonging to a whaler is the crow's-nest, which I may describe as a sentry-box at the mast-head. It is, perhaps, more like a deep tub, formed of laths and canvas, with a seat in it, and a movable screen, which traverses on an iron rod, so that it can instantly be brought round on the weather side. In the bottom is a trap-door, by which it is entered. Here the master takes up his post, to pilot his ship among the ice; and here, also, a look-out is kept, when whales are expected to appear in the distance.

Just consider how necessary it is to have a good shelter, when frequently the temperature of the air is from 10 degrees to 20 degrees below the freezing-point.

I must not forget to mention the means taken for preserving the cargo of blubber. This is done in casks, in which the blubber is placed after it has been cut up into very small portions. The casks are stowed in the hold, and some are placed between decks; and when there has been unusual success, so that there are not casks enough, the blubber is stowed away in bulk among them.

The mode of fishing, and the remainder of the operations, will be described in the course of my narrative.

In three more days we were all ready. The harpoon-guns were cleaned, oiled, and fastened, with their swivels, on the "billet-heads," in the bows of the boats. Each harpooner got a supply of gunpowder and percussion-caps; and all other requisites were put into the boats.

The crow's-nest had been got up to the main-topgallant mast-head; and in the afternoon we were ready, and eager to attack the first whale which should appear. In the evening the harpooners were invited down into the cabin, to receive their instructions for the season; and afterwards the steward served out a glass of grog to all hands, to drink "a good voyage and a full ship."

I had fully expected to see whales in such numbers, that we should have nothing to do but to chase and capture them; but in this I was disappointed, for not a whale did we meet; indeed, with the heavy sea then running, had we got hold of one, we could not have secured it. It was, I ought to say, towards the end of April, and we were in hourly expectation of being among the ice, through which, at that time of the year, it was expected a passage would easily be found to the northward.

We had seen several icebergs, which like their companion on which the corvette was wrecked, had early broken away from the main body, as also washing pieces and several large floes; but we had yet to learn what a field of ice was like.

It was night, and blowing very hard from the south-west. It was my watch on deck, and Mr Todd, the first mate, was officer of the watch. We were standing on a bowline under our topsails, a sharp look-out being kept ahead for danger. O'Connor and I were together, leaning against the bulwarks and talking. "Well, Terence," I said, "I would rather find myself homeward bound, after all that has occurred, than be obliged to be running into a sea in which we shall all the time be obliged to be cruising among ice."

"Oh, I don't consider much of that," he answered. "It's only a summer cruise, you know; and when we get back, we shall have our pockets stuffed with gold, and be able to talk of all the wonders we have seen."

"I hope we may get back. I have no fancy to spend a winter on the ice," I said.

"There are pleasanter places to live in, no doubt, Peter; but people have lived not only one year, but several years running in those regions, and have not been the worse for it," replied Terence.

Just then we were startled by the loud cry of "Breakers ahead!" Mr Todd in a moment saw what was to be done. "Wear ship!" he exclaimed. "Up with the helm. Gaff-topsail-sheets let fly. Drop the peak. Square away the after-yards."

While these and other orders were given and executed, in order to take the pressure of the wind off the after part of the ship, and to make her head turn from it, I glanced in the direction towards which we were running. A pale light seemed to be playing over it; and I could distinguish, amid the foaming breakers, huge masses of ice dashing about and heaving one upon another, any one of which, I thought, would be sufficient to stave in the sides of the ship, if not to overwhelm her completely.

At the same time a loud, crashing, grinding noise was heard, sufficient to strike terror into the stoutest hearts. But it must be remembered that we were all so busily engaged in flying here and there in the performance of our duty, that we had no time for fear. This is a great secret to enable men to go through dangers unappalled. Had we been compelled to stand inactive, our feelings might have been very different.

The ship wore slowly round; but still she seemed approaching the threatening mass. She plunged more violently than before amid the raging sea, and in another moment I felt certain we must be among the upheaving masses. Just then her head seemed to turn from them; but a sea struck her on the quarter and came rolling on board; a tremendous blow was felt forward, another followed. Cries arose from some of the men that all was lost, and I expected to find the ship instantly dashed to pieces.

Our good captain rushed on deck. He cast one glance aloft, and another at the ice. "She's clear, my lads," he shouted. The ship came round, and in another instant we were on the eastern or lee side of the floe, and gliding smoothly on in calm water through a broad passage, leading amid the main body of the polar ice.

Chapter Twenty Four

Our ship made good progress, considering the impediments in her way, towards the fishing grounds in the north, to which she was bound. Sometimes we had a clear sea; at other times we were sailing among patches of ice and icebergs, or through lanes penetrating into packs of many miles in extent, and from which it seemed impossible we should ever again be extricated. Our captain, or one of his mates, was always at this time in the crow's-nest, directing the course of the ship amid the dangers which surrounded her.

I shall not soon forget the first day of May, which I spent in the icy sea. It was as unlike May-day at home as any day could well be as far as the temperature went, though we were sailing through a sea tolerably free from ice.

"All play to-day and no work, my boy, for we are going to have a visit from a king and queen," said an old whaler, David McGee by name, as he gave me a slap on the shoulder which would have warmed up my blood not a little, if anything could in that biting weather.

"He must be King Frost, then," I answered, laughing; "for we have plenty of his subjects around us already."

"No; I mean a regular-built king," said old McGee, winking at some of his chums standing around, who had made many a voyage before. "He boards every ship as comes into these parts, to ask them for tribute; and then he makes them free of the country, and welcome to come back as often as they like."

"Thank him for nothing for that same," I answered, determined not to be quizzed by them. "But don't suppose, David, I'm so jolly green as to believe what you're telling me; no offence to you, though."

"You'll see, youngster, that what I say is true; so look out for him," was old McGee's answer, as he turned on his heel.

I had observed that for a few days past the old hands were busy about some work, which they kept concealed from the youngsters, or the green hands, to which class I belonged. Everything went on as usual till eight bells had been struck at noon, when an immense garland, formed of ribbons of all colours, bits of calico, bunting, and artificial flowers, or what were intended for them, was run up at the mizzen-peak. On the top of the garland was the model of a ship, full-rigged, with sails set and colours flying. Scarcely had it gone aloft, when I was startled by a loud bellowing sound, which seemed to come from a piece of ice floating ahead of the ship.

"What's that?" I asked of old David, who persevered in keeping close to me all the morning. "Is that a walrus blowing?" I thought it might be, for I could not make it out.

"A walrus! no, I should think not," he answered, in an indignant tone. "My lad, that's King Neptune's trumpeter, come to give notice that the old boy's coming aboard us directly. I've heard him scores of times; so I'm not likely to be wrong."

The answer I gave my shipmate was not very polite. One never likes to be quizzed; and I, of course, thought he was quizzing me.

"You'll see, lad," he answered, giving me no gentle tap on the head, in return for my remark. "I'm not one to impose on a bright green youth like you."

Again the bellow was heard. "That's not a bit like the sound of a trumpet," I remarked.

"Not like your shore-going trumpets, maybe," said old David, with a grin. "But don't you know, youngster, the water gets into these trumpets, and makes them sound different?"

A third bellow was followed by a loud hail, in a gruff, voice, "What ship is that, ahoy?"

Old David ran forward, and answered, "*The Shetland Maid*, Captain Rendall, of Hull."

"Heave to, while I come aboard, then; for you've got some green hands among you, I'm pretty sure, by the way your gaff-topsail stands."

"Ay, ay, your majesty. Down with your helm—back the main-topsail," sung out old David, with as much authority as if he was captain of the ship.

His orders were not obeyed; for before they were so, the gruff voice sung out, "Hold fast!" and a very curious group made their appearance over the bows, and stepped down on deck.

I was not left long in doubt as to whether or not there was anything supernatural about them. "There," exclaimed David, pointing with great satisfaction at them, "that big one, with the thing on his head which looks for all the world like a tin kettle, is King Neptune, and the thing is his helmet. T'other, with the crown and the necklace of spikes under her chin, is Mrs Neptune, his lawful wife; and the little chap with the big razor and shaving-dish is his wally-de-sham and trumpeter extraordinary. He's plenty more people belonging to him, but they haven't come on board this time."

Neptune's costume was certainly not what my father's school-books had taught me to expect his majesty to wear, and I had always supposed his wife to be Amphitrite; but I concluded that in those cold regions he found it convenient to alter his dress, while it might be expected the seamen should make some slight mistake about names.

Neptune himself had very large whiskers, and a red nightcap showed under his helmet. In one hand he held a speaking-trumpet, in the other a trident surmounted by a red herring. A piece of canvas, covered with bits of coloured cloth, made him a superb cloak, and a flag wound round his waist served him as a scarf. A huge pair of sea-boots encased his feet, and a pair of sealskin trousers the upper part of his legs. Mrs Neptune, to show her feminine nature, had a frill round her face, a canvas petticoat, and what looked very like a pair of Flushing trousers round her neck, with the legs brought in front to serve as a tippet. The valet had on a paper cocked-hat, a long pig-tail, and a pair of spectacles on a nose of unusual proportions. I had read descriptions of Tritons, the supposed attendants on Neptune, and I must say his valet was very unlike one. I might have been prejudiced, for I had no reason to feel any warm affection for him.

"Come here, youngster, and make your bow to King Neptune," exclaimed David, seizing me; and, with number of other green hands, I was dragged forward and obliged to bob my head several times to the deck before his marine majesty.

"Take 'em below. I'll speak to 'em when I wants 'em," said the king in his gruff voice. And forthwith we were hauled off together, and shut down in the cable tier.

One by one we were picked out, just as the ogre Fi-fo-fum in the story-book picked out his prisoners to eat them. There was a considerable noise of shouting and laughing and thumping on the decks, all of which I understood when it came to my turn.

After three others had disappeared, I was dragged out of our dark prison and brought into the presence of Neptune, who was seated on a throne composed of a coil of ropes, with his court, a very motley assemblage, arranged round him. In front of him his valet sat on a bucket with two assistants on either side, who, the moment I appeared, jumped up and pinioned my arms, and made me sit down on another bucket in front of their chief.

"Now, young 'un, you haven't got a beard, but you may have one some day or other, so it's as well to begin to shave in time," exclaimed Neptune, nodding his head significantly to his valet.

The valet on this jumping up, seized my head between his knees, and began, in spite of my struggles, covering my face with tar. If I attempted to cry out, the tar-brush was instantly shoved into my mouth, to the great amusement of all hands. When he had done what he called lathering my face, he began to scrape it unmercifully with his notched iron hoop; and if I struggled, he would saw it backwards and forwards over my face.

When this process had continued for some time, Neptune offered me a box of infallible ointment, to cure all the diseases of life. It was a lump of grease; and his valet, seizing it, rubbed my face all over with it. He then scrubbed me with a handful of oakum, which effectually took off the tar. Being now pronounced shaved and clean, to my great horror Mrs Neptune cried out in a voice so gruff, that one might have supposed she had attempted to swallow the best-bower anchor, and that it had stuck in her throat, "Now my pretty Master Green, let me give you a buss, to welcome you to the Polar Seas. Don't be coy now, and run off."

This I was attempting to do, and with good reason, for Mrs Neptune's cap-frill was stuck so full of iron spikes, that I should have had a good chance of having my eyes put out if she had succeeded in her intentions; so off I set, running round the deck, to the great amusement of the crew, with Mrs Neptune after me. Luckily for me she tripped up, and I was declared duly initiated as a North Sea whaler. The rest of my young shipmates had to undergo the same process; and as it was now my turn to look on and laugh, I thought it very good fun, and heartily joined in the shouts to which the rest gave way.

If any one got angry, he was soon made to cut so ridiculous a figure, and to feel his perfect helplessness, that he was compelled, for his own sake, to get back his good-humour again without delay. We had an additional allowance of grog served out, and what with dancing and singing, the fun was kept up till long after dark.

I need scarcely say that the representative of his marine majesty was no less a person than the red-whiskered cooper's mate, that his spouse was our boatswain, and the valet his mate. I had often heard of a similar ceremony being practised on crossing the line, but I had no idea that it was general on board all whale ships.

The fourth day of the month was a memorable one for me and the other green hands on board. The wind was from the westward, and we were sailing along to the eastward of a piece of ice, about two miles distant, the water as smooth as in a harbour. Daylight had just broke, but the watch below were still in their berths. The sky was cloudy, though the lower atmosphere was clear; and Andrew, who was walking the deck with me, observed it was first-rate weather for fishing, if fish would but show themselves.

Not ten minutes after this, the first mate, who had gone aloft into the crow's-nest to take a look-out round, eagerly shouted, "A fish! a fish! See, she spouts!" and down on deck he hurried with all despatch.

The words were scarcely out of his mouth before the crews of two boats had jumped into them, and were lowering them down, with their harpoons, lances, and everything else ready, not forgetting some provisions, for it was impossible to say how long they might be away. The chief mate jumped into one, and the second harpooner into the other, in which my friend Andrew went as line-manager.

Away they pulled. I looked over the side, and saw the whale a mile off, floating, thoughtless of danger, on the surface of the ocean, and spouting out a fountain of water high into the air. I fancied that I could even hear the deep "roust" she made as she respired the air, without which she cannot exist any more than animals of the land or air. Every one on deck follows the boats with eager eyes. The boat makes a circuit, so as to approach the monster in the rear; for if he sees them, he will be off far down into the ocean, and may not rise for a long distance away. With rapid strokes they pull on, but as noiselessly as possible. The headmost boat is within ten fathoms of the fish—I am sure it will be ours. The harpooner stands up in the bows with harpoon in hand. Suddenly, with tail in air, down dives the monster; and the faces of all around me assume an expression of black disappointment. It must be remembered that, as all on board benefit by every fish which is caught, all are interested in the capture of one.

"It's a loose fall, after all," said old David, who was near me. "I thought so. I shouldn't be surprised if we went home with a clean ship after all."

However, the boats did not return. Mr Todd was not a man to lose a chance. Far too experienced ever to take his eye off a fish while it is in sight, he marks the way she headed, and is off after her to the eastward. With his strong arm he bends to the oar, and urges his men to put forth all their strength, till the boat seems truly to fly over the water. On they steadily pull, neither turning to the right hand nor to the left for nearly half-an-hour. Were it not for the ice, their toil would be useless; but the boat-steerer looks out, and points eagerly ahead.

On they pull. Then on a sudden appears the mighty monster. She has risen to the surface to breathe, a "fair start" from the boat. The harpooner stands up, with his unerring weapon in his hand: when was it ever known to miss its aim? The new-fangled gun he disdains. A few strong and steady strokes, and the boat is close to the whale. The harpoon is launched from his hank, and sinks deep into the oily flesh.

The boat is enveloped in a cloud of spray—the whole sea around is one mass of foam. Has the monster struck her, and hurled her gallant crew to destruction? No; drawn rapidly along, her broad bow ploughing up the sea, the boat is seen to emerge from the mist with a jack flying as a signal that she is fast, while the mighty fish is diving far below it, in a vain effort to escape.

Now arose from the mouth of every seaman on deck the joyful cry of "A fall, a fall!" at the same time that every one jumped and stamped on deck, to arouse the sleepers below to hasten to the assistance of their comrades. We all then rushed to the boat-falls.

Never, apparently, were a set of men in such a desperate hurry. Had the ship been sinking, or even about to blow up, we could scarcely have made more haste.

The falls were let go, and the boats in the water, as the watch below rushed on deck. Many of the people were dressed only in their drawers, stockings, and shirts, while the rest of their clothes were in their hands, fastened together by a lanyard; but without stopping to put them on, they tumbled into the boats, and seized their oars ready to shove off. Among them, pale with terror, appeared poor Tom Stokes and another youngster in their shirts. They hurried distractedly from boat to boat. At each they were saluted by, "We don't want you here, lads. Off with you—this isn't your boat."

I belonged to the after or smallest boat, which was most quickly manned, and most easily shoved off; so that I was already at a distance when he ran aft and saw me going. "O Peter, Peter!" he exclaimed in a tone to excite our commiseration, though I am sorry to say it only caused loud shouts of laughter, "you who have gone through so many dangers with me, to desert me at last in a sinking ship!"

Poor fellow, aroused out of a deep sleep by the unusual sounds, he not unnaturally thought the ship was going down. I heard the gruff voice of the cooper's mate scolding him; but what he said I don't know. The scolding must have brought him and the other back to their senses; and they of course went below to get their clothes, and to return to assist in working the ship. On such occasions, when all the boats are away, the ship is frequently left with only the master, one or two seamen, and the rest landsmen on board.

The moment the fast-boat displayed her jack, up went the jack on board the ship at the mizzen-peak, to show that assistance was coming. Away pulled the five boats as fast as we could lay back to our oars. The whale had dived to an immense depth, and the second boat had fastened her line to that of the first, and had consequently now become the fast-boat; but her progress was not so rapid but that we had every prospect of overtaking her. To retard the progress of the whale, and to weary it as much as possible, the line had been passed round the "bollard," a piece of timber near the stern of the boat. We knew that the first boat wanted more line by seeing an oar elevated, and then a second, when the second boat pulled rapidly up to her. The language of signs for such work is very necessary, and every whaler comprehends them.

We now came up and arranged ourselves on either side of the fast-boat, a little ahead, and at some distance, so as to be ready to pull in directly the whale should reappear at the surface. Away we all went, every nerve strained to the utmost, excitement and eagerness on every countenance, the water bubbling and hissing round the bows of the boats, as we clove our way onward.

"Hurra, boys! see, she rises!" was the general shout. Up came the whale, more suddenly than we expected. A general dash was made at her by all the boats. "'Stern for your lives; 'stern of all!" cried some of the more experienced harpooners. "See, she's in a flurry."

First the monster flapped the water violently with its fins; then its tail was elevated aloft, lashing the ocean around into a mass of foam. This was not its death-flurry; for, gaining strength before any more harpoons or lances could be struck into it, away it went again, heading towards the ice. Its course was now clearly discerned by a small whirling eddy, which showed that it was at no great distance under the surface, while in its wake was seen a thin line of oil and blood, which had exuded from its wound.

Wearied, however, by its exertions and its former deep dive, it was again obliged to come to the surface to breathe. Again the eager boats dashed in, almost running on its back, and from every side it was plied with lances, while another harpoon was driven deeply into it, to make it doubly secure. Our boat was the most incautious, for we were right over the tail of the whale. The chief harpooner warned us—"Back, my lads; back of all," he shouted out, his own boat pulling away. "Now she's in her death-flurry truly."

The words were not out of his mouth when I saw our harpooner leap from the boat, and swim as fast as he could towards one of the others. I was thinking of following his example, knowing he had good reasons for it, for

I had seen the fins of the animal flap furiously, and which had warned him, when a violent blow, which I fancied must have not only dashed the boat to pieces, but have broken every bone in our bodies, was struck on the keel of the boat.

Up flew the boat in the air, some six or eight feet at least, with the remaining crew in her. Then down we came, one flying on one side, one on the other, but none of us hurt even, all spluttering and striking out together; while the boat came down keel uppermost, not much the worse either. Fortunately we all got clear of the furious blows the monster continued dealing with its tail.

"Never saw a whale in such a flurry," said old David, into whose boat I was taken. For upwards of two minutes the flurry continued, we all the while looking on, and no one daring to approach it; at the same time a spout of blood and mucus and oil ascended into the air from its blow-holes, and sprinkled us all over.

"Hurra, my lads, she spouts blood!" we shouted out to each other, though we all saw and felt it plain enough. There was a last lash of that tail, now faint and scarce rising above the water, but which, a few minutes ago, would have sent every boat round it flying into splinters. Then all was quiet. The mighty mass, now almost inanimate, turned slowly round upon its side, and then it floated belly up and dead.

Our triumph was complete. Loud shouts rent the air. "Hurra, my lads, hurra! we've killed our first fish well," shouted the excited chief mate, who had likewise had the honour of being the first to strike the first fish. "She's above eleven feet if she's an inch," (speaking of the length of the longest lamina of whalebone); "she'll prove a good prize, that she will." He was right. I believe that one fish filled forty-seven butts with blubber—enough, in days of yore, I have heard, to have repaid the whole expense of the voyage.

Our ship was some way to leeward; and as the wind was light, she could not work up to us, so we had to tow the prize down to her. Our first operation was to free it from the lines. This was done by first lashing the tail, by means of holes cut through it, to the bows of a boat, and then two boats swept round it, each with the end of a line, the centre of which was allowed to sink under the fish. As the lines hung down perpendicularly, they were thus brought up and cut as close as possible down to the harpoons, which were left sticking in the back of the fish. Meantime the men of the other boats were engaged in lashing the fins together across the belly of the whale. This being done, we all formed in line, towing the fish by the tail; and never have I heard or given a more joyous shout than ours, as we pulled cheerily away, at the rate of a mile an hour, towards the ship with our first fish.

Chapter Twenty Five

A cookery-book, in the possession of my good mother, advises one to catch one's hare before cooking it. On the same principle I deferred describing how a whale is disposed of till I had seen one caught; for I have heard that it is possible for a ship to return clean, or without having caught a single whale; and this might possibly, I feared, be our case. Every one on board, from the captain downwards, was now in good spirits.

We had got a fish; but it was necessary to secure it carefully alongside, lest it might sink even there, and be lost after all our trouble—such misfortunes having occurred to careless fishers. The first thing we did was to secure at the stern of the ship, on the larboard side, a tackle, which is called a nose tackle, from its being fastened to the nose or head of the fish. A tail tackle was secured to the tail of the fish, and this was brought on board at the fore-chains. Thus the head of the fish was towards the stern of the ship, and the tail towards the bows, the body being extended as much as possible. The right side fin, which was next the ship (it being remembered that the whale was on its back), was then lashed upwards towards the gunwale.

To "cant" or "kent," in nautical phraseology, is to turn over or on one side. The tackle, therefore, composed of many turns of ropes and blocks, which turns the whale over as the blubber is cut off, is called the "kent purchase" or tackle. One part was fastened to the neck of the whale, or rather the part of the body next the head—for a whale, even in courtesy, cannot be said to have a neck—and the other was tied to the head of the main-mast, the fall being passed round the windlass. The neck, or rather the part which would be the neck if it had one, is called the "kent."

From the size of the whale, it was impossible to lift it more than one-fifth part out of the water; and this was only done after heaving away at the windlass. Till this operation was performed, not one of us had rested from our labours.

"Knock off, my lads, and turn-to to breakfast," sung out the master in a cheerful tone. The order was obeyed with right good-will; and perhaps never did a more hungry crew of fishermen sit down to a more jovial meal. Breakfast was soon over, and, strengthened and refreshed, we prepared to turn-to at our task.

On going on deck again, I found that our booty had attracted round us many birds and fish of all descriptions, ready to prey on what we should leave. There were fulmars in thousands, eager to pounce down upon the morsels which they knew would be their share. They were of a dirty grey colour, with white breasts and strong crooked bills, formed to tear flesh easily, and able to give a very severe bite. Then there were numbers of the arctic gull, who may be considered the pirate of the icy regions, as he robs most other birds, not only of their prey, but of their eggs and young. The sea-swallow, or great tern, however, like an armed ship of size, bravely defends himself, and often beats off his antagonist; while the burgomaster a large and powerful bird, may be looked upon as a ship of war, before whom even the sea-swallow flies away, or is compelled to deliver up his prize. There were a few also of the ivory gull, a beautiful bird of immaculate whiteness. They are so timid that they dare not rest on the whale, but fly down, and while fluttering over it, tear off small bits, and are off again before the dreaded burgomaster can come near them.

But now to our prize. First, the harpooners secured to their feet what we called spurs, that is, spikes of iron, to prevent them from slipping off the back of the whale, on which they now descended. I and three other youngsters were meantime ordered to get into two of the boats, into which were thrown the blubber-knives and spades, bone-knives, and other instruments used in the operation in which they were about to engage.

Our duty was to keep alongside the whale, to hand them what they required, and to pick any one up who should by chance fall into the water. The specksioneer, or chief harpooner, took post in the centre of the rest to direct them. The fat is, as it were, a casing on the outside of the whale, so that it can easily be got at. With their blubber-knives the men then cut it into oblong pieces, just as a fish is cut across at table; and with their spades they lifted it from the flesh and bones, performing the same work on a larger scale that the fish-knife does. To the end thus first lifted a strap and tackle is fastened, called the "speck-tackle," by which those on deck haul it up. This operation is called "flensing."

As the huge mass is turned round and round by the kent-tackle, the harpooners continue cutting off the slips, till the whole coat of fat is removed. The fins and tail are also cut off; and, lastly, the whale-bone is cut out of the mouth. The whale-bone is placed in two rows in the mouth, and is used instead of teeth, to masticate the food, and to catch the minute animals floating in the water on which it feeds. Each side of bone consists of upwards of three hundred laminae, the interior edges of which are covered with a fringe of hair. Ten or twelve feet is the average size. In young whales, called "suckers," it is only a few inches long. When it is above six feet, the whale is said to be of *size*, a term I have before used.

The tongue of the whale is very large; it has a beard, and a very narrow throat. While I was handing a blubber-spade to old David, as I looked over the side of the boat, I saw a pair of bright green eyes glancing up at me with such a knowing, wicked look, that I drew back with a shudder, thinking it was some uncommon monster of the deep, who was watching for an opportunity to carry one of us off.

"What is it now, youngster? Have you bit your nose?" asked David, laughing.

"No," I replied breathlessly. "Look there—what is that?" I pointed out the eyes, which were still glaring up at me.

"That—why that, my green lad, is only a blind shark. Have not you ever seen one of them before?"

"Only a shark!" I exclaimed with horror, remembering all I had heard about sharks. "Won't he eat one?"

"No, not he; but just run a boat-hook into him, and try and drive him away, for he's drawing five shillings' worth of oil out of the fish every mouthful he takes, the glutton," said David.

I did as I was desired; but though the point ran right into his body, he only shifted his post a little, and made a fresh attack directly under the stern of the boat. I again wounded him; but he was either so engaged with gorging himself, or so insensible to pain, that he continued with his nose against the side of the whale, eating away as before.

I afterwards learned that this Greenland shark is not really blind, though the sailors think so because it shows no fear at the sight of man. The pupil of the eye is emerald green; the rest of it is blue, with a white worm-shaped substance on the outside. This one was upwards of ten feet in length, and in form like a dog-fish. It is a great foe to the whale, biting and annoying him even when alive; and by means of its peculiarly-shaped mouth and teeth it can scoop out of its body pieces as large as a man's head.

But the most persevering visitors during the operation of flensing were the sailors' little friends the Mollies. The moment the fish was struck they had begun to assemble, and they were now pecking and tearing away at the flesh with the greatest impudence, even among the men's long knives. One at last got between David's legs, which so tried his patience, that he took it up and flung it from him with a hearty shake, abusing it for running the risk of being hurt; just as a cab-driver does a child for getting into the road, without the slightest idea of injuring it. But the Molly would not take the hint, and with the greatest coolness returned to its repast, thinking, probably, that it had as much right to its share as we had to ours.

The Mollies do not evince an amiable disposition towards each other; and as the "krang" (such is the name given to the refuse parts of the whale) is cut off, they were to be seen sitting on the water by thousands tearing at the floating pieces, and when one morsel seemed more tempting than another, driving their weaker brethren away from it, and fighting over it as if the sea was not covered with other bits equally good. All the time the noise they made "poultering" down in the water, and quacking or cackling—I do not know which to call it—was most deafening.

My good friend Andrew pointed them out to me. He never lost an opportunity of giving me a useful lesson. "There," he said, "that's the way of the world. We are never content with what we have got, but must fight to gain something else. Now take my advice, Peter. Do your duty as a man; and when you light upon a piece of krang, stick to it, and be thankful that you've found it." I have never since been in a noisy, quarrelsome crowd, that I did not think of the Mollies and the krang.

I must not forget the green-eyed monster which had so startled me. The surgeon had got a hook ready, covered by a piece of blubber; and letting it fall quietly over the stern before its nose, the bait was instantly gorged. To hook a fish of ten feet long, and to get him on board, are two different things; and our good *medico* was very nearly drawn overboard in a vain attempt to do the latter without assistance, which, just then, all hands on board were too much engaged to afford. The line was very strong, or the shark would have broken it, as now, finding himself hooked, he had sense enough to struggle violently in order to get free.

I must confess that, when I came on deck after the krang had been cast adrift, I was not sorry to see my friend in that condition. After some trouble we got the bight of a rope over his head, and another round his tail, and hoisted him on deck. If a cat has nine lives, a Greenland shark may be said to have ninety. We cut him on the head and tail with hatchets, and knocked out any brains he might have possessed, and still he would not die. At last the surgeon cut him up, and hours after each individual piece seemed to have life remaining in it.

Sometimes when the tackles are removed the carcase of the whale sinks, and the fish at the bottom are alone the better for it; but at other times, as in this case, it floats, and not only the birds and sharks, but the bears find a hearty meal off it. This krang floated away; and afterwards, as I shall have presently to relate, was the source of much amusement. I ought to have said, that while the harpooners were flensing the whale, another division of the crew were employed in receiving it on deck, in pieces of half a ton each, while others cut it into portable pieces of about a foot square; and a third set passed it down a hole in the main hatches to between decks, where it was received by two men, styled kings, who stowed it away in a receptacle called the "flense gut." Here it remained till there was time for "making off."

Having now got our prize on board, the owners being probably 500 pounds richer, should we reach home in safety, than they were a few hours before, we set to work to make off the blubber, that is, to stow it away in the casks in the hold. For this purpose we ran out some miles from the ice, in smooth water, and hove to, with just sufficient sail set to steady the ship. While the skee-man—the officer who has charge of the hold—the cooper, and a few others, were breaking out the hold, that is, getting at the ground or lowest tier of casks, we on deck were arranging the speck-trough, and other apparatus required for preparing the blubber.

The speck-trough is an oblong box, with a lid, about twelve feet in length. The lid, when thrown back, forms a chopping-table; and it is covered with bits of whale's tail from end to end, which, being elastic, though hard, prevents the knives being blunted. In the middle of the trough is a square hole, which is placed over the hatchway; and to the hole is attached a hose or pipe of canvas, leading into the hold, and movable, so as to be placed over the bungs of each cask. A pair of nippers embrace it, so as to stop the blubber from running down when no cask is under.

The krang is the refuse, as I have said, and the men who separate the oily part from it are called "krangers." The "kings" throw the blubber in rough out of the "flense gut" to the "krangers" on deck; from them it is passed to the harpooners, who are the skinners. After the skin has been sliced off, it is placed on the chopping-block, before which stand in a row the boat-steerers, who with their long knives cut it up into oblong pieces not larger than four inches in diameter, and then push it into the speck-trough.

The line-managers are stationed in the hold, and guide the tube or lull to the casks they desire to fill. Finally, when no more can fall in, piece after piece is jambed in by a pricker, and the cask is bunged up. Sometimes not only are all the casks on board filled, but the blubber is stowed away in bulk in the hold, and even between decks; but this good fortune does not often occur.

It will be seen by any one who has read an account, that the process of preparing the cargo by the whalers in the southern seas is very different. Andrew Thompson had once been in a South Sea whaler, and he told me he never wished to go in another; for a wilder, more mutinous set of fellows it was never his ill-luck, before or since, to meet. This was, of course, owing partly to the captain, who was a rough, uncultivated savage, and totally unfit to gain any moral restraint over his men.

"I'll tell you what it is, Peter," said Andrew, as I sat by him in the forecastle that evening, listening to his yarns, "till the masters are properly educated, and know how to behave like officers and gentlemen, the men will be mutinous and ill-conducted. When I say like gentlemen, I don't mean that they should eat with silver forks off china, drink claret, and use white pocket-handkerchiefs. Those things don't make the gentleman afloat more than on shore. But what I like to see, is a man who treats his crew with proper gentleness, who looks after their interest in this world and the next, and tries to improve them to the best of his power—who acts, indeed, as a true Christian will act—that man is, I say, a gentleman. I say, put him where you will, ask him to do what you will, he will look and act like a gentleman. Who would dare to say that our good captain is not one? He looks like one, and acts like one, at all times and occasions; and if we had many more like him in the merchant service generally, we should soon have an improvement in the condition of our seamen.

"But I have got adrift from what I was going to tell you about the South Sea whalers. You see, the whales in those seas are generally sperm-whales, with blunt bottle-noses, altogether unlike the fish about here. There is not much difference in the way of killing them, except that one has not to go among the ice for them, in the way we have here, as they are met with in 'schools' in the open sea. What we call 'making-off' is there called 'trying-out.'

"You see, on account of the hot climates they have to come through to return home, and partly from the value of the blubber, they have to boil it to get out the oil; and for this object they have to build large stoves or fire-places with brick on deck, between the fore-mast and main hatchway; and above them are three or four large pots. The blubber is then, you see, minced up, and pitched into the pots with long forks. Just fancy what a curious scene there must be while the trying-out is going on at night—the red glare of the fires, and the thick lurid smoke ascending in dense columns round the masts! Any one, not knowing what was going forward, would think, to a certainty, the ship was on fire; and then the stench of the boiling oil, hissing and bubbling in the pots—the suffocating feel of the smoke— the fierce-looking, greasy, unwashed men—I say, those who have been in a South Sea whaler will never wish to go again."

I told him that I had no wish, after his description, ever to belong to one, though I liked the life, as far as I had seen of it, where I was.

"I have not a word to say against it, mate," replied Andrew. "But wait a bit till we come to boring and cutting through the ice, in case we are beset, and then you'll say that there is something like hard work to be done."

It took us two hours to kill our first whale, and four to flense it. We afterwards performed the last operation in less time, when all hands were more expert.

The next morning we again stood in towards the ice, to see if there was any opening through which we might force the ship, but none appeared. What was curious, we hit the spot to which the krang of the fish we had killed the day before had floated. We saw something moving on the ice, as we approached, besides the clouds of wild-fowl which hovered over it, and on the sea around.

We pointed it out to the second mate. He took his glass, and, putting it to his eye, exclaimed, "There's a big white bear has just been breakfasting, and has hauled up some of the krang on the ice, to serve him for dinner; but we'll try what we can do to spoil his sport."

In accordance with this resolution, he went to the captain and asked leave to take a boat to try and bring back Bruin, dead or alive.

"You may bring him back dead, but alive you'll never get him into that boat, depend on it," answered Captain Rendall, laughing. "However, take care he is not too much for you; for those bears are cunning fellows, remember; and I should advise you to take a couple of muskets, and some tough lances."

"Never fear, sir," answered the mate, preparing to lower a boat. "I don't think a boat's crew need, any day, be afraid of a single bear."

Volunteers being asked for, Terence and I, old David and Stokes, and three others, jumped into the boat, and pulled off towards where the bear was seated quietly licking his paws after his meal. The mate had a great idea of noosing him; and for this purpose he and David were each armed with a coil of rope, with a bight to throw over his head, like a lasso, while Terence and I were to take charge of the guns. The mate first made us put him on the ice some few hundred yards on one side of the bear, and then we pulled round to the same distance on the other. Each had a lance besides his lasso, and the mate had a pistol in his belt.

In case of extreme necessity, Terence and I were to fire, and then to land and come to their rescue. As soon as the two had landed, they began to move away from the edge, hoping thereby to cut Bruin off should he attempt to escape. He had, however, no inclination to leave his dinner; though, perhaps, had he not already eaten to repletion, he would not have sat so quiet while we approached.

We meantime pulled close up to the krang, among all the ducks and gulls. This Bruin did not mind, but sat still, looking quietly on. Of course I could then easily have shot him; but that was not the mate's object. All he did was to growl and show his teeth, as if he longed to have us all within his paws. This made us bolder and less cautious, so we got close up to him.

"We are still too far for me to heave the bight over his shoulders," cried Terence. "Just see if you can't get hold of his dinner with the boat-hook, and that will bring him nearer."

I luckily held my gun in my left hand, while with my right, as I sprang on the ice, I attempted to catch hold of the whale's flesh with the boat-hook. This was too much for the equanimity even of Bruin, and with a loud growl he sprang towards the boat, happily thinking me too insignificant for punishment. I immediately ran off towards the mate; while so great was the impetus which the bear had gained, that he went head-foremost into the water, just catching the gunwale of the boat as the men in her tried to shove off to avoid him.

Terence seized his musket, but it missed fire; and before either of the others could get their lances ready, Bruin had actually scrambled on board. No one can be surprised at their fright, nor that, as the bear came in on one side, they should jump out on the other. They were all good swimmers, so they struck out for the ice, on to which the mate and I hauled them, while Bruin floated away in our boat.

We thought he would have jumped out again, and attacked us: but he seemed perfectly content with his victory, and inclined for a cruise, as he sat, with the greatest composure, examining the different articles in the boat. How long he might have sat there I do not know, had not the mate ordered me to try my skill as a shot. It was a long time since I had had a gun in my hand, and my ambition was roused. I took a steady aim at poor Bruin's eye, and he sunk down in the bottom of the boat.

The whole occurrence had been seen from the ship by our captain, who despatched a boat to our assistance. We stood meantime, looking very foolish, on the ice; and those who had been in the water shivering not a little with the cold. After the boat had taken us on board, we pulled towards ours, with the bear in it. We half-expected to see him jump up, and, seizing the oars, pull away from us. Terence declared that he knew a man who said that such a thing had once happened, and that the bear, after a chase of many miles, got clean off with the boat; and that next year, about the same latitude, he was seen cruising about by himself, fishing for seals.

However, we got cautiously up to our boat; and there lay Bruin, breathing out his last. By the time we got alongside, he was quite dead. We all, especially the mate, got well laughed at for having had our boat captured by a bear.

"And so, Mr Derrick," said the captain, "a boat's crew can possibly be beaten by a bear, I see."

"They can, sir," answered the mate; "I own it; but if you'll remember, you said I should never get that bear into the boat, alive or dead, and I've done both."

"Not that," replied the captain. "He got himself in, and he got you out; so I don't see that you've fulfilled your promise."

However, Bruin was hoisted on board, and the mate secured his skin, which was what he wanted. Of course the adventure caused much joking afterwards, and the boat was ever afterwards called "the bear's boat."

Chapter Twenty Six

For several days, during which we captured another whale, we were cruising about, in the hopes of finding a passage through the ice. We were now joined by a squadron of six other ships, all bent on the same object that we were, to find our way across Baffin's Bay to a spot called Pond's Bay, which has been found, of late years, to be frequented by a large number of whales.

I have before forgot to mention the great length of the days; indeed, for some time past there had scarcely been any night. Now, for the first time in my life, I saw the sun set and rise at midnight. It was my first watch; and, as eight bells were struck, the sun, floating majestically on the horizon, began again its upward course through the sky. On the other side the whole sky was tinged with a rich pink glow, while the sky above was of a deep clear blue. I could scarcely tear myself from the spectacle, till old David laughed heartily at me for remaining on deck when it was my watch below. Now was the time to push onward, if we could once penetrate the ice. We had worked our way to the east, in the hopes of there finding a passage.

"Land on the starboard bow!" shouted the second mate from the crow's-nest. Still on we sailed, till we saw it clearly from the deck. Lofty black rocks were peeping out from amid snow-capped heights, and eternal glaciers glittering in the sunbeams. In the foreground were icebergs tinged with many varied hues. Deep valleys appeared running up far inland; and above all, in the distance, were a succession of towering mountain ranges, reaching to the sky. Still on we sailed.

"Well, lad, how long do you think it would take you to pull on shore now?" asked old David.

"Better than half-an-hour, in a whale-boat, with a good crew," I answered, thinking the distance was about four or five miles.

The old whaler chuckled, in the way he always did when he had got, what he called, the weather-gauge of me.

"Now I tell you it would take you three good hours, with the best crew that ever laid hand on oar, and the fastest boat, too, to get from this ship to that shore."

"Come now, David, you are passing your jokes off on a greenhorn," I replied. "Why, if the water was not cold, I don't think I should find much difficulty in swimming there, when we got a little closer in."

This answer produced a fresh succession of chuckles. Still on we sailed; and I confess that at the end of an hour we appeared no nearer than before.

"Well, what do you think of it now?" asked old David.

"Why, that there must be a strong current against us, setting off shore," I answered, wishing to show my knowledge.

He replied that there was no current, and that I was wrong. Another half-hour passed, and still we did not seem to have gained ground.

"What do you think of our being off Cape Flyaway, youngster?" asked David, pretending to be alarmed. "Did you never hear speak of that? The longer you sail after it the farther off it goes, till it takes you right round the world. If that's it, and I don't say it isn't, it will be long enough before we get back to old England again." Having thus delivered himself, he walked away, to avoid being questioned.

Tom Stokes, who was near me, and, as I have said, was very fond of reading, heard his remark.

"Do you know, Peter, I am not certain that what David says is altogether wrong," he remarked, in a mysterious manner. "I have just been reading in a book an account of a voyage made many centuries ago by a Danish captain to these seas. His name was Rink, but I forget the name of the ship. His crew consisted of eighty stout brave fellows; but when they got up here, some of the bravest were frightened with the wonders they beheld—the monsters of the deep, the fogs, the snows, and the mountains of ice—and at last they saw at no great distance a high picturesque land on which they wished to land, but though they sailed rapidly on, or appeared to sail, they got no nearer to it. This increased the alarm they already felt. One-half of the crew were of opinion that the land itself moved away from them; the others that there were some powerful loadstone rocks somewhere astern, which kept the ship back. At last Captain Rink finding a northerly breeze spring up, and being somewhat short of provisions, put up the helm and ran home, every one on board giving a different account of the wonders they had seen, but all agreeing that it was a region of ice-demons and snow-spirits, and that they would never, if they could help it, venture there again."

For some hours we continued much of Captain Rink's opinion, till at last I had an opportunity of asking Andrew what he thought about the matter. He then told me that, on account of the clearness of the atmosphere, and the brightness of the snow-covered hills or icy plains, they appear to a person unaccustomed to look on them to be very much nearer than they really are. He assured me that it would be a long time before I should be able to judge of distances; and that he had known a person mistake a few stunted shrubs appearing above the snow a few yards off for a forest in the distance, while land many miles off appeared, as it had to me, close at hand.

It was evening, or I should rather say near midnight, when we really got close in, when we found that the valleys were magnificent fiords, or gulfs running far inland, and that the rocks and icebergs were of vast height. As we sailed along the coast, nothing could be more beautiful than the different effects of light and shade—the summits of the distant inland ranges shining in the sunlight like masses of gold, and the icebergs in the foreground tinged with the most beautiful and dazzling colours.

Beautiful as was the scene, I had no idea that any civilised beings dwelt in such a region of eternal snows. What was my surprise, then, to find the ship brought to an anchor off a small town called Leifly, belonging to the Danes! They have several small colonies along the coast, at each of which are stationed missionaries engaged in the pious work of converting the Esquimaux to Christianity.

I thought that where we lay at anchor was directly under the overhanging cliffs; but I found, from the time the boat took reaching the shore, that we were several miles off. Several Esquimaux canoes came off to the ship to barter with us. One man sits in each boat, which is so long and narrow, that one is surprised it should be able to encounter the slightest sea. The whole is decked over, except a round opening, in which they seat themselves.

All these people were Christians; and in each canoe was a strip of paper stuck in a thong under the deck, on which were written, in Danish, passages from the Scriptures. They were comfortably dressed in sealskin coats, trousers, and boots, with a sealskin helmet. Their heads were large, with a narrow, retreating forehead; strong, coarse black hair, flat nose, full lips, almost beardless chin, and full lustrous black eyes—not beauties, certainly, but the expression was very amiable, and so was their conduct.

We had to lower a boat to assist them on deck when they came alongside, for otherwise they would not have been able to get out of their crank barks without capsizing. The way they manage is as follows:— Two canoes bring up alongside each other, the man in the outer one passing his paddle through a thong which stretches across the deck of the inner one, which it thus steadies till the owner can get out. The inner canoe is then hauled out of the way, and another pulls up on the outside. The last canoe is held by the gunwale till the occupant steps out. They all appeared ready to render each other this assistance. The canoe is called a "kajack."

The kajacks being hauled on deck, we began our barter. We had to give old clothes, red and yellow cotton handkerchiefs, biscuits, coffee, earthenware bowls, needles, and many other little things; for which they exchanged sealskins, sealskin trousers, caps, slippers, gloves, and tobacco-bags. These articles were very neatly sewed with sinew thread. Our negotiations being completed in the most amicable manner, they took their departure much in the way in which they had arrived.

I afterwards went ashore in the boat, and saw their huts, which were better, I am ashamed to say, than many I had seen in Ireland. Many of them were nearly built of the bones of the whale, which had an odd appearance. There were heaps of filth in front, and troops of ill-favoured dogs were prowling about them.

I saw some of their women, the elder ones being the most hideous-looking of the human race I ever beheld. They wore their hair gathered in a large knot at the top of the head; but in other respects they were dressed exactly like the men, in sealskin garments. Whatever business took us there was soon completed; and once more, in company with several other ships, we commenced our struggle with the ice-monsters of the deep. Our course was still northerly, as what is called the "middle ice" fills up the centre of the bay in impenetrable masses; and it is only by working round it to the north, where it has drifted away from the coast, that a passage to the west side can be effected.

Soon after sailing, we were frozen into a sheet of bay ice for some days. It was slight, and in many places could scarcely bear the weight of a man. Indeed, there were in every direction pools of water, which for some reason or other did not freeze. Our captain had been for some time in the crow's-nest, looking out for a sign of the breaking up of the ice, when he observed several whales rising in the pools. He instantly ordered the smaller boats to be lowered, and worked through and over the ice to the pools, with harpooners ready to strike any whale which might rise in them. Meantime he armed himself with a harpoon, and ordered others to follow with lances, each with ice-shoes on his feet.

The first man carried the end of a line, and the rest laid hold of it at intervals; so that, should any fall in, they might be able to draw themselves out again. We had not long to wait before a whale was struck, and out flew the line from the boat. So thin was the ice, that we could see the monster through it, as he swam along close under it. Away he went; but, losing breath, he knocked a hole in the ice with his head, to get some fresh air. We followed, but at first he was too quick for us, and had dived again before we came up with him.

We had to look out to avoid the place he had broken as we made chase after him. Our captain took the lead without a rope, going at a great rate in his snow-shoes. He saw the whale close under him, and had just got his harpoon ready to strike through the ice, when up came the fish under the very spot where he stood, and we saw him skip off in a tremendous hurry, or he to a certainty would have gone in, and perhaps have been drawn down when the whale started off again.

Instead of this, he boldly went to the very edge of the ice, and while the whale was blowing, he darted his harpoon deep into his neck. The whale continued his course, but so much slower than before, that we got up to him, and striking our lances through the ice whenever he touched it, we soon despatched him. As he had no means of breathing under the ice, he died quietly, and was dragged up by the line of the first harpoon which struck him; and, by breaking the ice so as to let the line pass, he was hauled up to the ship.

Scarcely was the first secured than a second one was struck, and away we went after him, hallooing, shouting, and laughing. The first man was a little fellow, though, I believe, he cracked the ice. At all events, we had not gone a hundred yards when in fell three men, one after the other; but they did not mind, and by means of the rope they were soon out again, and in chase of our prey.

Poor Stokes got in twice, and I once, to the great amusement of the rest; however, very few escaped without a wetting, so that the laugh was not entirely against us. We succeeded in killing the fish, and I do not know whether it was not as exciting as chasing him in the water; at all events there was more fun and novelty, and that is what a sailor likes.

A fair breeze at length sprung up, which, bringing warmer weather, and enabling us to spread our canvas with effect, we cut away the ice round the ship, and then she, with her strong bows, forced a passage through it. While the wind lasted, with every yard of canvas alow and aloft the ship could carry, we pressed our onward way—sometimes among floes, threatening every instant to close in and nip us; at other times with drift and brash-ice surrounding us; and at others amid open ice, with here and there floating icebergs appearing near us.

To one of these we had to moor, on account of a shift of wind, which blew strong in our teeth; and at first, when I turned into my berth, I did not sleep as securely as usual, from remembering Andrew's account of one toppling over and crushing a ship beneath it. However, I need scarcely say that that feeling very soon wore off. The objects gained by mooring to an iceberg are several. In the first place, from so large a proportion of the mass being below the water, the wind has little effect on it, and therefore the ship loses no ground; then it shields her from the drift-ice as it passes by, and she has also smooth water under its lee. Casting off from the iceberg, as did our consorts from those to which they had been moored, when the wind again became favourable, we continued our course.

We were now approaching the most dangerous part of our voyage, the passage across Melville Bay, which may be considered the north-eastern corner of Baffin's Bay. Ships may be sailing among open ice, when, a south-westerly wind springing up, it may suddenly be pressed down upon them with irresistible force, and they may be nipped or totally destroyed.

All this I learned from old David, who was once here when upwards of twelve ships were lost in sight of each other, though the crews escaped by leaping on the ice.

"Remember, youngster, such may be our fate one of these days; and we shall be fortunate if we have another ship at hand to take us on board," he remarked.

I never knew whether he uttered this not over-consolatory observation for my benefit, to remind me how, at any moment, the lives of us all might be brought to an end, or to amuse himself by watching its effect on me.

For a week we threaded our way among the open floes, when a solid field seemed to stop our further progress. This had been seen hours before, from the unbroken ice-blink playing over it. Our captain was in the crow's-nest, looking out for a lane through which the ship might pass till clear water was gained. After waiting, and sailing along the edge of the field for some time, some clear water was discovered at the distance of three or four miles, and to it our captain determined that we should cut our way. The ice-saws were accordingly ordered, to be got ready, with a party to work them, on the ice. I was one of them; and, while we cut the canal, the ship was warped up, ready to enter the space we formed.

The ice-saw is a very long iron saw, and has a weight attached to the lower end. A triangle of spars is formed, with a block in the centre, through which a rope, attached to the upper part of the saw, is rove. The slack end of the rope is held by a party of men. When they run away from the triangle, the saw rises, and when they slack the rope, the weight draws it down, as the sawyer in a sawpit would do. As the saw performs its work, the triangles are moved from the edge of the ice. As the pieces were cut, they were towed away, and shoved along to the mouth of the canal.

All the time we were at work, some of the men with good voices led a song, in the chorus of which we all joined; and I must say we worked away with a will. It was harder work when we had to haul out the bits of ice, the ship being towed into the canal. With a cheerful shout we completed our canal, and got the ships into a natural lane; and the rest following close upon our track, we worked our way along for many miles, by what is called tracking.

This operation is very similar to the way a canal-boat is dragged along a canal through the green fields of England, only that men have, in the case I am describing, to do the work of horses. A tow-rope was made fast to the fore-mast, and about a third of each ship's company were ordered to drag their respective ship ahead. Away we went, as usual, with song and laughter, tramping along the ice for miles together, and towing our homes, like snails, after us.

For several days we continued the same work; and afterwards, when we got out of the lanes, and the ice was found broken, or so irregular that it was impossible to walk over it, we had to carry out ice-claws, or what may be called ice-kedges, to warp the ship ahead. The ice-claws grappled hold of the ice, and the warp being then carried round the capstan, or windlass, we hove in on it, just as if we were heaving up an anchor, only that this work continued for hour after hour, and days and nights in succession, without intermission.

Ten days passed away much in the manner I have described. We then got into comparatively clear water for a few hours, during which time the other ships joined us. As there was no wind, we had to tow the ship ahead in the boats, so that there was no cessation of our labours.

"Well," I exclaimed to old David, "I suppose after all this we shall soon get into an open sea again."

"Don't be too sure of that, or of anything else, lad," he answered. "We have not yet got into the thick of it, let me tell you."

I found that his words were too true. The boats had been hoisted in, for a breeze had sprung up, and we were progressing favourably, when we came to some large floes. The openings between them were wide, and without hesitation we proceeded through them. On a sudden these vast masses were seen in motion, slowly moving round and round, without any apparent cause. The captain hailed from the crow's-nest, ordering the ice-saws to be got ready, and the ship to be steered towards one of the largest floes close on the larboard bow. The sails were clewed up, and the ice-claws being carried out, the ship was hauled close up to it; and while the captain and carpenters were measuring out a dock, a party, of which I was one, set to work with the saws.

There was no time to be lost. A moment too late, and our stout ship might be cracked like a walnut, and we might all be cast homeless on the bleak expanse of ice to perish miserably. The floes were approaching rapidly, grinding and crushing against one another, now overlapping each other; or, like wild horses fighting desperately, rearing up against each other, and with terrific roar breaking into huge fragments.

"Bear a hand, my lads; bear a hand, that's good fellows. We'll not be nipped this time if we can help it," sung out the officers in a cheering tone to encourage us, though the anxious looks they cast towards the approaching masses showed that their confidence was more assumed than real.

Whatever we thought, we worked and sung away as if we were engaged in one of the ordinary occupations of life, and that, though we were in a hurry, there was no danger to be apprehended. The dock was cut long-wise into the ice the length of the ship, which was to be hauled in stern first. As there was every appearance of a heavy pressure, the ice at the inner part of the dock was cut into diamond-shaped pieces, so that, when the approaching floe should press on the bows, the vessel might sustain the pressure with greater ease, by either driving the pieces on to the ice, or rising over them.

The crews of all the other ships were engaged in the same way, but, as may be supposed, we had little time to attend to them. Our captain was engaged in superintending our operations; but I saw him cast many an anxious glance towards our advancing foes.

For an instant, he ran to the side of the ship and hailed the deck. "Mr Todd," he said, "it will be as well to get some casks of provisions, the men's clothes, and a few spare sails for tents, and such-like things, you know, ready on deck, in case the nip should come before we can get into dock."

"Ay, ay, sir," answered the mate, not a bit disconcerted; and with the few hands remaining on board he set about obeying our commander's somewhat ominous directions.

I ought to have said that the rudder had at the first been unshipped and slung across the stern, as it stands to reason that when pressed against by the ice it should be the first thing injured. Still we worked away. We had begun to saw the loose pieces at the head of the dock.

"Hurra, my lads! knock off, and bear a hand to haul her in," shouted out the captain; "no time to be lost."

With a right good will we laid hold of the warps, and towing and fending off the ship's bows from the outer edge of the ice, we got her safely into the dock. We then set to work to cut up the pieces. We completed our labours not a moment too soon; for before we had got on board again, the tumult, which had been long raging in the distance, came with increased fury around us, and we had reason to be grateful to Heaven that we were placed in a situation of comparative safety.

Chapter Twenty Seven

We were safe—so the old hands said; but it required some time before one could fully persuade one's self of the fact. Not only were the neighbouring floes in motion, but even the one in which we were fixed. Rushing together with irresistible force, they were crushing and grinding in every direction, with a noise far more terrific than that of thunder.

The ship meantime, notwithstanding all our precautions, was driven back before the force opposed to her; and had it not been for the loose pieces under her stern, she might have been nipped in the most dangerous manner. One might fancy that the floes were pitted to try their strength against each other, though it would have been difficult to decide which was the victor.

I had read descriptions of earthquakes, and the commotion reminded me of them. Those who have crossed a large frozen pond or lake will remember the peculiar noise which even stout ice makes when trod on for the first time. Fancy this noise increased a thousand-fold, thundering under one's feet, and then booming away till the sound is lost in the almost interminable distance! Then the field began to tremble, and slowly rise, and then to rend and rift with a sullen roar, and mighty blocks were hove up, one upon another, till a rampart, bristling with huge fragments, was formed close around the ship, threatening her with destruction.

It seemed like the work of magic; for where lately there was a wide expanse of ice, intersected with lanes of clear water, there was now a country, as it were, covered with hills and rocks, rising in every fantastic shape, and valleys full of stones scattered in every direction.

In several places large misshapen masses had been forced up in a perpendicular position, while others had been balanced on their summits so evenly, that the slightest touch was sufficient to send them thundering down on either side.

Our own safety being provided for, we had time to look after our consorts. Most of them had managed, as we had done, to get into docks; but one, which had taken a more southerly course, appeared to heel over on one side, and to be in a most perilous condition.

The weather, which during the commotion had been very thick, now for an instant clearing in the direction where she lay, the first mate ascended with his glass to the crow's-nest, and on coming on deck he reported that the *Arctic Swan* seemed a complete wreck, and that the boats and the men's chests were scattered about round her, as if thrown on the ice in a great hurry.

"I fear it's a very bad case, sir; and if you'll give me leave, I'll take a party and see what help we can afford them," said Mr Todd to the captain.

Seamen are always anxious to render assistance to those in peril; and Captain Rendall having given his permission, plenty of volunteers were found ready for the somewhat hazardous expedition. I was one of them. The risk was, that during our absence the ice might begin to take off; and that we should be separated from the ship, and be left among the heaving and tumbling masses of ice. Of this probably the captain had not much fear, or he would not have allowed us to go.

To assist our return, and also to enable us to rescue any of the crew of the wreck who might be injured, the stern boat was lowered that we might track her up to them. Mr Todd, three other men, and I, formed the party. Away we went towards the ship, dragging our boat with no little difficulty among the hummocks and masses, with some risk of the blocks toppling down on our heads and crushing us.

As we drew nearer the *Arctic Swan*, an exclamation from the mate made us look up at her. "There they go," he cried; "I feared so—she'll never see old England again."

One mast fell while he was speaking, and the others followed directly after; and one fancied one could hear the crushing in of the ship's sides even at that distance. That, however, was not the case, for the ice had taken but a short time to perform its work of destruction.

When at length we got up to the ship, a scene of ruin presented itself, which, before I saw what ice was, I could scarcely have believed could have been wrought so speedily. Stout as were her timbers, the ice had crushed them at the bows and stern completely in, and grinding them to powder, the floes had actually met through her. Part of her keel and lower works had sunk, but the rest had been forced upwards, and lay a mass of wreck on the summit of the hummocks which had been formed under it.

The stern, by the concussion, incredible as it may seem, had been carried full fifty yards from the rest of the wreck. Two boats only had been saved, the rest had been crushed by the ice before they could be lowered and carried free. A few casks of provisions had been got up on deck beforehand, in case of such an accident happening, and they, with the two boats, were upon the ice.

The crew had escaped with the greatest difficulty — some having gone below to get their bags being nearly caught in the nip and crushed to death. At first their faculties were paralysed with the disaster; for the thick weather prevented them from seeing that any help was near, and they feared that they should have to attempt to escape in the two boats, which, even without provisions, would not have held them all.

British seamen are not addicted to giving way to despair, and their officers soon succeeded in rousing them, and in inducing them to set to work to take measures for their safety. Having stowed away the most portable and nutritious of their provisions in the boats, they began to make a strong raft, to carry those whom the boats could not contain, purposing afterwards, should the ice not break up before, to build a barge out of the fragments of the wreck.

They were so busily employed that they did not see our approach, and a loud shout we gave was the first intimation they had of it. They all started up to see who was so unexpectedly coming to their relief; and then responded to our cheer with a hearty good-will. They at once began lightening the boats, so as to be able to drag them over the ice to our ship; and some of the provisions we took into ours, as well as their clothes.

The master gave a last glance at the wreck of the ship with which he had been entrusted, and with a heavy heart, I doubt not, turned away from her for ever. After taking some food, in the shape of salt pork and biscuit, which we much needed, we commenced our return to the ship. Delay, we all felt, was dangerous; for, should the commotion of the ice recommence before we could regain the ship, we ran a great chance of destruction.

At length, however, after four hours' toil, we accomplished our journey in safety, and the shipwrecked crew were welcomed on board the *Shetland Maid*. Some persons might say that, after all, they had little to congratulate themselves on, for that the same accident which had happened to them might occur to-morrow to us. Though we were, of course, aware of this, I must say that I do not believe the idea ever troubled any one of us; and we all fully expected to return home in the autumn, notwithstanding the destruction which was, we saw, the lot of so many.

That night in the forecastle there was as much fun and laughter as if we had all come off some pleasant excursion, and our light-hearted guests seemed entirely to have forgotten their losses.

"Well, mates, it is to be hoped none of the other ships has met with the same ill-luck that yours has," said old David. "It will be a wonder if they have not. I mind the time, for it's not long ago, that nineteen fine ships were lost altogether, about here. It was a bad year for the underwriters, and for the owners too, let me tell you. I was on board the *Rattler*, a fine new ship, when, in company with many others, we were beset, not far from Cape York, by the ice driven in by a strong south-wester.

"Our best chance was to form a line under the lee of the heaviest floe we could pick out; and there, stem and stern touching each other, we waited for what was to come. The gale increased, and forced the floes one over the other, till the heaviest in sight came driving down upon us. The first ship it lifted completely on to the ice; the next was nearly stove in, and many of her timbers were broken; and then, getting more in earnest, it regularly dashed to pieces the four next it got foul of, sending them flying over the ice in every direction.

"We were glad enough to escape with our lives, which we had hard work to do; and then some hundreds of us were turned adrift, not knowing what to do with ourselves. We thought ourselves badly off, but we were many times better than the people of another ship near us. They had made fast to an iceberg, when it toppled right over, and crushed them and the ship to atoms. We were not alone; for not far from us another fleet was destroyed, and altogether we mustered nearly a thousand strong— Englishmen, Frenchmen, and Danes. We built huts, and put up tents; and as we had saved plenty of provisions, and had liquor in abundance, we had a very jolly time of it.

"The Frenchmen had music, you may be sure; so we had dancing and singing to our hearts' content, and were quite sorry when the wind shifted, and, the ice breaking up, we had to separate on board the few ships which escaped wreck."

"I remember that time well," said Alec Garrock, a Shetlander, belonging to our ship. "It was a mercy no lives were lost, either escaping from the ships, or afterwards, when we were living on the ice, and travelling from one station to the other. It seems wonderful to me that I'm alive here, to talk about what once happened to me. The boat I was in had killed a whale in good style; and when we had lashed the fins together, and made it fast to the stern of the boat, we saw that a number of whales were blowing not far off—I ought to say we were close under an iceberg. We, of course, were eager to be among them; and as, you must know, the stern-boat had just before been sent to us with one hand in her with another line, we wanted him to stay by the dead fish. He said he would not—if we liked to go, so would he; but stay there by himself; while sport was going on, he would not.

"At last we resolved to leave the small boat empty, and to take him in ours. To this he agreed. So, making the whale fast to his boat, and securing the boat to the berg, away we pulled, as fast as we could lay our backs to the oars, after a fish we saw blowing near us. Now what I tell you is true, mates. Not thirty fathoms had we pulled, when over toppled the iceberg right down on the boat, and we were nearly swamped with the sea it made. When we pulled back to look for the whale, neither it nor the boat was to be seen. You may fancy what would have become of us if we had been there!"

"There are none of us, to my belief; but have often, if we would but acknowledge it, been mercifully preserved by Providence," observed my friend Andrew.

"I won't speak of what has happened to myself; and Terence, and Peter here. No one will doubt, I hope, but that it was the finger of God directed you to take us off the iceberg; but every day some less remarkable case occurs. A block falls from aloft on the deck, where a moment before we were standing; a musket-ball passes close to one's ear; a topmast is carried away just as we have come off the yard; and fifty other things occur of like nature, and we never think of being grateful for our preservation. Talking of escapes, I once saw a man carried overboard by a line round his ankle as a fish was diving. We all gave him up for lost; but he had a sharp knife in the right-hand pocket of his jacket, and he kept his thoughts about him so well, that before he had got many fathoms down, he managed to stoop and cut the line below his foot, then striking with all his might, he rose to the surface."

"Did you ever hear tell of the Dutchman who had a ride on the back of a whale?" asked David. "He had just struck his harpoon into a fish, when, lifting up her tail, she drove the boat into shatters. He fell on his back, and got hold of his harpoon, his foot at the same time being entangled in the line. Away swam the fish on the top of the water, fortunately for him never thinking of diving. He stood upright all the time, holding on by his right hand, while his left tried in vain to find his knife to cut himself clear. Another boat followed, for the chance of rescuing him; but there appeared but little hope of his being saved, unless he could free himself. Just as the fish was going down, the harpoon shook out, and, jumping off its back, to which he gave a hearty kick, he struck out for the boat, and was picked up when he could swim no more. He is the only man I ever heard of who really has ridden on a whale's back, though there's many a tale told by those who have, which is not true."

"I've been on the back of a live whale more than once," said Garrock. "I mean when we've been fishing among bay ice, and the fish have come up through the holes to breathe. But I was going to say how last season we had a chase after a fish, which gave us more trouble than I ever saw before. It led us a chase for the best part of the day, after it had been struck. It dragged one boat, with twenty lines fast, right under a floe, and then broke away; and when we killed it at last, it had taken out thirty lines, which, as you know, is close upon six miles of line."

Thus yarn after yarn was spun. I do not attempt to give the peculiar phraseology of the speakers; but their stories, which I believe to be perfectly true, may prove interesting. For a whole week we were beset, and some of the green hands began to fancy that we should be blocked up for the winter; but the old ones knew better.

Every day the surface of the ice, where the nip had taken place, was examined with anxious eyes, in the hopes that some sign of its taking off or breaking up might be given. At length the pressure became less, the sound under the ice shrill and sharp, instead of the sullen roar which had before been heard; the fragments which had been cast above others began to glide down and disappear in the chasms which were opening around, and water was seen in a long thin line extending to the northward.

A lane was formed, with a wall of fragments on either side; the lane widened, the fragments rushed into the water, and the captain, from the crow's-nest, ordered the ship to be towed out of dock. The order was cheering to our hearts; and as we had plenty of hands, it was soon executed. All sail was made, and away we flew through the passage, in a hurry to take advantage of it, lest it should again close upon us. We succeeded in getting clear, and soon after were joined by our consorts, which had escaped the nip.

We made the land again to the northward of Cape York, and, when close in, were completely becalmed. The boats of each ship were ordered ahead to tow; and thus we slowly progressed along one of the most picturesque scenes it has ever been my fortune to witness in the arctic regions. The water was of glassy smoothness, the sky of brightest blue, and the atmosphere of perfect transparency; while around floated numberless icebergs of the most beautiful forms, and of dazzling hues, while all around was glancing and glittering beneath a bright and glowing sun.

One berg, I remember, was of enormous size. On the north side it was perpendicular, as if just severed from another; but, as we rounded it on the west, ledge above ledge appeared, each fringed with icicles reaching to the one below, thus forming lines of graceful columns, with a gallery within, appearing as if tinged with emerald-green. The summit was peaked and turreted, and broken into many fantastic forms. On the eastern side a clear arch was seen; and several small cascades fell from ledge to ledge with a trickling sound, and into the water with a gentle splash, which could distinctly be heard as we passed.

It must be remembered that in every direction arose bergs of equal beauty; while in the background were lofty hills covered with snow, tinted of a pinkish hue, and above them, of dazzling whiteness, ranges of eternal glaciers, towering to the sky. I could scarcely have believed that a scene of such enchanting beauty could have existed in the arctic regions, and was inclined to fancy, as I pulled at the oar, that they were rocks of Parian marble and alabaster, and that the galleries and caverns they contained were the abodes of fairies and the guardian spirits of those realms. But avast! what has Peter the Whaler to do with such poetical ideas?

On we worked our way northward. In clear weather, when a good look-out was to be had from the crow's-nest, we were able to make our way among the streams of ice; but in thick weather, when our course could not be marked out, we were sadly delayed.

At last, after keeping a westerly course for a few hours, we broke through all intervening barriers, and once more felt our gallant ship lifting to the buoyant wave of the open sea, or rather what is called the "north water."

The ice, by the warm weather, the currents, and the northerly winds, being driven out of Lancaster Sound and the head of Baffin's Bay to the southward, leaves this part, for most of the summer, free from impediments. In five days after leaving the eastern land, having passed the north of Lancaster Sound, we came off the famous fishing-station of Pond's Bay.

Chapter Twenty Eight

The whole coast, in most places, was lined with a sheet of ice some ten or fifteen miles wide, to the edge of which, in perfectly smooth water, our ship, with many others at various distances, was made fast.

Fancy a day, warm to our feelings as one at the same time of year in England, and an atmosphere of a brilliancy rarely or never seen at home, not a breath of air stirring the glassy surface of the shining ocean; while on the land side lofty mountains stretched away on either side, with the opening of the bay in the centre, the rocks of numberless tints, from the many-coloured lichens growing on them, rising as it were out of a bed of snow still filling the valleys even in midsummer; while mid-way, along the dark frowning crags which formed the coast, hung a wavy line of semi-transparent mist, now tinged with a crimson hue, from the almost horizontal rays of the sun, verging towards midnight.

These objects also, it must be understood, appeared so close at hand, that I could scarcely persuade myself that an easy run across the level ice would not carry me up to them; and yet all the while they were upwards of a dozen miles off.

Most of the watch were "on the bran," that is, were in the boats stationed along the edge of the ice, on the look-out for whales. A few hands only, besides myself, were on deck, taking our fisherman's walk, with our fingers in our pockets, and the watch below were sound asleep in their berths, when Captain Rendall, as was his custom, went aloft before turning in, to take a look-out for fish from his crow's-nest. We watched him eagerly. In a few minutes he hailed the deck, with the joyful news that at about ten miles off there was a whole run of whales, spouting away as fast as they could blow.

On the instant, instead of the silence and tranquillity which had before prevailed, all was now noise, excitement, and hurry. The sleepers tumbled up from below; the harpooners got ready their gear and received their orders from the master; the boats on the bran came alongside, to have their kegs replenished with water, and their tubs with bread, beef, and pork; while the more eager mates ran aloft, to assure themselves of the best direction to take.

In a few minutes five boats were pulling out towards the run, as if the lives of a ship's company depended on our exertions. "Hurra, my lads, hurra! give way," shouted our boat-steerers; and give way we did indeed.

Frequently, as we pulled on, we heard the loud blasts of the narwhals, or sea-unicorns, as they came towards the bay in shoals; and each time I fancied we must be close upon a whale, and that the sport was about to begin, so loud a sound did they make.

The sea-unicorn is, when full grown, from thirteen to sixteen feet long, and has a long spiral horn or tusk growing rather on one side of its upper jaw, of from eight to ten feet in length. The eyes are very small, the blow-hole is directly over them, and the head is small, blunt, and round, and the mouth cannot be opened wide. The colour, when young, is grey, with darker spots on it, and when full grown, of a yellowish-white. It is a very inoffensive animal. It is said to use its horn for the purpose of breaking through the ice to breathe, and neither to destroy its prey nor to defend itself. It swims very fast; when struck, dives rapidly, but soon returns to the surface, and is easily killed. We passed several shoals of them on our pull, before we got up to the run, near a small floe.

"There she blows!" exclaimed our boat-steerer, almost in a whisper, so great was his eagerness and fear of disturbing the fish, as a large fish appeared close to us. We had a fine burst; the harpooner was on his feet, and, his weapon glancing from his hand, struck the monster.

Instead, however, of diving, up he rose, clear almost from the water, his head first, seeming, as his immense bulk appeared against the sky, like some giant of the deep. We thought he was going to leap on to the floe; but, suddenly plunging his head beneath the water, his tremendous tail was lifted above us. I thought all was over. One blow from it would have annihilated us, and dashed our boat into a thousand fragments; but the fish, instead, dived directly down under the floe, his tail only splashing the water over us, and we were safe.

Then arose the exciting shout of "A fall, a fall!" Other boats came hurrying to our aid; but, alas, the line on a sudden slackened, and, with a blank face, the harpooner began to haul it in.

The fish had shaken himself clear of the harpoon, and escaped. Mighty must have been the force used, for the massive iron shaft was twisted and turned as a thin piece of wire might have been bent by a turn of the hand.

But, hurra! there are plenty more fish near; and with a will, little disconcerted, we gave way after them. One was seen at some distance from a floe, in which there was a crack. Now it is known that a whale generally rises close to the nearest floe; and if there is a crack in it, that part is selected instead of the outer edge. We got up to it before the fish appeared; our oars were out of the water; our harpooner standing up and watching eagerly every sign of the approach of our expected prey, guiding by signs the boat-steerer, who, with his oar, was silently impelling on the boat by sculling.

"Gently, boys—there's her eddy—two strokes more—now avast pulling!"

I could just see the head, and the large black mass of the monster's back, rising slowly from the water as he spoke, forming a strong contrast to the clear blue and white of the ice, and pure glittering sea. Then was heard the peculiar snorting blast, as she sent up in the air two watery jets; but in an instant we were upon her.

"Harden up, my lads!" shouted the harpooner; and a lusty stroke sent us almost on to the monster's back; then flew forth his unerring harpoon. For a few moments, but for a few only, the whale seemed prepared to die without a struggle: a convulsive quiver passed through its frame; then, lifting up its flukes, it dived down, like its predecessor, beneath the floe. The iron had sunk in, and, raising our Blue Jack, with a loud shout we proclaimed a fall. Out flew the line with tremendous rapidity. Now the harpooner, sitting on his thwart, attempted to check the fish by turning the line round the bollard; but so quickly did it pass through his hands, shielded by mitts, that, almost in spite of the water thrown on it, smoke ascended from the burning wood, while the bows of the boat were drawn through the underwash to the solid floe beyond.

At times we thought the boat's bow would have been drawn under the floe; again the line-manager let the line run out, and she rose once more, to be drawn down directly it was checked. But it was all-important to tire the fish, or otherwise all our line might be taken out before any assistance could come. Should this be the case, we might, after all, lose the fish. First one oar was elevated, to show our need of aid; then a second, a third, and a fourth, as the line drew near what is called the "bitter end."

"Hold on, Darby, hold on!" we shouted in our eagerness; for we feared we might have to cut, or that the boat might be drawn under. Our shipmates tugged away at their oars with all their might; the boats from every direction dashing through the water to the point where they thought the fish might rise. Our line at the very edge began to slacken—a sign that she had ceased diving. She appeared about a quarter of a mile off or more, at the edge of the floe.

The quick-sighted eye of the first mate was on her almost before she had reached the surface; and before she could again seek safety in the ocean's depths, another harpoon was plunged into her. We instantly began hauling in our lines; but before long she was off again, swimming away some depth below the surface, at a great rate, while we and the other boat were towed after her. Again the strain slackened, and she rose once more; but this time her foes were close to her. Another harpoon was struck, but it was needless. Without mercy lances were thrust into her on every side, till the shouts which reached our ears, as we slowly approached, hauling in our lines, proclaimed that our victory was complete. The fish was now secured, as I have before described, and made fast to a floe, while all but one boat made chase after another fish which blew temptingly near.

I ought to have said that, after securing the whale, all hands turned to with a right good-will to attack the bread and meat we had with us; for though whale-hunting beats hollow any other style of hunting, whether of deer, elephants, or tigers, yet it cannot by any manner of means be carried on without sustenance to the frame.

Away we went, then, the boat of the first mate leading. He, too, was successful in striking the fish. Three times she dived; but each time one or other of her enemies were upon her with harpoon and lances, while her eddying wake was dyed with blood, and a thick pellicle of oil, which attracted crowds of persevering Mollies to feast on it, marked her course.

She at last rose close to a floe, when we all rushed in upon her. The cry of "Stern all!" was given. Her death-flurry had come on. High up in the air she sent a stream of blood and oil, which fell thick upon us in showers of spray, and on a hummock which was near; and the edges of the ice were dyed of a crimson tint.

The weariness which began to oppress even the strongest, told us that we had had work enough, and that a second night was approaching. With shouts of satisfaction, we now began the task of towing our prizes to the ship. It was slow and wearying work; but every fish we took brought us nearer home, so we set cheerfully about it.

When we at length reached the ship, we found that we had been full thirty-six hours away, nearly all the time in active exertion; and yet, from the excitement of the work, neither did we feel unusually weary, nor were we aware of the time which had passed.

I must remind my readers that this could only happen in a latitude and at a period where there is little or no difference between night and day. Our fishing was most successful, partly owing to our good fortune in meeting with the fish, but owing also much to the sagacity of our captain and his officers.

Similar scenes were occurring every day; but though they were all nearly as exciting, and the interest of the sport was never decreased, but rather grew on us, yet, if I were to attempt to describe each chase, and how each fish was killed, my readers would weary with the account.

For the greater part of a month we remained in the bay; and now the fish becoming scarce, and the summer drawing to a conclusion, with a fair breeze we made sail to the southward.

I spoke of our having passed Lancaster Sound, a short way to the south of which Pond's Bay is situated. I did not mention at the time the interest with which I regarded that vast inlet—the mouth, one cannot help fancying, to the unknown sea which bounds the northern shores of the American continent. I certainly think more of it now, while I am writing, than I did then, because I have since become aware of the many gallant exploits which have been there performed, and the bold attempts which have been made to pierce through it to the seas beyond.

I need scarcely remind my readers that up that passage the veteran arctic explorer, Sir John Franklin, and his brave companions, are supposed to have proceeded. Under his command, the *Erebus* and *Terror* sailed from the Thames on the 26th May, 1845, to proceed up Davis's Straits, then into Lancaster Sound, and from thence, without stopping, to examine the coast, to push westward as fast as they could towards Behring's Straits.

Captain Crozier had command of the *Terror*; and the expedition was accompanied by the transport *Bonetto Junior*, commanded by Lieutenant Griffith, and laden with provisions, clothing, etcetera, to be put on board the ships in Davis's Straits. Both vessels were fitted with steam-engines and screw-propellers; but they did not go ahead with them more than three knots an hour. Lieutenant Griffith reports "that he left them with every species of provisions for three entire years, independently of five bullocks; they had also stores for the same time, and fuel in abundance."

The expedition was last seen by the *Prince of Wales* whaler, on the 26th July, in latitude 74 degrees 48 minutes north, longitude 66 degrees 13 minutes west, moored to an iceberg, and waiting for an opening in the great body of ice, which I described as filling the middle of Baffin's Bay, in order to reach the entrance of Lancaster Sound. All hands were well and in high spirits, and determined to succeed, if success were possible; but since that day they have never been heard of.

Year after year have those gallant men in vain been looked for, but not without hope of their return, nor without attempts made to discover and rescue them.

When the year 1848 arrived, and no tidings had been received of the lost voyagers, it was determined to send out three expeditions to look for them. One under Captain Kellett, who commanded the *Herald* and Captain Moore, who commanded the *Plover*; proceeded to Behring's Straits, and after continuing along the American coast as far as they could go, they were to despatch some whale-boats, to meet a second expedition under Sir John Richardson and Dr Rae, who were to descend the Mackenzie River, and there to examine the coast; while Sir James Ross, commanding the *Enterprise*, and Captain Bird, the *Investigator*, were to proceed at once to Lancaster Sound, and there to examine the coast as they proceeded.

After leaving deposits of food and directions in several places, these expeditions returned, without having discovered any traces of our missing countrymen.

Notwithstanding the ill-success of the first set of expeditions, others were without delay determined on. Captain Collinson was appointed to command the *Enterprise*, having under him Commander McClure in the *Investigator*; and on the 20th of January, 1850, they sailed from Plymouth for Behring's Straits, where they were to be joined by the *Plover*. They were to endeavour to reach Melville Island.

In the meantime, Dr Rae, who had remained in America, was ordered to continue his search along the northern coast; while the Government of the United States prepared an expedition for the same purpose. The British Government likewise fitted out four ships, under the command of Captain Austin, in the *Resolute*; the *Assistance*, Captain Ommanney; the *Pioneer*; Lieutenant Osborn; and the *Free Trader*—the two latter screw-propeller steam-vessels.

Two private expeditions have also started. The *Lady Franklin* is commanded by Mr Penny, a veteran whaling captain, who has with him a fine brig as a tender, called the *Sophia*. Captain Penny was to be guided by circumstances, in following the course he judged expedient. Besides this, the veteran explorer, Sir John Ross, has taken command of another private expedition. He is on board the *Felix*, a large schooner, and has the *Mary*, a tender of twelve tons, with him. They also are to proceed to Barrow Straits, and to examine various headlands on their way. The *Mary* is to be left at Banks' Land, as a vessel of retreat, and the *Felix* will proceed for another year as far as she can to the westward, examining the coast on the way.

These last expeditions have been fitted out in consequence of the energetic and persevering efforts of Lady Franklin, and the niece of Sir John Franklin, Miss Sophia Cracroft; and those who have seen them, month after month, indefatigably labouring in that, to them, holy cause, hoping almost at times against hope, yet still undaunted, persevering unweariedly, must feel and heartily pray that they may have their reward in the happy return of the long-missing ones.

I was unable to refrain from giving this brief sketch of a subject in which every man worthy of the name of Briton must feel the deepest and warmest interest; and I now resume the thread of my more humble narrative.

Chapter Twenty Nine

The return of darkness during the night gave us notice that we were advancing towards the south, and that the short arctic summer was drawing to a close. We could no longer continue our course, hour after hour without intermission, as before, the officers relieving each other in the crow's-nest, and one watch following the other through one long-protracted day.

It was impossible with any safety to proceed through that icy sea when darkness came on, and therefore each night we were obliged to make the ship fast to a floe till the return of daylight. But those nights were sometimes such as are not to be found in another realm. The bright moon floated in an atmosphere the most clear and brilliant that can be conceived, while the silvery masses of ice lay sparkling beneath it, as they floated on the calm and majestic ocean.

Then the sun at setting bathed the sea, the sky, the rugged mountains, the pinnacles of the icebergs, and the lower floes with colours and tints more beautiful and varied than the imagination can picture, far more than words can describe. But I should not dwell on such scenes, except that I wish to observe that God distributes His bounties throughout the globe with an equal hand; and that, barren and inhospitable as is that land, no less than in southern realms are His power and goodness displayed.

For about four days we had proceeded south, our course interrupted whenever we met with a whale; and if she was killed, we made fast to a floe till we had flensed and made off. Some of the smaller whalers had got full ships, and, with joyous shouts and light hearts on board, they passed us on their way home; and others, unwilling to wait, returned not full, so that we were nearly the last ship.

The weather continued beautifully fine, though now growing cold and chilly. We also had nearly a full ship, and were congratulating ourselves on soon being able to follow those which had preceded us; but, till we were quite full, we could not think of doing so while the ice continued open, and there was a chance of a fish. Consequently we were all on the look-out, and more eager than ever to secure our prey.

One afternoon, while we were under weigh, the cheering sound of "A fish, a fish! see, she blows!" from the crow's-nest, roused us all to activity. Two boats were immediately equipped and sent in chase. I was in one of them. While we were yet close to the ship, another whale was espied to the southward, at a very great distance. The prospect of getting two fish at a fall was more than could be resisted; and, while we were killing our fish, the master made sail to come up with the other. We were successful; and, with less difficulty than usual, killed the whale at the edge of a floe connected with the land, towards which it had gone for shelter. The whale was killed, and made fast to the floe, waiting for the return of the ship.

While we were all engaged in the chase and capture, no one had noticed the change in the weather. From a fresh breeze, sufficiently to the eastward to enable the ship to stand back towards us, it had fallen a flat calm: the sea lay stretched out before us like a dark shining glass, while an ominous stillness reigned through the air.

Andrew, who was line-manager in the boat to which I belonged, was the first to observe it, as we were assembled on the floe busily engaged in hauling in the lines. He said nothing; but I saw him look up, and, after glancing around for some moments, put his hand over his brow, and gaze earnestly forth in the direction the ship had gone. The anxious expression his countenance instantly assumed alarmed me; and, though he at once resumed his task of coiling away the lines, I saw that all was not right. I then cast my eyes seaward, to see whereabouts the ship was. I need scarcely say that I felt a very natural alarm, when I discovered that she was almost hull down.

Andrew again looked up. The anxious expression on his face had in no way diminished; but he was not a man to alarm or unnerve his companions by any unnecessary exclamation.

"Bear a hand, lads," he at length said. "The sooner we get in our lines, and tow the fish alongside, the better."

"I was thinking the same," said old David. "And I say the sooner the ship stands back to pick us up, the better for us. We couldn't get the fish alongside till long after dark, if she comes no nearer to us; and how she's to do that, without a breeze springs up, I don't know."

These few remarks scarcely interrupted the task in hand. When it was accomplished, however, and we had time to look round us, we all began to consider more about the difficulty of our position. I must explain that there were two boats, with a crew of five men each, so that we were ten in all. We had with us a few provisions and a cooking apparatus, with our pea-jackets to put on while waiting after our heating exercise.

The harpooners and the elder men now began to consult what was best to be done. David gave it as his opinion that the other boats had been led a long chase after a fish, and that the ship had followed thus far to the southward to pick them up, with the intention of returning immediately to us, when the calm so unexpectedly came on.

"There's no doubt about what has happened, mates; but I want to know what those who have had experience in these seas think is about to happen," said Andrew. "There's something in the look of the sky and sea, and the feel of the air, which makes me think a change is about to take place. I therefore ask whether we shall stay by the fish, or leave her secured to the floe, and get aboard as fast as we can."

In answer to this proposal, which was certainly wise, and perfectly justifiable, several opinions were given. Some were for getting on board without delay, others were for towing the fish towards the ship, and several were for remaining by till the ship should return, though the majority were for going back in the boats alone.

A more mighty Power than ours decided what was to be done; for, while we were still speaking, a sudden gust of wind came blowing along the edge of the ice from the northward, and throwing up the sea in so extraordinary a manner, that, had the boats been exposed to it, they could scarcely have lived. Then the wind as suddenly fell, and again all was calm as before.

"Now's your time, lads; we must get on board as quick as we can," shouted old David. While, accordingly, we were with additional care securing the whale to the floe, the sky, which was already overclouded, began to send down dense showers of snow, which so obscured the atmosphere, that the sharpest eye amongst us could no longer distinguish the ship. To attempt to get on board under these circumstances, would be more dangerous than remaining where we were; so, putting on our Flushing jackets, we got into the boats, and drew a sail over our shoulders, to shelter ourselves as much as possible from the storm.

The snow, which had begun to fall in flakes, now changed to a powder, so dense that it appeared as if night had already come on.

"It's very dark, Andrew," I remarked; "what can be going to happen?"

"Why, I'll tell you, Peter," answered David, who heard my question. "There's going to be a harder gale of wind than we've had since you came on board; and if the old ship don't stand up to her canvas, and fetch us before night, there are few who would wish to change places with us, that's all."

I did not by any means like this announcement, for I felt that this time old David was not joking with me. However, our only course was to remain where we were. If the gale did come on, we were safer on the ice than on the sea; and if it passed off, the ship would not fail to come and take us on board.

In the meantime, we were continually putting our heads from under our shelter, to cast anxious glances towards where we supposed the ship to be, and in every other direction, to discover if there was any opening in the thick cloud of snow which dropped around us. I say dropped, for I never before saw snow fall so perpendicularly, and in such minute powdery particles. The peculiar and oppressive gloominess which filled the air, made one feel that something unusual was approaching, otherwise I could scarcely fancy that in so perfect a calm any danger could be at hand.

For two hours we sat cramped up in the boat, and, in spite of our warm clothing, suffering not a little from the cold, which was greater than for some time past we had experienced. Suddenly the snow ceased, and with eager haste, Andrew, David, and some others jumped out of the boat and climbed to the top of the nearest hummock, from whence they could get a wider look-out than on the flat ice.

With feelings which it were vain to attempt to describe, we looked for the ship, and could nowhere see her. To the southward there was a thick mist, caused by the snow falling in that direction, and in this she was probably shrouded.

On looking to the north, we perceived in the horizon a bright luminous appearance, something like the ice-blink, but brighter, and which seemed to increase in height. David looked at it for an instant, and then shouted out, "Bear a hand, my lads, and haul up the boats—the gale is upon us!"

Suiting the action to the word, he rushed down from the hummock, accompanied by the rest of us, and we commenced hauling one of the boats up on the ice. While all hands were engaged at this work, and before it was completely accomplished, down came the gale upon us with terrific violence, almost lifting us off our legs, and hurling us into the now foaming and hissing sea. The snow, which lay thick on the ice, was lifted up and blown in clouds over us; the ocean, which before lay so tranquil, was now lashed into fury.

"Haul away, my lads, and run the boat up," shouted Andrew, his voice scarcely heard amid the tumult. We had taken out most of the things from the other boat, and, having secured the first, were about to haul her up, when a heavy sea, striking the ice, broke off a piece to which she was secured, and carried her and the harpooner belonging to her, who was standing near her, far beyond our reach. To have attempted to launch the boat to go to his rescue would have been madness. One loud, hopeless shriek was heard, and he sunk for ever.

We had little time to mourn for our poor messmate—our own condition occupied all our thoughts. At the same moment that the boat was carried away, the sea broke the whale from the lashings which secured her to the ice, and, without our having any power to preserve our prize, it was driven down along the edge of the floe, from which it gradually floated away.

"What's to be done now?" I asked, with several others, in a voice of despair.

"Trust in God," answered Andrew in a solemn voice. "Peter, remember we have been in a worse position before, and He saved us. He may, if He wills it, save us again."

"But how are we ever to get back to the ship, with only one boat to carry us?" asked some one.

"Captain Rendall is not a man likely to desert his people," observed David. "The ship will come back and take us off, when the gale is over—no fear of that, mates."

Notwithstanding the tone of confidence with which he spoke, I suspected that he did not feel quite as much at his ease as he pretended to be. Our position was indeed, I felt, most critical, though I did not express my fears. The gale might continue for days, and our ship, if she escaped shipwreck, which too probably would be her lot, would be at all events driven so far to the south, that she would find it utterly impossible to return. The ice, even, on which we stood, might any instant break up from the force of the waves; and if we could not retreat farther back in time, our destruction would be almost certain. We had a boat; but even in smooth water she could scarcely do more than contain us all, and in such a sea as was likely to be running for some time she could not live ten minutes. We could have no hope, therefore, of regaining the ship in her; and should we be compelled, therefore, to quit the ice, she could afford us no refuge.

We had a small quantity of provisions,—enough, with economy, to sustain life for two or three days, though not more than was intended to supply a couple of good meals, should we have been kept away from the ship a sufficient time to require them. We had some boats' sails, a cooking apparatus, two harpoons, spears, and two fowling-pieces, brought by the harpooners to kill a few dovekies for our messes. Several things, with a set of lines and harpoons, had been lost in the other boat.

For some time after the fatal catastrophe I have described, we stood looking out seaward, undecided what steps to take. The wrenching asunder of some huge masses of the ice, which the sea drove up close to the boat, and the violent heaving to which the whole body was subjected, showed us that we must rouse ourselves to further exertion. We had no need of consultation to judge that we must without delay get farther away from the sea; and, having laden our boat with all our stores, we began to work her along the ice towards the shore, which lay bleak and frowning some ten miles or so from us.

Our progress was slow; for the ice, though thick, was much rotted from the heat of the whole summer, and in some places it was very rough, while shallow pools of water constantly appeared in our path, and compelled us to make a circuit round them. When we had accomplished nearly two miles, it was proposed that we should wait there to see if any change took place in the weather. There was no longer a motion in the ice, and Andrew and David gave it as their opinion that there was consequently no danger of its breaking up so far from the edge, and that we might remain there in safety. Night was now fast approaching; and the gale, instead of abating, blew with greater fury than at first.

The exertion had somewhat warmed us; but the moment we stopped, the cold wind whistled through our clothing, and showed us that we must prepare some shelter for the night, if we would avoid being frozen to death.

Another point we also discovered was, that we required some one to take the lead, and to act as chief officer among us. The remaining harpooner would, by right, have taken command; but, though expert in the use of his weapon, he was not a man by character or knowledge well fitted to command the respect of the rest of us. This we all felt, as he probably did also, as he raised no objection when David proposed that we should elect an officer whom we should be bound to obey, till we could regain our ship, should we ever be so fortunate so to do.

Three were first proposed, but Andrew Thompson was finally selected; for, though he was known not to have so much practical experience as several of the others, his firmness, sagacity, and high moral character were acknowledged by all.

"And now, my lads," he said, when he had modestly accepted the office, "the first thing we must do is to build a snow-wall, to shelter us from the wind; and as soon as the wind moderates, we'll have up a flagstaff on the top of the highest hummock, to show our friends where to look for us."

According to this advice, we set to work to collect the snow, which did not lay more than three inches thick on the ice. We first made it into cakes, about four times the size of an ordinary brick, and then piled them up in a semicircular form, the convex side being turned to the wind. Over the top we spread a boat's sail, which was kept down by lumps of snow being placed on the top of it. The canvas was also allowed to hang over a couple of lances lashed together in front, so that we had a very tolerable shelter. The snow was scraped away from the interior; and such spars and planks as we could get out of the boat were spread at the bottom, with a sail over them, to form our bed.

These arrangements were accomplished as the long twilight turned into total darkness. We lay down, and prepared to pass the dreary hours till the sun rose again as best we could. I thought of the time I had spent on the iceberg, and, remembering Andrew's words, I did not despair. I slept, as did my companions, many of them with the careless indifference to danger which has become the characteristic of most British seamen.

I was awoke by the excessive cold, though we kept as close together within our shelter as we could, for the sake of the warmth. My companions were still asleep, and I was afraid if I moved of arousing them. The storm still raged furiously without, and I could not again compose myself to sleep for the noise it made.

I lay awake, listening to its whistling sound as it blew over the ice, when I fancied that I heard a low grumbling noise, like a person with a gruff voice talking to himself. At last this idea grew so strong on me, that I crept quietly to the curtain in front of our hut, and, lifting up a corner, looked out. The stars were shining forth from the sky, and there was a thin crescent moon, by the light of which I saw a white monster leaning over the gunwale of our boat, examining, it appeared to me, the things in her. I was not long in recognising the visitor to be a large, white, shaggy polar bear. He first took up one thing, and, smelling it and turning it over on every side, replaced it. When, however, he came to a piece of beef, or anything eatable, he without ceremony appropriated it, and was thus rapidly consuming our slender store of provisions. "This will never do," I thought to myself. "If this goes on, we shall be to a certainty starved."

We had fortunately brought the two guns into the hut, that they might run no risk of getting damp. They were both loaded; and, drawing back, I got hold of one, hoping to shoot the bear before he was disturbed. If I aroused my companions first, they to a certainty would make some noise, which would probably frighten away our visitor, and we should lose both the bear and the provisions.

When I again put my head from under the sail, he was still at work. I was on my knees, and had got the gun to my shoulder, when he saw me. He was fortunately on the other side of the boat; for no sooner did his eye fall on me, than he began slowly to walk along the side, holding on by the gunwale, evidently intending to get close to me. "My best chance is to hit him in the eyes," I thought, "and blind him. If he once gets hold of me, he'll give me a squeeze I shall not like."

Before he had moved many steps I fired full in his face. The report of the gun, and the loud growl of rage and pain uttered by the brute, instantly awakened my companions. They started to their feet, but had some difficulty to understand what had happened. The bear, on being wounded, nearly fell headlong into the boat; but, recovering himself, he endeavoured to find his way round to the spot where he had seen me.

"A bear, a bear!" I sung out. "Get your lances ready and run him through." Most fortunately I had hit the monster so directly in the eyes, that he could not see his way, and this prevented him from rushing directly on me; for though I might have leaped out of his way round the back of the hut, he would in all probability have seized upon one of my half-awake companions.

This momentary delay gave time to Andrew to spring to his feet, and to draw out a lance from under the sail. He appeared at the entrance of the hut, just as the bear, slightly recovering himself, was rushing forward, with his mouth open and covered with foam, and a stream, which I could see even in that light, trickling down his face. His paws were stretched out, and in another instant he would have had me in his deadly clutch, when Andrew dashed at him with his spear. The bear seized the handle, and endeavoured to wrench it from his assailant; but the iron had entered his breast, and, in his attempt to rush on, it pierced him to the heart.

The rest of the party were by this time awake, and, armed with whatever they could first seize, and seeing what had happened, they all set up a shout of triumph, every one of us forgetting entirely for the moment the very precarious position in which we were placed.

We had several reasons to be satisfied with having killed the bear. In the first place, had he put his snout into our hut while we were all asleep, he might have killed some of us; secondly, we had saved most of our provisions by our discovering him; and what he had taken was amply repaid by the sustenance his flesh would afford us, and the use to which we might turn his skin, for bedding or clothing, should we have to remain any time on the ice.

"Our friend there has given us a lesson to keep a better look-out in future," remarked Andrew. "If it had not been for Peter, he might have carried off every bit of our food; so we must take it by turns to keep watch. I'll stand the first."

"And I the second, willingly," I exclaimed. "I've no inclination to sleep, and if I did, I should be fancying all the time that the bear had me in his grasp."

So it was arranged each man should take an hour at a time, as near as could be guessed, and thus all would have plenty of rest, and be fit for work in the daytime.

Before the rest turned in again, we drew the carcase of the bear close up to the hut, so that, if any of his fellows should come near him, they might to a certainty be seen, and shot without difficulty.

Extraordinary as it may seem, the rest of the people were very soon asleep again. Andrew and I were the only two awake. The gun which had been fired was reloaded, and, having placed the two close at hand, we sat down just inside the curtain, leaving only a small aperture on either side of it, through which to look out. We also placed a couple of lances within our reach, that, should any more bears visit us, as we hoped they might, we might have a better chance of killing them; for their flesh, though rank, is not unwholesome, and, at all events, it would enable us to support life as long as it lasted, independently of the value of their skins.

After we had made our preparations, Andrew advised me to lie down and to try to sleep; but I told him that I was too much excited, and that it was impossible, and that, if he would allow me, I would much rather sit up and watch with him; or, if he liked, I would watch while he slept, and would call him if anything occurred.

"Neither can I sleep, Peter," he answered: "You and the rest have chosen me to guide you, and I doubly feel the responsibility of my office; for I need not tell you that I think our position very bad. From the first time I saw you, I found that you were well educated, and I since have had reason to place confidence in you. Now, Peter, I am afraid that, when we are surrounded with far greater difficulties than we have yet met with, some of these poor fellows will lose heart, and sink under them, unless their spirits are kept up, and a good example is set them. I therefore rely upon you to assist me, by showing that, young as you are, you do not shrink from danger, and that you place a firm reliance on the power of God to deliver us, notwithstanding all the appearance to the contrary."

I told Andrew that I thanked him for the confidence he placed in me, and that I hoped I should not disappoint his expectations.

"I know you will not, Peter; but I tell you that our courage will be severely tried," he answered.

"Why, don't you think the ship will be able to take us off?" I asked.

"I do not think she will, Peter," he replied. "Before the gale is over, she will have been driven very far to the south; and it will take her so many days to beat back, if the wind should continue foul, that Captain Rendall will consider we must have perished, and that the attempt would be useless, and that he should not be justified in thus risking the safety of his ship."

"What hope, then, have we?" I asked.

"My greatest hope is, that we may be seen by some other ship passing after the gale has moderated," he answered. "If that fails to us, we must endeavour to pass the winter on shore. Others have done so before now; and I do not see why we should not manage to live as well as the ignorant natives who inhabit this country."

"If we had powder, and shot, and fuel, and timber to build a house with, I should say we might do it," I answered; "but as we have none of these things, I am afraid we shall be frozen to death as soon as the cold sets in."

"The natives live, and we must try to find out how they contrive to do it," was the tenor of his answer.

Miserable as the night was, and slow as the hours seemed to drag along, they at last passed away. We had no further visits from the bears, nor were we otherwise disturbed. When daylight came, there was nothing in the prospect to cheer our hearts. On one side there was a sheet of ice covered with snow, with high rocky cliffs beyond; and, on the other, the wide expanse of ocean, still tossing and foaming with the fierce storm which raged over it.

Chapter Thirty

Our companions slept on, and, while they happily were able to forget the hardships and dangers which were in store for them, we could not find it in our hearts to awake them. At last, one after the other, they awoke. As they did so, they went and looked out at the dreary prospect I have described, and then returning, sat themselves down in gloomy silence in the hut.

On seeing the discontent, not to say despair, which their countenances exhibited, I remembered the conversation I had with Andrew in the night, and determined at once to try and follow his advice; so I went and sat down with the rest.

"Well, mates, things don't look very pleasant, I'll allow, but they might be worse, you know," I remarked.

"I don't see how that can be," answered one of the most surly of the party. "Here are we left by our ship, without food or a house, at the beginning of the winter; and it's cold enough, I've heard, in these parts, to freeze up every drop of blood in the veins in ten minutes."

"Andrew and Terence, and Tom and I, were once much worse off, when we were left on the iceberg," I observed. "As for food, too, we've got a good lump there, which came to our door of its own accord. We've every chance of taking plenty more; and I've heard say the country is full of game of all sorts. Then, as for a house, we must try and build one, if no ship comes to take us off. Mind, I don't say that none will come; only if we are left here, we need not fancy that we are going to die in consequence."

"Faith, Peter's the boy for brightening a fellow's heart up," exclaimed Terence, rousing himself from the despondency which he, with the rest, had begun to feel. "Why, mates, perhaps after all we may have as merry a winter of it as if we got home, though they do say the nights are rather long at that time."

Terence's remark did more good than mine. There was something inspiriting in the tone of his voice; and in a few minutes all hands were ready to perform their best,—at all events, to do what Andrew considered for the public good. He first ordered us to have breakfast, for we had been in no humour to take any supper the night before. We accordingly brought in our provisions, and were about to commence on them, when I suggested that we should preserve them for times of greater necessity, and begin, instead, upon the bear.

"But how are we to cook him?" asked some one. "We can't eat him raw, and we've got no oil for the kitchen."

The kitchen was the cooking apparatus I have spoken of. It was simply an oil lamp with several wicks, and a couple of saucepans, a kettle, and frying-pan to fit over it. The crude oil drawn from the last fish we had killed served for it.

"As to that, lads, he'll supply the oil to cook himself with," remarked Andrew. "Let us skin him and cut him up at once, and then he'll be all ready to pack if we want to travel from this place."

We soon cut up the bear, very clumsily I will allow, for there was no butcher among us; and collecting the fattest parts to serve as fuel for our lamp, we soon had some bear-steaks frying away under our noses. We took a very little of our biscuit in addition, but Andrew advised us to economise it to the utmost.

The skin was taken off as neatly as we could manage the work, and then, having scraped the inside clean, we hung it up in front of our hut to dry. We spent the whole day anxiously looking out for some sign of the gale abating, for we knew that every hour of its continuance would send our ship farther and farther away from us; but in the evening it blew as hard as it had done at the first.

The wind was too high, and cut us too keenly, to allow us to go from under shelter of our hut in search of seals; but we were not entirely idle. In the first place we drew the boat up to it, and secured our remaining provisions. We also cut up the flesh of the bear into long strips, that they might more easily dry in the air; besides this, we heightened the walls of our habitation, and sloped them inward, so as to enable the sail to cover the hut more completely.

The greater number of the men, however, showed little inclination to work, preferring to pass the day sitting crowded together in the hut in a sort of dreamy forgetfulness of the present, without speaking or moving. I own that few positions could be much more disheartening than ours; but I saw the necessity of keeping the intellects awake, ready for active exertion, if we would save our lives.

We cooked some of our bear-steaks for supper, and boiled up a little cocoa; so that for food we might have been worse off. We found also that the lamp, small as it was, diffused a warmth throughout the hut, which enabled us to pass the night much more agreeably than we had the previous one.

The bears seemed to have been aware of the fate of their brother, for none came near us. Another morning dawned; and though the gale still blew strong, it had somewhat abated; but yet it was still necessary to keep under shelter.

"As soon as the wind drops we must go sealing," remarked Andrew. "If we could get a good number of seals, or unies, or walrus, we might keep our lamp burning all night and day through the winter. Their flesh is not bad to eat; and then, you know, we can make boots, and caps, and jackets of their skins. We must look out to get them before the cold sets in."

"Then you think we shall have to winter here?" I asked.

"If the gale had taken off yesterday, I should have expected our ship back; but now I do not think she will attempt it," he answered positively. We were standing outside the hut, some way from the rest. "However, two ships were left in Pond's Bay when we came away, and they may see us as they pass, or we may pull off to them if the sea goes down. Peter, we should be thankful that things are no worse. Cold and inhospitable as is this country, we have the means of existing in it, if we have sense to employ them. Even now the wind has dropped and the sea has gone down. It will be as well to get our signal-post up, in case either of the ships should pass."

I agreed with him; and calling Terence to accompany us, we told the rest that we were going to the edge of the ice to see how things were, and to set up a signal.

Our flagstaff consisted of a spar, with a lance handle as a topmast, and the flag was the jack used in the boat to show that a fish was fast. We took also some line, to serve as shrouds for the staff. We three set off, then, not without some difficulty in advancing; for the wind was still so strong, that we were almost taken off our legs.

The distance, however, was not so great as we expected, for the sea had broken off the edge of the ice for full half a mile. Some of the pieces had been washed away, and others had been hurled far up on the surface, so as to form a high and rugged wall. We had taken the precaution of bringing two hatchets with us; and having selected the highest hummock near the sea, we chopped the summit of it perfectly level. We then cut out blocks of ice, and piled them up, till we had built a pyramid some ten feet high. We left places on which we could stand, to enable us to do this. We then planted our staff in the centre, and secured the shrouds to some large blocks of ice we had dragged up for the purpose.

We thus formed a very conspicuous mark, but we felt that it was too probable the ship might not pass near enough to see it. For some minutes we contemplated our work, and then prepared to return to our companions. Just then Terence happened to turn his eyes to the north-east. He stopped and looked eagerly out. "A sail, a sail!" he exclaimed; "she's coming down right before the wind."

"It's the only way she could come, mate," said Andrew, not in the least way excited by the announcement. "But are you sure you see a sail? Don't you think it may be the wing of a seafowl?"

"'Tis too steady for that," answered Terence. "If we get to the top of the flagstaff hummock, in another minute or so we shall know to a certainty." In spite of the cutting cold wind to which we were exposed, we stood for several minutes eagerly watching the white spot which Terence asserted was a sail.

I asked if it might not be an iceberg; but Andrew said an iceberg never travelled fast before the wind, because, although a great deal of it was exposed above the water, there was a much larger proportion below, on which, of course, the wind had no influence; and he wound up his observation by pronouncing the spot to be the topsail of a ship.

"Huzza, then, mates, we shall get off this time," shouted Terence, who had no wish to winter in the arctic regions.

"We must not be too sure of that," answered Andrew. "Let me ask you, even if we are sure, how are we to get off with the sea there breaking on this sheet of ice? We must not let our hopes blind us to the truth."

"You are always croaking, Andrew," said Terence in a vexed tone. He was, like many another man, without much hope, and who, the smaller it grows, is the more inclined to be angry with the person whose plain-speaking tends still further to decrease it.

On came the ship, scudding at a great rate before the gale, right down along the edge of the floe. She seemed, as well as we could then judge, to be about three miles off. We were obliged to descend, and to run about to keep ourselves warm; but every instant one of us was climbing to the top of the hummock to watch the progress of the stranger. She was drawing near when some of our companions discovered her; and we now saw them come hurrying along over the ice towards us, forgetting everything in the expectation of being able to escape from our perilous situation.

By the time they reached us she was just abreast of us, running under her fore-topsail at headlong speed before the wind. How anxiously we watched her, expecting her every instant to heave to; but she glided onward, unconscious of the agony and despair she was creating in our hearts. We waved our hats; we pointed to our signal staff; we leaped up on the hummock; we even, in the extravagance of our eagerness, shouted out at the top of our voices, as if sounds so faint could reach her. But all we could do was vain. On she passed in her course, as if we were not in existence.

"Fire our guns," said Andrew; "they might possibly be heard." But in their hurry our companions had left the guns at the hut.

All hope of making ourselves seen or heard was now abandoned; the ship flew by, and soon her hull sank below the horizon. Some of the men, on this, gave way to impious exclamations of discontent, but Andrew checked them. "It is God's will that we remain here, mates," he said. "How do we know but that it is for our benefit that we are left where we are? That ship, which we are now so anxious to be on board, may before the night be crushed beneath an iceberg, or perhaps dashed to pieces on the rocks in sight of home, while we may yet be destined to see again our country and our families. Believe me, mates, all is for the best; and though we don't see the way we are to escape, it may now be ready for us."

The tone of religious confidence in which Andrew spoke, contributed much to revive the spirits of our companions. The gale was also rapidly decreasing, and hopes were therefore expressed that, should the last ship appear, the boat might be able to reach her, even though she might be too far off to see our signal. However, day drew on, and no ship appeared. The returning darkness warned us that we must get back to our hut without delay, or not only might we not be able to find it, but it might be visited by our friends the bears, and our remaining provisions might be destroyed. We accordingly hurried back, and were only just in time to prevent the latter catastrophe; for, as we got to the hut, we observed three large objects moving over the snow towards the land. They were no doubt bears, who, when they saw us running up, had been frightened away from the food, to which their keen scent had attracted them. I rushed into the hut for a gun, intending to make chase after them; but Andrew told me to desist, as I should not have the slightest chance of killing one, and that they might possibly turn upon me and destroy me.

The third night we spent in our hut was much colder than the former ones, though there was less wind. One of us by turns kept watch, as before. I was asleep, and it was Terence's watch, when I was awakened by a loud noise like thunder, and a shout from him which made all the party start on their feet. The noise continued. It too much reminded us of that we had heard when the ice, in which we had been beset in our passage through Baffin's Bay, had begun to break up.

"What's the matter now?" exclaimed several voices.

"The floe must be separating, and we are perhaps going to be drifted away from the shore," remarked old David, "But never mind, mates, we can't be much worse off than we were, and a short cruise won't do us any harm."

"How can we tell that the floe will not break up into small pieces, or perhaps drift out and join the middle ice?" I inquired. I thought such a thing might possibly occur, and I wished to secure our retreat on shore.

"There is little doubt that the floe is separating," said Andrew. "But at all events we can do nothing while it remains dark. As soon as daylight appears, we must decide, without loss of time, what is to be done."

The noise continued for a considerable time, then all was silent; and I suppose that the piece we were on had already begun to drift away from the main body of ice. I fancied, even, that I could feel a peculiar undulating movement, as if it was acted on by the waves. As soon as morning dawned we eagerly looked out. At first there appeared to be no change; but, as the light increased, we found that between us and the main ice there was a wide passage of nearly a quarter of a mile.

The floe we were on was about a mile across in the narrowest part, and two or three miles long. It seemed, while we watched the land, to be advancing towards the northward and eastward. Our flagstaff was on the same piece, and was not disturbed. But another object met our sight which engaged all our attention. It was a sail to the southward. With what deep anxiety we watched her, I need scarcely say.

"Which way is she heading?" was the general cry.

"To the southward," exclaimed old David. "She'll not come near us, depend on that, mates; so we need not look after her. She must have slipped by in the night or in the grey of the morning, or we should have seen her."

"But don't you think she may be the *Shetland Maid* come to look for us?" I asked. "Who is certain that she is standing away from us? for I am not."

One or two sided with me; but the others were of opinion that the stranger was standing from us.

Meantime the floe drifted out to sea. There was no immediate danger, and we might have remained as secure as we were before, provided it did not come in contact with any other floe, which, had it done, it would probably have broken into fragments, and we should have forthwith perished. All hands were too busy watching the ship to think much on this subject. We watched, but we watched in vain.

If she was our own ship, Captain Rendall must have fancied that he had come as far north as he had left us; and seeing the ice broken and changed, and floes drifting about, he must have thought we had perished. At all events, after an hour's earnest watching, the most sanguine were compelled to acknowledge that the top-sails were gradually again sinking in the horizon; and before long they were out of sight, and all hope of escaping that year was at an end.

By this time we had been, as it were, somewhat broken in to expect disappointments, so no one expressed his feelings so strongly as on the former occasion. We were also obliged to think of means for securing our present safety. Two things were to be considered. If we remained on the floe, should it break up we must be destroyed; besides this, we could procure no food nor fuel.

After Andrew had heard all of us express our opinions, he resolved to quit the floe and retreat to the main ice. "We'll stay on the edge of it for one day, or two if you wish it, and we'll keep a bright look-out for a ship; but it's my opinion that the last has passed, and that we had better make up our minds to winter on shore. The sooner we begin our preparations the better chance we have of weathering out the time."

This plan being agreed to, two hands were sent to unstep the flagstaff and bring it forward, while the rest of us dismantled our hut, and dragged the boat to the edge of the floe nearest the shore. It was time that we should be off, for the channel had already widened to half a mile. Though the water was perfectly smooth, the boat, with all our party and our stores, had as much in her as she could conveniently carry.

A quarter of an hour served to carry us across, when we again hauled our boat up; and choosing the highest hummock in the neighbourhood, we again erected our flagstaff. Before, however, we began to build a hut, we examined the condition of the ice round us, to ascertain whether there was a probability of another floe breaking away with us. On finding it, according to the opinion of the old hands, perfectly secure, we put up a tent in the same manner as the last, though of rather a larger size. This done, we cooked and ate the first food we had tasted that day, for we had been too busy all the morning to think of eating.

Andrew then urged us to make diligent search for any of the oil-giving fish which we could catch. Accordingly, armed with our harpoons and lances, we set out, leaving one hand to guard the boat and to keep a look-out for a passing sail.

We first kept along the edge of the ice; but meeting with no success, we turned towards the land to look for any pools which might exist in the ice. After looking about for some time, we came to one nearly the eighth of a mile across. In it were a shoal of narwhals or sea-unicorns, every now and then rising above the water to breathe, and then diving down again in search of prey. Could we have brought the boat so far, we should have had no difficulty in killing them, but now it depended how near they would rise to the edge. It was tantalising to watch them and not to be able to get hold of any.

We divided into three parties, for we had as many harpoons; and at last one rose within reach of David's weapon. He launched it forth, and struck the fish in the neck. Down it dived rapidly; but it soon had to return to the surface, when we hauled it towards the edge and despatched it quickly with our lances, after which we hauled it upon the ice. In the same manner another was afterwards killed. These were indeed prizes; for, though not so valuable as the seals, their flesh and oil were most welcome.

We found that they were too heavy to drag over the ice whole, so we cut off the blubber and some meat, and left the kral for the benefit of the bears. The horns would, under other circumstances, have been valuable; but we could not afford to burden ourselves with more than what was absolutely necessary.

We at last got back to the hut with our prize; and the hand who was left to watch reported that no sail had appeared. We had now an abundance of oil, so that we were able to dress the flesh of the bear in it, as also to keep up a light in the hut all night long. The next day, if the *Shetland Maid* did not return, and if no other ship appeared, we were to form our plan for future operations. All that day the look-out hummock was occupied by one of our party with his eye anxiously looking seaward; but hour after hour passed away, and no sail appeared.

What a sinking at the heart, what a blank, desolate feeling came over us, as our last hope vanished! Hitherto we had been buoyed up with the expectation of relief; now the most sanguine felt that the last whaler had departed for the season.

It was my turn to look out just before it grew dark. The floe on which we had floated for so long had now drifted a considerable distance off, and had broken into three almost circular pieces. As I watched, it was met by several other floes of equal magnitude, which were revolving, some in one direction, some in another, without any apparent cause. Then began a most furious contest between them,—hurled together, they overlapped and crushed on each other, till in the course of a few minutes they had broken into a thousand fragments. I was indeed thankful that we had not remained on the floe in the hopes of being seen by a ship.

Darkness coming on, and it being impossible any longer to distinguish objects at a distance, I returned to the hut. I found my companions sitting round our kitchen in the hut, and discussing plans for the future. Some were still anxious to get on to the southward in the boat, in the hopes of overtaking some whaler which might have stopped to fish; but Andrew strongly urged them at once to abandon all hopes of escaping that year, and at once, while they had health and strength, and the weather remained moderate, to make preparations for the winter. He showed the extreme improbability of our overtaking ships which must have been driven very far to the south by the gale, as also the danger of being swamped should the slightest sea get up; while, should we not succeed in our attempt, we should be worn out, and, incapable of providing for the future, must inevitably be destroyed.

I voted with Andrew, and also spoke in favour of his plan, showing, from what I had read and heard, that, notwithstanding the cold, with good management we might preserve our lives and our health throughout an arctic winter. At last this plan was agreed to by all, and we lay down once more to sleep away the time till daylight.

We were up by dawn; and, having laden our boat with all our stores, we commenced our toilsome journey. Our purpose was to make the land, and then to travel along over the ice till we should arrive at some valley, or at the mouth of a river, where we might hope to find some clear water and opportunities of catching fish.

Though the land appeared quite near, it was late in the day before we reached it. What, then, was our disappointment to find not even a beach on which to build our hut for the night! The high black cliff came completely down to the sea, and was fringed by masses of ice piled up against it, so that we could not even reach it without difficulty and danger. Our only course, therefore, was to continue along under it, till we should meet with the opening of which we were in search.

I ought to have said that we had protected the keel and bilge of our boat by securing some spars along them, so that she was able to pass over the ice without damage; but the labour of dragging her was very great, and some even proposed leaving her behind rather than have the trouble of conveying her, till Andrew reminded them that on her might depend our only means of procuring food, and of ultimately escaping next year.

We performed a distance of nearly three miles along the shore, under the same lofty unbroken cliffs; and then Andrew called a halt, and we made our usual preparations for passing the night.

Chapter Thirty One

For three days we travelled on; and, supposing that we advanced ten miles a day, for thirty miles not a break of any description appeared in the overhanging cliffs on our right. The men had begun to grumble; and those who had wished to proceed in the boat by water, asserted that, if their advice had been followed, we should have made greater progress with less fatigue.

Andrew told them in answer that if they would but keep up their spirits, and persevere for one day longer, we should in all probability come to some opening where we might get on shore, and near which, if the sea was smooth, we might launch the boat and try to get some more fish. This encouraged them; and the following morning, with renewed spirits, we continued on our way.

As the day drew on, there appeared but little chance of Andrew's promise being fulfilled, for, far as the eye could reach, was the same unbroken line of cliff. It was drawing towards sunset, when I caught sight of what appeared to me a ship thrown on her beam-ends, close under the cliff. The rest laughed at me, and telling me I must be deceived, asked me how a ship could get there.

I answered I was certain that I was not mistaken, and pointed out to them the object I had seen. It appeared to me, when I first saw it, as in a sort of shallow cavern under the cliff; but before we could make any progress towards it, the shades of evening completely obscured it, and long before we could reach it we were obliged to encamp.

We talked a good deal about it as we sat round our lamp in our usual ice cottage; and I dreamed all night that a strange ship had appeared, and that we were to go on board in the morning.

When the morning did really come, I eagerly looked out for the first rays of light falling on the object I had seen. It was now more clear than ever. I first pointed it out to Andrew.

"Well, if that is not a real ship, those are very extraordinary marks at the foot of the cliff," he observed. "Peter, I believe you are right. It is a ship, and it may prove the means of our preservation."

Without waiting for any meal, although Andrew insisted on the boat being dragged with us, we advanced towards the supposed ship. David certainly did not believe she was one. "If that's a ship," he remarked. "I don't see how the natives would have spared her. They would have been swarming about her like bees, and would have pulled her all to pieces long before this."

"I still say she's a ship, and that we shall see before long," I answered.

It is extraordinary how the imagination helps out the vision in a case of this sort. I believed that there was a ship, so I saw her; another man did not believe that there was a ship there, so could not perceive her.

We travelled on for three hours before all doubts were set at rest by the appearance of a large ship, thrown, as I said, on her beam-ends, but with her masts and rigging still standing. An overhanging cliff projected to the south of her, and within it was the cavern in which she lay, so that she could only be seen from the point from which we had advanced towards her.

This providential circumstance instantly raised our spirits, and we could not help giving a loud shout of joy, as we hurried on to get on board her. Even should we find no provisions, we could not fail of obtaining numberless things which would prove of the greatest value to us.

As we got near her, her condition at once told that she had been lost amongst the ice; and probably thrown up on to a floe by another striking her, she had drifted afterwards into her present position. For some minutes we stood round her, examining her with a feeling approaching to awe. She looked so shattered and weather-worn, and of a build so unusual, that I fancied she might have been there frozen up for centuries.

At last Terence climbed up her sides, followed by all of us. Her decks were uninjured, and were thickly covered with snow, which had contributed, I suppose, to preserve them. Her masts and lower rigging were standing, though the topmasts had gone over the side. David pronounced her to be a Dutch whaler; and such, I believe, she was. Her hatches were on, and even the companion-hatch was drawn over, which made us think that the crew had remained on board till she was driven into her present position, and had afterwards quitted her with the intention of returning.

This opinion was confirmed when we went below. We found the cabin in good order and the furniture uninjured, for the water had not reached it. On going into the hold we discovered an abundant supply of provisions in casks; but all her tubs were empty, which showed us that she had been wrecked on her outward voyage, before having taken a fish. Her boats also were gone, which showed the way in which her crew had escaped from her. When I first went below, I half expected to find all her people frozen to death, as I had heard of such dreadful occurrences having taken place.

Several books and papers were found in the cabin, but as none of us could read Dutch, we were unable to learn anything from them; but Andrew and David were of opinion that she had been there five years at least, perhaps longer.

Having taken a cursory glance throughout the ship, our appetites reminded us that we had eaten nothing that morning, so we set to work to examine the condition of the stores on board. The meat in the casks was perfectly good, and so even was the biscuit and flour, which had been preserved, I conclude, by the cold from the weevils and the rats. The only animals which had visited the ship were the bears. They had not failed to scent out the good things she contained, but not having been clever enough to lift the hatches off, they had, fortunately for us, been unable to appropriate them.

We were not long in knocking the head out of a cask and in collecting materials to form an abundant meal, which we had not enjoyed for so many days. The cook's caboose was still uninjured on deck, and his pots and kettles were hung up inside it, with a store of coals and wood ready chopped up. We accordingly lighted a fire, and two of the men, who professed to be the best cooks, prepared our breakfast.

In the cabin we found in jars and canisters a profuse store of tea, coffee, cocoa, sugar, and several sorts of preserved fruits and sweetmeats; indeed there was an ample supply of everything we could require. The cabin was, of course, very much on one side, and moreover very chilly; but, for the pleasure of sitting at a table, we carried our meal down there to eat it.

Andrew took care not to let the opportunity pass by of reminding us that our heartfelt gratitude was due to the Great Being who had so mercifully guided our steps to this spot, where, without trouble or risk, we might provide ourselves with the necessaries of life.

After breakfast I saw some of the men hunting busily about the ship; and from their look of dismay, when, getting hold of a brandy cask, they found the contents had run out, I guessed that their object was to enjoy themselves for a short time by drinking, and I am afraid that many of our party would not have refrained from doing so to excess.

I told Andrew, who was still in the cabin examining the lockers what I had remarked.

"Never mind," he answered. "All the glass bottles containing spirits or liquid of any sort have also burst with the cold, so that there is no fear of any of them getting drunk. There are a few stone bottles with hollands, and as they were only partly filled they seem to have something left in them; so I will hide them away in case they should ever be required."

We had just concealed them in a locker in the captain's state-room, as his sleeping cabin is called when some of the rest returned, grumbling very much at having found nothing to drink. Andrew reproved them mildly for their discontent, when we had been thus led so mercifully to the means of preserving our lives.

"If you had discovered any liquor you might have made merry at first," he observed; "then you would have become worse than the brutes, without sense; and lastly, you would have been left without strength or energy to bear the difficulties we shall have to encounter. Let me tell you, lads, the liquor you are so fond of only gives you false strength just for a short time after you have drunk it, and then leaves you much weaker than at first. To my mind, people in this climate are very much better without spirits; and in any other climate for that matter. There are times, when a person is almost frozen or overcome with weakness, when they may be of use; but in most cases we are better without them." Andrew's reasoning had some effect on his hearers, particularly when they found themselves forced to follow his advice whether they would or not.

We now all assembled together in the cabin to decide on what we should do. Some were for remaining on board, and making ourselves as comfortable as we could; but Andrew at once pointed out the madness of such a proceeding. He argued that even in summer the position under the cliff was excessively cold; that the ship was in no way fitted to serve as a habitation during the winter, when there were days no person could be exposed for ten minutes together to the air without suffering; and that, although there was an abundant supply of salt provisions, unless we could procure some fresh meat, our health would materially suffer.

"My advice, mates, is," he continued, "that we travel along the coast as we first intended, till we arrive at the sort of place we were in search of when we fell in with this wreck. When we have found it, we will at once build a warm house, and then set to at hunting and fishing till the animals desert the country, and the sea is frozen over, and the long winter nights set in. We will, however, first build some sledges, such as the natives use, and we will carry on them all the things we require from the ship to our station. If any one has a better plan to offer, let him propose it."

"I think Andrew's plan is the one to follow, and I propose we set about it without delay!" I exclaimed.

"And so do I," said Terence.

"And I don't see that it's a bad one," observed David.

"And I think it a good one," said Tom Stokes.

The rest offered no opposition; indeed they did not know what else to propose. I must observe that now when we had nothing to do with whaling, in which the others had more experience, Andrew fully showed his superiority and fitness to command, so that we all readily obeyed him whenever he thought fit to issue any orders. However, as he felt that he only held his authority on sufferance, he judged it best, as in the present instance, to consult all hands before the formation of any fresh plan for proceeding.

The whole day was spent on board in examining the ship, and in forming our plans, and in making some of the preliminary arrangements. The first of them was to build a couple of sledges, which Andrew showed us how to do, very similar to those used by the Esquimaux. We also packed up some tea, cocoa, and sugar, as also some meat and bread to serve us for present use, till we could bring up the remainder to our winter station.

Among other valuable articles were some carpenter's tools and two fowling-pieces, some canisters of powder, with a supply of shot, thus giving us the means of killing any game we might meet with. It was, as I said, very cold; but as there was a stove in the cabin, we lighted it, and soon got the cabin comfortably warm. Probably, had we been left to our own devices, we should have all gone to sleep without keeping any watch; but Andrew ordered one of us to keep watch by turns throughout the night, both to supply the stove with fuel and to guard against fire. Had it not been for this precaution, we might have slept away some of the valuable hours of daylight.

As soon as we had breakfasted, Andrew gave the signal for us to start. Some wanted to leave the boat till we had found the spot we were in search of; but he insisted on its being brought along, showing that we must have her at our station, both to enable us to catch fish and to assist us in escaping on the following summer; and that, as she was laden and prepared for the journey, it would be wise to bring her at once.

We could only drag one sledge with us, and on that were placed a few additional stores. Having closed the hatches, we once more left the ship. We travelled on the whole of that day and the greater part of the next, without meeting with a fit place to fix on for our winter station. Some of the grumblers declared that we never should find it, and that we had much better go back to the ship.

The prospect was certainly very discouraging, and even Andrew was beginning to think that there was no help for it but to return, when, on reaching a high black rocky point, we saw a bay spreading far back and surrounded by hills of only moderate height, from which the snow had melted, leaving exposed a variety of grasses and lichens which clothed their sides. I shouted with joy on seeing this to us cheering prospect. To people under different circumstances, the view might have appeared bleak and gloomy enough.

On getting round the point, we landed on firm ground for the first time since leaving our ship; and, strange as it may seem, I felt as if half our difficulties and dangers were over. On climbing up the nearest hill, we saw that a stream, or rather river, ran into the centre of the bay, and that from its mouth to the sea there was a clear channel. Nothing could have been more in accordance with our wishes. We might here be able to supply ourselves with fish, and from the appearance of the country, there would probably be an abundance of game.

We continued along the ice till we saw, a little above the beach, a level spot on the side of the hill, well sheltered from the north. Andrew pointed it out. "There, my lads, is the place where we must build our house, and we must make up our minds to live in it for the next ten months or so at least," he observed. "We will therefore make it as comfortable as we can, for we shall not be able to shift our quarters when once the frost sets in, let me tell you."

We proceeded up to the place he indicated, and under it we hauled up our boat on the beach. On a further examination of the spot, we resolved to establish ourselves there, and immediately set to work to erect a habitation which might serve us till our winter-house was ready. For this purpose we collected some large stones which had been washed down from the neighbouring cliffs, and rolled them up the hill. With these as a foundation, with the addition of earth and small stones and turf, we in the course of a couple of hours had raised a wall very much in form like those we had been accustomed to form of snow. Our sail served as a roof; and in an excursion made by some of the party a short distance among the hills, a quantity of a low shrubby plant was discovered, admirably suited for a mattress till we could get bedding from the ship.

Andrew assured us that we had every reason to be thankful that our position was so good; and so I think we had, for it most certainly might have been very much worse. But those who stay at home at ease by their warm firesides would not consider a residence in a hut on the side of a bleak hill, throughout a winter within the Arctic Circle, as a position much to be envied. Everything, we must remember, is by comparison; and I again repeat, we had good reason to be grateful.

The first thing the next morning, off we all started with the sledge, to commence the work of bringing the things from the wreck. The distance was twelve miles, so that we could at the utmost only take one trip in the day. We were all in good spirits, for we had slept soundly and had enjoyed a good meal; but before long, some of the men began to grumble at the distance.

"I don't see why we couldn't have chosen some place nearer the wreck to build our house," said one.

"It's a pity the ship weren't driven ashore nearer the bay," cried another.

"Now, for my part, I'd rather let the things remain where they are, than have to bring them all this way," exclaimed the worst grumbler of the party.

"Or, as I said before, we'd better by half take up our quarters on board," put in one of those who had advocated that measure at first.

"Now, let me tell you that you are an ungrateful set of fellows to talk as you do," exclaimed Andrew, who had listened to all that was said. "You saw yourselves that there was not a spot of ground nearer than the place we have chosen fit to winter in; and as to complaining that the ship is no nearer the bay, why, if she had been driven into any other spot than the exact one where she is, she would have been seen by the Esquimaux, and plundered of everything she contains. You'll soon find the want of everything we can get from the wreck; and if any one chooses to winter aboard her, we'll leave him plenty to eat, but if he isn't frozen to death we shall have him back with us before very long, that I know."

Most of the party sided with Andrew on this as on other occasions, and the grumblers were silenced. As we were perfectly unencumbered, we advanced at a rapid rate, and in about three hours we got up to the ship. We scrambled up the sides by the chain-plates, and were all soon on deck.

"Hillo, who left the companion-hatch open?" exclaimed Terence, who was the first who got aft. No one recollected who could have been guilty of the neglect. "No matter, there's no chance of any one having been here while we were away," cried Terence, as he jumped down the companion-ladder.

He had not got down many steps before he sprung up again in a great hurry, with a face of terror, his head shoving back the next man who was following him, and sending him sprawling on deck, while a loud angry growl was heard issuing from the cabin.

"Och, murder!" he exclaimed. "There's Davy Jones aboard, as sure as my name's Terence O'Connor."

"Shut to the hatch there!" shouted David to some of us who were standing abaft the companion. We drew it over just in time to prevent a white head and a pair of sharp claws covered with shaggy hair from protruding out of the hatchway. At the same moment David, who had a lance in his hand, thrust it down, and again a fierce snarling growl was heard.

"Why, mates, we seem to have caught a bear," observed Andrew, who had come aft to see what had happened.

"We may have caught a dozen, for what I know," answered David. "And provided they haven't eaten up the flour, and sugar, and beef we left here, the more there are the better."

While he was speaking he was pronging away with his spear down the companion-hatch, and the growling grew louder and fiercer.

The bear was now severely wounded and enraged to the utmost; for in spite of the enemies he might have guessed were ready to receive him, he tried to force his way up. "Hand a gun here, and we'll see if we can't settle him," cried David; but the guns had been left leaning against a block of ice outside the ship, and before we could recover them the bear had made another attempt to get out of the trap. Evading the points of the lance, he had seized the handle in his teeth, and then climbing up the ladder, he forced the top of the hatch off with his head, and seemed about to take the deck from us. Andrew, however, had got another lance, and just as his terrific claws were close to David's shoulder, he gave him a severe wound in the neck. At the same moment I ran up with a gun, and firing into his mouth, he fell dead across the hatchway.

That he was not alone we were convinced by the appearance of another shaggy monster, who now shoved his head up to see what his companion was about. As he showed his head from under the dead body and opened his mouth to growl, David plunged his lance into it with such force that he fell mortally wounded down the ladder, carrying the weapon with him. We had some work to drag the dead bear out of the way, he was so heavy a fellow.

"Are there any more of them?" cried Terence, who, discovering that they were mortal foes, had completely recovered from his fright. He spoke as he was peering into the cabin, and about to spring down the ladder. "Och, yes, here comes another."

And sure enough a third bear appeared at the doorway, with a look which seemed to ask what we wanted there. As he was too sagacious to come within reach of our spears, and our remaining gun was loaded only with small shot, we scarcely knew how to despatch him. It would have been very dangerous to descend the ladder, for one pat of his paw was sufficient to tear any man's arm off; so we had to enrage him by shaking our lances in his face, and then pretending to run away to induce him to follow us.

At last we succeeded almost too well; for with a speed of which I did not think a bear capable, he clambered up the ladder, and was making for the side of the ship with the sensible intention of escaping, when we closed in upon him and caused him to stand at bay. He looked at us savagely, singling out one of us to attack, and then rushed upon David; but the old whaler's lance was ready, and the bear received a mortal thrust in his breast. Notwithstanding this, he rushed forward grinning savagely; but David sprung out of his way, and another lance pierced him to the heart.

We had thus secured some very valuable prizes, and we even hoped there might be more of them below, provided they had not eaten up the stores on which we counted. Not one liked to be the first to go down till we had ascertained whether the cabin had any more occupants. At last none appearing. Terence with cautious steps descended the ladder, ready to spring up again should another bear show his face. Stepping over the carcase of the bear, which lay at the foot of the ladder he looked in. Presently he shouted to us to follow, and we all quickly descended,—anxious to see what damage the bears had committed.

Fortunately all our stores had been returned to the lockers, and they had broken open only one, and had got hold of a jar of brown sugar and another of flour, which, in their clumsy endeavours to eat, they had sprinkled about the cabin. We calculated from this that they had not been there long; for if they had, they would have routed out everything eatable they possibly could get on board.

As it was, our carelessness had been productive of more good than harm, for the skins of the beasts would make us some warm clothing, while their flesh would afford us food for a long time, if we could get no other fresh meat.

Our first care was now to construct a number of hand sledges, for the conveyance of our stores to our winter quarters. The small ones were made so that one person could drag them over the smooth parts of the ice; and on having to pass any rough portions, two or three persons might tackle together, passing one sledge after the other.

To carry the woodwork for our house, we were obliged to form a large sledge, which would require nearly all the party to drag it forward. Taking care to close all the hatches, we loaded our sledges with provisions, blankets, and some additional clothing, and set forward on our return to the bay.

Chapter Thirty Two

We travelled briskly along over the ice, our encounter with the bears affording us abundant matter for amusement. I forgot to say, that not having time to flay them, we had shoved them down the main hatchway, to wait till the next day. Now and then one or other of the sledges, not carefully constructed, would come to pieces, and we had to wait while it was being repaired; otherwise we got on very well, and, I suspect, faster than if we had not had them to drag after us. At length our journey was almost accomplished, and in a few minutes we expected to arrive at what we already had begun to call our home,—it was, indeed, the only home we were likely to have for a long time to come.

We had rounded the rocky point, and were dragging our sledges towards our hut, when what was our surprise to see a group of human beings, clothed from head to foot in skins, standing round it, examining it apparently with much curiosity! On seeing us they drew up in a line, and advanced slowly towards us down the hill. They numbered twice as many as we did; and as they had arms in their hands, Andrew ordered us to stop, to see what they would do.

"Show them that we wish to be friends, lads, and place your lances and the guns on the ground," said Andrew.

We did as he directed, and instantly the Esquimaux, for such we saw they were, threw aside their spears and knives, and cried out, "*Tima, Tima!*" and advanced with outstretched arms towards us.

We uttered the same words and advanced also. We soon saw by the expression of their countenances that they were amicably disposed towards us; and from their manner of behaving, we suspected that we were not the first Europeans they had met.

They all appeared comfortably clothed. The men wore deerskin jackets with hoods to them, to be drawn over the head; their trousers were generally of sealskin, made to reach below the knee, and their boots were of the same substance, with the hair inside. Some of them had shoes over their boots, and an under-jacket of deer-skin. The dress of the women was very similar, except that their jackets had long flaps behind, reaching almost to the ground, and were pointed in front. There were several children, who kept in the background, and they were all dressed exactly like the older ones; and funny little beings they were, reminding one forcibly of hedge-hogs, or rather of little bears and dancing dogs.

They advanced slowly in a line as we walked forward; but when we had got near enough to see each other's faces they stopped. Whatever sign we made they instantly imitated; and there was a merry, good-natured expression in their countenances, which gave us great confidence in the friendliness of their disposition. Seeing this, we walked forward and put out our hands; they did the same; and presently there was as warm a shaking of hands between us, as if we were the oldest friends each other had in the world.

This ceremony being over, they accompanied us to the hut, which we examined with some little anxiety, to see if they had taken anything away; but nothing was disturbed. The few things, also, which had been left in the boat had not been touched.

"You are honest fellows, that you are," exclaimed Terence, shaking them all round again by the hand, at which they seemed mightily pleased. We talked away at them, and they talked to us for some time, making all sorts of signs and gestures; but at the end of it all we were not much the wiser, for neither of us could understand a word each other said.

However, we did not want them clustering round us while we were unpacking our sledges, and we were in a hurry to stow our things away before night; so Terence undertook to draw them off. He managed it by taking one by the hand, and making him sit down at a little distance and seating himself beside him; then, making a sign to the first to sit quiet, he led another to the spot, and so on till they all were seated. They then remained very quiet, looking on with an expression of the greatest surprise at the various things we produced. It was almost sunset when they got up, and again shaking hands, took their departure over the hills. By this we supposed that their habitations were at no great distance.

The next morning we were up by daybreak to return to the ship; and as we did not think it wise to leave our property without a guard, Terence and Tom were selected to remain, with two of the guns, to shoot any game which might appear, or to defend themselves if necessary. The ship had not been visited; and having laden our large sledge with some wood from the wreck for building the house, and two small ones with provisions, we set forward on our return.

Terence reported that the Esquimaux had again visited the hut, and had invited him and Tom, by signs, to accompany them over the hills; but that, on his shaking his head and sitting still, they had understood that he could not leave his post, and they went away.

As soon as we had taken some food, Andrew urged us to set about building our winter house without delay, lest the severe frosts should come on before it was finished. The plan he proposed, and which was adopted, was to divide it into two compartments, one for a store-house, the other for our dwelling and cooking room. The latter was fifteen feet square and eight feet high, with a sloping roof, and a hole, with a trap in the top, to let out the air and to serve for a chimney. All this would require a great deal of wood, besides the turf and stones with which we also proposed to build it. We had no means of forming windows; but, as we had heard it was always night during the winter, we thought we should not want them.

The next morning we were off again for the wood, as well as some bears' flesh and some of the other provisions. Terence, who managed so well with the natives, remained as before, and he reported that they had come, and seemed much surprised with the work we had performed; that they had examined the tracks of the sledges and the additional stores, and then, after a great deal of talking, had returned from whence they came.

The following morning we were disturbed by a loud noise of dogs barking and men shouting; and on looking out of our tents, we saw our Esquimaux friends looming through the twilight, each of them accompanied by a troop of seven dogs harnessed to a sledge formed of the jaw-bone of a whale and sealskins. They came close up to us, talking very rapidly, and pointing in the direction in which the ship lay.

When we prepared to start on our daily expedition, they showed their evident intention of accompanying us. David and some of the other men did not like this, and were afraid that if they saw the ship they might appropriate everything on board; but Andrew assured us that he was certain they had no such intention, and that their purpose was to assist us, otherwise, as they might easily have tracked us along the ice, they would have set off by themselves.

The Esquimaux laughed very much when they saw us trudging along with our clumsy heavy sledges; and calling their dogs to stop with a *Wo Wo-hoa*, just as a carter does in England, they beckoned each of us to get on to a sledge behind each of them, and placing our sledges on theirs, away we drove. Off went the dogs at full gallop, they guiding them with their whips and their voices along the smoother portions of the ice. It was amusing and very exhilarating to feel one's self whirled along at so rapid a rate, after being so long accustomed to the slow movements of our own weary feet, and our spirits and courage rose accordingly.

Their sledges were between eight and ten feet long, and about two wide. The runners of some were of the jaw-bones of a whale, and of others of several bones lashed together. To prevent the wearing out of the runner, it is coated with fresh-water ice, composed of snow and ice, rubbed and pressed over it till it is quite smooth and hard.

The dogs are harnessed with thongs of sealskin, passed over the neck and fore-legs, and leading along the back. Great care is taken to select a good leader, who goes ahead with a longer trace than the rest, and in the darkest night, by keeping his nose to the ground, can always find out the right track. The driver uses a whip with a lash many feet in length, but he guides his team more by words than blows; and it is amusing, when the leader hears his own name called, to see him looking round for his master's orders.

As we drove along, I bethought me I should like to learn the name of my companion; so I pointed to myself, and pronounced my own name several times, "Peter, Peter, yes, I Peter;" and then I touched him, and nodded for him to speak.

He quickly understood me, and uttered the word Ickmallick; and when I repeated it, he seemed much pleased. After this, whenever I touched anything, he always mentioned the name, and so did I; and in that way in the course of our drive we had both of us learned something of each other's language.

When they arrived at the ship, they appeared very much astonished; and we could only account for their not having seen her, by supposing that they had come from inland, or from the south, and that their fishing excursions never took them in this direction. Their astonishment was much increased when they clambered on board and descended into the cabin; and they seemed almost afraid to touch the numberless strange things they saw. A looking-glass was hanging up; and by chance one catching sight of his face in it, he was riveted to the spot; then he began to move slowly and to make grimaces, which he continued to do, increasing the rapidity of his movements, till he broke into shouts and shrieks of laughter, till most of his companions assembling around him, they became convulsed in the same extraordinary manner.

As we had no time to lose, we covered up the glass, which quieted them; after which we led them into the hold, when no sooner did they see the dead bears than they rushed up to them, and began examining them minutely to see how they had been killed. After this they treated us with much greater respect even than before, evidently admiring the prowess which had enabled us to overcome so many of the few enemies with whom they have to contend. We immediately set to work to remove the lining of the ship, the bulkheads, and such other woodwork as we thought would prove useful to us in building our house. The Esquimaux gave us to understand by signs that they would carry it for us; and as we threw it over the side of the ship, they packed it on the sledges, each sledge carrying six or seven hundredweight. They seemed to fancy that the ship was ours, and that we had come in her; and of course we did not wish them to think otherwise.

Among the things in the cabin, we had discovered a number of knives, hatchets, cotton handkerchiefs, and other articles, which had evidently been brought for the purpose of trading; and some of them we now produced, and signified that we would bestow them on them, as rewards for carrying our property. The way we did this was to load one of our own sledges,— one of our men dragged it on some little way, and then Andrew, pointing towards the bay, went up to him and gave him a knife or a handkerchief. As a hatchet was three times as valuable, he dragged the sledge three times before he received it. My friend Ickmallick's black eyes sparkled when he saw this, and his countenance was wreathed with smiles for two reasons— first, for the pleasure of comprehending what he meant, and also at the thoughts of receiving so large a reward for his labour.

We were so pleased with the honest countenances and manner of these people, that we had no fears about entrusting the wood and other heavy things to them. If we had known how scarce and valuable wood is to them, we might have hesitated more before we did so.

Among our other labours, we skinned the bears; and, reserving the more delicate portions of the meat, we gave the rest to them. To our surprise, they immediately began to eat large lumps of it raw, though we had lighted the caboose fire to cook our own breakfast, and offered to cook for them.

Some they divided among their dogs; and, as soon as masters and beasts had devoured their meal, they set off together towards the bay, leaving us still busy on board. When they were gone, we were not quite satisfied that we had done wisely in giving them the things. They might, knowing them to be ours, carry them off; or they might have misunderstood our signs, and fancy that we had given them to them. However, the thing was done, and we must abide by the consequences.

We calculated, at the rate they travelled, that they would easily make two journeys in the day; so we employed ourselves in getting loads ready for them on their return. We were not disappointed. In little more than two hours they made their appearance; and so well had they understood us, that those to whom we had promised knives or handkerchiefs for carrying one load held out their hands for them, while those who were to make three for the hatchets signified that they had performed part of their contract.

We now entrusted some of them with the bears' flesh and skins, and with some casks of salted meat; and we also piled up, outside the ship, a load of wood for each of them, to see if they would come and take it. As soon as they were off, we followed with the more valuable stores; but, as we trudged slowly along, we envied their more rapid means of conveyance, and agreed that we would get them to carry us as well as our stores on the following day.

We had got about two-thirds of the way, when they appeared before us with a fresh relay of dogs. They had come out expressly to meet us; and, putting us and our loads on their sledges, away we trotted quickly towards the hut. We were much delighted when Terence informed us that everything had been safely delivered into his hands.

The next morning we set to work in earnest about our house, and, as we all worked, we progressed much to our satisfaction. During the day the Esquimaux arrived with the loads of wood we had left prepared. They did not show any intention of visiting the ship when we were not there to deliver the things to them; indeed, after watching us at work for a little time, they all went away.

I have not space to describe our proceedings minutely. We first got our storehouse completed, and all our things stowed away in it; and then we built our dwelling-house, and surrounded it with clods of turf, fancying that we had constructed a very comfortable edifice. The Esquimaux paid us daily visits, and carried us to the ship to bring away whatever we required. We were always careful to shut down the hatches before leaving, to keep out the bears; and this they seemed to consider some religious ceremony, for they never attempted to visit the ship during our absence.

I never met with people, in any part of the world, who possessed a more peaceable friendly disposition—such perfect honesty and constant good-humour, with a very fair amount of intelligence. Their courage and perseverance are expended in overcoming the beasts which form their subsistence, and there are few opportunities of developing their intellectual qualities; but in many respects they are, in my opinion, far more civilised than a large proportion of their brethren in the south, who claim to be the most enlightened nations in the world.

Chapter Thirty Three

We had been all so busy in building our house, and in bringing our stores from the ship and in stowing them away, that none of us had wandered a quarter of a mile from our location. The Esquimaux seemed perfectly to understand what we were about; and when they saw that our work was completed, they came with their sledges and made signs to us that they wished us to come and pay them a visit at their abodes.

By Andrew's advice, five of us were to go first, and the remainder were to go on our return. Terence and I and David, and two other men, signified our willingness to accompany our new friends. I stepped into Ickmallick's sledge, and the rest were accommodated in those of the others; and the dogs being told to get up and step out, off we set at a good rate along a valley in which the snow already laid pretty thickly. As there were no fields, or hedges and ditches, we were able to follow the most convenient track, though certainly not the shortest, for we twisted and turned among the hills for the sake of getting a level road so as to treble our distance, as we found afterwards that we could reach the spot to which we were bound almost as speedily on foot.

The Esquimaux location was on the shore of a little bay, opening on a deep fiord to the south. It was a sheltered and romantic spot; and in some respects, we at first thought, superior to the one we had chosen. As we turned round a point of rock we came in sight of a number of tents of some size, arranged along the shore at regular distances from each other. As we appeared, their inhabitants rushed out to meet us—men, women, and children—while the dogs, no insignificant part of the establishment, hurried up the hill to get out of our way, not liking our appearance, or perhaps their masters' whips, which were used with no sparing hand.

We drove up to the tents in fine style, and were welcomed in the most cordial manner. These tents were supported by a pole of whalebone, about fourteen feet long, placed perpendicularly in the ground, with four or five feet projecting above the roof. The sides and roof were formed of the skins of seals sewed neatly together. The tents were about seventeen feet long, and at the entrance about seven feet wide, increasing towards the farther end, where the bed-places were situated, where they are about nine feet in width. The beds were formed of a shrubby plant strewed over about a third of the tent, and kept separate by pieces of bone laid across from side to side. The doors opened towards the south-west. They also were formed of a bone framework, with the skins stretched on them, and were made to overlap each other. The entrance to the tents was much the lowest part. The skins were pegged down to the ground with curved bits of bone, also parts of the whale; indeed, everything about the tents may be said to have been made of skin and bone, as in truth were all the articles we saw in the possession of our friends.

It was worthy of remark how well these people adapted their mode of living to the circumstances of the country, and how ingeniously they made use of the very few objects they had the means of obtaining. I thought to myself, suppose a civilised man, or indeed a whole army of civilised men, were to be placed in this region, not having been accustomed to whaling and sealing, as my companions were, every one of them would perish within a few hours, or days at the utmost; and these people, who are called savages, have contrived to supply themselves with all the conveniences and necessaries of life. We felt that had we not discovered the wreck, and afterwards fallen in with them, we might have fared very ill indeed.

When we got off the sledges, our new friends invited us to enter their tents. I went into Ickmallick's, where he introduced me to his wife and children. She was young, and had a pleasant amiable expression of countenance, which made me feel quite at home. She was employed in cooking the family meal. Her fireplace was composed of a few stones in the corner of the tent, with a lamp of oil and moss in the centre; and over it was suspended a small stone vessel of an oblong shape, and larger at the top than the bottom, containing a mess of sea-horse flesh, with a quantity of thick gravy. The dinner was just ready; so all of us sitting round in a circle, with the dish in the centre, we set to. I had become in no ways particular, or I might not have relished my meal, for there was rather more blood and dirt in the mixture than might have been wished for; but some of the ribs were very palatable, though I should have preferred some bread and salt and potatoes with them.

I considered my appetite good; but Mr and Mrs Ickmallick and their interesting family distanced me far, and in a few minutes each of them had eaten more than would have served me for the whole day.

The dish out of which we were eating was made of whalebone, one piece being bent for the sides, and another flat piece being used for the bottom, and sewn so neatly together that it was perfectly water-tight. The knives they used were made of the tusk of the walrus, cut or ground sufficiently thin for the purpose, and retaining the original curve of the tusk.

In the tent I observed a number of the weapons they use in the chase. The spears or darts employed in killing seals and other sea animals are something like harpoons, consisting of two parts, a spear and a staff.

The latter is of wood when it can be obtained, and is from three and a half to five feet in length; and the former is of bone, ground to a blunt point. The lines attached to the spears are cut out of sealskin, well stretched and dried, and then coiled up like a rope. To serve as a float, a large bladder is used.

Most of the ladies had their faces tattooed, and some their hands; and I certainly did not think it improved their beauty, though I suppose they did. The children were fat and rosy, and really interesting-looking, and so were some of the younger girls; but my gratitude for their hospitality prevents me saying anything about the elder ladies. Their jet-black glossy hair hung down carelessly over their shoulders, and was not tied up like that of the people we had seen on the Greenland coast. They carried the younger children on their backs, in little sacks or hoods, just as the gipsies do in England.

The women were under five feet in height, and few of the men surpassed five feet four, five, or six inches. The complexion of the young women was very clear, and by no means dark; their eyes were bright and piercing, and their teeth of pearly whiteness, though their lips were thicker and their noses flatter than people in England consider requisite for beauty.

From the quantity of clothes they wore, both men and women appeared a much larger people than they really were, especially the children, who looked like little balls of skins.

When we came out of the tents we found the air very cold; and to warm himself, Terence began to jump about and to snap his fingers, singing at the same time. This seemed particularly to strike the fancy of our hosts; and in a little time men, women, and children had joined us in a reel, and we were all dancing and singing away furiously, till we could scarcely move for fatigue.

It made us all very merry, and improved the intimate terms on which we were with our friends. As the sun was sinking low, we made signs that we wished to return home; but they signified that they could not part so soon from us, and that we must pass the night at their huts. As we felt perfect confidence in them, and were willing to see more of their habits and customs, we determined to remain. We had some more singing and dancing, and they were highly delighted at seeing Terence and another man dance an Irish jig, they carefully noting every movement that was made.

As soon as it was over, two of them got up, and amid shouts of laughter performed a very good imitation of the dance. When the dance was over, we were invited into the tents to partake of some more of their savoury messes, they probably thinking that as we had eaten so little, according to their notions, the first time, we must be hungry again. They pressed us much to eat more; and Ickmallick selected what he considered the tit-bits, and watching his opportunity, endeavoured to pop them into my mouth, not at all to my satisfaction, though I endeavoured to conceal the annoyance I felt lest I should hurt their feelings, for I saw it was done with the kindest intentions.

The meal was scarcely over when notice was given that a herd of sea-horses, or walruses, or morse, as they are sometimes called, had come into the fiord, and were at no great distance from the bay. The opportunity of catching some of these animals, so valuable to the Esquimaux, was not to be lost, so, seizing their spears and lines, they hurried down to the beach.

Here their canoes were placed bottom upwards on two upright piles of stones, about four feet from the ground. This is done to allow the air to pass under them, and to prevent them from rotting. They are about seventeen feet long and rather more than two feet wide, decked over, except a hole in the centre in which the rower sits, and round this there is a high ledge to prevent, the sea washing in. Two feet of the bows float out of the water. The timbers or ribs, which are five or six inches apart, and the stem and stern, are of whalebone; and they are covered with the skins of the seal or walrus sewed neatly together. When driftwood can be found, they employ it. The paddle is double, and made of fir, the edges of the blade being covered with hard bone to secure them from wearing.

With the greatest caution the Esquimaux lifted their canoes into the water, to prevent them rubbing against the rocks, and they then helped each other in, we assisting the last man. I observed that each of them took a few handfuls of sand with him in the canoe. As we stood on the beach, we could see the walruses blowing like whales as they came up the fiord, and our friends eagerly paddling out towards them. The canoes went along as fast as a quick-rowing gig.

The walrus may be said to be something like a bullock and a whale, and it grows to the size of an ox. It has two canine teeth twenty inches long, curving inward from the upper jaw; their use is to defend itself against the bear when Bruin attacks it, and to lift itself up on the ice. The head is short, small, and flattened in front. The flattened part of the face is set with strong bristles. The nostrils are on the upper part of the snout, through which it blows like a whale. The fore-paws are a kind of webbed hand; they are above two feet long, and may be stretched out to the width of fifteen to eighteen inches. The hind feet, which form a sort of tail-fin, extend straight backward. They are not united, but are detached from each other. The termination of each toe is marked by a small nail. The skin of the animal is about an inch thick, and is covered with a short yellowish-brown coloured hair. The inside of the paws in old animals is very roughened, from having to climb over the ice and rocks. Beneath the skin is a layer of fat, the thickness varying in different seasons.

The canoes were soon among the herd, and several of the animals were immediately struck. Instead, however, of darting away, each of the wounded animals made at the canoes, and their occupants had to pull hard to keep out of their reach. When the other walruses saw this, they also swam towards the canoes to the assistance of their companions, and a regular contest commenced between man and beast.

The men, by the clever twists and turns they gave their canoes, managed to keep out of their way, the wounded animals all the time growing weaker and weaker; and whenever any of those untouched approached so near as to endanger the canoes, they threw a handful of sand so dexterously in their eyes, that the enraged animals were blinded and confused, and immediately swam off.

I regretted that we had not our firearms with us, as we might very soon have killed a large number without difficulty, provided the report did not frighten them away.

It was quite dark by the time the canoes returned to the beach, each towing in triumph the dead body of a walrus. On hearing of their success, the people who remained on shore set up shouts of joy, and hastened down to carry off the blubber and the more delicate morsels for their next day's meal. The greater portion of the flesh was stowed away in holes in the bank, lined with a coating of snow, and thickly covered over with large stones, so that no animal could get at them. They have no fear in this climate of their food being destroyed by vermin or small insects.

We thought our friends had done eating for the day, but the temptation of some fresh blubber was too great to be resisted, and to our astonishment they again set their pot on to boil, and ate till they could eat no more.

Terence and the rest of my party fared in the same way, in their respective tents, which I did. Ickmallick, when he had done eating, made a sign to me to occupy a corner of the family couch; and the whole family were soon snoring away and making a no very harmonious concert, when a dozen or more dogs sneaked in and took up their quarters at our feet.

The lamp was left burning all the night. It is a shallow crescent-shaped vessel of potstone, or what is called soapstone from its soapy feel. The wick is composed of dry moss, rubbed between the hands till it is quite inflammable. It is disposed along the edge of the lamp, on the straight side, and a greater or smaller quantity lighted, according to the heat required or the fuel that can be afforded.

I was much pleased by observing the clever way in which the lamp is made to supply itself with oil, by suspending a long thin slice of whale, seal, or sea-horse blubber near the flame, the warmth of which causes the oil to drip into the vessel, until the whole is extracted.

The wick is trimmed by a piece of asbestos stone, and a quantity of moss is kept ready to supply the wick.

Immediately over the lamp is fixed a framework of bone, from which the pots are suspended; as also a large hoop of bone, having a net stretched tightly within it. Into this net are put any wet things which require drying, and it is usually filled with boots, shoes, and mittens. The lamp kept up a pleasant heat in the tent during the night, and without it we should have suffered much from the cold, as it was freezing hard outside.

The first thing my hostess did in the morning was to set on the cooking-pot. The toilet was made as rapidly as that of a family of bears, for all they did was to get up and shake themselves. Before they went out, however, they pulled on some shoes over their boots to keep their feet dry, for it had been snowing hard in the night. I was very little inclined to partake of the breakfast, though I did my best to eat a little to please them.

We now explained to our friends that we wished to return; and they showed their willingness to comply with our wish by catching their dogs and harnessing them to their sledges.

In every part of the world the dog is the faithful companion and servant of man, but especially so in these icy regions. I do not know how the Esquimaux could exist without dogs. Not only do they drag heavy weights for long distances at a great rate, but they by their excellent scent assist their masters in finding the seal-holes; and they will attack the bear and every other animal with great courage, except the wolf, of which they seem to have an instinctive dread.

In appearance and colour they much resemble the wolf; but the latter when running always carries his head down, and his tail between his legs, as if ashamed of himself, while they always hold their heads up, and their tails curled handsomely over their backs.

In the winter they are covered with hair three or four inches long and a thick under-coat of coarse wool, so that they can withstand the severest cold, if protected from the wind by a snow wall or a rock.

Their masters treat them very roughly; and, when food is scarce, they leave them to pick up any garbage they can find. They often beat them unmercifully; but in spite of ill-usage the dogs are much attached to them, and, on their return from a journey, show as much pleasure, by jumping up and trying to lick their faces, as any well-bred hounds in England. If they show a disposition to stray, a fore-leg is tied up to the neck, so that they tumble down when they attempt to run.

The females are tended by the women, and treated with great care, and the puppies are often fed with meat and water at the same time as the children. Consequently, when grown up, they always follow women more willingly than men; and when they are drawing a heavy load, a woman will entice them on by pretending to eat a piece of meat, and by throwing her mitten before them on the snow, when, mistaking it for food, they hurry forward to pick it up.

We afterwards purchased a number, which we found very useful for hunting, as also for drawing a sledge; though we never managed them as well as the Esquimaux did.

A drive of a couple of hours carried us back to our house, where we found our companions well, and ready to accompany our new friends on a visit to their tents. We employed ourselves during their absence in thickening the walls of our house, and in getting our boat ready for hunting seals, in order to lay in a good supply of oil for winter use.

We had no time to lose, for every day the weather was getting colder and colder, and the days shorter, and we might expect the winter speedily to set in.

All this time, it must be remembered, there was no want of ice and icebergs on the sea, and snow on the ground; but still, when the sun shone, the air was pleasantly warm to our feelings, long accustomed to constant exposure to sharp winds, which would have chilled the blood of most of our countrymen accustomed to live at home at ease.

We found our house at night colder than we expected; and we resolved to catch as many animals as we could with warm skins, to make ourselves clothing.

The next morning, while the rest of us were engaged about the house, Tom Stokes, who had gone some way along the beach to watch for any seals which might appear, came running back, declaring that he had seen a fierce-looking wild man grinning at him over a hummock of ice, and that he must be one of the mermen he had read about, but which he did not before believe to exist. He said that when he first saw him, he was in the water; that he came out on the ice, and put up his fist, and made faces at him, and that, though he hove a stone at him, he did not seem to care.

"I'll see what this merman is," I observed, taking up a gun loaded with a bullet, and following Tom to the spot.

There, sure enough, was an ugly black-looking monster; but instead of a merman, it was a walrus. I got round so as to have a fair shot at its side, and knocked it over sprawling on the ice. It had not strength left to crawl off the ice, and Tom and I going up to it, despatched it with our spears. We summoned the rest, and dragged it home on our big sledge in triumph. We never ceased afterwards to joke Tom about his ugly merman.

Chapter Thirty Four

We fancied that we had got everything comfortable for the winter, which now, about the middle of October, began to set in with severe earnestness, with heavy falls of snow and strong northerly winds. Our house, on which we had so much prided ourselves, did not keep out the cold blast as we expected; and though we covered ourselves up with blankets, and sails, and skins, and kept up a constant fire in the little stove we had brought from the cabin of the wreck, we were almost perished with cold.

It was after a very severe night, and we were consulting what we should do to keep warm, that we saw the sledges of our Esquimaux friends come dashing along down the valley towards us. We were anxious to return the hospitality they had shown us so we asked them into the house and stirred up our fire, threw some more wood on it, and put on a pot of lobscouse to regale them.

They could scarcely restrain their feelings of dismay when they saw this waste of wood, to them so precious a thing, and by signs they entreated us to desist; reminding us that they had cooked their meat in a very different way. However, as the pot began to boil, there was no necessity for putting more wood on.

They then tried to show us, by significant gestures, that they thought we should be frozen to death in our house when the cold increased. To do this, they shivered very much, then shut their eyes, and stretched out their limbs till they were rigid, and looking round at the walls, shook their heads, as much as to say, "This will never do." Then they smiled, and explained that they could soon show us how to manage.

Having selected a level spot near our house, they beat the snow on it down till it was quite hard, and then marked out a circle about twelve feet in diameter. They then, from under a bank where the snow had drifted thickly and was very hard, cut out a number of slabs like large bricks, about two feet long and six inches thick. These they placed edgeways on the spot marked out, leaving a space to the south-west for the door. A second tier was laid on this, but the pieces were made to incline a little inwards. The top of this was squared off with a knife by one of them who stood in the middle, while the others from without supplied him with bricks.

When the wall had been raised to the height of five feet, it leaned so much that we thought it would certainly fall in; but still our friends worked on till they could no longer reach the top. The man within then cut a hole in the south-west side, where the door was intended to be, and through this the slabs were now passed. They worked on till the sides met in a well-constructed dome; and then one climbing up to the top, dropped into the centre the last block or keystone.

The rest of the party were all this time busily employed with their snow-shovels in throwing up the snow around the building, and in carefully filling any crevices which might have been left.

While we stood looking on with amazement at the rapidity and neatness with which the work was executed, the builder let himself out as a mole does out of his mole-hill. He cut away the door till he had formed a gothic arch, about three feet high, and two and a half wide at the bottom. From this door in the same way two passages were constructed about twelve feet long, the floor of them being considerably lower than the floor of the hut, so that one had to creep up through them into the hut.

We were wondering how they were to see through the thick snow, when from one of the sledges a large slab of fresh-water ice was produced; and the builder cutting a round hole in one side of the roof, it was let into it to form a window.

After the window was cut, the builder remained inside for a short time, and then invited us to enter. He had collected the snow on one side to form the beds for a family. Round the remaining portion seats were formed, and a place for holding the cooking-lamp.

Indeed the house thus rapidly formed was perfect in every respect. The light which came through the ice was like that transmitted through ground glass, very soft and pleasant, and tinted with the most delicate hues of green and blue. A domed room of the most shining alabaster could not be more beautiful. We found that our friends intended to take up their abode near us; for as soon as they had finished one hut, they began upon others, making signs to us that the first they intended for our occupation.

We would rather, perhaps, for some reasons, that they had selected a spot at a greater distance; but they were so honest and good-natured, that we had little cause to complain. Andrew suggested that though we might not use the hut they had built, we might take a lesson from them, and cover in our house with snow of the same thickness as their walls, procuring from them slabs of ice for the windows.

No sooner was this proposed than we set about the work, at which, when our indefatigable friends observed it, they were so pleased that several of them came to assist us in forming the bricks of snow; and in a short time a thick wall was run up, which made a very sensible difference in the temperature of our room. The next day we covered in the roof, leaving only a very small opening for the chimney. We also built a deep portico before the door, with a second door to it, which prevented the wind from whistling in as it had before done.

Besides this, we built a courtyard to our house, with the walls eight feet high, to protect us from the wind; and at last we began to flatter ourselves that we might be tolerably comfortable, though we had to own that, notwithstanding all the means we had at our command, the Esquimaux were better able to make themselves so.

Our fire, from the constant care it required and the difficulty of procuring fuel, gave us most trouble; so remembering the lamp we had seen in the tents, we resolved to adopt a similar plan.

We had been so busily engaged in improving our own house, that we had not remarked the progress made by our friends in the construction of their habitations. They now invited us to enter them again, when we found all the families established comfortably in them.

After creeping through the two low passages, each with its arched doorway, we came to a small circular apartment, of which the roof was a perfect dome. From this, three doorways, also arched and of larger dimensions than the outer ones, led into as many inhabited apartments, one on each side, and the other facing us as we entered.

The scene presented by the interior was very interesting. The women were seated on the beds at the sides of the huts, each having her little fireplace or lamp, with all her domestic utensils about her. The children crept behind their mothers, and the dogs, except the female ones, which were indulged with a part of the beds, slunk out past us in dismay.

The roof and sides of the inner rooms were lined with sealskin, neatly sewed together and exactly fitting the dome, which gave the whole a very comfortable nest-like appearance. On examination we found that the beds were arranged, first by covering the snow with a quantity of small stones, over which were laid tent-poles, blades of whalebone, and other similar-shaped things; above these a number of little pieces of network, made of thin slips of whalebone; and lastly, a quantity of leaves and twigs. Above all was spread a thick coating of skins, which could not now by any chance touch the snow, and a very comfortable couch was the result.

The lamps were the same as those used in the tents, and were quite sufficient to afford ample warmth to the apartments. Indeed, had the heat been greater, it would have caused the snow to melt, to the great inconvenience of the inhabitants.

I have already described some of their domestic utensils—their pots hollowed out of stone, with handles of sinew to place over the fire; their dishes and plates of whalebone; and their baskets of various sizes, made of skins; their knives of the tusks of the walrus; their drinking-cups of the horns of the musk-ox; and their spoons are of the same material. They also make marrow spoons out of long, narrow, hollowed pieces of bone, and every housewife has several of them tied together and attached to her needle-case.

Every person carries a little leathern case, containing moss well dried and rubbed between the hands, and also the white floss of the seed of the ground-willow, to serve as tinder. The sparks are struck from two lumps of iron pyrites; and as soon as the tinder has caught, it is gently blown till the fire has spread an inch around, when the pointed end of a piece of oiled wick being applied, it soon bursts into a flame, the whole process occupying a couple of minutes.

While speaking of their domestic habits, I may remark that in summer they live on the flesh of the musk-ox, the reindeer, the whale, the walrus, the seal, and the salmon, besides birds and hares, and any other animals they can catch; but in the winter they seldom can procure anything but the walrus and small seal, so that they suffer often from hunger. Then I am sorry to say they are very improvident, and eat to repletion when they have a good supply, seldom thinking of saving for the future.

This is their great fault. I should say that they are a most amiable, industrious, and peaceful people, whose minds are well prepared to receive the truths of Christianity, though at present they appear to have little or no notions whatever of any sort of religion, and none of a Supreme Being.

The children, from their pleasing manners, took our fancy very much. They never cry for trifling accidents, and seldom even for severe hurts. They are as fond of play as other children; and while an English child draws a cart, an Esquimaux has a sledge of whalebone, and instead of a baby-house it builds a miniature snow-hut, and begs a lighted wick from its mother's lamp to illuminate the little dwelling.

Their parents make for them as dolls, little figures of men and women habited in the true Esquimaux costume, as well as a variety of other toys, many of them having reference to their future occupations in life,—such as canoes, spears, and bows and arrows.

Grown people as well as children use the drum or tambourine in their games. They are fond of notching the edges of two bits of whalebone, and whirling them round their heads to make a humming sound, just as English boys do; and they also make toys like wind-mills, with arms to turn round with the wind.

From an early age boys are taught habits of industry; and when not more than eight years old, their fathers take them on their seal-catching expeditions, where they learn how to support themselves during their future life. They are frequently entrusted, even at that early age, to bring home a sledge and dogs several miles over the ice; and at the age of eleven boys are to be seen in water-tight boots and mocassins, with spears in their hands and coils of line on their backs, accompanying the men on their fishing excursions.

The village had been established a few days when my friend Ickmallick proposed that I should accompany him in an expedition in search of game inland. The Esquimaux had not yet seen us use our guns; but, from having discovered that we had killed the bears and the walrus by some means unknown to them, they were impressed with an idea that we were able to kill any animals without difficulty.

Andrew having no objection to my going, I supplied myself with a store of provisions to last me several days, with a skin and a couple of blankets, a cooking-pot and cup; and with my gun in my hand, I took my seat on my friend's sledge. Besides the six dogs which drew it, we were accompanied by two brace of hunting dogs, those in the team being also equally serviceable for running down game. Ickmallick had some walrus flesh and blubber for himself and the dogs, and a dish for our lamp. He was armed with a bow and arrows, a spear, and a knife.

I had become possessed of a dog of the name of Tupua, a very fine animal, who had grown very much attached to me, in consequence of my feeding him regularly and treating him kindly. He now followed the sledge with the rest of the pack. Ickmallick cracked his whip, and off we went over the hard frozen snow at a rapid rate. Where we were going to I could not tell, except that our course was about west and south-west.

The first day we saw no game of any description. We travelled, I suppose, about thirty miles; for though sometimes we went along over the hard snow very fast, at others we had to go over very rough ground, and to climb hills. Had I not seen the snow-hut built before, I should have hesitated about accompanying my friend, on account of not knowing how we were to pass the nights. I was, however, not surprised to see him set to work behind a sheltered bank, and in the course of half-an-hour, with my assistance, run up as comfortable a hut as under the circumstances of the case we could desire, with a lamp burning within, and a luxurious bed ready, while another hut, close to it, was run up for the dogs. The dogs being fed, and our pot having produced us a savoury mess, of which my companion ate by far the larger portion, we went to bed and slept soundly till the morning.

We had started about two hours when the sharp eyes of my friend discovered the traces of two musk-oxen on the steep side of a hill. Immediately jumping off the sledge, he unyoked the dogs, and commenced building a hut over it, which might also serve us at night. He then let slip his dogs, who went off at full speed and were soon out of sight, as the nature of the ground did not allow a very extensive view. I let go mine also. But being unaccustomed to walking in the snow, I could not keep up with Ickmallick; so he slackened his pace, refusing to leave me behind, though I urged him to do so, lest we should lose our expected prey. He assured me, however, that the dogs would take very good care of their own business. We went on, therefore, laboriously enough for two hours, over a very rugged country, and through deep snow, when, finding that the footsteps of the dogs no longer followed that of the oxen, he concluded that they had got up with the animals, and were probably holding one or both at bay.

We soon found, on turning a hill, that this was the fact; when the sight of a fine ox at bay before the three dogs cured my fatigue in an instant, and we went off ourselves at full speed to the rescue.

Ickmallick, however, kept the lead, and was in the act of discharging his second arrow when I came up. We saw that it had struck on a rib, since it fell out without even diverting the attention of the animal from the dogs, which continued barking and dodging round it, seizing it by the heels whenever they had an opportunity or when it turned to escape, and then retreating as it faced them.

In the meantime it was trembling with rage, and labouring to reach its active assailants, but, experienced as they were in this service, unable to touch them. It was easy to see that my companion's weapons were of little value in this warfare, or at least that victory would not have been gained under many hours, as he continued to shoot without apparent effect, finding his opportunities for an aim with much difficulty, and losing much time afterwards in recovering his arrows.

I therefore thought it was time to show what I could do with my mysterious weapon, and putting in a ball, I fired at the animal at about fifteen yards from it. The ball took effect, and it fell; but rising again, it made a sudden dart at us, very nearly catching me as I sprang aside. Fortunately there was a rock rising out of the ground close to us. Behind this we dodged, when the ox, rushing at it with all its force, struck its head with tremendous violence against it.

The animal fell down, stunned for a moment, with a crash which made the hard ground echo to the sound. On this Ickmallick leaped forward and attempted to stab it with a knife; but it was instantly up again, and he was obliged to run for shelter behind the dogs, which came forward to renew the attack. Bleeding profusely as the animal was, its long hair down its sides being matted with blood, yet its rage and strength seemed undiminished, as it continued rushing forward and butting with the same ferocity as before.

In the meantime I had reloaded my gun behind the rock, and was advancing to take another shot, when the animal darted towards me, to the great alarm of my friend, who thought I should be killed. He called to me to return to my shelter, but I had time, I felt, for a cool aim. I fired, and the animal fell not five yards from me. The sight of his fallen enemy made my companion scream and dance with joy, and on his coming up it was dead.

On examining it, we discovered that the last ball had passed through the heart. From the habits of the Esquimaux, I expected that my friend would have lost no time in extracting a dinner out of the ox; but I found that I had done him injustice, and that his prudence was more powerful than his stomach.

He was satisfied with mixing some of the warm blood with snow, thus dissolving as much as he required to quench his thirst; and he then immediately proceeded to skin the animal, knowing very well, what I might have recollected, that the operation would shortly become impossible in consequence of the severity of the cold, which would soon freeze the whole into an impracticable mass.

For the same reason he divided the carcase into four parts, that we might be better able to lift it. As we were unable to carry off our prize, we built a snow-hut over it, setting up marks that we might know the spot again. We however took away a small portion for a meal, which on reaching our abode we cooked, and found excellent.

We were up by daylight to go in search of the other ox, the traces of which we had seen. We searched for it for two hours, when we discovered it grazing on the top of a hill free from snow. There was only one path by which it could escape. That we occupied; and as we advanced rapidly towards it, our shouts and the loud barking of the dogs alarmed it.

First it seemed as if it would rush at us, but its heart failed it and it turned and fled. There was a precipice before it; but it either did not see it, or fancied that it could leap to the bottom in safety. We observed it disappear, and I thought it was lost, and on reaching the edge of the cliff it was nowhere to be seen. My friend, however, beckoned me to accompany him, and winding down the hill, we found the animal at the bottom of the precipice, killed by the fall.

It was cut up in the same way as the first, and a snow-hut was built over it.

We employed the next day in bringing up the flesh and skins of the oxen to our hut; and fortunate it was that we did so, for it snowed so hard that I do not think we should otherwise have been able to find the spot where we had left them. We were out looking for more oxen, when, being on some high ground, I saw some dark objects to the north, advancing over the snow in a line which would bring them to the foot of the hill where we were.

I pointed them out to Ickmallick, but his keen eye had perceived them. They were a herd of deer migrating to the south. They travelled on at a rapid rate, not stopping to graze, nor turning to the right hand nor to the left. My companion pulled me by the sleeve, and urged me down the hill, where he beckoned me to take up my post behind a snow wall, which he with the greatest rapidity threw up.

We had scarcely knelt down when the herd appeared in sight, dashing onward. I waited till I could get a good shot, and fired at a fine buck. I hit him, but he continued his course with his companions. We thought he was lost to us, but he very soon dropped behind the rest. On this Ickmallick let slip the dogs, which he had held all the time in leashes. They were very soon at the stag's heels, and brought him to bay. He was a fine object as he stood conspicuous on the white sheet of snow, now tinged with the blood which flowed from his side, his antlers still raised in defiance at the dogs barking round him, and yet scarcely daring to attack him. Though deserted by his companions, he fought nobly; but he was already exhausted by loss of blood, and could no longer ward off the attacks of the dogs at his throat.

At last he sank, and we were just in time to prevent him from being torn to pieces by the ravenous dogs. A stroke from Ickmallick's knife put an end to his torture, and gladly would I have avoided the reproachful glance of his eye as the weapon struck him. This unexpected good fortune made my companion resolve to return home; and he seemed to regret that he had not brought another sledge to carry back our game.

The deer was prepared as had been the oxen, and going back to the hut for a sledge, we conveyed it there before night.

Ickmallick, to my astonishment, made a dish of the vegetable contents of the intestines, which he seemed to consider very excellent, though I could not prevail upon myself to taste it.

The next morning we started on our journey homeward. I could not recognise the face of the country, it was so covered with snow; and still less could I have found my way against the heavy snow which was driving in our faces.

It was slow work, for we had in several places partly to unload the sledge and to go forward, then to return for the remainder of our property. It was, however, satisfactory to feel that we were independent of inns and innkeepers, and that we had ample means of making ourselves comfortable at night. As usual, when it began to grow dark we built our hut, lighted our fire, cooked our supper, made our beds, and were very soon fast asleep.

I awoke at the usual hour, feeling rather oppressed with the heat. I then aroused my companion, whose slumbers were heavy after the five or six pounds of solid flesh he had devoured, and inquired what was the cause of this. He pointed to the door of the hut, which I found was completely blocked up with snow. He laughed to show me that there was nothing to fear, and began making preparations for breakfast.

On further examination of the state of things, I found that we were snowed in, but to what depth I could not say, further than that, as six to seven feet frequently fell in the course of a night, I supposed, as was the case, that we might be buried beneath that depth of snow. This seemed to make no difference to Ickmallick, for he ate away as heartily as usual, and then packed up our goods in preparation for departure.

Having accomplished this task, he began cutting away the snow, so as to form a passage just large enough to admit his body. When this was done, we crept through it into the cold bleak air, and it took us a considerable time before we could enlarge the cavity sufficiently to get out the sledge and dogs with our goods. The heat, with the wear and tear of the journey, had somewhat damaged the runners of the sledge, and we had to melt some snow and to rub it hard over them before the conveyance was fit to proceed. The day closed in before we reached home, but Ickmallick knew the road too well, as did his dogs, to make it necessary to stop.

I fancied that I recognised the cliffs of the coast in the distance, when suddenly just before us I saw some pale lights, like those from gigantic glow-worms, rising out of the ground. The dogs came to a standstill; and voices of welcome rising from the interior, showed me that we had arrived at the village, now covered to the roofs of the huts by snow. The lights I saw were emitted through the ice windows in them. I walked on to our own house, where I found all my companions well; and before long Ickmallick brought in half the deer and a quarter of one of the oxen, which he seemed to consider my share of the produce of the chase.

Chapter Thirty Five

We thought that we had known what cold was when the winter first began; but when a strong northerly wind commenced, having passed over either a frozen sea or sheet of snow, then we really felt how hard it could freeze. Even the Esquimaux kept within their snow-huts, and we could not venture beyond the shelter of our snow-wall, without instantly having our faces frost-bitten.

It was not till the last day of November that we entirely lost sight of the sun, and the long arctic night commenced. But the night of that region cannot be compared to the dark, gloomy nights of more southern climes. Overhead the sky was generally beautifully clear, and the moon and stars shining on the snow gave a light scarcely less bright than that of day.

About noon, also, there was always a twilight, and in clear weather a beautiful arch of bright red light was seen over the southern horizon. Besides this, the aurora borealis frequently lighted up the sky with its brilliant hues, like some magnificent firework on a grand scale. I watched a very beautiful aurora one night in the south-west, which extended its glowing radiance as far as the zenith.

Fancy a bright arch suddenly bursting forth in the dark-blue sky, sending up streamers of many hues—orange, crimson, and purple—while bright coruscations were emitted from it, completely obscuring the stars in the neighbourhood! Two bright nebulae afterwards appeared beneath it: and about two o'clock it broke up into fragments, the coruscations becoming more frequent and irregular till it vanished entirely.

Even during the coldest weather, provided there was no wind, we could enjoy ourselves in the open air; but the slightest wind made us feel a smarting sensation all over the face, with a considerable pain in the forehead. We could not touch our guns in the open air without our mittens; and when by accident one of us put his hand to anything iron, it felt as if it was red-hot, and took off the flesh exactly in the same manner.

We were very comfortable in our house, but we had to make some alterations. We found it better to stop up the chimney of our stove, and to use the same sort of lamp as the natives, which we were able to do, as we were well supplied with seals and walrus. The Esquimaux used to hunt the walrus throughout the winter, and would frequently venture out to sea on floating masses of ice to attack them, trusting to the wind to bring them back again with their prize.

When a walrus is struck near the edge of a floe, the hunter fastens the line of his harpoon round his body and places his feet firmly against a hummock of ice, in which position he can withstand the very heavy strain of the struggling animal.

Seals are taken in a less dangerous way, but one which requires very great perseverance. As seals require to breathe, they have to make holes in the ice for this purpose, and the Esquimaux watch for them as they are thus employed. Immediately that a man discovers by listening that a seal is working beneath the ice, he builds a snow-wall about four feet in height to shelter him from the wind, and seating himself under the lee of it, deposits his spear-lines and other implements upon several little forked sticks inserted into the snow, to prevent the slightest noise being made in moving them when wanted. He also ties his own knees together with a thong, to prevent any rustling of his clothes.

To ascertain if the seal is still at work, he pierces through the ice with a slender rod of bone with a knob at the end of it. If this is moved, he knows that the animal is at work; if it remains quiet, he knows that he has deserted the spot.

When the hole is nearly completed, the hunter lifts his spear with its line attached; and as soon as the blowing of the seal is distinctly heard, and the ice consequently very thin, he drives it into him with the force of both arms, and then cuts away the remaining crust of ice to enable him to repeat the wounds and to get him out. A man will thus watch for hours together, with a temperature of 30 degrees below zero.

We were able to kill a good many with our guns at a distance as they lay on the ice, when no one could have approached near them. Our sporting, on the whole, was tolerably successful, for we killed a quantity of ptarmigan, grouse, and other birds, besides several white hares. We also killed several foxes and a quantity of wolves which came prowling round our house, and would, I doubt not, have carried off any of our dogs or provisions they could have got at.

Thus the winter passed away without any adventures particularly worth recording. The sun was below the horizon for about six weeks; and though only for a short period at a time, we gladly once more welcomed the sight of his beams.

Our Esquimaux friends continued on very good terms with us; and with our assistance they were always well supplied with food. Andrew took great precautions about our health, and advised us to take daily some of the pickles and preserved fruits we had discovered, to assist in keeping off the scurvy,—as also a daily supply of fresh meat, whether of fish or flesh; and we very soon got over any objection we might have had to seal's blubber dressed in Esquimaux fashion.

During calm weather we paid numerous visits to the ship, to bring away things we might require; and we were able to afford our friends what was to them an almost inexhaustible supply of wood. Without the aid of our saws and hatchets they could not cut away the stout timbers and planks; and as we had removed the bulkheads and lining of the ship, with the remaining spars, their honesty was not as much tempted as it otherwise might have been.

Our time did not hang on our hands nearly as heavily as might be supposed. We in the first place employed ourselves in manufacturing the skins of the animals we killed into garments of all sorts,—mittens, hoots, jackets, and caps,—so that we were all of us clothed from head to foot very much in the fashion of the Esquimaux.

We took some trouble to trim our jackets and caps with fur of different colours as they do, and the effect produced was very good. We also made models of sledges and canoes, and of all the articles used by our friends, which seemed to please them very much, though I confess they were not more neatly made than theirs, in spite of our superior tools.

When tired of work we used to sit round our lamp at night, and narrate our past adventures, or invent stories, some of which were very ingenious and amusing, and were well worth writing down; indeed, I regret that my space will not allow me to give some which I remember very well, for I took pains to impress them on my memory, thinking them worth preserving. If my young friends express any wish to hear them, I shall be very glad at some future time to write them down for their amusement.

But the subject which naturally occupied our chief attention was the means we should take to regain our native land. We could not hope that any whalers would visit the coast till August at the soonest, and even then it was not certain that they would come at all. David, who was our authority on such matters, said that he had known some years when the ships could not pass the middle ice through Baffin's Bay to Pond's Bay; and that, consequently, we might have to pass another year in that place, unless we could escape through our own exertions.

On this the idea was started of building a vessel, and attempting to reach Newfoundland in her, or to try and fall in with some whaler at the entrance of Davis' Straits.

I cannot say that I very much approved of this plan. I had great confidence in Andrew's discretion, and I knew both him and David to be experienced seamen, but neither of them knew anything about navigation—indeed David could neither read nor write; and though we might possibly be able to find our way through the ice, when once we got clear we might lose it, and be wrecked on a worse coast than the one we were desirous of quitting. How also could such a vessel as we had the means of building be expected to withstand the slightest pressure of the ice? and, from the experience we had had, I did not think it likely we should be able to get to the south without encountering some of those fearful contests in which we had seen other vessels destroyed.

However, day after day we talked about it; and at least it served to beguile the time, though nothing definite was determined on. We had unfortunately no books, for those we found in the ship we could not read. I had, however, a small note-book in my pocket, and with my pencil, which I used very carefully, I kept a sort of journal across the leaves of the foreign books, thus turning them to some account.

Had it not been for Andrew, I am afraid that few of us would have shown any attention to our religious duties; but he by degrees drew the minds even of the most thoughtless to the subject of religion, till all acknowledged its importance and beauty. He explained to us, to the best of his power, the truths of Christianity, of which most of us had before a very slight and imperfect knowledge. He also proposed that we should unitedly offer up our prayers to Heaven every morning and evening; and from that time we never failed in that important duty.

As I think over the prayers used by that good man, although the words and sentences might have been somewhat unpolished, I feel that the sentiments could not have been surpassed by the most highly educated clergyman—for this reason, that they came from an enlightened mind with an earnest spirit. No words, indeed, could be more appropriate to our condition than those he used.

Early in February the sun again made his appearance, and the day, including twilight, might be said to last from eight o'clock to four, so that we had not a very much shorter day than people in London. The weather, however, was colder than ever, and we were less able to be exposed to the air for any length of time than during the dark months.

About the middle of March there were slight signs of a thaw, the snow being glazed over in the evening, as if the sun had had some effect on it. We also felt a sensible improvement in the temperature, and were soon able not only to wash our clothes, but to dry them in the open air, an operation which rather astonished our Esquimaux friends.

Early in May there was a perceptible twilight at midnight, so that we felt the summer had once more begun.

A little later, ptarmigan, grouse, and other birds made their appearance, and the Esquimaux reported that they had seen the tracks of deer and musk-oxen. Still, far out to sea there was the same dreary flat expanse of ice, covered with a sheet of snow.

I ought to have mentioned that for the sake of being nearer the edge of the ice, where seals could be caught, some of our friends had built for themselves snow-huts on the ice. For this purpose they completely swept away the snow, leaving a flooring of clear ice, which was of the richest and most splendid blue that nature affords. I thought to myself, with these simple materials what a magnificent palace might be built, far surpassing any other style of edifice!

The increasing warmth of the weather now enabling us to work out of doors for several hours together, it was once more seriously proposed that we should begin to build a boat, or, as some insisted on calling her, a vessel, to carry us home. I asked Andrew what he thought on the subject, for he had not expressed any very strong opinion either one way or the other. He replied that he thought there could be no harm in trying to build a small vessel; that we had an abundance of materials and tools, with provisions; and that if we could contrive to make her seaworthy, we might manage to reach one of the places to the south constantly visited by whalers; but if not, we must be content to wait till some ship might pass in the autumn.

He owned that he, for one, should not be inclined to venture out of sight of land; and that, provided we took a good supply of provisions with us, our firearms and powder, our harpoons and lances, after the experience we had had, we could not come to much harm, even if we were compelled to weather out another winter in the arctic regions.

Chapter Thirty Six

Having determined to build a vessel, we set to work with great energy; and we hoped by ingenuity and perseverance to make amends for our want of skill and knowledge.

Our first task was to break up the wreck, and to convey it piecemeal to the bay; and in this work we were ably assisted by the Esquimaux, who understood that whatever portion we did not require was to be their perquisite. They also shrewdly suspected that we should leave them, if we went away, many of the other treasures we had in our possession. I believe, however, that they really had formed a sincere regard for us, and were sorry to find that we were about to depart; at the same time that they consoled themselves, as more civilised people are apt to do under similar circumstances, with the reflection that we should leave something behind us.

We first had to carry to our store the remainder of the salted provisions; which, had they been left a single night on board after the hatches were removed, the bears would inevitably have got hold of. We then carried off such part of the deck as we required, with some of the timbers and planks.

As we could not get at the keel, we were obliged to content ourselves with the mainmast, to serve as a keel for our new vessel. We laid her down close to the beach just above high-water mark, with a carriage-sledge under her, so as to be able to launch her over the ice. Our intention was to make her a vessel of about sixteen to twenty tons, which was as large as our materials would allow, and to rig her as a schooner for the same reason, and because she would thus be more easily handled.

After much discussion as to the ways and means, we laid down the keel and set up the stem and stern. We next commenced on the ribs, which puzzled us much more to shape them, so as to make the sides of the form we wished, and one side to correspond with the other. However, there is an old saying, that "Where there's a will there's a way;" and though not always true, it was so in our case, though we expended six times as much labour and time as we should have done had there been a good carpenter among us to superintend our work. We were unwearied in our labours; we worked all day, and a great part of the night too, for we all felt that on getting it done in time depended our escape from those icy regions that year.

I have described our imprisonment as passed more pleasantly than we could have expected; but yet none of us desired to spend another winter in the same way, and most of us had some friends or relations whom we wished again to see, and to relieve from the anxiety they must be feeling on our account.

We should have worked on Sundays, but Andrew Thompson urged us to desist. Some of the men answered that we were working in a good cause, as we should the sooner be able to return home.

"It is the Lord's day, and He says we shall not work on it," answered Andrew. "Therefore it is wrong to work on it; and depend upon it He never intends us to do wrong that good may come of it. We are building a vessel, which we think may be the means of saving us; but He may have arranged differently, and after all our labour it might prove our destruction."

Terence, Tom, and I at once said we would follow Andrew's advice; and one or two of the others added that they were not going to work for us if we chose to be idle, so the Sabbath became a day of rest. The Esquimaux wondered when they observed this, and inquired why every seventh day we desisted from work, though so anxious to get our ship built.

Andrew then explained to them that we were commanded to do so by the God we worshipped, and that if we disobeyed His laws He would be angry with us, and that we could not expect to prosper.

Our knowledge of their language was unfortunately far too imperfect to enable us to impart any of the great tenets of Christianity to them; but I do believe that this reply, and the exhibition of obedience to the commands of a Being whom none of us saw, yet willingly obeyed, opened their minds, more than any sermon could have done, to receive those truths whenever they may be offered to them.

Many a time in their snow tents will those untutored savages, during the long night of winter, talk of the God of the Kablinae (the Europeans), and worship Him unknowingly in His works. They are people of inquiring minds, very capable of receiving instruction; and from their habits and dispositions, I feel assured that were the great light of the gospel placed before them, they would gladly receive its truths, and be brought into Christ's flock of true believers.

Should there be no other result from the gallant attempts making to discover a north-west passage round the continent of America, than that by those means people have become acquainted with the condition of vast tribes hitherto little known, and thereby it has been put into the hearts of some of Christ's true soldiers to carry His gospel among them, glorious indeed it will be.

Who can say that the finger of God has not directed our brave countrymen to those regions for that very purpose, although they themselves are ignorant of the influence which impels them; and that, it having been shown how easily the rigours of an arctic winter may be withstood, ere long missionaries may be on their way to reside among the northern, as Christian men have for long resided among the southern, tribes of Esquimaux for the same holy purpose?

We got on very briskly with our vessel. She was not very sightly, certainly, but we thought she would be strong, which was of more importance. After much discussion we determined to give her a round stern, as more likely to withstand a blow from the ice. Her floors were very flat, which was very much owing to the shape of the timbers, which we could not alter; but this was not a fault, as she would better have borne being thrown on the ice.

When we came to planking her, we found great difficulty in making the planks fit the ribs, as any one conversant with shipbuilding may suppose; and we had to fill up under the planks in many places, to secure them to the timbers. We resolved that she should be very strong; so we almost filled her with beams, and double-planked her over after having caulked the first planking.

We had less difficulty in laying down the deck; but for the size of the vessel it was very thick and not very even. Provided, however, it was water-tight, we cared nothing for other defects.

We built up some strong high bulwarks, not forgetting to leave ports of good size to let the water run off should a sea break on board us. We got two spars from the lower yards of the ship which served for masts, and set them up with shrouds, though, as most of the rigging of the ship was rotten, we had some difficulty in finding a sufficient quantity.

We rigged her with a fore and aft mainsail and fore-sail, and a square topsail and a fore staysail and jib, the bowsprit steeping up very much, so that when she pitched there might be less chance of its being carried away.

It is not an easy job to cut out a sail well, though there appears to be no difficulty in it; and I must own that ours did not look very well when we first set them, but by alterations, and making several patches, we got them to stand fairly at last.

We were prudent and made two suits, besides keeping a supply of canvas among our stores.

Our yards and gaffs were somewhat heavy, as we had no proper-sized spars to make them from. We found a good supply of rope on board the ship, from which we fitted our running rigging. At last we had a vessel of some twenty to five-and-twenty tons, in all appearance ready for sea.

The last and not the least important task was to select the stores and provisions we should require, and to make the casks to hold the water tight. Had we had carpenter or blacksmith among us, much of our labour might have been spared; but it must be remembered that we had only a few tools, to the use of which none of us were accustomed, and that nearly every nail we employed we had to draw from the planks and to straighten.

By the end of August our task was accomplished, and it was with no little satisfaction that we walked round and round our vessel to survey our work.

The next thing to be done was to move her over the ice to the centre of the bay, where about two miles off there was open water. When once we could get the cradle on which she rested on the ice, we thought our task would be easy; but to set it going was the difficulty. We tried every means we could think of, but the heavy mass would not move.

An ordinary-built vessel of fifteen tons could not have weighed a third of what ours did. At last we bethought ourselves of cutting away the ground under the cradle, and of placing slips of ice for it to run on. With infinite trouble and no little risk we succeeded in doing this. We gave a shout of joy as we saw our craft moving towards the ice. She glided slowly at first, but her speed increased. She dashed on; and before she reached the ice, while yet on the beach, the cradle gave way, and with a loud crash she fell over on her side. We were in despair, and some gave vent to their feelings in expressions of bitter complaint.

We might shore her up, and afterwards cut a channel for her through the ice, if she had escaped injury; but it would be a work of time, and the season for proceeding to the south might be lost.

Most of the Esquimaux had gone away to catch salmon, and on hunting expeditions, but a few remained; and though they expressed great regret at our misfortune, they seemed glad that we had less chance of leaving them.

Andrew was the only one among us who was calm. "Come, my lads," he said, "there's no use looking at what's happened without trying to set matters to rights again. If we stand here all day without putting our hand to the work, we shall not get the craft on an even keel."

His taunting words aroused us to exertion; and it was proposed to get the vessel up by driving wedges of ice under her bilge, and since the cradle could be of no further use, to build a way for her to the water, or to where the ice might be thin enough to allow us to break it, so as to form a channel for her to float through.

We laboured away very hard; but our want of scientific knowledge made us despair of accomplishing the task. The first day we did nothing—the next we set to work again, but performed little of the proposed work.

"It's of no use, I see," grumbled David. "We may as well make up our minds to spend the rest of our days here."

While he was speaking, and all hands were standing doing nothing, I happened to turn my eyes to the northward, and there I saw what appeared to me a high land, covered with towers, and houses, and church-steeples, with trees and rocks on either side. Under the land, however, appeared a thin line of water, and dividing it a broad gap, as it were the mouth of some wide river or fiord; but what most attracted my attention was an inverted ship, which appeared above it under all sail.

I at once guessed that this extraordinary appearance was caused by refraction; but the figure of the ship puzzled me. It was so perfect in every respect, that I was convinced that it could not be an ocular illusion, and that there must be some real ship, and that this was her reflection in the clouds. I pointed her out to my companions; and when they saw that all the objects were continually changing and that she remained the same, they were of the same opinion. We therefore resolved to watch, and to get the boat ready to shove off to her should a ship appear; at the same time the great uncertainty of what might really be the case prevented us from feeling any exuberance of joy. It was already late in the day, but none of us could sleep, so eager were we to keep a look-out for the strange ship.

Hour after hour passed away, and still no vessel appeared to relieve our anxiety. Some of the men at length grew weary of watching, and threw themselves on their beds to sleep.

"It was, after all, to my mind but a fancy," exclaimed Terence, entering the hut with a discontented air. "The figure we saw in the sky was very like a ship, I own; but still I'd bet anything it was no ship at all."

Andrew and I still held that it was a ship.

"Come, mates," said David, who had been looking out as eagerly as any of us; "I've sailed these seas man and boy, thirty years and more, and so I've a right to have my say. Now I've often seen just such a sight as we saw yester-even; sometimes we fell in with the ship we saw up in the clouds like, and other times we looked for her and she never appeared, so we supposed that it must have been an iceberg in the figure of a ship which we had seen. Therefore what I say is, that what we saw may be a ship. But if she was a ship, then she ought to have been off here by this time; but if it was an iceberg, then there's no use troubling our heads about it."

David having thus authoritatively delivered his opinion, walked into the hut and threw himself on his bed, thereby proving that he considered the appearance we had seen merely the reflection of an iceberg.

I, however, still held to my first opinion, that a real ship alone could have created a figure so perfect in the clouds. Then it must be remembered that I had seen it first, and that the appearance may have somewhat altered before the attention of the rest was called to it. I, however, was so far biassed by David's opinions, that I went and threw myself on my bed. I slept, but it was very lightly; and all the time I fancied that ships were gliding before me, and that their crews were beckoning me to come on board.

At last, so strong was the impression on my mind, than I got up and went to our look-out place on the top of the nearest hill. Great, alas! was my disappointment, when the same dreary expanse of ice and water met my eye, without a sail anywhere to be seen.

One thing struck me, that the whole surface of the sea was as calm and unruffled as the intervening ice, and that no breath of air was stirring in the heavens. The sun rose as I watched, gilding the pinnacles of the icebergs, which still remained fixed in the bay, casting a silvery hue over the masses of snow yet unmelted on the hills, and making stronger than ever the contrast between the pure white of the snow-covered ice, and the deep blue of the tranquil ocean.

"At all events," I thought, "no ship can approach us from any quarter unless a breeze should spring up, and till then I may rest in peace." So I again turned in, and slept as soundly as I had ever done in my life.

I was aroused by my companions, who summoned me to come and assist them in launching our vessel. We all set to work again with a will, and after infinite labour we got her once more shored up; but to drive her towards the element on which we intended her to float, was another affair.

At last we thought that we had succeeded. If we could but move her a few more feet she would be on the ice. Once more she glided on; but on reaching the ice the impetus she acquired was so great that the shores gave way, and with greater force than before she fell over on her side, and in spite of the stout timbers and thick planking, from the imperfection of our workmanship she was fairly bilged.

We were most of us differently affected. Some gave way to despair, and uttered imprecations on their ill-luck, as they called it—others actually wept with grief—while Andrew looked on with calm composure.

"Mates," he said, turning to those who were loudest in their impious expressions of discontent, "I have always said that everything happens for the best; and in this case, depend upon it, we shall find it so. From the damage our vessel has suffered from the slight shock she received, it is clear she could not for a moment have withstood a common nip; and let me ask you, is it not better to remain here even for another year till a ship takes us off, than to be thrown on a sudden on a floe, with only our whale-boat to preserve us, and perhaps without time to save our clothes or provisions? Let us, rather than be discontented, believe that God, in this as in everything else, has ordered all for our good."

The calm confident tone in which Andrew spoke had a great effect on his hearers, and not another word of complaint was uttered. While we were at work, we had not noticed that a breeze had sprung up. One by one we were retiring to our hut, when on looking seaward I observed that the whole surface of the ocean was broken into crisp waves; and glancing my eyes to the northward, there I beheld what no seaman could doubt for a moment were the topgallant-sails of a large ship.

I rushed into the hut where my companions were sitting, most of them with their heads sunk between their knees, brooding on our misfortune, except Andrew, who stood with his arms folded, meditating on our future plans, and asking assistance whence alone assistance could be given.

"A sail! a sail!" I exclaimed. My voice aroused them from their lethargy. They looked at my countenance, and seeing that I was in earnest, like madmen they rushed from the hut. Every eye was turned towards the point I indicated. There, sure enough, was the sail I had seen; and without waiting to secure any provisions, we hurried down towards the boat, but Andrew called us back.

"We should not go empty-handed, mates, among our new friends, nor quit those who have treated us so hospitably without a word of farewell," he exclaimed. "There is yet time enough to do what we should do, and to pull out into the offing before the ship is off here."

Ashamed by his mild reproof, we went to the tents of our Esquimaux friends, who still remained near us; and explaining that a ship, by which we hoped to return to our country, was in sight, we bade them understand that if we did not return, all the property we left behind was to be theirs. We saw tears falling from their eyes as they wrung our hands when we stepped into the boat, which they assisted us to launch over the ice.

We had loaded her with as large a supply of provisions as she could carry, and with our guns and the little ammunition which remained. Once in the boat, we gave way with a will, and pulled boldly out to sea, with our jack at the end of a spar of three times the usual length.

On came the stranger. O how our hearts beat as we saw her hull rising out of the water!

On we pulled, so as to place ourselves directly in her course, that there might not be a possibility of her missing us. Various were the conjectures as to what nation she belonged; for it was soon seen she was not English by the cut of her sails, and as she drew nearer, by her build. Some said Danish, others Dutch, and others French.

The last proved right; for, as we got within hailing distance, once more the voices of civilised men struck our ears. We could not understand the question put to us; but when we sung out that we were Englishmen, who had lost our ship, a voice in our own tongue told us to come on board. With joyful hearts we pulled alongside, and found ourselves on board the *Saint Jean*, whaler, belonging to the port of Bordeaux.

The cargo of our boat, as Andrew had supposed, was not unwelcome, and secured us a warmer reception than we perhaps might otherwise have experienced. The *Saint Jean* was nearly full, and was one of the few ships which had that year succeeded in reaching Pond's Bay; so the second mate, who spoke English, informed us. Most of them, afraid of the early setting in of the winter, had already gone to the south, and must have passed out of sight of land. Thus, had we not seen the ship, we should probably have had to pass another winter in the arctic regions.

I will not stop to describe our voyage to the south. It was in some respects favourable for the greater part of the distance; but the crew were in a sickly state, and our services were therefore of much value.

The captain and first mate both fell ill; and I have reason to suspect that our reckoning was not kept with proper accuracy. Six weeks had passed since we had got on board, when a heavy gale sprung up from the north-west. As the night drew on it increased in fury, though, as we had got everything snug on board, we hoped to weather it out.

It was the opinion of the mates, for the master was too ill to attend to his duty, that we were well to the southward and west, and that we might keep away for our port. Instead, therefore, of laying to, we ran on before it. The weather was very thick, and we could scarcely see a hundred yards ahead.

Day was just breaking, and we Englishmen were all on deck together, from being placed in the same watch under the second mate, when Terence, who was forward, sung out with a startling voice—

"Land right ahead, land on the starboard bow!"

The Frenchmen understood the cry—all hands sprang on deck. The mate ordered the helm to be put a-port and the yards to be braced up, in the hopes of being able to beat off. It was too late; we were completely embayed. Land appeared broad on either bow.

To have beaten off with less sail than we carried would have been hopeless; but still there was more than the ship could carry. The masts went by the board. Fortunately the mizzen-mast went first, followed by the main-mast, or the ship would have broached to, and every soul of us would have been swept from her decks. Andrew sprang aft and put the helm up again, calling on me to assist him; while the rest ran forward, to look out for a clear beach to run the ship on, for by this time we saw that we were too near to attempt to anchor with any chance of saving the ship.

In moments of sudden peril the French are apt to lose command over themselves; at all events, such was the case in the present instance. And yet these men had gone through all the dangers of an arctic voyage; but then they were dangers for which they were looking out. Even now they were brave—that is to say, I do not think they turned paler than any of us; but they ran here and there, not knowing what to do nor comprehending the orders of their officers, while we were cool and did our best to save ourselves.

We kept the helm a-starboard, and steered to a spot where there appeared to be less surf; but it was a fearful choice of evils. In two or three minutes the ship struck; it must have been on a rock, for she trembled throughout, and the foremast went by the board. All hands had run aft, knowing what must occur. Again she lifted and flew forwards several yards, but it was to strike with more violence; and the following sea, before most of us could secure our hold, came rushing furiously on board, and sweeping everything before it.

I found myself lifted off my feet, and whirled round among the foaming billows. I knew nothing more till I felt my arm grasped at by some one; and when I returned to consciousness I was on the beach uninjured, with Andrew leaning over me.

I asked for our companions; he shook his head sorrowfully. Three of them were missing—poor Tom and two others. Nearly all the Frenchmen were lost. We two, Terence, David, and the two others, and six Frenchmen, were the only ones who had escaped. Before the ship struck we had instinctively thrown off our shoes and the greater part of our clothing, so that we had nothing on but our shirts and trousers; and as none of the bodies of our unfortunate shipmates nor any clothes were washed on shore, we had no means of supplying ourselves.

We suspected that we had been cast away on the west coast of Ireland; and we found, on inquiry of some people who flocked down to the shore, that we were not wrong. I am sorry to say, that so eager were they in hunting for whatever might come on shore, that they seemed little disposed to afford us any assistance. The Frenchmen were anxious at once to proceed to Dublin, where they might get relief from their consul; and Andrew and the rest wished to go there also, to cross over to England or Scotland, and Terence because he belonged to that city.

I, however, was eager to return home direct. The yearning to see my parents and brothers and sisters again was stronger than I could repress I felt sure, also, that Captain Dean and Mary, to whom I had given my father's address, would have communicated with him, and that I should receive some news of them.

With sincere regret I parted from that excellent man, Andrew Thompson, and with not much less from Terence and the rest; but the two first promised to write to me as soon as they got to their homes.

I set off alone, and a stranger, without shoes, hat, or jacket, to beg my way across Ireland. Some disbelieved the tale I told of my disasters, and turned me from their doors; but others gave me bread and meat, and the poorest never refused me a potato and a drink of milk, for their eyes, accustomed to real misery, could discern that I spoke the truth.

At length, just after dark, I reached the well-known gate of my father's grounds. I walked through, and with knees knocking together from over-excited feelings I approached the house. I looked up at the windows—not a light was to be seen, nor a sound heard. My heart sunk within me; I feared something must have happened—what, I dared not ask myself. I sat down on the steps, fearful of inquiring.

At length I gained courage to ring the door-bell. It was answered by a loud barking of dogs from within, but no sound of a human voice. Again I rang, and after waiting some time, in my impatience I began to knock fiercely with my fists. I stopped, for I heard a window opening, and a voice inquiring from above what I wanted. It was old Molly Finn, the housekeeper. I recognised her in a moment. I told her who I was, and entreated her to tell me where my family were gone.

"Och, ye idle spalpeen, get along with ye, with your lying tales about being Master Peter, who has been dead these two long years or more," she exclaimed, in a voice of anger. "Get along with ye, I say, or I'll let the dogs out on ye."

"If you mean to let Juno and Pluto slip, you are welcome," I answered, my anger beginning to rise. "They'll at least know me, and that's more than you seem inclined to do, Molly."

"Just come nearer here, and let me ax ye a few questions, whoever ye are," she said, in a softer tone.

"Tell me first, Molly, where are my father and mother, and brothers and sisters—are they all alive and well?" I exclaimed.

"Well, then, there's no harm in telling ye thus much; they are all well, and gone to Dublin for Miss Fanny's marriage there to a fine gentleman who's worthy of her. And now, what have ye got to say?"

"Thank Heaven!" I exclaimed, and burst into tears, and sobbed till my heart was like to break. It was the giving way to affections long long pent up, like the icy ocean in winter; within my bosom.

"Och, it must be Master Peter, whether dead or alive!" exclaimed the old woman, disappearing from the window.

I had some notion that bars and bolts were being withdrawn, and in another instant a lantern was flashed in my face. It was instantly thrown down, and I found myself hugged in the dear old creature's arms, and several of my old four-footed favourites leaping up and licking my face, she coming in for some share of the said licking, and thinking it was me all the time returning her kisses.

Tim, the stable-helper, the only other person left on the premises, was now roused up from his early slumbers, and added his congratulations to Molly's. We went inside the house and shut the door, and I rushed round to every room before I could sit down to eat. As may be supposed, there was no great supply of delicacies in the house; but there were potatoes and buttermilk, and bacon and eggs, and what wanted I more?

Molly had actually cooked my supper, and talked of making my bed, before she discovered how badly I was clothed. As for the bed, I begged she would not trouble herself, as I assured her I should have the greatest difficulty in sleeping in one, and I at last persuaded her to let me have a mattress and a blanket on the floor. I did however, contrive to sleep, and awoke to find old Molly sitting by my side.

"Och, the dear boy, there's no doubt of ye now, Master Peter!" she exclaimed. "Ye talked of them all in your sleep, and looked just like yourself, ye did; and I'll stand bail that no one but ye could have done that same."

I got a piece of soap from Molly, and going to a tank there was in the yard under the pump, by Tim's aid I soon made myself cleaner than I had been for a long time; but we had a sad puzzle about the clothes, for my father and brother had left none. Tim had only those he wore on his back and a coarse suit; and money, I found, was scarce with Molly.

After hunting about in every direction, she routed out from an old chest some, with which she came to me in great triumph, saying they were my own; and so I found they were, but they were some I had thrown aside as being far too small before I went to sea. At last I bethought me, that as no money was to be had without much inconveniencing Molly, I would continue my journey as I had begun it; and I would present myself to my family as I was, in the character of a seaman who had known the lost Peter, and had brought some tidings of him, thus breaking gradually to my parents the fact that I was still in existence.

I proposed, however, disguising myself somewhat to prevent their recognising me. Molly liked my plan; so filling a bag with food, and borrowing ten shillings from her to help me on my way with greater speed than I could otherwise have made, I immediately started on the road to Dublin. Travelling sometimes on a car, sometimes in a waggon, where I contrived to get some sound sleep, and oftentimes on foot, in three days I reached the capital of Ireland.

Beggars in rags excite no remark in any part of Ireland; so, scantily clothed and careworn as I was, I passed through the streets unobserved. I was on my way to the house my family had taken, when I observed, walking leisurely along, a person whose figure and gait I felt certain I knew. My heart beat with eagerness. For some time I could not catch a glimpse of his face; so I ran on, and passing him, turned back to meet him. I was not mistaken—it was my kind friend Captain Dean.

My heart beating violently, I walked up to him, and said, calmly enough, "I have sailed with you, Captain Dean; but I don't suppose you remember me, sir."

"No, indeed I do not; though I am not apt to forget those who have been any time with me," he replied, looking at me very hard.

"It's a long time, sir; but perhaps you may remember a lad of the name of Peter Lefroy, to whom you were very kind," I said, my voice faltering as I spoke, for I was longing to inquire after Mary.

"I remember him well, poor lad. He was lost with a whole ship's company in the North Sea, upwards of a year ago. But what do you know of him?" he asked.

"Why, sir, I know that he was wonderfully preserved, and now stands before you, Captain Dean," I exclaimed, no longer able to contain myself. "And tell me, sir, oh tell me—Mary, where is Mary, sir?" I blurted out, feeling that I could not speak again till I heard of her.

"Peter—Peter Lefroy, my good lad!" he ejaculated, seizing my hand and gazing earnestly in my face. "It is you yourself I ought to have known you at once; and Mary—she would know you—she is well, and with your own sisters, for she is to be one of Miss Fanny's bridesmaids. But come along, this will be a day of rejoicing."

Captain Dean, on our way to the house where my family was living, to which he was bound when I stopped him, told me that he had some time back communicated with my father; and that a month ago, having made a voyage to Liverpool, where he was obliged to have his ship repaired, he had come over to Dublin with Mary to show her something of Ireland. He had accidentally met my father, and introducing himself to him, all my family had shown him and Mary the greatest kindness; and he added that my sisters had formed a warm friendship for her.

My heart beat when I heard this; but I did not trust myself to say anything. "And now, Peter," said Captain Dean, as we reached the door, "I will go in and break the joyful news to all hands."

What a tumult was in my heart, as for ten minutes I walked up and down before the house, waiting to be summoned! At length Captain Dean opened the door, and beckoning to me, pulled me in. "They all suspect the truth," he observed. "But I would not tell them till I had got you all ready to show; so now I'll go back and tell them I have brought a lad who will let them know all about the long-lost Peter."

They heard him speak, and guessing what was the case, they came flying down the stairs; and before I had got through the half, I was once more in the loving arms of my truest and best friends. Even my mother did not faint, though she sobbed aloud for very joy that her truant son had returned.

One sweet little girl hung back from the eager crowd. I espied her, and breaking through them, she received a not less affectionate greeting than had my sisters.

With my subsequent life I need not trouble my readers.

"Well, Peter," said my father, after I had been washed and clothed, and had put on once more the appearance of a gentleman, "you have come back, my lad, poorer than you went away, I fear." He made this remark with the kind intention of filling a purse my sisters and Mary had given me.

"No, father," I answered, "I have come back infinitely richer. I have learned to fear God, to worship Him in His works, and to trust to His infinite mercy. I have also learned to know myself, and to take advice and counsel from my superiors in wisdom and goodness."

"Then," said my father, "I am indeed content; and I trust others may take a needful lesson from the adventures of *Peter The Whaler* ."